PRAISE FOR THE GRAY MAN NOVELS

"Never has an assassin been rendered so real yet so deadly. Strikes with the impact of a bullet to the chest . . . not to be missed."

—*New York Times* bestselling author James Rollins

"Hard, fast, and unflinching—exactly what a thriller should be."

—#1 *New York Times* bestselling author Lee Child

"Vivid action scenes . . . this is still a must for espionage thriller fans."

—*Publishers Weekly*

"Writing as smooth as stainless steel and a hero as mean as razor wire . . . *The Gray Man* glitters like a blade in an alley."

—*New York Times* bestselling author David Stone

"The latest in the Gray Man series continues to demonstrate why Greaney belongs in the upper echelon of special-ops thriller authors."

—*Booklist* (starred review)

"The action is almost nonstop, with nice twists right to the end. . . . This is good, Clancy-esque entertainment."

—*Kirkus Reviews*

"Mark Greaney continues his dominant run."

—The Real Book Spy

TITLES BY MARK GREANEY

THE GRAY MAN

ON TARGET

BALLISTIC

DEAD EYE

BACK BLAST

GUNMETAL GRAY

AGENT IN PLACE

MISSION CRITICAL

ONE MINUTE OUT

RELENTLESS

RED METAL
(with LtCol H. Ripley Rawlings IV, USMC)

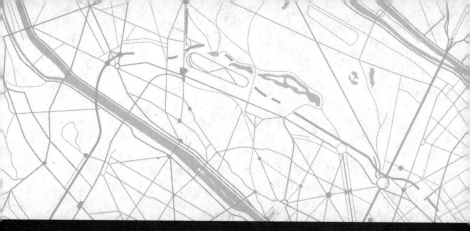

RELENTLESS

MARK GREANEY

BERKLEY
NEW YORK

BERKLEY
An imprint of Penguin Random House LLC
penguinrandomhouse.com

ISBN: 9780593098974

The Library of Congress has catalogued the Berkley hardcover edition of this book as follows:

Names: Greaney, Mark, author.
Title: Relentless / Mark Greaney.
Description: New York : Berkley, [2021] | Series: The gray man ; vol. 10
Identifiers: LCCN 2020044404 (print) | LCCN 2020044405 (ebook) |
ISBN 9780593098950 (hardcover) | ISBN 9780593098967 (ebook)
Subjects: GSAFD: Spy stories. | Suspense fiction.
Classification: LCC PS3607.R4285 R45 2021 (print) |
LCC PS3607.R4285 (ebook) | DDC 813/.6—dc23
LC record available at https://lccn.loc.gov/2020044404
LC ebook record available at https://lccn.loc.gov/2020044405

Berkley hardcover edition / February 2021
Berkley trade paperback edition / August 2021

Printed in the United States of America
3rd Printing

Cover images: running woman © Stephen Mulcahey;
running man © James Wragg—both from Trevillion Images
Interior art: Black-and-white Paris map © Nicola Renna / Shutterstock.com
Book design by Kelly Lipovich

For Allison.
9-26-20
I love you.

ACKNOWLEDGMENTS

I would like to thank Joshua Hood (JoshuaHoodBooks.com), J.T. Patten (JTPattenBooks.com), Rip Rawlings (RipRawlings.com), Chris Clarke, Jon Harvey, Ashley Goodner, Dr. Jon Griffin, and Allison Greaney.

I'd also like to thank my agents, Scott Miller at Trident Media Group and Jon Cassir at CAA, along with my editor, Tom Colgan, and the remarkable staff at Penguin Random House: Sareer Khader, Jin Yu, Loren Jaggers, Bridget O'Toole, Jeanne-Marie Hudson, Christine Ball, and Ivan Held.

Strength does not come from physical capacity.
It comes from an indomitable will.

—MAHATMA GANDHI

CHARACTERS

COURTLAND GENTRY: Code name Violator; former CIA paramilitary operations officer; CIA contractor, Poison Apple program

MATTHEW HANLEY: Deputy director for operations, CIA

ZACK HIGHTOWER: Code name Romantic; former CIA paramilitary operations officer; CIA contractor, Poison Apple program

ZOYA ZAKHAROVA: Code name Anthem; former SVR (Russian Foreign Intelligence Service) officer; CIA contractor, Poison Apple program

SUZANNE BREWER: Operations officer, Programs and Plans, CIA

CLARK DRUMMOND: Former NSA computer scientist

RIC ENNIS: Former CIA operations officer; intelligence officer for Shrike International Group

SULTAN AL-HABSI: Code name Tarik; deputy director of the Signals Intelligence Agency, United Arab Emirates; son of the crown prince of the UAE and the ruler of Dubai

SHEIKH RASHID AL-HABSI: Father of Sultan; prime minister of the United Arab Emirates; crown prince of the UAE and ruler of Dubai

RUDOLF SPANGLER: Owner of Shrike International Group; former executive, East German Ministry of State Security (Stasi)

ANNIKA DITTENHOFER (MIRIAM): Shrike International Group employee; former German military intelligence officer

DR. AZRA KAYA: Turkish/German doctor of internal medicine

CHRIS TRAVERS: CIA Special Activities Division (Ground Branch) paramilitary operations officer

KEITH HULETT: Code name Hades; mercenary; former U.S. Army Special Forces

HAZ MIRZA: Former Iranian Quds Force commander; Iranian Quds sleeper agent

KAMRAN IRAVANI: Member of MeK (People's Mujahedin Organization of Iran); anti-regime operative

MAKSIM AKULOV: Russian mafia assassin; former soldier; Spetsnaz; Vega Group; Federal Security Service of the Russian Federation

SEMYON PERVAK: Russian mafia assassin

INNA SOROKINA: Russian intelligence asset for Solntsevskaya Bratva; former officer, Foreign Intelligence Service of the Russian Federation

ANYA BOLICHOVA: Russian intelligence asset for Solntsevskaya Bratva

RYAN SEDGWICK: U.S. ambassador to Germany

PROLOGUE

The asset sensed trouble, both a threat to his operation and a threat to himself, and it immediately occurred to him that he was screwed.

The American had been trained through decades of fieldwork to miss nothing, to question everything. While most people lived in a world of black and white, he saw shades of gray, and he knew how to navigate his way through them. It had kept him alive thus far, but he did not yet know if he'd identified tonight's problem in time for his training to save him now.

It was a small thing, but to the asset it was unmistakable. Simply put: his target's mannerisms were all wrong for a wanted man.

This target had tradecraft. Just like the asset, both of them had spent most of their lives doing this shit. The target would know to have his head on a swivel; it would be second nature by now, and the fact that the fifty-five-year-old American moved through the market street stalls alone this warm Caracas evening, idly looking over handmade leather goods and wall art, without a care as to what was going on around him, meant to the asset that this just might be an attempt to lure him into a trap.

The asset did not overreact in the face of this danger. Instead he turned slightly to his left, ending the foot-follow, and strolled lazily into an alley, leaving the throngs of marketgoers behind. He feigned nonchalance, but all his senses were on fire, his mind racing, secure only in the knowledge that he needed to get the fuck out of here.

Now.

He only picked up his pace when he was out of sight of the market.

This was the time for action, not reflection, but as he moved quietly alone through the dark, the asset still couldn't help but wonder what had gone wrong. How the hell did he get made? He was new to Caracas; this wasn't his turf, but still he was confident in his abilities to blend in with the crowd, *any* crowd.

But clearly he *was* blown, nothing else made any sense, and his only objective now was to minimize the damage to the overall op by contacting his masters as soon as he was clear.

He was fifty yards away from his rented Toyota Hilux, just down Calle Cecillio Acosta, on the far side of the heavily trafficked street, and he knew that by climbing into his vehicle and pulling a U-turn he could be on the Francisco Fajardo Highway in just minutes.

The asset thought he was home free.

He was not.

Eight men, Venezuelans by the look of them, government goons by the smell. These weren't cops. No, from the weight of their bearing and their obvious confidence, the asset took them for state security. They had that air of authority, that posture of coordination, and their sharp eyes locked onto him as they closed the distance in the alleyway.

He didn't see guns, but there would be guns. The asset knew that no one in this situation would approach him without a firearm.

The American could have drawn his own weapon; he kept a 9-millimeter Walther PPQ inside his waistband, but this wasn't that kind of an op. He could throw some fists if things got rough, but he wasn't going to start shooting Venezuelan spooks.

Not because he gave a shit if any of them lived or died, really. These dudes were government thugs of a dirty regime. But he couldn't shoot them because he knew he'd be strung up by his masters if he turned this into a bloodbath. The gun was under his shirt to handle unavoidable street crime, not to create international incidents.

The asset didn't speak much Spanish, so his words were in English when he got close enough to the men, who were now blocking his path in the alley. "All right, boys, what's on tonight's agenda?"

One of the hard-eyed plainclothed men walked up to him, his hands empty and out to his sides, and when he got within striking distance, he threw a right cross.

The American asset read it all the way. He ducked under it and then came up behind the swing, pounding the man in the right kidney with a powerful left hook that dropped the Venezuelan to the ground like a sack of wet sand.

Another man had moved forward; he swung a stainless steel telescoping baton, but the American spun away from the movement, sidestepped the blow, and hammered this man with an uppercut into his jaw.

But the others had taken the opportunity to close in, and they were on him before he could reload for his next punch. They came with fists, feet, and knees, and then small saps and more batons. The asset gave as good as he got, for a moment anyway, dropping a third man and momentarily stunning a fourth with an elbow to an eye socket, but a metal truncheon from nowhere took him in the back of the neck. The American fell to the ground, covered his head, rolled into the fetal position, and did all he could to weather the blows.

They had him, he knew it, and as far as he was concerned, he deserved to get his ass kicked for somehow fucking this up.

The American never lost consciousness—he was a tough bastard—but he did lose track of time. After the pounding he was hooded and thrown into the back of a car, dragged and frogmarched and all but carried into a building with steel doors that clanged shut with a sound that told him he wasn't going anywhere for a while.

He was no longer an asset. Now he was a prisoner.

He was pushed into a room, another door shut behind him, and then his hood was removed. Four men forced him into a chair with iron cuffs built into the armrests, and they locked him down.

A tough-looking younger member of the roll-up crew grabbed a bottle of water from a shelf, opened it, and poured it over the top of the American's head, washing away a little sweat and blood but annoying the prisoner just the same.

His ribs hurt, the back of his head was cut, and both his eyes had been blackened, but his thick, muscular body seemed to remain intact, and for this he was glad.

The prisoner just sat there while the water and blood ran off him, and then a grizzled older man stepped in front of him and knelt down.

In English the man said, "You don't speak Spanish, do you?"

The asset shook his head.

"You have been detained by SEBIN. You will only insult me if you deny knowing who we are."

The prisoner *did* know SEBIN, but he had no problem insulting this guy, so he denied it. "Never heard of you. I'm a tourist. Is this how you treat visitors down here?" He was playing cool, but it was an act. SEBIN was Servicio Bolivariano de Inteligencia de Nacional, the Bolivarian National Intelligence Service, both the FBI and CIA of Venezuela, and if the American harbored any doubts about his predicament before, *now* he knew for certain he was fucked.

He spit blood on the floor and said, "Why don't you tell me why you arrested me for walking down the street of your lovely country?" He was playing dumb, and it occurred to him he'd probably be playing dumb for a very long time.

But before anyone replied to his question, the door across the room opened and a man entered from a dark hallway. As he stepped into the light over the chair, the prisoner recognized the figure.

Clark Drummond. The target he'd been tailing through the market.

Drummond was fifty-five, a computer scientist and software engineer at the National Security Agency. Or he had been, anyway, before he disappeared one year earlier. A boating accident, or that was the quite reasonable assumption made when his twenty-six-foot Sea Ray power craft was found bobbing capsized in the Chesapeake Bay after a thunderstorm.

But here he was. Low-profile in Venezuela, obviously supported by the local intelligence service, and brazen enough to walk right in here among them like he was running this whole damn country.

Drummond sat down in a chair in front of the prisoner and flashed a smug smile across his face. "You must be incredibly confused right now."

"You think?" the prisoner said. "Are you from the State Department?

These assholes just came out of nowhere and started beating the shit out of—"

Save it," Drummond said with a little smile. "You know I'm not consular affairs. You know who I am and . . . unfortunately for you, *I* know who *you* are."

The prisoner did not respond, but his mind was racing nonetheless. *Never change your story. No matter what, never change your story.*

"I also know who sent you," Drummond continued. "The Agency somehow found out I'm still alive, and I had been hoping to avoid that." He put his hands on his knees and sat upright. "They'll send another asset down here. Hell, they'll probably send a rendition team at this point. Whatever. SEBIN will roll up the next batch of CIA, just like you got rolled." He grinned even more broadly now; his confidence seemed genuine to the American in front of him. "Matthew Hanley can keep trying, but he will never drag me home in chains."

The prisoner cocked his head. *Play dumb, stay dumb.* "Who's Matthew Hanley?"

Clark Drummond rolled his eyes as his smile faded. "You're a bit of a bore, aren't you? Hanley runs CIA ops and . . . obviously . . . Hanley runs you. Or he did anyway. You won't be running anywhere any time soon."

Clark Drummond stood, then started for the door, but turned back. "He didn't tell you what I have, did he?"

The prisoner did not respond.

"He didn't tell you I left the U.S. last year with tools that made me all but rendition proof. When you showed up on cameras in my neighborhood, I saw you myself, and SEBIN was alerted. They were on your ass within hours."

The prisoner hid his anger well. He hadn't been told that the man he'd been sent to find was in possession of the means to easily identify him. That would have been useful information, to be sure, and he would have conducted his surveillance differently had he known.

But still, he said nothing, because nothing he could say would matter. He was destined for a dank and nasty Venezuelan prison cell; the rest was just noise.

Drummond continued to the exit, but he stopped in the doorway and again turned back around to the shackled American. "Hanley fucked you, Hightower. You never stood a chance."

The steel door slammed shut a moment later, and Zack Hightower's shoulders and head slumped forward. He was a beaten man. He had no idea how it had happened, but he was a beaten man.

ONE

Templeton 3 Annex is almost impossible to find if you don't already know about it. Nestled deep in a sterile office park in an unincorporated stretch of Prince George's County, Maryland, just a few minutes south of Joint Base Andrews, the front door simply reads: Palmer Holdings, LLC.

But there was no Palmer, there were no holdings, and the office space behind the door housed no limited liability company.

Templeton 3 Annex is the bland code name for a clandestine medical facility run for personnel of CIA black operations, those deemed too covert for regular medical care, and not only was Templeton 3 physically hard to find, even deep within CIA operations, only a very few knew about it at all.

No one had ever come through the door to Palmer Holdings accidentally, but if someone had they would have been turned away by the pair of men in nondescript security guard uniforms sitting behind the desk. A well-trained eye might be curious as to why men so obviously young and fit would be working the security D-list here in an out-of-the-way office park, but a visitor would get no farther into the building without passing the pair—and the Heckler & Koch MP7 Personal Defense Weapons they kept out of sight but within reach.

But at four fifty a.m. on a rainy Tuesday in August, someone with the right credentials *did* come through the door, and he stepped up in front of the two guards. Though surprised by both the time of the visit and the identity of the visitor himself, they disengaged the electronic lock to a door, which the large man in the dripping raincoat passed through. Here he encountered another pair of guards sitting in a snack room guarding yet a third door. After an okay radioed by the lobby crew, the lunchroom team asked the visitor to put a hand on a scanner, and then, when the locks popped open, the men escorted the visitor down a wide staircase and into the basement of the four-story building.

A short hallway led to more security, and the men here didn't bother to hide their weapons. Submachine guns dangled from their necks as they stood up from the table by door number four and again examined the visitor's credentials, even though, after two other checks, it was simply pro forma.

The fourth door opened, and the early-morning visitor finally stepped inside the heart of Templeton 3.

Visitors from Langley were not a particularly uncommon occurrence, but a visitor at four fifty in the morning was, so the doctor working the graveyard shift here was startled to his feet. Eugene Cathey stood at his desk, computer monitors all around him, stiffening a little in an attempt to hide the fact he'd been caught dozing.

And when he recognized the big man in the wet raincoat, he only stiffened more. As far as Dr. Cathey knew, Matthew Hanley, deputy director for operations for the Central Intelligence Agency, had never been here in person.

For this reason, and also due to the time of day, Cathey immediately sensed trouble, and he wasn't wrong.

In lieu of any greeting, Hanley asked, "How's the patient?"

Dr. Cathey looked to his nurse, also now standing nearby, and she excused herself into another room.

"Stable, but certainly not ready for operational status," the doctor replied.

Hanley heaved a sigh, then looked towards a closed door across the darkened and sterile space. There was a small window in the door, and through it he could just make out a hospital room, dark inside save for the glow of a few electronic monitors.

"Explain."

Cathey cleared his throat and came around his desk, standing in front of it now. "He took a knife just below the clavicle. Deep. Somehow, the blade missed the subclavian artery, so he survived, but by the time he was brought here he couldn't operate his upper left extremity. We identified the problem: the knife damaged the nerves of the brachial plexus. They have since healed to a large extent, although he does have some residual numbness and tingling in his left hand."

"He's right-handed," Hanley said.

Cathey cocked his head, paused a moment, then continued. "We're confident the nerves will completely heal in time; they aren't the problem. The problem is, the knife wound below the patient's clavicle developed an infection. A small piece of the blade broke off in his collarbone and held on to the bacteria even after a course of heavy antibiotics. I had to go in and clean it out, which I did, but he's got sixteen fresh stitches, he's got the pain from the procedure, and he's still fighting the infection. It's likely in the bone, and it will take a lot of IV antibiotics to diminish it. He'll be fine, but he needs time."

"How much time?"

"A few more weeks."

Hanley sighed again. Looked around at the machines and monitors and other equipment that lined the walls behind a small nurses' station. Several other hospital rooms ran down the hallway, but their doors were open and their lights off.

There was only one patient at Templeton 3.

Hanley said, "What if he doesn't get a few more weeks?"

"Why wouldn't he get—"

"If I take him out of here right now. What will happen?"

Dr. Cathey lifted his chin, a mild show of defiance. "In my professional opinion, your man will get very sick and die."

Hanley rubbed his wide face with a hand like a catcher's mitt. The doctor couldn't tell if he was worried or just annoyed. "How long until he gets sick, assuming the worst?"

And with that question it became clear to the doctor that the DDO wasn't concerned about the health of the man in the next room for any reason other than that he was impatient to get his asset back in the field.

Cathey did not hide his disdain now. "That requires speculation, and I don't—"

"I need you to speculate."

Cathey hesitated, then answered back with a twinge of anger. "Okay. You take him out of here, give him pills instead of the IV antibiotics. That will, *maybe*, suppress the infection somewhat, but it won't cure it. Within one week . . . two at the outside, he could be on his back, dangerously ill and in need of the nearest ICU."

Matt Hanley nodded, more to himself than to the doctor, then began moving for the door. "Plenty of time."

The doctor surprised both himself and the DDO by reaching out and taking Hanley by the arm. "I'm not sure I'm being clear enough about his condition."

The deputy director stopped. "I need him, Gene. I need him more than he needs to sit here. It's just as simple as that."

Cathey was emboldened by his anger. "Get someone else."

Hanley sighed again. "I *did* get someone else." He said nothing more, just let the comment hang in the low light, the sound drifting off over the noises of the computers and monitoring equipment outside the hospital room.

"Look," the doctor implored. "These assets. *Your* assets. You're running them too hard, not giving them enough time to recuperate after whatever the hell is done to them in the field." He continued, "You bring them in here broken, and you don't give me long enough to fix them. The woman last month. She wasn't cleared back into active status, but your people came and collected her anyway."

"I needed her. I need *him*," he said flatly. "He's tough. He'll be fine."

"Are you a medical doctor, Director Hanley?"

Hanley licked his lips, then ran a hand through his graying blond hair. "There's an old joke. A soccer player gets knocked unconscious in a game, the trainers drag him off the field and check him out when he comes to. The coach comes over, whispers to the trainer, asks if the player is okay. The trainer says, 'He can't remember his name.' The coach replies, 'Then tell him he's Pelé, and put his ass back on the field.'"

Dr. Eugene Cathey just stared at the DDO.

Hanley clarified. "The point I'm making is this. If we tell the asset he's fine, he'll be fine."

"With apologies, Director Hanley, that's not how medicine works."

"Well, in this case, it's how American national security works." He looked back to the door. The matter was settled, and both men knew it. Hanley asked, "Is he awake now?"

"I don't know. But when he *is* awake, he just stares into space. There's a TV in there. Internet. But I haven't seen him do anything in nearly three weeks other than sit and gaze at the wall, listening to music on the radio. I have concerns about his psychological cond—"

"This guy doesn't need a shrink," Hanley replied flatly, and then under his breath he said, "It's too late for that." He started forward again; the doctor had let go of his arm, but he called out to the DDO as he walked away, one final attempt to fulfill his Hippocratic oath.

"You brought me into this to give you my unvarnished opinion."

Hanley stopped again. "No, I brought you into this to keep my assets operational. Look, doc, I don't do this shit because I'm an asshole. I do it because I have crucial work that needs doing. Now, will you let me take him or not?"

The doctor, deflated, walked back over to his desk and sat down. "You can do whatever you want, and I can't stop you."

Hanley continued towards the door. "Just wanted to double-check that you understood our relationship."

TWO

Matt Hanley stepped inside the small ward, finding a space even darker than the room he just left. The air was cool despite the fact that several machines whirred and hummed along the wall on either side of a bed.

The patient's eyes were open but glazed, and he lay back on his bed on top of the covers. He wore burgundy tracksuit bottoms with no shirt, and bandages were wrapped around his left shoulder and upper chest area.

A full beard, dark brown with just a few flecks of gray, hung from his face. His hair was nearly to his shoulders and messy.

To Hanley's surprise, a radio somewhere in the room played what he took to be country music.

Both men's eyes met.

Hanley said, "You look good, Court."

CIA contract killer Courtland Gentry, code name Violator, blinked slowly now, his first sign of life. Softly he replied, "I'll bet."

Hanley looked around for the source of the music. The radio was across the windowless room on a wire shelf. "You like country?"

"That's not country. That's Drive-By Truckers. That's rock."

Hanley shrugged. "Sounds like country. You mind turning it off?"

Court produced a small remote that had been hidden in the bedsheets, and the music stopped.

"How are you feeling?"

Court turned away from the older man and stared at the wall. "Like I got stabbed in the chest with a knife."

Hanley pulled a rolling chair over and sat down on Court's left. He grinned suddenly; his voice boomed now, and it rang with levity. "It was your shoulder, kid. Just below your collarbone. Don't make a meal of it."

Gentry didn't smile. "Right."

"Dr. Cathey tells me you're just about healed up."

Gentry's languid eyes turned back to Hanley; they stared the deputy director down but gave away no malice. "Cool," was his only reply.

He wasn't buying what Hanley was selling; that much was clear.

"You feel like talking?" Hanley asked, and Court shrugged his good shoulder.

"Is this about Los Angeles?"

Court had done a job in LA a few weeks prior. Hanley had been furious about the way things had ended up, but he'd needed his best man on another operation, so he let it slide and extracted him from Southern California, intent on throwing Court back into the field immediately.

But on the transcontinental flight back to the East Coast, the doctor on board called the DDO and told him Gentry's injuries were too grave to send him anywhere but to an ICU.

So Hanley had scrapped his plan to use Gentry, and he sent Zack Hightower down to Venezuela instead.

"No, this isn't about LA," Hanley replied. "In fact, how about we never bring that shit up again? Might be good for our long-term relationship."

"Suits me," Court said, his head sinking back into the pillow. He closed his eyes.

Hanley's loud voice was out of place in the small, quiet room. "Here's the deal, kid. Not gonna sugarcoat it. I need you, and I need you yesterday."

Court's eyes opened back up, and he looked down at himself on the bed. "You need . . . *me*?"

"Yep. In Caracas. Zack was down there, working an op, and he got rolled up."

Court sat up now, wincing with the pain in his shoulder as he did so. "Federal police?"

"They've got him in El Helicoide, a detention facility run by the Bolivarian National Intelligence Service."

"Spooks. Shit." Court reached to a rolling bedside table next to him and lifted a plastic cup of water, took a slow sip, then asked, "How'd he get rolled?"

"We aren't certain."

"You aren't *certain*, or you don't have a clue?"

Hanley didn't pause for long before saying, "We don't have a clue."

"And . . . what? You want me to just pop down there and liberate him?"

"Negative." Hanley shrugged. "We'll get Zack out, eventually. He's tough, he'll be fine. Hell, he'll be playing poker with the warden in a month." With another dismissive heave of his shoulders, he added, "He's not the priority right now."

Court put the water down. He understood. "The mission he failed. You're sending me out on that."

"Correct."

"Zack has been doing this bullshit for a long time, Matt. I doubt he screwed up."

"We're trying to determine where the fault was. But we don't have time to work that out now."

"So, you're sending me in without knowing if there is a compromise?"

"We change up the op. You insert differently than Zack, you make your own plan, do your own thing. Look, this needs to be done, and it needs to be done now."

"What's the mission?"

"Personnel extraction of a noncompliant actor."

"So . . . kidnapping."

"Whatever," Hanley said, sweeping his hand through the air. "An American national, in Caracas. We need him here for questioning."

"Why?"

Hanley sighed a little. It was his go-to whenever Court frustrated him. He wanted his men to salute and move out, not to ask questions. Still, he said, "The target is Clark Drummond. You know who that is?"

Court cocked his head a little. "The NSA big shot who died last year?"

Matt Hanley shook his head. "No, the NSA big shot who *didn't* die last year. An officer working at Caracas station saw him three and a half weeks back in La Castellana neighborhood. Just stumbled upon him in the street walking out of a bank. Our man lost Drummond in the crowd but was sure it was him. We sent case officers out all over La Castellana looking for him, but one by one they were rolled up by SEBIN on trumped-up charges and quietly deported. I told Caracas station to spare their remaining case officers, and I sent in Zack instead."

"And they rolled him up just the same."

Hanley rubbed his face again. "Eventually, yeah. Zack was on Drummond for a couple of days. He got an ID on his residence to the southwest of the city, and then he tailed him through a market in town to see if he was meeting with anyone. And then Zack got popped. Yeah, Drummond had good physical skills to identify surveillance. Even though he was NSA he worked in the field all over the world for decades. His tradecraft was solid, according to all reports. But still . . . I don't understand it.

"SEBIN had the local agency guys and gals pegged. That, I get. But Hightower has never worked Caracas, he wasn't working with the embassy while down there, and he's not even CIA anymore. There is no record of him anywhere working for the Agency in the last five years."

"Right. He's a Poison Apple asset. Off book."

"Exactly."

Now Court's own voice rose to match Hanley's. "Like me."

Hanley exhaled slowly, looked around the room. "Got any coffee?"

"Shit. Sorry. Where are my manners? Cappuccino? Macchiato?"

The two men stared at each other in the dim light until Court said, "It's five a.m. Breakfast comes at seven. *That's* when I get coffee."

Hanley let it go. "Look, we don't understand the compromise in Venezuela totally, but I think if you get into Caracas on your own, with no Agency affiliation, then you'll be fine."

Court sipped more water. Finally, he said, "What do you want with Drummond?"

"We want to know what he's up to, if he's working for another entity, either a state actor or a criminal enterprise."

"He's not working for the Venezuelans?"

"We don't think so. He might be helping them out in exchange for safe harbor, but he's not giving them the good stuff. Drummond has a skill set. Special talents that he could employ. Things that make him uniquely valuable. But we've seen no hint of these talents showing up in Venezuela's intelligence community. No, he might be living in Caracas, SEBIN might be protecting him, but he's been using his real skills for someone else."

"No sightings of him at all in the past year?"

"Not once." He added, "But he's not the only one."

Now the man in the hospital bed looked confused. "Not the only one, *what*?"

"He's not the only member of the intelligence community to have dropped off the map in the last year. There is a pattern developing, men and women retiring, then disappearing. Americans, Brits, French, Australians, Israelis, and a South African. A dozen now, more or less."

"Sounds like someone, either a state actor or a big corporate intel firm, has a headhunter out there picking up talent on the down low."

"Yeah," Hanley said. "It sounds a hell of a lot like that. But who? And why? And why did Drummond have to fake his death?"

Court said, "I want to know what makes Drummond so important to you."

Hanley didn't hide his annoyance now. "You know, kid, Zack didn't ask all these questions."

"And here we are." Apart from the humming of medical machinery, the room fell silent.

Finally, the DDO nodded. "Touché. When he was at NSA, Drummond had access to certain . . . information. Game-changing information. The intel he had could possibly be weaponized. Damned dangerous if it fell into the wrong hands. That's all I'm prepared to tell you."

Court wasn't fazed by the paucity of information. On the contrary, he was accustomed to it. "And you think he might have passed on this information?"

"We don't know where he's been the past year, so we don't know what he's been up to. Get down there, get past SEBIN, stick a gun in Drummond's ribs, and make him talk. Snag his hard drives, his phones, that sort of shit." He rubbed his face again. "Look, it's going to be tough, but you're the Gray Man. You've got this."

"Despite your rosy prognosis of my condition, we both know you're getting me at fifty percent. Half a Gray Man."

"I'll take him. Let's go."

Court didn't move. "And what do I do if Drummond won't talk?"

"Drummond was assigned to us a few years back when we were looking for you. He pioneered some documentary and facial recognition software that we tried to use to track you, but you were too slippery." Court said nothing. "When Drummond sees that the Gray Man has been sent, he'll know his only chance for survival is to comply with whatever you say. He'll spill it all."

"People are unpredictable, Matt. Desperate people even more so."

It appeared to Court that Matt Hanley hadn't considered the prospect of Court failing on his mission. The DDO seemed to think about this problem for the first time, taking several moments, just sitting in the dim, before responding. Finally, he said, "If he won't talk . . . if you've exhausted everything, and I mean *absolutely* everything—then get all the physical intel you can collect, and then remove the compromise."

"Kill him," Court said.

Hanley shrugged his linebacker shoulders once more. "Kill him."

Gentry leaned his head back on his pillow, looked at the ceiling. Then he himself shrugged. "Sure, boss, why not?"

The patient winced with pain as he kicked his legs off the side of the bed. Hanley stood quickly and began looking for the younger man's clothes.

THREE

The engine of the massive American-made International MaxxPro armored fighting vehicle growled like a lion eyeing its next kill as it rolled through the darkened streets of the port city of Aden. Traffic was light but consistent at ten p.m.; a curfew was in place, though many ignored it. The civil war here in Yemen had been raging for six years, but Aden was rebel-run now and currently spared from much of the fighting, and many locals took advantage of this uncommon calm to leave their homes.

The moon was out, but the hills to the north blocked some of its glow, so when the big armored truck flipped off its headlights just before turning south onto Saidi Street, it was all but invisible.

In the back of the vehicle, just behind the driver, the leader of the force of nine drummed gloved fingers over the upper receiver of his M4 rifle. The weapon lay across his knees, its suppressor just inches from the small gunport in the armored vehicle, which he could open if he needed to fire into the street. Looking out the thick starboard-side window, just above the gunport, he watched as his MaxxPro turned onto Mualla Street. There were apartments up and down the road, and many of the residents were out and about, as evidenced by the large amount of foot traffic on the sidewalk visible to him.

Other locals sat in chairs in front of little shops, or stood on apartment balconies.

A voice came over the team leader's headset. "Mercury for Hades."

Still looking out the window, the man with the rifle in his lap depressed the push-to-talk button on his interteam radio and spoke English in a midwestern accent through his headset. "Go for Hades."

From the front seat Mercury said, "Shitload of folks out tonight. Intel said it would be quiet by now."

The operator next to Hades, his second-in-command, didn't transmit over the radio, but as he looked through the window on his right, he spoke in a southern drawl. "We good, boss?"

Before he could answer, a voice crackled over both men's radio headsets. "Mercury to Hades. Target in sight. No security visible at the front gate."

The team leader nodded in resolution, then answered his second-in-command. "We're good." He clicked his radio. "Execute."

The vehicle pulled to a halt seconds later, twenty yards from the entrance of a gated office complex next door to the public works building. The property consisted of a pair of identical three-story structures, surrounded by a high privacy fence and a sliding steel gate.

Eight men piled out of the big MaxxPro, leaving only Mercury behind the wheel.

Hades brought his rifle's optic to his eye and crossed the street, third in a line of four operators. They flagged their barrels across a pair of older locals walking by dressed in ankle-length robes, quickly evaluating them as potential enemies. Then, after discounting the threat the pair posed, the Americans moved their focus to a group of four younger civilians standing next to a sedan with an open hood, smoking cigarettes while watching the heavily armed men who had just emerged from the heavily armored vehicle.

The young men did not move a muscle—they weren't idiots—and soon the Americans had passed them by, heading south along the street towards the office complex.

While they were still ten yards from the front gate, one of the four men who had taken a position around the MaxxPro spoke over the net. "Thor for Hades. I got a cluster of military-aged males eyeing us from an alley entrance, west side, two blocks south of your poz. How copy?"

Hades kept his trigger finger straight across the receiver of his rifle, one-handing his gun while clicking his radio with the other. "Solid copy. If they brandish, you light 'em up."

"Roger that."

The four-man assault element stopped in front of the gate. Three men covered as the fourth, the breacher, began setting a small charge on the lock. He'd just finished arming the device when gunfire boomed on the street.

The Americans dropped to their kneepads and identified muzzle flashes two blocks south of their position.

Americans at the MaxxPro began returning fire; incoming and outgoing bullets raced in both directions, ricocheting off concrete walls. Civilians dropped and huddled behind cover; others ran around blindly, frantic for refuge.

Others died where they stood, spinning down to the asphalt.

Hades squeezed off short bursts into the general area of where he'd seen the flashes. In the low light he saw bodies running, falling onto one another, diving into shops and alleyways, desperate to get away from the wall of gunfire generated by eight rifles operated by well-trained shooters.

Hades's M4 ran dry, and he ducked behind a small panel van near the gate to reload. As he triggered the bolt catch release with a click impossible to hear through all the shooting, he tapped his mic with his other hand. "Mars!" he called, giving the call sign of the man who had placed the charge on the lock. "Go secondary! Go secondary!"

Without hesitation the breach man rushed back to the gate. With the charge still attached to the lock next to him, he yanked off his backpack and pulled it open. From it he retrieved a smaller pack weighing almost twenty pounds, and this he also opened. Inside he turned a dial on the apparatus housed there, pressed a button, then hefted the pack and the device it held, flinging it over the gate and into the tiny forecourt of the office complex.

Mars turned, lifted his rifle, and began shooting down the street with one hand while triggering his push-to-talk button with the other. "Thirty seconds!"

Hades chimed in immediately from his position behind the van just a few yards away. "Exfil!"

The gunfire picked up as the men at the gate all began bounding back across the street to the armored vehicle, firing towards the alleyway as they went. Hades dropped someone looking over a balcony railing up the street; he hadn't seen a weapon but shot the man out of an abundance of caution.

Mercury shouted next to him, "Frag out!" as he threw a baseball-sized grenade. It bounced and skittered along the sidewalk, knocking into food stalls and small folding tables set up on the pavement, and then it detonated next to a man attempting to shelter under a parked panel truck.

The security team expended magazine after magazine, lighting up the street to the south and firing a few bursts to the north, not at targets but simply as a means to suppress any potential fire from that direction.

A two-door hatchback turned onto the road three blocks away, and Thor sprayed it with copper-jacketed lead from his M249 Squad Automatic Weapon. The driver of the hatchback slammed on his brakes, then threw his little vehicle into reverse, but before he made it more than a few meters back up the side street, the gas tank ignited and the rear of the car burst into raging flames.

Thor stopped firing to let Hades and the others pass in front of him on the way back inside the armored vehicle, and as soon as the four men of the assault element scrambled back into the MaxxPro, the four-member security squad outside the truck broke contact with the targets to the south and climbed in, as well.

The last hatch was shut twenty-six seconds after the breacher initiated the timer on the explosive, and Hades was still counting off the seconds in his head when he shouted over the mic, "Drive! Drive!"

The truck lurched forward.

Next to Hades, his second-in-command spoke up again in his southern drawl. "We're gonna catch it!"

Hades slammed his hands over his hearing protection. "No shit!"

When the thirty-second mark hit, the noise of the detonation was unreal, even inside the armored car and even with ear pro worn by the entire team. The shock wave of the blast enveloped the vehicle; debris pelted the armor and the thick Plexiglas ports. A man inside the cab of the vehicle flew into Hades, who was then slammed hard against the inner starboard-side wall.

But the big American truck continued racing to the south, out of the kill zone.

"Everybody good?" Hades shouted into his mic. It took a few seconds for a reply, and it came in the form of Hades's men counting off, some shouting their response under the effects of the concussion and the adrenaline of the attack and its aftermath.

They were all okay, and soon the back slapping, fist bumping, and high-fiving erupted in the confined space, but while this was going on, Hades looked out onto the street as the dust cleared and saw the bodies of civilians lying on the sidewalk. Many of them had been killed right where they had sheltered to stay out of the gunfire that preceded the explosion.

The bomb had been composed of ten M112 demolition blocks: C-4 plastic explosives wired together for simultaneous detonation. It had created a colossal blast, designed to kill those in the office complex, but it did not discriminate. No one inside the blast radius who was not housed in an armored vehicle stood a chance.

Civilians lay dead and maimed wherever he looked.

Also killed, Hades was pretty sure, were three high-ranking members of Al-Islah, a Yemeni political party, who had been meeting inside the office complex at the time of the blast.

The Al-Islah men were the targets. All these other victims, just collateral.

The collateral didn't bother Hades and his team—at all. They'd achieved their objective tonight. And achieving their objective meant a satisfied client and, almost assuredly, more work.

While all nine had been former members of elite American military units, they didn't serve the U.S. flag any longer. Hades and his men instead worked for an Israeli-owned company registered in Singapore, with a contract to provide direct-action combat arms to their client.

Their targets tonight were, as far as Hades and his team were concerned, terrorists.

And their client was the United Arab Emirates.

These were mercenaries, conducting targeted killings on behalf of the monarchy of the UAE, just one of the dozen or so factions involved in the Yemeni conflict.

Americans assassinating foreigners in a foreign land for a foreign power.

Yemen was a strange war.

Hades's raiding party was just two klicks out from the airfield when a call came in to his sat phone. The noise of the vehicle meant he only felt the unit's vibration; he couldn't even hear the ring. He pulled the device out of a pouch on his belt, then checked the number. While his team looked on, he removed his ear protection and his radio headset, then put the phone to his ear.

"Yeah?"

The men around him stared, wondering why he'd be taking a phone call when they were still in the process of extracting from a target location.

"Yes, sir," he said, and then they knew. Hades was talking to his contact in the Signals Intelligence Agency, the Emirates spy organization. The man, code named Tarik, was Hades's boss.

And when Tarik called, Hades answered.

The American said, "Repeat your last, I didn't make that out." The rest of the small force leaned closer, trying to discern some information from this end of the call.

Finally, Hades said, "Sorry, sir, it sounded like you said 'Caracas'?" A pause. "Caracas . . . like *Venezuela*?"

The rest of the raiding party within earshot looked to one another in confusion.

Hades nodded. "Roger that, sir. Caracas it is." He ended the call and slipped the device back into its pouch. Once he had his headset back on, he said, "That eighty-minute flight to Abu Dhabi we were gonna take has turned into a sixteen-hour flight to South America. We'll stop in Lisbon for fuel, but otherwise, it's gonna be nine smelly motherfuckers in a Learjet staring at one another for the next day."

Mars said what everyone else was thinking. "Why the hell would the Emirates want us in Venezuela?"

Hades said, "Ours is not to reason why." After a pause he said, "I haven't got a clue. I was told we'd be given instructions en route."

One of the men, call sign Ares, said, "Bet we're gonna go kill some shithead."

"Yeah, that's a pretty safe bet," Hades replied.

The fat, squat armored vehicle rumbled on through the night, delivering the American killers for hire to the flight that would take them to their next mission.

FOUR

TWO WEEKS EARLIER

The brunette seemed wholly unaware of the fact that dozens of heads turned in her direction as she entered Restaurant Quarré at the Hotel Adlon Kempinski Berlin. She passed the businesspeople, the diplomats, and the well-heeled tourists, ignoring their stares as she moved in a straight line through the waiters and guests, making her way towards a cluster of tables in the back.

She was stylish yet understated, appropriate for a business meeting at a five-star hotel in a major European capital city. She wore a Ralph Lauren blue silk-blend dress, slingback Chanels with a nude toe, and oversized Gucci sunglasses that she removed only when she was almost to her table, placing them in a case and then into her red clutch.

She was in her early thirties but could have passed for younger, her brown hair slicked back in a bun and her makeup minimalist. The expression on her face as she walked conveyed the same quiet confidence as her classic styling.

The Kempinski is on Unter den Linden, a two-minute walk to the Brandenburg Gate, and next door to the U.S. embassy. There was no more luxurious hotel in this giant city, and though the woman was actually staying in a three-star hotel on Alexanderplatz, she, at least, was getting the opportunity to visit the Kempinski for her lunch meeting at Quarré.

The brunette recognized the man she'd come to meet from a brief video-conference they'd had the week prior to discuss a job opportunity for her with the man's firm, and she steered towards his white tablecloth–covered banquette.

He stood when she arrived. He was tall, attractive, well into his forties, with a full head of hair that was considerably more salt than pepper.

"Mr. Ennis," she said, extending her hand.

Ennis had a strong handshake, bordering on rude, but he smiled charmingly as he clenched down. "Miss Arthur? Please, call me Ric."

The brunette squeezed back just as hard. "Fine, Ric, then call me Stephanie."

"Stephanie."

The brunette noticed a little smile on his face as he repeated her name back to her.

They sat and the waiter poured from a teapot that had been steeping on the table. The waiter then correctly sensed that the pair needed a moment before ordering.

When he was gone, the brunette said, "Thank you so much for meeting with me today."

Ennis replied, "Honestly, you are exactly the type of person we've been trying to recruit to take our company to the next level, to make it the pre-eminent corporate intelligence firm in Europe."

"I would love the opportunity to put the analytical skills I learned in my ten years with the National Security Agency to good use."

Ennis smiled again. "I have no doubts that your skills will come in useful." He poured sugar into his tea as he continued. "I've read your CV, but you haven't read mine. So . . . I'll fill you in. Born in San Diego, I was in the Air Force—intelligence, of course—four years, made captain but picked up a noncombat injury that forced me out. Went back to college, got a master's in applied intelligence at Georgetown, was recruited by the CIA. Spent a decade in different operational postings, then made the leap into corporate intelligence. I've been over here with Shrike International Group for three years now. I'm proud of the work we do, and let's just say my bank account isn't complaining." He winked. "We pay a hell of a lot better than the U.S. government, not that that will come as any big surprise."

Stephanie nodded at this as she sipped her tea, then asked, "What can you tell me about the work itself?" She had a distinctive Minnesota accent; her CV stated she was born and raised in Minneapolis.

Ennis, in contrast, was one hundred percent Southern California. "You will remain here in Berlin. Our office space is down in Potsdam, but you'll never see it. Your work will be done remotely."

"Remotely?"

"Yes. If we bring you on board, you would be working out of a suite here on the fourth floor."

Stephanie was surprised. The Adlon Kempinski was a five-star hotel. Were they really going to make it her office?

"But . . . why not put me at headquarters?"

"We try to keep our operation more horizontal than vertical. You'll work for me. Other than technical support personnel, it's doubtful you'll meet anyone else at Shrike Group." He added, "It keeps threats to a minimum."

"Threats?"

Ennis regarded the younger woman a moment. "The work we do is sanctioned by the nations in which we work. But this work does pit us against certain bad actors. Criminal organizations. States whose actions our clients are attempting to understand. That sort of thing. We face cyber threats, electronic surveillance threats, we even have some human intelligence threats our countersurveillance desk has to keep an eye out for."

Stephanie placed a hand over her chest, a look of mild surprise. "You make it all sound very cloak-and-dagger."

Ennis laughed at this. "I'm sure you can handle it." He paused, then said, "NSA at Fort Meade? That's like working at corporate headquarters. With Shrike Group, it will feel to you like operating in the field. It's faster-paced, and yes, there is some intrigue involved. Goes with the territory."

"And what about Shrike Group's clients? Who are they?"

Ennis held a finger up. "You will never know who our clients are, but you will also never have a doubt about your mission and its morality. Our clients are most interested in the things many Fortune 50 companies are concerned about. Terrorism, crime, and the like. Your targets will be the same targets the United States has around the world. Despots, criminal organizations, enemy states."

Stephanie said, "Okay, the client list is protected, I can respect that. But what about the targets? Specifically, Ric, who will *I* be targeting?" With a smile she added, "If I get the job, I mean."

"If you get the job, your target could be anyone or anything related to private sector security. We hope to expand our client base very soon, so we need people with a wide range of talents. At the outset, however, your target will be the Islamic Republic of Iran. Our clients are energetic in protecting themselves from that rogue state."

Stephanie's confident smile only grew. "As you know, I've been working counterintelligence, focusing on Iranian cyber intrusions, for quite some time. I am certain I will be an asset to your firm."

Ennis did not respond to this. Instead he opened up his menu, and Stephanie followed his lead. As he perused it, he said, "We do have one slight concern, however, and we'd like to clear that up before we bring you on board."

He didn't seem terribly troubled, but still the brunette folded her menu closed. "Please. Tell me."

Ric Ennis smiled at her an uncomfortably long time. Stephanie cocked her head, her eyes narrowed.

Finally, the American said, "You will come to learn something that will serve you well. We are very, very good at what we do. If you are going to work with Shrike Group, you would do well to respect our abilities and our reach." He added, "Our access into other intelligence organizations around the world, for example."

"I'm . . . not following, but this is beginning to sound a bit ominous."

Ennis's face and tone darkened, but only a little. "That all depends on you."

"I'm listening," Stephanie said, but her confident voice had vanished.

Ennis said, "We know who you are."

The attractive woman crossed her arms in front of her, a subconscious display of defensiveness. "What do you mean by that?"

Ennis leaned forward, spoke softer now. "Your name is not Stephanie Arthur, and you are not, in fact, an electronic intelligence analyst at the

National Security Agency. Your credentials check out, and you look a great deal like the real Mrs. Arthur, but I am assuming that's just makeup and dyed hair. I say that, because you are very clearly not eight and a half months pregnant, and Stephanie Arthur left her position on maternity leave last month." He paused for effect, then with a flourish he opened his napkin and put it in his lap before saying, "She's due in September. A boy, our U.S. sources confirm.

"Anyway, *you* . . . simply put, are not *her*."

The woman inhaled an almost imperceptible gasp.

When she offered no other immediate reply, Ennis said, "Denying this would seriously undermine my confidence in you."

She uncrossed her arms and placed her hands on the table. After a moment she said, "I . . . do not deny it."

"Good. We headhunted Mrs. Arthur, confidentially, and she showed no interest in our approach. And then you came along, and you managed to impersonate her. You responded to us as her, and you made it all the way until now before being called out. Impressive stuff, really."

"I hope you will let me explain. I *do* have the skill set you need, and I would be a great asset to your team. I just have certain . . . motivations for concealing my true identity."

Ennis leaned almost fully over the banquette table now, rested the arms of his suit on his flatware, unconcerned.

"We know your motivations, too."

She gave a dubious side glance. "I would be amazed if you did."

He reached out and put a hand on top of hers. His grip was firm; his skin, clammy. "Then, sweetheart, prepare to be dumbfounded."

The woman said nothing.

"Your real name is Zoya Feodorovna Zakharova, and until very recently you were a star employee of Sluzhba Vneshney Razvedki Rossiyskoy Federatsii. I don't need to translate that for you, but it's important *you* know that we at Shrike International Group have assets in the Russian Foreign Intelligence Service who were able to confirm your true identity. Now, how about we drop the Stephanie, and I start calling you Zoya?"

She answered slowly. "Yes, sir. Zoya is just fine."

Ennis seemed to notice her discomfort, and he also seemed to take some pleasure from it. He let the moment hang, then said, "You left the SVR under . . . how shall I put it? *Murky* circumstances."

The woman's lips trembled as she responded. "There was nothing murky about it. They tried to kill me. And if they find out I am here, they will come here, and they *will* kill me."

Ennis winked at her. "And now you know why I haven't tasted the tea."

Zoya Zakharova looked down at her teacup. She understood the man's cruel joke. Russia had recently poisoned a prominent critic with tea laced with polonium, and not for the first time. The radioactive isotope killed the victim only after many agonizing weeks of suffering.

Now Ennis leaned back. He was comfortable, secure, reveling in the moment. "You have nothing to worry about, Zoya. If anything, this little lie of yours has only established your bona fides even more. We didn't understand why Stephanie Arthur would leave NSA to come to us. Yes, we pay more, but if money was her main enticement, she wouldn't be working for a GS salary in the first place, would she? Usually there is some other reason when someone on a strong upwards trajectory jumps ship. But you? With you, now we understand completely why you are here and using a legend. I don't blame you. If the Russkies had a kill order on me, you can be damned sure I'd conceal my true identity."

"Yes," Zoya said, but she looked no less concerned. Her eyes darted around the room, as if assassins would rain down on her any second.

"Relax," Ennis said. "Our relationship with the SVR is not a two-way street. We received information about you, but we provided absolutely no information about you to them. They don't know you are in Berlin, and they don't know you are with us. If we hire you, they will never know."

Zoya nodded, sipped her tea again. Her hand trembled slightly as she did so, rattling the cup against the saucer as she placed it back down. "So . . . despite the fact I used a false identity to secure a position in your firm, you are still considering hiring me. Why?"

"We like to have the confidence that our employees will uphold our company's mission statement to hold our work in the strictest confidence. We value discretion above all, and that means we value people we trust to be discreet. You can earn trust over time, or you can come to us with some sort of . . . *compromise*, something that instills in us the immediate faith that you will not leave, you will not tell a tale about us and what we've been doing together, that you will remain loyal and reliable."

"You like to control your employees by having something on them." The comment was delivered by Zoya without anger or contempt.

Ennis shrugged. "Something like that. You came to us via our white side operation." He smiled now. "A woman with your skill set, we see you as being more suitable to our black side."

Zoya raised her eyebrows. "There is a black side to Shrike Group?"

"There is. You aren't an analyst, Zoya. You are a field operative. As am I. Soon we will have a need for another field operative, and I'd like to have you trained up in advance of this need."

"I am very interested."

"Excellent." He paused several seconds, forcing Zoya to wait on his next statement. She got the impression he enjoyed making her squirm. Finally he said, "I'd like to offer you a contract position in our clandestine division."

Zoya's smile had returned. "Then I accept."

"You will be run outside of Shrike International, a hidden asset. Paid via offshore accounts, given targeting assignments by me and me alone. At the moment we are finishing up the contract of our principal client. There are a couple more weeks of work involving Iranian activities in the EU, and then we will be done with that. We will fold you in immediately, give you an easy surveillance assignment or two, and then, in a few weeks, once we move away from Iran and focus on other intelligence matters, you will be ready to jump in feetfirst."

"Excellent."

She did not say what she was thinking, what Ennis must have *known* she was thinking—that she was being hired into a company for the simple reason that the company could make a single phone call and reveal her identity and her location to men and women intent on killing her unless she did exactly what they told her to do.

Ennis said, "We look forward to a long and fruitful relationship. You'll start tomorrow."

With this, Ennis reopened his menu, and Zoya followed suit.

As the two of them perused the lunch offerings, she did not hide her apprehension. She thought of everything that could go wrong, and she felt Ennis's eyes on her, certain he was picking up little cues about her fear. A quickened pulse throbbing in a vein on her forehead, a slight reddening of her cheeks, the faintest tremor in her hands.

Only when she was certain Ennis's attention was fully on his menu did she relax a little, tell herself it was going to be all right, and then get her mind back on her mission.

And she did have some reason for her comfort.

So far, at least, everything had gone exactly according to plan.

FIVE

Zoya Zakharova left Quarré after lunch and passed under the Brandenburg Gate, west on Strasse des 17. Juni, slipping her Gucci shades over her eyes as she strolled through a warm sunny afternoon along the wide sidewalk next to the trees of the Tiergarten. This was the opposite direction from her hotel in Alexanderplatz, but it was a nice day, she had the time, and she needed to make a very private phone call.

Zoya was thirty-three years old, and, though Russian by birth, she now worked for Matthew Hanley, deputy director for operations of the CIA. But it would not be accurate to say Zoya worked for the Agency herself. No, she did contract work for Hanley's completely off-book program, code named Poison Apple.

Ric Ennis had been correct that she was not who she said she was, and though she had acted astonished and distressed when he told her that he knew her true identity, the plan had revolved around him finding this information out.

But this plan was not Zoya's plan, and right now, despite willing her stress away more or less successfully over lunch, she again harbored serious misgivings about this entire damn op.

She strolled down to the Soviet War Memorial, then stepped away from several tourists milling about, pulling her phone out of her Dior purse along with an earpiece as she walked. Standing in the shade, she placed a call and slipped the earpiece in under her dark hair.

The international ring tone chirped a moment, and then the call was answered on the other end.

"Brewer."

Suzanne Brewer was CIA, Programs and Plans department. She was also Zoya Zakharova's handler, though neither of them liked or trusted the other.

Zoya responded to Suzanne in the exact same manner she always did these days. Coolly, and with only the necessary communications.

"Anthem," she said, giving her Poison Apple code name.

Brewer's voice betrayed a strong dislike for her asset, as well. "Iden check."

Zoya kept her eyes open, scanning the faces and actions of everyone in sight, unsure whether any threats were close or not. She replied with, "Identity Alpha, Alpha, X-ray, Uniform, seven, three, Yankee."

"Confirmed." Brewer immediately asked, "How did the meeting go with Ennis?"

Again, Zoya had absolutely no interest in verbosity. "I'm on the team."

"You've been hired at Shrike International Group?"

"Yes."

"As Stephanie Arthur?"

"No. As you expected, they ID'd me. They have contacts in the SVR, I guess."

"So, my plan worked," Brewer said, satisfaction in her voice.

But Zoya displayed little of Brewer's enthusiasm. "Your plan to get me killed."

"You're one to talk."

Brewer was referring to an incident between the two of them several months earlier in Scotland. Brewer had been badly injured in the altercation, and she blamed Zoya for it.

The residual mistrust between the two women crept into every single communication between them.

Suzanne Brewer said, "This is the best possible outcome. They think that they have their hooks in you. That they own you. Believe me, Anthem, they will fold you into the darkest corners of that organization."

"I believe that has already happened."

"What does that mean?"

"I am going to the black side, denied personnel, contract stuff. Offshore accounts and encrypted coms. If the missing intelligence officers from around the world are, in fact, here in Europe and working for Shrike, then this is probably where we will find them.

"Ennis described a horizontal structure to the firm, not a vertical one. He is my contact; he said I'd be interfacing with technical specialists here and there but I won't be setting foot in corporate HQ, and I won't be meeting anyone above him."

"We need answers. Whatever it takes, Anthem."

Zoya repeated her handler's words. "Whatever it takes? What does that mean, exactly?"

"If Ennis is your only access route up the chain at Shrike Group, then I suggest you concentrate on him. What I *don't* want is for you to be waltzing around Berlin for the next month doing irrelevant corporate intelligence ops for a private company. There is a ticking clock involved."

"Meaning?"

"It means our intelligence capabilities on Iran need to get a hell of a lot more robust, and quickly. If the Israelis are trying to fan the flames with Iran, we need the answers, and soon."

"I know how to do my job," Zoya replied flatly.

"I used to believe that. Then you made a critical and nearly deadly error. I'm watching you, and I'm directing you. I don't like it and you don't like it, but Hanley, for some reason, *does* like it, so let's just both do our jobs."

"I'll get back to it, then."

The Russian disconnected the call, then headed to the street to wave down a cab. "*Suka.*" *Bitch,* she said under her breath.

SIX

PRESENT DAY

The tiny 1981 Cessna 206 Amphibian flew low and lights out over the moonlit ocean, buffeted by rough air. It banked hard to starboard, nearly standing on its wing as it turned south in the darkness.

Just sixty feet above the water, the pilot leveled his wings again as he put the nose on 120 degrees, then pushed the throttle forward and descended even more.

Fifty feet. Forty. Thirty-five.

Court Gentry was the lone passenger on board and he sat in the co-pilot's seat, staring out into the darkness. He and the pilot were shoulder to shoulder, but they had barely spoken a word during the two-hour flight, and neither of them said a word as they approached the Venezuelan coast, just a couple of miles ahead.

Court could just make out a thin stretch of lighter gray in the black distance. It grew and grew, and then moments later they went "feet dry," racing over a beach at thirty feet, the single-engine aircraft churning the warm salty air at full throttle.

The strip of stark-white sand was the only landform Court had been able to make out in the darkness, but within moments the pilot began banking again, left and right, and he alternately climbed and dove while doing so.

Court turned to look at the pilot and was comforted by the shape of the ATN PS15 dual-tube night vision goggles attached to a mount on a head-band and positioned just in front of the man's eyes.

The passenger was happy he couldn't see a thing out of the windscreen in the cloudy evening now, but he was damn glad the pilot could. He knew they were winding through a forested mountain range, and they were likely a lot closer to impacting with terrain than he'd ever want to know.

He and the pilot had only met a few hours earlier at Oranjestad airport in Aruba, but the man and his aircraft had come well vetted and highly recommended.

Other than some surveillance gear, weapons, and other small items, Court wasn't using any CIA assets on this operation. He had his own contacts and his own methods of support while operating in the field, including a clearinghouse on the dark web known to only a select few, where men and women could procure a specific category of goods and services, almost *any* good or service one could imagine.

Court used it from time to time when he had a special need. The laundry list of skills on offer was impressive. Undersea transfer of goods from Colombia, paramilitary fighters for hire in Myanmar, political assassination in Japan. And Court had been pleased to see earlier in the day that airborne insertion of personnel into Venezuela was listed—even if it came at a high price.

Those few hundred on Earth who knew of and used the clearinghouse also knew that all the buyers and sellers were carefully assessed and rated on their abilities by other buyers and sellers. Court could read reviews of providers, though no names were anywhere to be found in the data, and this gave him some peace of mind when he contacted the pilot earlier in the day and arranged for the late-night air transport of one man into the Caracas area, and then ground transport to a location to the south of the city.

No, Court didn't know this son of a bitch next to him—Court's internal defense mechanism meant the man was a son of a bitch until proven otherwise—but he had no doubts that the pilot was incredibly skilled.

Court imagined that this man and this plane had made many incursions into Venezuela over the past several years, sneaking in intelligence officers, sneaking out drugs or other contraband to sell on the black market, or even helping Venezuelan citizens escape the misery of the economic and political stranglehold on their nation.

The Cessna weaved through the mountains for more than a half hour, Court's stomach contents fighting to stay down all the while. And still there was no conversation between him and the pilot. Once or twice the clouds above cleared enough for starlight to filter in, and Court could briefly make out terrain. Thick woods of pine whipped by outside his starboard-side window, seemingly one hundred feet or less from ripping off the wing and turning the tiny seaplane into a rolling ball of fire and twisted metal across the mountainside.

The underlying nausea he felt wasn't Court's only malady. He was weak and tired; he knew he was in no way fit to be operational right now. He understood that the infection was much better than it had been, but he also knew it wasn't gone, and it wasn't going to go away unless he got daily infusions of antibiotics.

But he was here on Hanley's orders, and as tough as tonight was going to be for him, he knew things would only get tougher if he defied the CIA on this.

Again.

Court had spent years working for the Agency, first as a singleton operative, sent in deep cover, alone, to fulfill CIA objectives around the world. And then he was assigned to a team of paramilitary operations officers, working in the coveted Special Activities Division on Task Force Golf Sierra, and there he and his mates conducted renditions, assassinations, recovery missions, and anything else that called for a team of Agency trigger pullers.

And then, some five years ago now, Court Gentry's life changed in an instant. Task Force Golf Sierra suddenly turned on him, tried to murder him. He fought his way out of the United States, realizing the CIA had a kill order out on his head, though he had no idea why. It took four years to reconcile with the Agency, and in that time he worked off grid as an assassin for hire, accepting only operations he felt to be righteous and worthy.

Now he was back with the Agency, more or less, as a contract agent, working in a program called Poison Apple. He and the other two agents in the program were deniable assets for Matthew Hanley, sent out on missions where any CIA fingerprints were forbidden.

Court had also taken a few freelance gigs recently—again, only objectives that satisfied his personal moral compass—and while Hanley had not approved of any of them, Hanley always knew that Court would come back and be a "good soldier" when he was done with his private crusades.

And now, even though he felt like shit, it didn't matter; Hanley had come calling, and Court knew he needed to make him happy.

Especially after screwing him over the last time.

His team leader back when he was on TF Golf Sierra had been Zack Hightower, the man now languishing in a cell here in Venezuela. Court knew he'd be within a few miles of Helicoide prison on his operation here, and he also knew that his proximity to Hightower wouldn't help Hightower's predicament one damn bit.

Court wasn't here for him, so Zack was shit out of luck.

This was a tough business. Friendships and loyalty got you nowhere; Court knew this better than anyone.

On paper, Court's mission here in Venezuela was not particularly complex. Go to some asshole's house, get around his security, and scare him into coughing up the information Hanley needed.

Don't have to be in top physical condition to pull that off, he told himself.

He also told himself he'd get back to Maryland in a couple of days, and then he'd resume his treatment. For now, he just had to focus on his objectives.

They banked left and right for several minutes more, sometimes gently, and sometimes the pilot yanked so hard on his controls it felt to Court as if the man were trying to turn his aircraft on the head of a pin.

And then he noticed the plane seemed to be in a steady climb, and for this reason only, he decided to end the silent treatment.

"I thought we were staying below radar."

The pilot did not answer.

Court waited a moment more, and then when the Cessna increased its rate of climb, he turned to the man and spoke more authoritatively.

"What are you doing?"

The pilot was Hispanic, under forty, short, bald-headed, and built like a fire hydrant with a human head on top. He kept his night vision goggles focused out the windscreen as he answered. "You want me to talk, or you want me to fly?"

Court felt his mission was in jeopardy now, and his tone conveyed his concern. "I want you to do both."

"This shit isn't easy, you know."

"Really? So *that's* why you're charging me fifty grand?"

"That's *exactly* why I'm charging you fifty grand."

"Tell me why we are climbing."

"So we don't hit the peak of that mountain right in front of us. That okay with you, amigo?"

Court peered ahead; he saw nothing but blackness. "How far?"

"Don't worry about it, I've got this."

"But won't we show up on radar?"

The Hispanic sighed, annoyed that he had to account for his actions. "Venezuelan air defense systems are good along the coast—gotta fly below eighty feet, lower even—but they can't cover these valleys that well. We're fifty miles inland now. We're fine."

"Okay," Court said, but he had no way of knowing if this guy was right or wrong.

The pilot clarified now. "We're fine, *unless* we hit that mountain."

The man was a smartass, Court could see, but he respected that. The flight finally leveled off, they dove down for a minute, and then they leveled again and continued on in silence.

It was not yet eleven p.m. when the Cessna 206 Amphibian banked gently to the left, and the pilot pulled back on the power and set the flaps. They flew slower and slower, and Court could tell from the instruments that they were descending, but only when they were less than fifty feet from landing did he see the glassy shine of a large body of water below him.

This was the Agua Fria reservoir, deep in Macarao National Park, just southwest of the city of Caracas. It was secluded, especially at this time of night, but shortly before the plane's pontoons made contact with the surface, Court saw a light flash on, dead ahead, perhaps a quarter mile distant.

"Is that for us?" Court asked the pilot.

"Why you always gotta talk when I'm concentrating?"

The man didn't seem worried in the least by the light, so Court dropped it.

The touchdown was smoother than Court expected, especially after the weaving, bumpy flight, and they taxied to a dock with a single light on a pole. The pilot cut the engines and the airplane floated closer, and soon Court saw a lone man appear on the dock out of the darkness. The pilot opened his door, stepped out on the pontoon below his seat, and pulled a rope from a hatch there. He tossed one end of the line to the stranger, and the man just held it in his hands; he didn't tie it off.

Court hefted his pack over his right shoulder; it was nearly forty pounds of gear but felt much, much heavier due to his sickness. He climbed out of the aircraft and onto the dock, nodded once to the pilot.

"I'll contact you for extraction."

There was no reply, and then the man on the dock tossed the line back to the pilot, and the seaplane began floating slowly away from the dock while the pilot stood on the pontoon, pulling one of several gas cans from the rear of the cabin to begin refueling.

Court didn't wait around. Together he and the other man began walking towards a small Honda four-door.

"*Habla Español, amigo?*"

"*Poco,*" Court responded. In fact, he spoke Spanish well enough, but he wasn't looking for conversation.

"My name is Diego," the young man said. "I am from Barquisimeto, but I know Caracas well. It will take us forty minutes to get to your destination. It's not too far."

"Good," Court said, and he followed the young man to the lone car parked near the dock.

"What's your name?" the man asked.

Shit, Court thought. *The last guy wouldn't talk, and this dude won't shut up.*

"Call me Carlos."

"Carlos?" the Venezuelan said, perplexed. "You are Latino?"

Court didn't answer, he just kept walking.

"You look like you could be Latino. But you don't talk like a—"

"I'm not looking to make friends tonight." Court opened the back door, threw his pack inside, and climbed into the front passenger seat.

The young man didn't seem hurt by the exchange, but he said nothing else as they began driving through the night.

SEVEN

San Antonio de Los Altos is a hilly, green residential suburb of Caracas, lying just south of the sprawling metropolis and full of upper-class properties laid out among the thick trees and brush, connected with narrow and steeply winding roads.

At two a.m. Court squatted in the thick foliage halfway up one of the hills, smelled the oranges in the trees around him, sweetening the pungent scent emanating from the rotting flora of the rainy season. He wore a uniform of tiger camouflage and a backpack along with black combat boots, and high-tech ear buds that both muffled loud noises and enhanced soft noises. He held binoculars to his eyes as he looked up at a whitewashed Colonial mansion high above him on the sheer hillside.

The large house appeared simultaneously regal and dilapidated, the white walls covered in mold and thick vines, but Court evaluated the building as structurally sound. He had just completed a twenty-minute 360-degree reconnaissance of the property, exhausting himself as he did so. Then he'd settled into this hide to scan the home on the hill from the rear.

This hide was some hundred feet below the building, but he was able to make out a portion of the large, wraparound, tile-floored veranda on the second level, and the big windows there, and he realized there were a lot of good ways to access the interior of the property undetected.

But he wouldn't be using any of them, because he was worried that climbing the foliage-covered gradient would be too much for him in his weakened state, especially because he needed to be ready for anything once inside the building.

He wiped a heavy sheen of sweat from his brow. San Antonio de Los Altos sat at a mile in elevation, so the air was cool, but Court's forehead poured perspiration and his hairline ejected thick steam.

The evening might have been mild, but his infection raged inside him.

Court wasn't in the mood for this shit. He was no fool, he knew he was sick, and his shoulder wound felt like he'd had surgery that morning instead of the previous week. He could function, he could move quickly in short bursts if he absolutely had to, but it was like he was operating underwater.

After another minute in his hide evaluating his options, Court decided his best course of action would be to walk around to the front of the residence, head up the steep winding driveway, and enter through the front door.

Not his regular modus operandi; in fact, it was roughly the opposite of how he liked to do business. Stealth was his specialty. Forgoing stealth today was a necessity; it was *not* a preference.

He rose and moved through thick brush, almost tripping over tufted vines, and then made his way back out onto the winding street. He walked around towards the driveway to Drummond's house, his eyes peering at the scene ahead through a small night vision monocular because there were no streetlights to light the way.

Drummond was thought to have security, and Court certainly wasn't looking to get into anything hand-to-hand tonight. This meant that, if it came down to it, he'd be reaching for a gun. He had two choices on him: a .22 caliber suppressed Walther pistol snapped into a shoulder holster under his left armpit, and a larger Glock 19 that he carried on his hip, which, while also suppressed, was still a hell of a lot louder than the .22.

Hanley had ordered Court to make certain his operation went off quietly and cleanly. *Well,* Court said to himself, *I might be able to give him quiet.* But this wasn't going to be clean, at all.

Clean was too much effort.

At the foot of the drive, he lowered himself to his kneepads and put his eye back in the thermal monocular. Scanning the scene ahead, he registered a lone man, obviously part of the protection force, sitting on a chair with his feet on a small table on the whitewashed stone front porch.

A continued scan showed no one else around, although Court was certain he'd run into others before long.

One dude asleep at the front? That can't be it, can it?

Court waited a minute more, searching for any heat signatures and listening through his hearing enhancers for any threat. He heard nothing alarming other than a few bats racing by in the sky, and he saw nothing through his glass save the thermal register of the guard and a single, small monkey, high in an araguaney tree near the home.

He rose and began climbing the steep driveway.

Court had spent two decades learning how to walk silently as if his life depended on it, because his life had *actually* depended on it. He made his way into the grasses to the side of the drive, avoiding the gravel, moving slowly with no light to guide him, measuring his footfalls as he neared the Colonial mansion.

Looking through his thermal as he climbed, he saw that the man at the front door hadn't moved at all. Court pocketed the device because it did give off a small amount of light, and then he crept forward, slowly and carefully.

When he was just twenty yards from the sentry in the chair, he thought he detected the faint sounds of classical music coming from the open second-story windows of the house ahead. This surprised him—it was past two a.m., after all—but he told himself he'd use the sound as additional cover for his approach.

It was clear to Court that, despite the fact that whoever Drummond had helping him had only two days earlier captured a man going after their protectee, they were utterly unprepared for someone else to make a similar attempt. It made no sense to him, unless of course they'd had some sort of advance warning of Hightower along with the CIA Caracas station officers before they appeared.

At the foot of the stairs to the porch, he kept one hand hovering over his Walther while with the other he pulled an eight-inch-long stainless steel cylindrical device from his chest rig, one of three held by the webbing there.

It was a Dermojet needleless automatic injector, capable of pushing a dose of whatever medicine had been loaded into it through bare skin via a quick, high-pressure blast of air.

Court eyed his victim, sleeping soundly in front of him, as he readied the device in his left hand.

Clean and quiet, Hanley had instructed. Maybe he could do clean after all, he told himself, but then his rational brain took back over.

Surely to God it's not going to be this easy.

Clark Drummond had become a cynical and bitter man in the past few years, and he no longer loved much in this world, but his love for Schubert had proved to be undying. The Austrian composer's 1816 work, Symphony no. 5, played over the speakers as the American milled about the second-floor library of the old Colonial mansion, perusing the shelves full of books. He brushed his fingers across old tomes that he had no interest in reading, his head moving gently with the subdued music.

He liked the look of this room, the feel of these books. Even though this mansion was in utter disrepair and he worried about breathing in an excessive amount of the heavy mold he smelled, he enjoyed his evenings in the place, thinking about the luxury of the property that had been sullied only by the hands of time.

But though this place did have its charms, he wasn't happy here.

Venezuela, he thought as he stepped back over to his desk in the corner. *Why the hell am I in Venezuela?*

This old house was not his. Venezuelan intelligence had put him up here, and they would continue to do so as long as he continued to help them. If he stopped, if he left, then he had no idea what lengths the regime might go to in order to bring him back or to make him pay for his defiance.

So he had decided to make the best of the situation, and he did what he could to enjoy himself, like staying up most evenings until the first glows of morning, working on his computer at his desk here in the library, or simply drinking gin and tonics and listening to music.

This was an arrangement of convenience between himself and the Venezuelan regime, and Drummond took advantage of the conveniences extended to him. Like this massive library that, while creaky and dusty and moldy and gloomy, gave off an unmistakable air of importance.

He also took advantage of the old stereo and the wide array of classical vinyl on the shelves among the books, even if many of the records were scratched or hopelessly warped from the warm, wet tropical air.

And there was one more positive aspect of his life here in hiding.

The woman.

Drummond had started to go back to his desk, but he stopped himself and turned back around when he heard the sound of footsteps in the hallway, shuffling over the music. As the Fifth Symphony's menuetto began, an attractive brunette in her forties entered the library, a fresh gin and tonic in her hand. Wearing a short skirt and a blouse that gave no hint she would be going to bed any earlier than Drummond, she kissed him as she handed him his sixth cocktail of the evening. She kissed him again, turned, and left to the sound of strings pouring out of the bassy old speakers like running water.

Alejandra was Drummond's girlfriend, or at least that was what he liked to call her. He was no fool; he knew she was actually "on the job." She wasn't a prostitute but an intelligence operative of some sort. She'd appeared in his life, a "chance" encounter in a grocery store, the day after he agreed to terms with the regime to provide technical assistance to SEBIN.

Clark Drummond had been in the spy game too long to believe in such coincidences.

Still, Alejandra was smart and interesting and always there for him, and though Drummond himself was no great prize, the good-looking Venezuelan woman never met his annoyed countenance with anything other than a pleasant demeanor.

She was working him, this he knew, but the truth was, he liked it.

He sipped the gin as he left the desk area in the corner and sat down in a worn leather chair in the middle of the room, facing both the open

French doors leading to the rear balcony and the pair of large speakers against the wall. He closed his eyes now, a slight and rare smile across his lips. He allowed himself this moment of peace. After the problems he'd encountered the past year, at least it was good to finally be safe.

And he *was* safe, of this he was certain. He didn't think much of the guards provided to him by Venezuelan intelligence, but he wasn't worried. He'd been notified well in advance of that goon Zack Hightower's arrival, and he'd been notified in advance when those foolish officers from CIA's Caracas station had tried to tail him before that. Since capturing Hightower two days earlier, he'd gotten no wind of anyone else being sent into the area, so he felt comfortable that tonight would be nothing more than an enjoyable time relaxing to classical music.

He waved a hand in the air in time with the symphony, as if he were the conductor of the orchestra, and he waited for the fourth movement to begin.

EIGHT

The sleeping guard at the front door woke up, but he did so far too late to make a play for his weapon. Court was on him before he could make a sound, covering his mouth and knocking him off the chair. Together they went down to the stones; Court lay on him with all his weight, pressing his free hand down onto the younger man's mouth.

The guard fought back, but he was saddled by surprise, panic, and his disadvantaged position, so his defense was weak and only lasted an instant. Court forced the Dermojet against the man's neck, pressed the trigger, and a full dose of propofol fired through the Venezuelan's skin and directly into his bloodstream.

It was a fast-acting sedative, one of the CIA's best drugs for taking down an opponent in a nonlethal manner.

The man continued to struggle, but for only a few seconds. Then the movement stopped abruptly, and the man went limp under Court, his head lolling to the side.

Court sat up on his rear now and grabbed at his sore shoulder, certain he'd probably already popped a stitch or two, even though falling on top of some sleeping jackass was hardly a real fight.

Shit, he told himself. *It's gonna be a rough night.*

He pulled himself to his feet and headed for the front door. He found it unlocked, and this would have made his ingress a breeze except for the fact that the door hung awkwardly on its hinges, and the bottom dragged across the threshold. He stopped as soon as the volume of the scraping grew, and he squeezed himself inside and gently shut the door behind him.

Court drew the Glock and moved with it at the ready now, through a low-lit foyer with worn hardwood floors. There was light coming out of a room on his left, so he headed that way, but found the going difficult due to the creaky boards under his feet. This home looked pretty nice on the outside, Court had thought, and it was spacious and elegant, but he could tell the old place was practically held together with baling wire.

The music wafted down from upstairs, and he prayed it covered all the sounds the house made to announce his arrival.

He approached the room with the light, ignoring the stairs up to the second floor for now. With dexterity learned through training and application, he holstered the larger pistol and drew the smaller Walther .22, which he aimed at the light as he advanced.

At this stage, Court was not hunting for Drummond; he was hunting for Drummond's security. The CIA had just made multiple attempts to track this wanted man, so as far as Court was concerned, there was no way this place wouldn't be crawling with bodyguards.

And in the kitchen he found what he was looking for. A pair of young men, facing away, both dressed in polo shirts and black tactical pants. One wore a pistol in a shoulder holster, and the other had a Micro Uzi with its stock folded, slung around his neck and hanging across his back.

Both men stood at a counter, spoons in hand, eating ice cream out of a cardboard carton.

Idiots, he thought. For the first time this evening, Court liked his chances at getting through this mission without popping all his stitches.

Court moved closer, along the wall, his .22 caliber pistol in one hand and the stainless steel Dermojet in the other.

Finally, one of the two bodyguards took his last bite of dulce de leche, put his spoon on the counter, and turned around. To his credit, he didn't move or make a sound when he saw the man in tiger camo pointing the suppressed pistol at him. Instead he just reached out to his partner, squeezed him on his arm to get his attention, then raised his hands in the air.

The second man turned around, saw the threat, and began to lower his hands to his Uzi. Court did not fire, he only lifted his weapon higher, pointing it right between the man's eyes, and he shook his head once.

The second bodyguard took his hands away from the Micro Uzi hanging against his torso, and he, too, raised his hands slowly.

Court stepped a little closer, but only so he could keep his voice down. In Spanish he said, *"Quisia dormir, o quisiara morir?"* *Would you like to sleep, or would you like to die?*

The men looked at each other, and then the man with the pistol croaked out the Spanish word for "sleep." *"Dormir,"* he said, but he didn't seem particularly thrilled about it.

"Bueno," Court replied, and then he held up the syringe in his left hand. *"Una vez para tu amigo, una vez para usted. Haz lo."* *One time for your friend, one time for you. Do it.*

Court tossed it underhanded, and the bodyguard caught it.

The Venezuelan understood that Court was ordering him to inject his partner with a shot of the medicine and then to inject himself. He was reluctant, and Court could empathize, but when Court shifted his pistol back to the man holding the syringe, the bodyguard nodded. He looked at the jetted tip, then back up to the stranger.

"Que es?" *What is it?*

Court's Spanish was good, but not great. *"Solo dormir, amigo. Media hora, nada mas."* *Only sleep, friend. A half hour, no more.*

Neither man looked convinced, but they both seemed to recognize that their options were nonexistent. The man with the pistol injected the man with the Uzi in the arm, then closed his eyes and stabbed himself in the right triceps, dropping the syringe on the floor afterwards in a weak show of defiance.

Once done, they both looked at Court, unsure of what to do now.

"Sientase en el piso." *Sit on the floor.* The men quickly complied. Court listened to the classical music coming from upstairs as he stood there for a moment. Both of the guards seemed to feel the drug at the same time, and in less than fifteen seconds they were both lying on the floor by the kitchen sink, unconscious.

Court disarmed the pair, then left them there with their ice cream and their dreams, and he made his way into the large foyer of the home. He was about to stick their weapons in a closet, but he decided against opening the door, worried that the hinges might be as rusty and loud as the ones at the front door. He slung the Micro Uzi; shoved the pistol, an HK VP9, into a dump pouch on his hip, then climbed a staircase to the second floor. As he'd imagined, the steps protested each footfall, and he could only hope the symphony playing upstairs would mask his approach.

He started down a dark and narrow hall in the direction the music seemed to be coming from. He made it only a few steps when a woman stepped out of a bathroom on his right.

She stopped when she saw the man with the gun in the dim hall in front of her.

She was small, attractive, and she wore a white blouse and a dark-colored skirt. She didn't appear to be armed, but she also didn't look to Court like a girlfriend, some sort of attendant for Drummond, or anything of the like. Her intelligent, calculating eyes, even in this shocking moment for her, tipped him off that she was something else.

Not a bodyguard . . . No, she was a spook.

He advanced on her, placed his hand over her mouth, and, pulling her skirt up to her hip, injected her in her right thigh. Her stifled screams were muffled even more when Court pushed her backwards into the bathroom and kicked the door shut with the heel of his boot. She was a fighter, and she pushed back, but he kept her mouth covered and held her up against the wall.

She went limp in his arms finally, and he laid her gently on the broken tile next to the tub. He found no weapons on her, so he left her there and turned again for the hallway.

There were only a few minutes left in Schubert's fourth movement, and Clark Drummond told himself he'd finally go to bed when it was over. He was focused on the music now, fixated even, until he felt a presence directly behind him, standing over him as he sat in the leather chair. He assumed it was Alejandra because the security men from SEBIN wouldn't dare disturb him this late at night.

He was about to speak to her, to invite her to join him for the rousing Allegro vivace, when he was tapped gently on the top of his head with a metal object.

He rose, drink in hand, then turned back in the direction of the door.

And stood face-to-face with an armed man in tiger camouflage. Panic welled inside him and he dropped his glass, shattering it on the hardwood.

"Who . . . are . . . you?"

"I'm that thing you've been telling yourself could never happen."

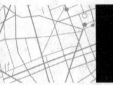

NINE

Drummond immediately looked to the hallway, then out the open doors to the veranda. Court was accustomed to this. Often when he confronted someone with bodyguards, their first thought, after the stabbing pain in their heart that came with the shock, was to check and see what the hell had happened to the assholes they'd been paying to keep them safe.

Court said, "I counted three security men. Did I miss anyone?" Drummond did not respond, so he added, "I'd sure hate for somebody to come in here and surprise me while my finger's on the trigger of the gun pointed at your face."

"There were only three tonight," the former NSA man said finally. "But my . . . my girlfriend is here in the house."

"She's fine," Court replied, not bothering to nitpick about Drummond referring to the obvious SEBIN minder as his girlfriend. "The guards will be fine, too. Not that I think you really give a shit."

Drummond still had not moved. He nodded, then puffed up his chest a little. "Those guards. They are Venezuelan intelligence. You fucked with the wrong people, friend."

"That's funny. I was about to say the same thing to you."

Court stepped around the leather chair, then around Drummond himself, and took a seat facing the door to the hallway, directly in front of his target.

The Glock 19 with a suppressor attached rested on his thigh, the business end pointed towards Drummond, and Court's finger hovered just outside the trigger guard.

The only light in the room save for the LEDs on the stereo was a little moonlight and a floor lamp between the chairs. Court pulled the chain on the lamp, and the room dipped into near darkness.

Now the older American looked searchingly out to the rear veranda.

Court said, "No one's coming to save you. Sit down."

Reluctantly, Drummond did so. Court could see worry in the man's eyes, but he saw little of the panic that usually came with someone who thought he was about to die.

Now the NSA specialist asked again, "Who . . . are . . . you?"

"Don't you recognize me?"

Drummond sniffed. "No. Why would I? You obviously know who I am. You should know that I don't interface with people like you on the operational side."

Court cocked his head at this. *Operational side? The operational side of what?* Court had been in the CIA's Directorate of Operations, but Drummond would be well aware Court was no longer an Agency employee.

Court said, "I hear you were involved with hunting me down a few years back. They did, at least, show you a picture of your target, didn't they?"

Drummond sniffed out a little laugh. "I don't have a clue what you are talking a—"

He stopped speaking suddenly, and when he spoke again, the word came out in a gasp. "Violator?"

Court sat motionless at the mention of his CIA code name.

After several seconds Drummond said, "I don't believe it."

"You *do*," Court countered. "I can see it in your eyes."

Drummond sat and stared for a long time, until he finally nodded, as if reluctantly accepting the reality before him. Then he said, "Berlin sent you?"

Berlin? Court didn't know what this meant, but he stored the information for later. When Court did not reply, Drummond sat up straighter in the chair.

"You can't kill me."

Court drummed his fingers across the grip of the Glock on his knee. "I disagree."

"No . . . I mean, they still need me. Nobody else can do what I do. They want you to bring me back. They wouldn't let you kill me if you wanted to."

Court was confused now. "Wait. *Who* needs you? Berlin?"

"Berlin," Drummond confirmed, then cocked his head. "Who else?"

"I don't know anybody in Berlin. I was *not* sent by someone who needs you. I was sent by someone who needs to silence you."

Drummond shook his head. "You're lying. There are only two groups on Earth that have a problem with me that could be solved by a man like you. There's Berlin . . . and there's the CIA. And I *know* you aren't CIA. As you said, they were after you, and I provided some technical assistance on the biometric and documentation side back when I was at NSA."

Court knew his ability to scare Drummond into spilling his guts today depended on him selling the fact that he came from Langley. So, he did the one thing he rarely did in the field.

He told the truth.

"I work for DDO Hanley. Outside the lines. It's a relationship that helps him do things that he otherwise wouldn't be able to do on behalf of America."

Drummond appeared poleaxed by this information. "What *things*?"

"Snuff out traitors, for example."

"You're . . . you're a deniable asset?"

Court responded with, "I'm always deniable. I try to be an asset, when I can."

Drummond was now, Court could tell, sufficiently terrified. In an almost reverent whisper he said, "Hanley sent the motherfucking Gray Man after me." Still in disbelief at this fact, he said, "Matt's always been a thorn in my side, but he's also a friend."

"He *was* a friend. Then you disappeared from NSA with state secrets. Trust me, right now, he's pretty much just a thorn in your side."

"So . . . what? You're supposed to shove me into a shipping crate and haul me back to Langley?"

Court realized now was the time to push even more fear into Drummond's mind. He shook his head. "Nope."

"Really? Just a talking-to? Well, you can go to hell. I'm not talking."

Court's brown eyes darkened now. "When someone just needs a talking-to, I'm not the guy they send."

Drummond shook his head back and forth several times at this, a show of certitude. "No. No way. Matt wouldn't send the Gray Man to kill me."

"I'm here to tie off a loose end. If you won't help us understand who you peddled your wares to, then we have no choice but to minimize any further losses and to send a message to others in the intelligence community about the cost of treason."

Drummond pulled his hands from his face, looked out the French doors to the veranda again, at the black sky.

"So . . . if I talk, if I'm transparent now, you'll let me live?"

Court shrugged. "I have execute authority. I'll make the call."

"Will you get me out of Venezuela?"

"I'll make that call, too."

Drummond deflated fully, nestled his head back in his hands. To Court he looked like a beaten man, but Court was ready for him to try to fight, to run. He'd seen how men act in desperate times, like cockroaches caught out in the light, like wounded animals cornered.

He had to be ready for anything, but in this case, he got the outcome he'd hoped for.

"I'm trusting you, Gentry. I know you fucked over the Agency once, but if Hanley took you back, then you must have made amends. I also know you aren't evil. You did what you were told to do, more or less, and then when you turned rogue you only went after bad actors. What I'm saying is . . . I'm expecting you to do the right thing here, and hold up your end of the bargain."

Court simply replied, "I have a tendency to reward good behavior."

Drummond kept his head in his hands as he said, "I was approached by a woman in D.C."

"What woman?"

"Her name was Miriam. A pseudonym, I figured that from the beginning, but a good Jewish name. Old Testament spelling of Mary."

"Jewish?" Court asked, surprised by this.

"She was Israeli intelligence, though she never said that outright. Not

Mossad, something darker. I don't have to tell you Jerusalem has sub rosa groups that are blacker than the Mossad."

Drummond was right, he did not have to tell Court.

"Go on."

"A classic bump. I should have reported it, but it was innocuous enough and it didn't even surprise me. I had been vocal about my . . . *disappointment* with my superiors with regard to our intelligence sharing with Israel. Of course they were going to approach me.

"Miriam spent months selling me on the idea that Europe was going to relax economic sanctions on Iran, and that new cash flow would go into Iran's quest for regional dominance. And she was right. Last year, EU sanctions were cut in half, and there's pressure to lower them even more.

"And she wanted to hire me to help get the sanctions reinstated. Strengthened. I'd heard rumors at NSA that Israel was trying to get us to go along with their initiative, but official U.S. government policy was that America did not want to get pulled into any more spying in Europe that could piss off the EU, and we were holding steady with our policy on Iran."

Gentry sat quietly for a moment, listening to the late-night calls of howler monkeys out in the trees. Finally, he spoke. "And what was Clark Drummond's official policy?"

"There are many of us in the government who think we've gone weak on our enemies. We have capabilities to deal some serious intelligence blows, but certain friendly countries have been basically made off-limits. Our enemies are very active in these nations, and our efforts are hampered."

"Like Germany?"

"Exactly like Germany. We got caught spying on the upper tiers of their government years ago. Now CIA, NSA, all the U.S. agencies, treat German soil with kid gloves. The new U.S. ambassador to Germany is openly hostile to the CIA, just like his pal the president of the United States. Meanwhile, Iran has convinced the EU to lower sanctions, and the Iranians are using that money to build nukes. Iranian spies and diplomats are running around Europe, trying to get more trade and even lower sanctions, which will mean more euros for the Shia tyrants."

Drummond reached for his gin and tonic. Court watched the movement, ready to heft his pistol again if necessary.

The older man sipped and said, "I finally told Miriam I wanted in. She offered me one point three mil a year, but there was a caveat. I had to make a copy of PowerSlave and get it out of the U.S."

"PowerSlave?" Court asked.

Drummond looked up at him with suspicion now. "Hanley knows I have it, which means you would know what that was if you were really sent by Hanley."

Court didn't miss a beat. "Hanley doesn't tell me shit."

Drummond eyed Court in the dim for a moment, then nodded and put his head back in his hands. "Yeah, okay. That sounds like Matt." He continued. "PowerSlave is what I designed at Fort Meade. It's the code name for a secret NSA program, a database-linked software application."

"You're boring me," Court said.

Drummond ignored him. "The name and image of every single existing or former intelligence officer in the U.S. intelligence community. All seventeen agencies." He looked proud suddenly. "Still bored, Gentry?"

Court wiped sweat from his forehead as he flexed his jaw muscles in anger. "You gave Israel our NOC list?"

"PowerSlave is not just NOCs. It's all intelligence agency employees, either official or nonofficial cover. And it's not just the list, either. It's all their biometric data, as well. I added the complete database into a program you can run against facial recog data; any camera you can hack into, you can use. If an American spook passes a camera I have access to, it will trigger an alert to PowerSlave.

"It uses biometric algorithms to query the face in front of the camera with the database, then uses high-level machine learning to run data against known actors. It accounts for plastic surgery, disguises, everything. It can't be spoofed."

Court nodded. "And that's how you rolled up Hightower."

He nodded.

"I wormed into all the cameras around here; Zack didn't stand a chance." Drummond added, "I know Hightower was your team leader back with Golf Sierra. What was it they used to call you guys? The Gangster Squad?"

"The Goon Squad."

"Right," Drummond said.

Court was thinking about what a dick Hanley was to send Zack up against a guy in possession of the means to identify him via biometric data. He cleared his head of his anger. "Back to Miriam. She wanted you to fake your death?"

"She helped me stage the accident in the Chesapeake. I was on a private jet to Germany that afternoon. She put me up in a farmhouse in Potsdam, guarded twenty-four-seven by armed Israelis. She gave me a team of tech experts, all private sector men and women: a Brit, a couple of Germans, an Israeli, and a woman from Lithuania."

"What was Miriam's objective?"

"At first, she wanted PowerSlave to help them ID U.S. intelligence personnel from Berlin station. America had been pushing back against Israeli covert ops, thinking that for some reason Israel was trying to goad Iran into attacking the West. But my work with Israel wasn't about war, it was about sanctions, so I was totally on board with helping Israel combat the Americans on that. Everyone on my team was."

Court looked at his watch, mindful of how long the men and the woman around the house would remain under the effects of the propofol. He said, "You seem pretty proud of yourself for the work you were doing over there. That raises the question . . . Why are you here?"

There was new stress in his voice. "Because people started dying."

Court cocked his head. "In Iran?"

Now Drummond shouted, the stress overtaking him fully. "No! On the fucking streets of Berlin!"

TEN

"What people?" Court asked.

"People working for the Israelis." Drummond's face darkened. "People working with me. We hacked into Iranian intelligence servers in several European embassies, we were able to see some of their personnel files. We thought this was all going to be used to target spies for surveillance, or to get them deported by the host countries. But that's not what happened."

"What happened?"

"Miriam came to me and told me they wanted to be able to alter files in the Iranian servers. I agreed, at first. It was theoretically possible to do, and it could help turn the screws on the embassy spooks. But when my team and I got the targeting list of files they wanted to change, we knew something was wrong."

"Why?"

"We were turning regular consular affairs guys into Iranian spooks, and Iranian spooks into consular affairs guys. We were, basically, creating false positives and false negatives in their systems. This meant that America, Germany, anybody else who broke into the Iranians' servers, they wouldn't be able to determine who was an IO and who was regular embassy staff."

"What was Miriam's objective with that?"

"She didn't say, but it looked like she wanted Quds Force personnel and other Iranian officers to move freely within Europe, even though they were on a watch list.

"To me, and to my colleagues, this was absolutely wrong. It could hurt friendly nations' capabilities versus Iran. It had nothing to do with the stated goals I was brought over from the U.S. to achieve. I'm not a traitor, no matter what Hanley told you. I'm an achiever, and I thought Israel was actually going to do something to cripple the mullah's power in Iran, while we in the U.S. have been playing patty-cake with them for forty years."

"What did you do when they asked you to alter the databases?"

"My lead software engineer, Tony Hutchens, went to Miriam and demanded to speak to someone above her. He was persistent. He insisted on hard proof that this was, in fact, an Israeli intelligence initiative we were all involved with. He thought we were actually working for the Iranians the entire time, which, of course, was crazy. Hutchens, like an idiot, threatened to go to *Spiegel* or *Stern* or some other German publication to tell them what we were doing, what we had done."

Court said nothing now, because he knew something more was coming.

Drummond went on. "And then, nine hours later, Tony Hutchens died of a heart attack in his car outside a restaurant in Charlottenburg."

"You think he was murdered?"

"Would you believe a coincidence like that?"

"I didn't know Tony Hutchens, so I couldn't say."

"He was thirty-four, he wasn't about to drop dead on his own. Someone killed him."

"So, you ran?"

"Not when Tony died." He paused. "I ran when Gretchen died."

"Shit," Court said now.

"Gretchen Brust. She was Swiss, not Israeli, but she was a case officer. The Israelis like using foreign talent, I guess. She ran a human intelligence cell for them in Zurich. I only met her a few times in the course of our work—they keep their cells separate—but our two groups coordinated on a . . . a thing. Anyway, she came to my apartment in Berlin one night after Tony's heart attack and told me she thought he'd been murdered. She said her cell was actively working against Swiss intelligence in Zurich, and she'd had enough. She went to Miriam, complained about overreach. Miriam told her she'd kick her complaints up the chain of command. But nothing happened." He held up his hand. "That's not true. Something *did* happen. She grew a tail."

"Someone was following her?"

Drummond nodded. "Middle Eastern men, that's all she knew."

"What happened to Gretchen?"

"Stabbed to death in the street four blocks from my place. Her purse was taken, but that was just for show. I knew that if they had been following her, then they probably knew she'd come to see me. I had to get the hell out of there.

"I played along for another day, just long enough to upload PowerSlave on a remote server based in Romania. Then I flew to Buenos Aires. Made my way here a week later."

Court wasn't writing any of this down. He'd been trained to keep large amounts of information memorized. "Miriam. What else can you tell me about her?"

"Not much. Nice looking. Midthirties, I'd guess. Serious. A good intelligence officer, which means I barely knew her. I received orders via encrypted message, exchanged files on a dark web link, text messages and calls via double encryption services. I had a bank account in Luxembourg to draw funds from as I saw fit. It was like that the entire year I was in Berlin."

Court was incredulous. "And you didn't see that as shady as fuck?"

Drummond sighed; he was clearly pained by what he'd done to his life by running from America to work for some opaque organization. "The mission was good, at first. When it wasn't good, I left. I didn't do one single thing over there that I regret."

Court rolled his eyes. "When the mission was good, that was just them feeling you out, grooming you to do the dirty work. You get that, right?"

"I see that now, yeah."

"Was this even an Israeli operation?"

Drummond shook his head, but he didn't seem sure. "I . . . I still believe so."

Court countered, "It could have been anybody with a lot of money and a high level of sophistication."

Drummond agreed. "Yeah. There was a *lot* of money involved, and the few people working for them that I had dealings with were all first-rate. But most were Israeli, the mission was Iran. I just assumed—"

Court checked his watch again and then he stood, startling Clark Drummond in the process. "Hanley is going to need to find this Miriam. How will he do that?"

"I have a picture. I took it covertly, shortly after her first bump." He looked over to his computer.

Court said, "I'll give you a number to text it to. Print it out, as well. I want the hard drive to that computer, too. Anything else?"

"We always met at Ben Rahim coffee shop, near Alexanderplatz. She loves Middle Eastern coffee, I guess. I could tell the staff there all knew her, so she was a regular. Might be a good place to start."

Drummond went over to the computer now; as he logged in, he said, "Call Hanley, tell him I want to come home. I've got more to trade if you bring me in. SEBIN is not going to be happy about what happened tonight. I'm no longer safe in Venezuela."

"I'll call him as soon as we're out of here. Those guards will be waking up soon, and they're gonna be pissed."

Court stepped to the veranda to look out over the rear of the property and the hills around. It was all but black outside, even though his eyes had had time to adjust with the low lighting in the library.

"You've got a car, I assume?" he asked back into the library.

"Yeah. A Wrangler. It's in the garage. We can't go to the airport, though."

"No shit," Court replied. "Some asshole gave the Venezuelans the means to identify any intelligence asset coming or going through their immigration."

"You're safe from PowerSlave, Gentry," Drummond countered. "You were too black to be on any list, anywhere. Even when I was on the hunt for you I wasn't allowed to upload any of your stored biodata onto the master server. Me, on the other hand: the Venezuelans have a ton of ways to ID me, especially since I've been working with the government here for the past few months."

Court began to turn away from the open French doors. "We're not going to the airport. I've got another way out of—"

But then his head swiveled back outside. As he was turning away he thought he'd detected movement in the darkness down the hill, but he wasn't sure. Quickly he pulled his thermal monocular out of a chest pouch and held it to his eye.

First he saw only a few howler monkeys in the trees, but as he scanned over to the left he picked up more heat signatures. There were four of them, moving up the driveway on the other side of a cluster of tall brush, ascending quickly until they disappeared around the side of the house to his left.

These four men had been spaced evenly. Their movements had been tight and practiced; one bounded while another rushed forward, took a position, and then was followed by the man behind.

Their tactics were familiar to Court.

These guys weren't Venezuelan security goons. No way.

These were special forces of some sort, and Court had never heard much that impressed him about Venezuelan special forces, so he assumed them to be foreign.

"Turn off the stereo," he demanded.

The laser printer to the left of the desk hummed as Drummond turned to Court. "Why?"

Court did not answer. He drew his suppressed .22 in a flash and spun, fired once into the glass panel of the stereo receiver near Drummond's desk. The music stopped abruptly.

The printer disgorged a single page, and then it went quiet, as well.

The room fell silent.

Drummond looked terrified now. "What the hell are—"

"Shut up."

Just then Court picked up a faint noise through his hearing enhancers. It was the long scraping sound of the front door opening.

Court said, "We've got company."

"Your people?" Drummond asked.

Court shook his head as he holstered the .22. "I don't have people. Hanley sent me here alone."

"Who is it, then?"

"My only guess is that you were right to worry about the boys in Berlin coming for you."

Court rushed towards the door to the hall, lifting up the Venezuelan guard's Uzi that had been hanging from a sling over his shoulder as he did so. He unfolded the tiny stock, pulled back the charging handle on the top of the receiver, and let it go, chambering a 9-millimeter round.

Drummond held his hands up. "Wait a second. You aren't actually going to fight them, are you?"

Court looked out with the weapon at his shoulder, found the space in front of him clear, then moved back into the library, shutting and locking the door as he did so. Sarcastically, he said, "Do you think I can talk them into surrendering?"

Drummond's terror increased by the second. "They won't kill me. They *can't* kill me. They have PowerSlave now, but they know that I'm the one who built it, I'm the only one who can operate it effectively. They need me."

Court said, "Trust me, I'd rather run than fight, but first I need to know what I'm up against. Get into the bathroom and wait till I call for you."

Drummond moved to the bathroom in the corner near his desk, while Court crouched low and then moved out onto the veranda, staying out of the line of sight in case there were others with eyes on the back side of the home. Peeking through the railing at the terrain below, he decided that though he really didn't want to go down the steep hill, especially with an older, untrained man in tow, he didn't see that he had any choice.

He wiped the film of sweat off his brow, even though the late-night air was cool at this altitude. He had twenty meters of rope in his backpack, and it was fewer than ten down to the hillside. He was confident he could make this work, although the thought of having some asshole holding on to his back, his arms pressing against the dozen stitches in Court's shoulder, didn't appeal to him in the slightest.

He attached the carabiner hanging on one end of the rope around the metal railing of the veranda, then threw the black line over the side.

He was almost back to the French doors to collect Drummond when he heard a new sound, loud and immediate. It was something clanging down onto the veranda, metal striking ceramic tile, then bouncing against a wooden chaise lounge to Court's right.

He recognized the sound, and he recognized the danger.

Throwing himself through the doorway he screamed, "Grenade!"

ELEVEN

The explosion on the veranda ripped through the windows and sent shrapnel into the room, just feet above Court's body on the floor. Metal fragments shredded the thin wooden walls. Smoke, dust, and other debris blew in and filled the darkened library with a haze.

It had been a high-explosive grenade, not a stun grenade, and this told Court that Drummond had severely overvalued the importance placed on him by his former employers.

Court rose and ran for the bathroom now. Adrenaline overcame the lethargy caused by the infection, and he moved as quickly and as adroitly as ever. He slid into the bathroom, knowing without a doubt that he'd torn the remaining stitches below his collarbone in the process, and as he winced with the fresh pain, he turned to the NSA man. "You hurt?"

Drummond knelt against the wall, next to a large, cast-iron, claw-foot bathtub.

"They can't kill me, they need me!" the older man repeated.

A second grenade detonated, this time just outside the open doors to the veranda.

Court coughed dust, then said, "It's starting to look like these guys didn't get that memo, chief. If they're slinging frags your way, they aren't worried about your health."

Drummond accepted Gentry's logic. "Get me out of here. Please!"

There were only two ways to safety as far as Court could tell: going through the door to the hallway, or going over the side of the veranda. The hallway would have enemy there, he had little doubt of this, but he was equally certain there were bad guys outside, as evidenced by the grenades lobbed in his direction.

Court made his decision quickly, and though it was hardly ideal, he determined it to be the lesser of two evils. They'd go for the hall, then the stairs, then the front door, then Drummond's Jeep. He had three pistols and a fully automatic Micro Uzi Pro loaded with thirty rounds. He had the guns and ammo to make this work; as long as he was alive, he could fight.

"Follow me," he said. "Head low."

Drummond grabbed him by the arm. "Listen. If I don't make it, find Miriam. Israel wouldn't kill me. Whoever she's working for, it's someone else."

"Got it."

They made it halfway across the library to the door, and then gunfire began tearing through the bookshelves on their left, emanating from the hallway. Court grabbed Drummond and threw him to the ground, then slammed down on top of him, returning short bursts of fire with the Uzi one-handed in the direction of the incoming rounds.

His rounds ripped into books and the wall, but he didn't think the Uzi was powerful enough to penetrate with enough force to be deadly in the hallway, so he concentrated his fire on the closed hallway door. He expended his magazine quickly, hoping he was taking out at least one enemy on the other side in the process.

The Uzi ran empty; Court threw it aside and pulled his Glock pistol with one hand while he climbed up to a crouch, yanking Drummond with him by the collar of his shirt. They began moving forward again, and they were steps away from the hallway door now.

It exploded in front of them from a breaching charge; wood blasted through the library, narrowly missing the two men there. The concussion slammed into both Drummond and Gentry, but since Court had been in front, he fell all the way to the floor, while Drummond only stumbled back into the middle of the large room.

Books began burning in the shelves near the doorway.

Court took his concentration away from the NSA computer scientist for an instant to fire more rounds into the smoke-filled hallway, and when he climbed back to his feet, he turned to see that Drummond had begun running for the veranda.

Good idea, Court thought. Exfiltrating through the hallway was obviously too risky; they were going to have to jump over the railing and roll down the hillside.

Court turned back to face the doorway to provide suppressive fire for Drummond's escape, but after only a few rounds something appeared out of the dark haze in front of him. Right before Court's eyes, he saw a small green satchel tossed into the room. It landed on the floor just feet from the chairs where he'd been sitting with Drummond minutes before.

He knew what it was, and he knew he was fucked.

It was a satchel charge. Probably twenty times the power of the grenades that had been exploding outside the library. Drummond was on the veranda now, probably in the line of fire of shooters out there, but Court saw no way to get to him. He screamed, "Bomb! Get over the side!" and then he turned and took four rushed steps before diving headfirst into the bathroom, straight into the big iron tub against the wall.

Just as he slammed down against the bottom of the tub, he was engulfed with an impossible sound and light. His world shook, he flipped upside down and then back up, his wrecked body crashing like a pinball against the floor and walls of the bathtub, and he was thrown hard against his left side before coming to rest again facedown with his mouth on the drain.

The motion stopped abruptly, his ears rang, and he groaned in agony. Everything hurt. A second later something crashed down on top of his back, hard, and though there was too much dust in the air to see anything, he recognized that the material that hit him was plaster and wood.

Through the fog in his brain that came from the concussion of the detonation, Court thought that a portion of the ceiling had collapsed onto him. As he tried to push it off, the dust and smoke cleared a little, and soon in the low light he realized he'd fallen through the second-floor bathroom during the blast, kept alive only by the heavy tub, and now he and the tub were covered with building material on the ground floor.

He felt wet blood dripping from his nose, slickening the bottom of the tub where his gloved hands were pressed under his chest.

Above him, through the screeching ring in his ears, he heard voices, and he thought they were speaking English.

And then he passed out.

TWELVE

Hades followed Mercury and Atlas through the black smoke filling the library, rising from the bookshelves to the right of the door. They realized quickly that Mars's satchel charge had collapsed a large portion of the floor of the library and the bathroom. Water shot from pipes, and dust and smoke rose from a twenty-foot hole in the hardwood.

The three men covered different portions of the room with their rifles, until Mars entered behind them. He looked at his handiwork and said, "Shit. Sorry, boss. Little overkill, I guess. House is a piece of shit."

Before Hades could respond, a voice came through his headset. "Thor for Hades. I have one unknown subject on the rear veranda. Looks unarmed. Do I take the shot?"

Thor was in overwatch on a nearby hillside and had a better view of the veranda than the men in the smoke-filled room. Hades headed to the French doors, now ripped and shredded; glass and plaster and wood were everywhere. He pressed his transmit button. "Negative, hold for target ID."

"Holding," came the terse reply.

Hades spun out through the ruined doorway, sweeping his rifle right to left. He saw a middle-aged man on the veranda in front of him, with one leg over the railing. The American mercenary raced forward and grabbed the man by the arm, then swung him off the rail and down to the ceramic tiles. He held his gun on him and actuated the weapon light in the man's face.

It was Clark Drummond, his target.

The older man shouted in panic. "You can't kill me! Call your masters! You can't—"

"Oh, okay," Hades said, and then he shot Drummond twice in the chest from a distance of three feet, and then a third time between the eyes. Blood and tissue splattered across the tile.

Hades clicked his mic and spoke authoritatively. "Target is KIA. Mercury, pull the hard drive from that computer."

"Roger that, snagging it now."

Hades broadcast to all elements now. "Are we clear?"

One at a time his men began responding, each assuring that their area was clear of any hostiles.

But only five of his seven men counted off.

"Hades for Ares. Hades for Atlas."

After a few seconds a reply came. "Atlas for Hades. Ares is down! Say again, Ronnie's down!"

"Where are you?"

"Hallway."

Hades found Atlas on his knees over Ares, a thirty-eight-year-old Kansan named Ronnie Blight. Atlas had ripped off the man's body armor and was now performing frantic chest compressions.

Hades shined his light on Ronnie now. A jagged bullet wound had opened his neck; blood was everywhere, but he didn't seem to be bleeding from the hole any longer.

"Heart's stopped," Hades said. "He's dead."

Atlas sat back on his haunches, giving up on the compressions. His gloves and bare forearms were covered in blood. "Shit!" he shouted in frustration.

Hades sighed, looking down at his fallen man. Just then he began to feel the heat from the growing fire in the library reaching him out here. He knelt down and took the corpse under his arms, began lifting him up to drag him towards the staircase. Ares's head hung back, his eyes open, and blood stained the forearms of Hades's tunic. But he'd only begun to move him when Atlas squeezed him on the shoulder. "We gotta exfil, boss. This whole place is gonna go up in flames."

But Hades was barely listening. He transmitted to his men, even though most of them were within a few feet from him, standing over the body of their comrade. "Anybody see any other hostiles?"

"That's a negative," Mercury replied as he came out of the burning room, slipping a computer hard drive in his bag as he did so. "Gunfire came through the door, tagged Ronnie as we covered Mars while he prepped the C-4. I never saw the shooter."

"Me, either," said Atlas, then added, "but I caught a pistol round in my plate right before Ronnie dropped."

Several feet away from the cluster of men around the body, Mars came out of the bathroom, having just rechecked it for hostiles. He brushed the doorway with his right arm as he exited, and then he winced with pain. He touched his gloved hand to a spot right below his elbow on his forearm.

"Shit, guys. I took one, too. Not bad."

Atlas stepped over to him to check it out, pulling out his flashlight as he did so. He put it away when he saw that the growing firelight would provide plenty of illumination.

"Yep. That ain't shit, bro, but you definitely got lucky."

Hades put Ronnie Blight's body back down in the hallway, and stood back up. "Three of us got hit? By Drummond?" He turned and moved quickly back into the burning library. He ducked below the ever-thickening smoke and sprinted back to the veranda. Here he found Zeus already searching Drummond's body.

"No weapon, boss. He either lost it or tossed it."

As Hades weighed the slim possibility that Drummond might actually have been the man who killed Ares and shot both Atlas and Mars, the voice of Thor, still positioned on the opposite hillside with a long gun trained on the veranda, came over the net.

"Thor for Hades. Be advised, I've got four squirters movin' down the driveway. They're staggering along like they're hurt or on drugs or some shit. No weapons visible. I got a shot if you want me to waste 'em."

"Negative," Hades said. "Intercept. I'll come to your poz." He then rallied his remaining men, and they all began climbing down the rope hanging from the veranda, leaving their dead comrade behind to be consumed by the growing fire.

Court Gentry woke slowly, shook his head to clear it, then felt the lumber and plaster pressing down on his back. He pushed with all his might and after several seconds managed to free himself, though when he looked around he saw it was too dark to make out much of his surroundings.

Water from burst pipes somewhere above rained down on him, and though he smelled smoke, he could see no light from a fire here. He climbed out of the tub, pushing his way through flooring that had collapsed with him, and slowly oriented himself.

He was dazed still; his hearing protection had saved him from burst eardrums, but the jarring impacts had taken a toll on his already weakened body. He had to reach out to a wall to hold himself up as he shook the haze and exhaustion from his brain several more times. He wasn't badly hurt, he realized, especially after what had just happened, though the surgical wound in his shoulder screamed in agony and blood dripped from his nose.

He didn't know if Drummond had made his way off the veranda, but he knew he had to go and find out.

He'd lost the Glock and the Walther somewhere during the explosion, but he did have the HK VP9 he'd taken off the bodyguard in his dump pouch. He drew this and headed for the stairs.

Seconds later he was back in the upstairs hallway, kneeling low to stay out of the thick smoke. He saw a body outside the doorway to the library; the man had been stripped of his weapons by his mates, so Court just moved past him, then directed his attention to the fire raging in the last place where he'd seen Drummond.

Shit.

Court didn't go directly into the fire. Instead he found a bedroom across the hall, pulled the comforter off the bed, went into the bathroom, and threw it in the tub there. He turned on the shower and let it run over the fabric, then looked back over his shoulder only to find the bedroom filling quickly with smoke as the fire spread. He dropped to his knees to stay below the rising black cloud, then sloshed the comforter around in the water for a few seconds, making certain the entire thing was soaked. Then he rose again to his feet, pulling the heavy waterlogged comforter around his shoulders and head as he moved towards the fire-engulfed library.

Moving into the room, he looked immediately towards the veranda but couldn't see it through the smoke and flame, so he dropped to his knee-pads and began crawling, still holding the wet comforter around him for protection.

But as he made his way to the doorway outside, he stopped his advance. There, some twenty feet away from him, a clearly dead Clark Drummond lay on the tile.

Court shifted his attention to the far wall of the room. To the right of the old executive desk there, the floor had caved in, taking bookshelves, most of the bathroom, and Court down with it. But when he checked the desk, he was happy to see both the computer and the printer still there on a waist-high stand.

The heat was all but unbearable, so Court rose, ran for the printer, and snatched the one sheet of paper on top. He stuck it in his dump pouch without looking at it, then reached for the computer. Upon inspecting it, though, he saw that the back had been removed. He felt around inside and realized the hard drive was gone.

"Dammit," he said to himself. Hanley was going to blow a fucking gasket.

He considered checking all the drawers in the desk but almost instantly decided against it. He had no choice now; the acrid smoke and the flames were forcing him out of the library. Forgoing any more of his rushed sensitive site exploitation, he turned and made his way towards the veranda, though he couldn't see anything in front of him.

Once outside he found that the flames behind him were still too hot to bear. He threw off the comforter and ran for the railing, passing Drummond's corpse as he did so. He fell over the side of the veranda, landed on the steep gradient of the jungle hill thirty feet below, and began rolling down, faster and faster.

Mercifully, he came to rest in especially thick jungle foliage, and here he spent nearly a minute coughing and wiping soot out of his eyes.

His camo pants were burned below the knees, but he didn't feel like he'd been burned himself. Still, his wound stung as hot as the fire he'd just braved, and his body was racked with pain and exhaustion.

He vomited into the brush around him, ravaged by both his sickness and the smoke.

Tonight was a nearly complete mission fail, no doubt about it, but now the only thing he could do was cut his losses and get out of the country without getting caught.

Court rose slowly, stiffly, and began moving down the jungle hill, some forty yards away and obscured by trees from the driveway on his left.

At the bottom of the driveway, three men and a woman were on their knees with their hands behind their heads. Thor guarded over them with his rifle as Hades appeared out of the darkness behind the prisoners. He wore a large shemagh bandana around his neck, and this he pulled up to cover the lower half of his face as he stepped in front of them.

Looking at the four, he instantly took the woman in the dark skirt as the one in charge due to the fact that she was older than the men and possessed an air of authority. He said, "English?"

"Yes," she replied, her face straight ahead and her fingers still laced together behind her head.

"Who are you?"

"SEBIN. Venezuelan intelligence." She looked up to the man now. Unafraid. "Who are *you*?"

Hades didn't answer. "Which one of you killed my man?"

The woman shook her head. "These are bodyguards. They were disarmed, and we were all drugged. We didn't shoot anybody."

Hades cocked his head. "Who disarmed you? Who drugged you?"

One of the young security men said, "He was fast. He was alone. He knew what he was doing."

Hades narrowed his eyes. "One guy?" He wasn't buying it.

But all four nodded, and to Hades they appeared adamant.

"What did he look like?"

The woman shook her head. "Not like you. Not like any of you. He looked . . . normal."

"That's it?"

"A gringo. That's all."

Now the American mercenary sighed audibly. "A gringo." He thought things over a moment, then said, "I don't like losing a dude. I'd love to shoot you four as payback, but I don't have approval for that shit." He considered using the sat phone to call his masters in the Middle East to see if he could terminate Venezuelan intelligence officers. But he decided against it. "Fuck it," he said. "Stay right here for twenty minutes, then get up and go."

Mercury had collected the panel truck the team had arrived in, and he pulled up now. Hades and the others climbed in, and then the truck backed out of the driveway and began hurtling down the hillside towards Caracas.

THIRTEEN

The massive Russian-built Mi-17 helicopter raced low, flying north over flat Yemeni scrubland in the dark, until the dawn's early light opened up the sky and hinted at a massive expanse of desert ahead.

In the back, a man looked out a portal in the cabin imagining this very area two years earlier, when the heaviest fighting took place in the region, and then he shut his eyes, shuddering from the thought.

He'd not seen it himself; he'd been in Aden, to the west, at the time, but out here in the desert, not far from where he now flew, his brother had lost his life.

The man in the Russian helo was Sultan al-Habsi, but he had adopted the code name Tarik in the field. He was forty-seven years old, and he was the deputy director of operations for the SIA, Signals Intelligence Agency, the spy service of the United Arab Emirates.

After a moment, Sultan opened his eyes again and looked around the cabin, telling himself that, as the chief clandestine intelligence officer for the UAE, he would not think of his older brother Zayad today, only his mission.

He took a few deep breaths and realized that although a little sadness had crept into his thoughts, his overwhelming sensation was one of excitement. This was a great day, the beginning of his life's purpose.

He would make his father proud, and his father was the crown prince of Dubai and the ruler of the United Arab Emirates.

Sultan al-Habsi might have been his father's son, but he had been created by the CIA. The elder al-Habsi had been supported by the Agency for decades, and the son was brought along through academia and through the UAE military with an eye on a career in the intelligence services of his nation.

It was his destiny.

The Americans had always maintained good working relationships with the UAE in intel matters, but after 9/11, the necessity for "friends" in the Middle East grew exponentially, as did the amount of money the Agency was willing to spend on its allies' intelligence services. At the time the UAE had little to offer, but the Americans decided their needs in the region were so great, they would design and build up an entire spy service for the Emirates, and then they would train local personnel to staff it.

The son of the ruler of Dubai was on every list the Americans had for quality candidates. He was unknown, having eschewed what little spotlight there was on the royal family in Dubai. He was smart, a polyglot, and well educated. And his father wanted him in the role.

Sultan spent months in the United States training with the CIA, and then he moved up the ranks of the SIA quickly, finally being chosen by his father to lead covert ops five years earlier.

Rashid al-Habsi had told his son what he wanted from the outset. As far as the father was concerned, the chasing of Al Qaeda on behalf of the Americans was just a sideshow; AQ was no great threat to Abu Dhabi and Dubai and Muscat. No, the real threat was Shia expansion; it had been so since the 1970s and it would be so until the day Iran was wiped from the face of the Earth. At that time, the Iraqi Shias and Lebanese Shias and Syrian Shias and any other Shias anywhere on the planet would again know their place: as impotent outsiders.

That was the goal of Rashid al-Habsi, and thus it also became the goal of all three of his sons. Zayad, the oldest, became an army infantry colonel. Saed, the youngest, worked in the diplomatic corps for the nation in Yemen, and the middle child, Sultan, took over the operational wing of the nation's intelligence services.

All three brothers were in Yemen during the UAE's proxy war there. Saed, the diplomat, worked at the embassy in Sana, and had been killed in a rocket attack three years earlier. And then, just over a year ago, Colonel Zayad al-Habsi, Sultan's older brother, was killed in combat near the town of Ataq, when sappers made their way into his command post and detonated suicide vests.

The two surviving Rashid men, father and son, knew without question that the Houthi rebels had not coordinated either of these two attacks on their own. It was obvious the work had been done by the Islamic Revolutionary Guard Corps, specifically their clandestine unit known as Quds Force.

Neither seventy-year-old Rashid nor forty-seven-year-old Sultan had needed any more incentive to despise Iran, but the deaths of Zayad and Saed only poured gas on the flames of their hatred.

As his helicopter landed on the sand-strewn helipad at Ataq airport, his mind was now keenly tuned to his objective this morning. He wanted to be in and out of here in an hour, no more, and then head directly back to Dubai. There was still much to plan, but Sultan knew the importance of strong leadership in cajoling the rank and file into sacrifice, so he'd made this trip in person.

He climbed off the aircraft, accompanied by four Signals Intelligence operatives, as well as Hades and three more of the American mercenaries he had working for him. The Emiratis climbed into one large armored SUV with a driver waiting behind the wheel, and the Americans folded into an identical model that trailed behind.

The Americans were here to serve as additional bodyguards for al-Habsi, although none of them knew exactly where they were heading this morning. But Sultan knew, and when they took off south from the airport, every fiber of his being tingled and itched, so ready was he to get on with it.

The drive was less than ten minutes. Just south of the N17 highway, on the far side of a hill that shielded it from the road three hundred meters distant, they turned down a gravel drive before cresting the hill and continuing down on the other side.

And then he saw it. Sultan's destination was a clandestine prison, a black site run by the UAE's Signals Intelligence Agency. He had never been here in person, but he'd read the names and histories of every one of the prisoners kept here, and *they*, not his SIA staff at the location, would be his audience this morning.

The SUVs ground to a halt on the gravel road near the low and nondescript, yet large, concrete building.

Sultan walked up to Hades and his men as soon as they climbed out of their vehicle. "You will remain here."

Hades nodded, then cocked his head a little. "You gonna tell me where *here* is?"

"This is a holding facility for Iranian forces captured during the war. I am here on an intelligence collection mission. That's all you need to know."

If the American mercenary had any questions as to why the UAE's intelligence chief would need to come in person to interrogate some prisoner in the middle of a war zone, he made no mention of it. He and his men fanned out, kept their hands resting on the rifles across their chests, and looked out to the distance for any threats.

The guards outside the front doors to the facility lowered their weapons, and Sultan and two of the SIA men headed through the building and out into the small asphalt courtyard in the center.

Here a group of prisoners had been assembled; they stood in a sloppy line, and many shielded their eyes from the sun, having only just moments ago been allowed out into the light this morning. They wore clean white jumpsuits, all had new sandals on their feet, and four armed guards ringed the perimeter with weapons.

Sultan looked at the men, walking up and down the line as if at a parade inspection. He was pleased. He knew they had all been given double rations, and exercised every day, for the past five weeks. They were still POWs, but they were all in fighting shape.

He had personally chosen every one of the men for his mission, wading through dossiers on the fifty-two prisoners here, selecting only fifteen for the operation he had in mind. They were the cream of the crop, or at least the best enemy soldiers the UAE had managed to capture alive.

Tarik knew who these men were. They were the true believers. Iranian fighters who were only too happy to race off to Yemen to fight with the Houthi rebels against America, the Jews, the Saudis, and the UAE. They weren't intelligence agents, they weren't intelligence officers, they were gunmen, but they were directly tied to Quds, and that made them perfect for Sultan's objectives.

These men had been captured on the battlefield and kept here, some for years. They were committed and angry, and for Tarik they would be a difficult-to-manage, but incredibly potent, weapon of war.

He raised his fist in the air in front of them and shouted, *"Allahu akhbar!" God is greater!*

The fifteen men just stared at him in confusion. Some had assumed they were about to be shot when they were brought from their cells and lined up, although others thought it would just be another day in the courtyard doing calisthenics.

"Allahu akhbar!" Tarik shouted again. These men spoke Farsi, not Arabic, but while *Allahu akhbar* was Arabic, it was a ubiquitous chant.

The second time around some of the men repeated it softly.

Tarik shouted a third time, and now all voices joined in. The men were no less confused, but they were, at least, aware this stranger was trying to build a chorus.

Sultan put his arm down now. In Farsi he said, "My name is Tarik." He spoke passable Farsi, a product of years of training, focusing on one nation, on one foe.

"My brothers. It is a great morning. You all have earned your freedom."

The men looked at one another in utter confusion now, some still shielding their eyes from the orange sunrise.

He continued. "But you are not going home to Iran. Instead you will join me, your Muslim brother, in the existential fight against the West. We will deliver a blow straight into the heart of Europe, and together we will bring the Kaffir to their knees."

Still, no one spoke. They'd all been sufficiently psychologically damaged while in captivity to the point where no leader rose among them to question the stranger with the Arabic accent.

"You are no longer prisoners," Sultan al-Habsi continued. "You are confederates in our struggle. Mujahedin. Together we will combine our abilities, and we will be victorious, *inshallah!*"

One man finally spoke up. "The heart of Europe, you say?"

"Balé." Yes, Tarik answered in Farsi.

"We will fight?" asked another.

"You will fight bravely, my brother. You all will. I have selected a righteous target, the destruction of which will do so much more to our mutual enemy than ten thousand of you brave fighters could accomplish here in Yemen."

A new man spoke up. "You are Emirati. You are our enemy."

Sultan had been expecting this. "Here, yes. I have been your enemy. That is true. But our mutual foe is of much greater importance to me—and should be to you—than any quarrel we have between one another. Tehran has left you here to die, and that is a disgrace, but Tehran will shine with prideful eyes on you for what you are about to achieve."

"What is our target?" the same man asked.

"You will be armed and briefed, and you will be transported and housed. Then, a short time from now, you will conduct a coordinated attack in Germany. In Berlin. But your target, my brothers, is the nation that put you here. That took your lives from you."

"Saudi Arabia?" one asked.

"UAE?" said another.

Tarik shook his head. "America."

There was a pause, and then some fresh chants of *Allahu akhbar,* this time without Sultan having to lead the choir.

When the voices died down, one man stepped forward.

"I will not fight for your cause."

Al-Habsi walked over to him, stood close. "You refuse to join your comrades, to wage holy war on the Great Satan?"

"If my commander orders me to, I will. But my commander is not here. Only you. A Sunni."

Al-Habsi nodded thoughtfully, then turned and looked to the director of the black site. In Arabic he said, "You heard his wish. Put him back. Do not punish him. He is free to give his life away for nothing, instead of giving his life for the jihad."

Guards rushed forward, took the man roughly by the arms, and dragged him back through a doorway in the corner of the courtyard. The fourteen remaining men watched this, and then all eyes turned back to the one called Tarik.

"He will not be joining us. A pity for him, but better this than to have a weak-willed fighter on your shoulder as you enter battle."

"Is this a martyrdom operation?" a man at the end of the line asked.

Tarik walked to him, looked him over, then said, "If it is?"

The man's chin rose, his eyes narrowed. "So be it, *inshallah.*"

The Emirati put his hand on the prisoner's shoulder and gave it a squeeze along with a broad smile. "The answer to this question is, I do not know. It is my wish that we complete our mission, achieve our objective, and remain in this world for any fighting that follows. But the truth is, you might all die in glorious combat."

He looked up and down the row of men, and he realized that, with only the one exception who had been returned to the darkness, he had chosen his fighters well. They hated him, that would never change, but he was giving them a chance for purpose, and for that they would die for him if the mission called for it.

And, more importantly, looking these men over, he knew one more thing. Each and every one of them was a killer. He could see it on their faces.

Sultan left the prison a half hour later, certain that he had the proxy fighters he needed.

Now, he just had to get them into Europe without them being detected, because they were known Quds operators, and anything they did would inevitably leave a trail back to Iran.

FOURTEEN

PRESENT DAY

Just after eleven a.m. Court sat at a wooden table on the patio of el Refugio de Aguila, a German restaurant all alone alongside the highway just outside the town of Miranda. He had a half hour to kill before climbing back into his driver's car for the ride to the reservoir, and then another several hours to wait until nightfall for the flight in the Cessna seaplane back to Aruba.

And, as far as he was concerned, he was using his time wisely.

A bottle of pale lager, his second, rested on the table in front of him. A basket of half-eaten sausages sat next to it.

The food and drink were good, a nice coda to an exceptionally shitty morning, but he was putting off the one thing he really needed to do.

Call Hanley.

And when he *did* call Hanley, he knew then the shit would *really* hit the fan.

He looked down to his phone on the table. After a moment he reached down for it, but his hand bypassed the phone and he hefted his beer instead.

Not yet, he told himself.

He'd spent an hour in the jungle before being picked up by the driver for the ride back in the direction of the reservoir. While waiting for the pickup, he'd poured antiseptic into his open surgical wound and rebandaged the bloody hole. He'd taken his antibiotics and some mild painkillers, but he ignored the myriad cuts and bruises he'd sustained falling through the floor of the home and then, a few minutes later, crashing down the hillside.

He'd then changed out of his tiger camo and into a pair of jeans and a dingy gray T-shirt. He'd considered calling Hanley then; he'd had the time to do so, but he needed to get control of his emotions and come up with a strategy for delivering the bad news to the DDO.

After finishing his second beer, however, he told himself he could put it off no longer. Court ordered a third, then lifted the phone, opened an encrypted communication app called Signal, dialed the number from memory, and immediately reached the deputy director on the seventh floor of CIA's headquarters in McLean, Virginia.

Hanley opened with, "Identity check."

"Lima, Victor, Golf, Papa, eight, fiver, Bravo."

"Iden confirmed," Hanley said. And then, "Status?"

"My status is nominal." And then he sighed to himself. There was no way to sugarcoat this. "But Clark Drummond is dead."

"Did you—"

"No, I didn't do it. I tried to get him out of there, but he was intercepted by a tier-one team. They starched him. Execution style."

"Dammit, Violator! I told you I needed this done quietly."

"Don't look at me. This team was after Drummond, I just happened to get in the middle of it."

"Who was the enemy?"

"Unknown. They suffered one KIA that I am aware of."

"Did you, at least, get any pocket litter from the body that can help with the ID?"

Court wasn't going to go into detail about the backpack of Composition Four detonating just feet away from him, about the partial building collapse, about the raging fire. Hanley wouldn't care, anyway. Instead Court said, "You know, there wasn't a hell of a lot of time for me to be searching the pockets of dead assholes. Things move a bit faster in the field than you might remember."

If Hanley was annoyed at Court's jibe, Court couldn't pick up on it, because Hanley was so obviously annoyed at his agent's failure in Venezuela that nothing else came through.

"What about Drummond's phone and his hard drives?"

Court paused while the waitress brought him his lager, and he paused a little longer to take a long pull from it.

Then he said, "Negative to both. I did get a little intel, though, including the name and photo of an unknown who is definitely involved."

Court told Hanley about Berlin, about Miriam, about the death of Drummond's colleagues. About Drummond's assertions that they were actually spying on EU countries and not just Iranians in the EU. Hanley took it all in, but he clearly wasn't satisfied.

"*Anything* else?"

"Yeah," Court said. "Just an FYI. You sent Zack straight into a trap."

The pause was brief. "I guess you're saying that Drummond gave Power-Slave to the Venezuelans?"

"Not exactly. He had the Venezuelans feed him immigration data every day, and he ran it through PowerSlave on his own. When Zack came through the airport, he had the computer watching for him on cameras near his house."

"Yeah, that makes sense."

"How did you not consider that a possibility beforehand?"

"I did consider it. I determined it was an acceptable risk."

"Did Zack get a vote?"

Hanley didn't answer this. He just breathed into the phone a moment, then said, "I can send a plane to you, assuming you're out of Venezuela."

"What about Drummond? Berlin? Everything that I just told you?"

Hanley paused, then said, "We'll deal with it."

Court sat there, looking out at the highway, thinking about what Hanley was *not* saying. Finally, he barked out an angry laugh. "You've been holding out on me, haven't you? You already knew about all this."

"No, not entirely. But nothing you just told me comes as a great surprise. We've been aware of a possible Israeli intel initiative in Berlin targeting Iran, despite denials from Mossad that they have any involvement in it. We didn't know Drummond was caught up in it, but the relationship you describe between him, his handler, and the work they were asking him to do sounds very much like what we have been hearing from other sources. For some reason, and in some way, they were able to keep Drummond in hiding, whereas others operated more overtly."

"Overtly?"

"There is an intelligence concern in Europe called Shrike International Group; it seems to have private sector ownership, but that gets very murky very quickly. It was started by Rudolf Spangler, an ex-Stasi asshole, but word is he isn't involved with the firm at all anymore. The consensus is his company has been taken over as a deniable Israeli operation spying on Iranian intelligence efforts in the EU.

"Shrike has been hiring some of the best analytical and technological talent from intel agencies around the world. Overtly. These aren't the missing IC personnel, just IC personnel who were recruited out in the light to come and work in Germany for a private firm. From what we can tell, the company's objectives all seem to involve Iran."

"What's the problem with Israel spying on Iran? Israel is an ally, right?"

Hanley gave another sigh, but Court didn't think this one was directed at him. He said, "Jerusalem is trying to draw Iran into a war with the West. They have been at it for years. They do whatever they can to stir the pot. Monthly bombing raids into Iran or Lebanon, for example, trying to get an overreaction out of Tehran. Israel is also furious, beyond furious, that the EU eased sanctions on Tehran last year.

"Yeah, Israel is an ally, but it's still my job to keep tabs on them to make sure whatever this initiative in Berlin is, it's not an operation to stir the hornets' nest even more.

"If the missing intelligence officers around the world are *also* affiliated with Shrike, in a covert fashion, then that is new information and we'll have to figure out what to make of it. If the Israelis are snagging IC personnel for some sort of offensive mission in the EU . . . against EU nations . . ." He paused. "This could be bigger than we thought.

"We've been suspicious of Shrike, but we haven't been able to pick up any solid intel that they were operating against anyone other than Iran. Mostly cyber, analytic, and atmospheric stuff. Definitely no meat-and-potatoes spy shit, from what we've ascertained." Hanley's voice deepened.

"Unfortunately, Violator, you are bringing out no proof, and you are bring-ing out no Clark Drummond."

Court rubbed his tired eyes. He felt like he had the flu, and he knew his infection was cooking inside him. But he shook off the feeling and said, "You need to get someone infiltrated into Shrike Group."

"Really, Violator? Is that what we need to do?" Hanley snapped. "No shit." He added, "I already have an asset on the inside."

Court nodded, then cocked his head. "Hopefully it isn't someone from Berlin station. Drummond said PowerSlave was up and running in Berlin. If Shrike is associated with the work Drummond was doing, then they would be able to peg your asset before he ever got near any intel."

"It's not someone from Berlin station," Hanley replied.

Court picked up on this. "Who is it?"

"You should know better than to ask me who—"

Court had been hunched over, but now he bolted up in his chair. "You can't send any official Agency assets, which means you are probably send-ing an off-book agent. Another Poison Apple agent. As far as I know, there are three of us. I'm right here, and Zack is in a prison twenty miles from here, so that means there is only one person who could be in Berlin right now."

Hanley sighed into the phone. In an almost reluctant tone he said, "You are correct. Anthem is in play in Berlin."

Court closed his eyes and squeezed the phone hard. There was so much wrong with this. Anthem was Zoya Zakharova, the Russians wanted her dead, and Court was in love with her.

His heart began to pound.

He chose his words carefully now. "Matt . . . listen carefully. The team sent here last night after Drummond. They came in hard and ruthless. They knew their shit. They might have been American, definitely ex–special operations forces. If Zoya is working over there in Berlin, without a net, in deep cover, and if all this shit is, in fact, tied together, then she is very much in danger."

"It's a dangerous occupation, what you all do."

"What *is* her cover? Drummond described a well-run intelligence organization. If Zoya gets made by the oppo, then you know she'll be in extreme—"

"She's *been* made," Hanley barked. "*That's* her cover."

Court held the phone even tighter in his hand. Forcing calm into his voice, he said, "I'm going to need you to explain that."

"We wanted her to be ID'd as a rogue Russian intelligence asset. A woman without a country, desperate for work. That's the only way we can be sure Shrike Group would trust her enough to bring her into their black side."

Court waited for a new cluster of diners to pass him on their way to a table on the other side of the deck. When they were out of earshot, he said, "Matt, I don't have to explain this to you, but I will anyway because it seems you have lost your fucking *mind*. If these bastards running this shady private intelligence shop realize Zoya Zakharova is there, in Berlin, then it's just a matter of time before the Russians get wind of it. And when the Russians *do* get wind of it, it won't be any time at all before they send hitters to Germany to deal with her. I don't care what crazy errand she is on for you; she won't be able to do it because she'll either be dead or on the run."

Hanley repeated himself. "It's dangerous work, what you do."

Son of a bitch, Court thought. But he just said, "Let me go help her."

"Denied. Look, Berlin station is working this on the periphery; they don't know about Anthem, but they have eyes and ears on the operation. At the first sign of any compromise of Anthem, you know I'll pull her out of—"

"Who's handling her? Let me do that, at least."

Hanley laughed now. "*You?* You're a field asset, not a desk jockey."

"I know her capabilities. I know the threats. You can get me up to speed on the op."

"Denied, Violator. She already has a handler."

Court closed his eyes and rubbed them with fingers wet from the condensation on the beer bottle. "Brewer? Brewer is running her?"

"Affirmative."

"How's *that* going?"

Hanley hesitated before replying. "'Bout like you'd expect."

"That bad?"

"They are both good at their jobs. They don't have to be friends."

"Right. Look, Matt. I want to go to Berlin."

"Court, you aren't ready to be deployed anywhere. You need to get back into Dr. Cathey's care."

"Why? I was ready to fly to Caracas and shoot it out with a dozen gun monkeys, otherwise you wouldn't have pulled me out of the medical ward in the first place, right?"

"You *weren't* ready, obviously. You were all I had. Zoya was working her way into Shrike Group so I could keep tabs on the Israelis, and Zack got his dumb ass popped down in Caracas by local-yokel counterintel guys. I put you in, you got about five percent of what I needed you to get, and now you want to rush off on your next op? Look, Court. Your infection needs another few weeks of treatments."

"Give me one week, Matt. One week, and then I'll pull myself out." When Hanley did not immediately respond, Court said, "I am going, and you can't stop me. What you need to do is decide if you want to put me in play with your blessing, or if you want to run this alone."

"Is that a threat?"

"It's an offer. I protect your asset over there so she can unravel this little mystery she's mixed up in without having to deal with Russian assassins on her ass. She'll never even know I'm there." Court smiled. "I'm the Gray Man, remember?"

"You're half a Gray Man, remember?"

Court hacked out a phlegmy cough, wiped his mouth and then his face with his paper napkin. "It's just countersurveillance work. I can do that shit in my sleep. Let me go watch her back."

Hanley's pause was long enough for Court to motion for the check and pull a wad of bills out of his pocket while he waited. Finally, the DDO said, "One week from today you are back in Maryland, under Dr. Cathey's care. You got it?"

Court nodded. "Got it."

"It is absolutely imperative no one finds out she has confederates watching her back. You have no operational role whatsoever other than running countersurveillance for her, from a distance. You do that, and we just pray to God everything else works out."

"Thanks, Matt, I won't let you down." Then he added, "Again."

He hung up the phone and headed out of the roadside restaurant, heading to a dusty parking lot where his driver was to pick him up.

This entailed passing an auto repair shop, and he scanned the eaves of the building, searching for cameras. He did this automatically, and with the care of both a man with a lot of training and a man with an intense vested interest in keeping his mug out of any cameras, lest he fall prey to the PowerSlave system that had snared Zack. He'd been told by Drummond his face wasn't in the database, but he had no idea if that was true or not.

He headed on to the parking lot, fully unaware that the owner of the repair shop, after dealing with numerous break-ins that began with his outdoor cameras being destroyed, had instead placed a high-quality Bluetooth security camera on a display shelf inside the building, pointed out a grimy window.

Gentry had ducked and dodged fifty cameras since arriving in Venezuela the night before, but it was the fifty-first that got him.

He slept in the right seat of the Cessna seaplane for most of the ninety-minute flight back to Aruba, and as soon as they landed, the aircraft taxied to a fixed-base operator and the pilot shut off the engine. Court was about to climb out, but instead he reached over and put his hand on the pilot's forearm. The man turned his way.

Court said, "I need to book another flight. As soon as possible."

The pilot didn't seem surprised that his quiet passenger was immediately rehiring him. "Caracas again?"

"Negative. Leipzig." Court was ultimately heading to Berlin, but he wouldn't tell this pilot his true destination. He knew that if he could get to Leipzig, then he could climb aboard an ICE, Germany's high-speed train, and get from the airport to Berlin's central train station in less than an hour and a half.

The pilot flashed him a bemused expression. "You think this Cessna can make a transatlantic hop?"

"Of course I don't. But I'm guessing you can recommend someone. I'll pay you a finder's fee, but I need to leave Aruba tonight."

The pilot seemed to think it over a moment. Finally, he said, "How much of a finder's fee are we talking about?"

Court realized he had judged this guy well. "Ten grand."

"Fifteen."

Court would be using Hanley's money, at least until Hanley cut off the spigot of funds.

He said, "Done."

To this the pilot replied, "The flight will be twenty-five thousand, plus the rental of a midrange executive jet. There is a Hawker 1000 at the airport in Aruba available. That will make the trip with a stop in the Azores. Fifteen hours, give or take."

Court cocked his head. How did this guy come up with all this without even talking to the pilot? He thought it over a moment. "Let me guess . . . *you're* going to fly me to Leipzig."

"Give me a couple hours to get it arranged and a couple hours to sleep. We'll touch down in Germany in less than a day. Don't forget the finder's fee."

"A finder's fee for finding yourself? You didn't have to look very hard, did you?"

The pilot grinned for the first time since Court met him the day before. "You look like a man who needs something, and needs it now. We're all just trying to make a living out here, amigo."

FIFTEEN

The man in apartment 3C jolted upright in his bed, looked around the small room, and then lowered back down slowly. He listened to the rain beat against the window next to him for a moment, and then, like most mornings, he wondered where the fuck he was.

Is this still Minsk? No . . . it's Warsaw. I've been in Warsaw for weeks.

He asked himself if the fog in his brain was from the early hour or from the pain raging between his temples.

He looked to the clock on the wall. It was almost nine a.m.

So . . . it wasn't the hour.

He'd drunk too much last night, again, and the bite in his stomach from all the vodka competed for supremacy against the pounding in his head. He had an ulcer; this he'd been told, and he'd also been told drinking himself to sleep each and every night would do nothing to improve his condition.

But Maksim Akulov didn't give a shit about his body anymore.

He shook his head in an attempt to clear it, then reached for a cigarette, lit it, and blew smoke straight into the air above his bed.

It had been a rough night. The rough nights were lining up one after another these days.

It wasn't just the drink, and it wasn't just his health. Well, not just his physical health, anyway.

It was the dreams. The dreams had haunted him again.

The fucking dreams.

They stopped with the morning; he'd grown so accustomed to them he only needed to open his eyes to send the nightmares packing for another day. But they'd be back tonight, he knew, and he also knew there was no sense in worrying about things he could not control.

Maksim Akulov was a survivor. He had survived an abusive father. He had survived special forces training. He had survived Chechnya. He had survived Georgia. He had survived Dagestan. He had survived Syria. He had survived Ukraine. He had survived wounds, sickness, every dangerous place, and every dangerous mission his nation had thrown his way.

But these days, the only danger he felt was from the demons in his mind.

And with each passing day they grew in strength and in number.

The forty-three-year-old Russian knew what he needed to do to make the nightmares stop. He needed new challenges, a new purpose, in the real world. The problem, as he saw it, was not that he had the nightmares. The problem was that he had nothing else to devote his time to *but* the nightmares, so they owned his soul.

He didn't have to wonder about the origins of his dark subconscious. Akulov was an assassin, after all; he'd seen things, done things, that he would never be able to erase from his memory banks.

But walking a razor's edge between life and death was the only existence he had known for many years.

He'd been in the Russian army, a member of an exclusive Spetsnaz unit, and then he had been hired into domestic intelligence, the FSB. There he worked in Vega Group, the most elite covert fighting force in the nation. After a few years kicking doors and bashing heads on behalf of the white, blue, and red flag that he wore on his shoulder, however, he was asked to resign his federal position and to go to work as a civilian.

For the Russian mafia.

He became a hit man for the Solntsevskaya Bratva, working Moscow and St. Petersburg at first, then taking foreign jobs in Central and Western Europe. It didn't take him long to recognize that most of his targets were political in nature, so he put together without anyone telling him officially that he still worked for the Kremlin, no matter who put the money in his bank account.

He didn't care. He was doing what he was good at, all he was good at, and he found value in that. He justified his life by saying he followed orders, and the morality of the orders didn't weigh on his shoulders but on the shoulders of those who gave them.

He didn't believe any of that bullshit anymore, but it had sure sounded good at the time.

He climbed out of bed and walked over towards the spartan kitchen on the far wall of the studio apartment, and along the way he grabbed the TV remote and flicked on the news; it was in Polish, reminding him again he wasn't in Minsk any longer. The job he'd done in Belarus ended six weeks earlier, so for six weeks he'd been here, lying low, thinking, drinking, and, unfortunately, dreaming.

He put the teakettle on, fished through the dirty dishes for a not-too-dirty cup, and readied it with a tea bag and a spoon.

His motivations had changed since his early years, when he cared only about executing his orders. Now his only motivation was the desire to work for the sake of work itself, to focus and distract, to take his mind off anything that was not the job.

Akulov saw himself as an *akula*, a shark. Sharks must keep swimming or they die, he'd been told once, and he felt the same. As long as he was killing, as long as he was pursuing his next victim, then he would be free of the screaming in the night.

But the thrill was gone. Now it was just the momentum.

Swim or die.

He'd become introspective, especially after the past six weeks of near hibernation, alone with his thoughts. He knew how this would all end now. He'd die in the field, and when it happened, it would be beautiful.

Death in the field was preferable to life in the loony bin. This he told himself every day.

Akulov had spent two years, against his will, at Mental Hospital Number 14, Branch 2, in Moscow. He didn't learn much there, but he did learn that he was unusual in that he welcomed death, and the only reason he was still alive was that he enjoyed the prospect of killing just slightly more than the prospect of dying.

Before the teakettle whistled, his mobile phone buzzed in his pocket, surprising him. He looked down at the number and his heart began to pound along with the throb in his temples.

In Russian he said, *"Da?"*

The reply came in Russian, as well. "Maksim, how are you?"

He rubbed his eyes, straightened his back, and brought some power into his voice. "I am fine." It was Ruslan, and Ruslan *never* called unless there was a job.

"I have a job."

Maksim threw his cigarette into the sink and began pacing his little flat. And just like that, the wounded, beaten man had come fully back to life. *"Khorosho."* Good, he said.

"I can send the details to the drop box, I just need to know you and the team are ready for this one. It's big, comrade."

Maksim had never been readier. His team? Well, his three colleagues were also here in Warsaw, also lying low and growing moss, and whether or not they wanted to get back to work, Maksim knew that was exactly what they needed.

"We are all ready, sir."

"Very well, then. You have never let me down before. I expect your best performance. The target is . . . deserving of the full measure of your talents."

"He will get the full measure of my talents," Maksim assured, then said, "Where is he?"

"The target is a she, and *she* is in Berlin."

Maksim Akulov hung up the phone and rushed to his computer in the kitchen, ignoring the teakettle as it began to wail. All the remnants of last night's horror show in his brain had drifted away, the headache seemed to subside with the rush of adrenaline, and he concentrated fully on his job.

Akulov opened his encrypted drop box and looked over the dossier. "Perfect," he said with a smile so faint it was nearly imperceptible, though it was the widest smile he'd worn in months.

SIXTEEN

The morning temperature in Dubai hit 108 degrees and the humidity hovered near ninety percent. The eight Americans who filed down the jet stairs looked weathered and worn; black soot was visible on the cheeks of virtually all of them, in sharp contrast to the rings around their eyes where they'd been wearing goggles during the hit on the house in Caracas nineteen hours earlier. Their hair was a mess, both from the helmets or ball caps they wore during the mission and from the bedhead picked up from lying awkwardly on cabin chairs or on the cabin floor, men packed nuts to butts in a luxury aircraft poorly suited for troop transport.

The leader of the team, call sign Hades, was last off the bird, and when he came down the stairs, he filed in with the others near the hatch of the cargo hold, ready to grab his heavy ruck of gear and his rifle. He was as tired as the rest of the team, if not more so, and he also had the additional burden of knowing he'd lost one of his men.

Hades rubbed his eyes, avoiding the sun and the glare off the aircraft as best he could, then reached up as his MultiCam rucksack was handed down.

Just like with the rest of the team, all of Hades's tactical gear and clothing were in his massive Osprey pack. Now he wore dingy linen pants, flip-flops, and a red loose-fitting Hawaiian shirt. The seven other men all wore civilian clothing, as well, but their beards, mustaches, fit physiques, and ages gave them away as some sort of a fighting force.

But there was no one here to see them. They'd parked in an out-of-the-way portion of the tarmac, and other than the pilot and copilot, there wasn't a soul in sight.

Until a black Mercedes passenger van rolled into view, coming from the direction of an airport entrance reserved for government personnel. The Mercedes parked in front of a nearby hangar, and a Middle Eastern man in a gray suit and tie climbed out from behind the wheel and opened the rear door.

"Somebody call an Uber?" Mercury quipped, but no one laughed. They were beat from the thirty-five-hour round-trip flight and the fight in Caracas, and their spirits had taken a hit with the death of Ronnie Blight. Joking and ribbing one another was a thing with this team of mercs, but today Mercury's tired attempt fell flat.

Hades moved with his men, squinting in the sun because his Oakley shades were still tucked deep in a pouch in his pack. He headed for the black Mercedes van that would take them all, he assumed, to the apartment building where they resided two to a room here in Dubai. But just before he folded himself into the van behind the others, a silver BMW 8 Series Gran Coupe pulled up, and the driver of this vehicle climbed out and opened a rear door.

Hades handed his pack off to Thor and headed to the BMW. "Catch you guys in a bit. Clean and secure your gear before you rack out." He knew where he was going; he'd been through this before. He'd be meeting with his employer, and he was damn glad. He had a few things he needed to get off his chest about the shit show they'd just experienced.

As he rode in the back of the sleek four-door coupe, it wasn't lost on him that he hadn't bathed in two and a half days. The rich leather looked brand-new; the wood paneling around him seemed to have been buffed to a brilliant shine that very morning.

And Hades looked down at his hands, dirt in the cracks like spiderwebs, even though he'd worn gloves, and he saw a faint smear of Ronnie's blood on his forearm, even though he'd worn a long-sleeved tunic.

Hades's real name was Keith Hulett, but no one on his team called him that. He hailed from Fort Wayne, Indiana, the son of a soybean farmer.

Hulett had been a master sergeant in the U.S. Army before joining his current company several years before, working his way through security contracts in the Middle East, Latin America, and Asia. He'd moved up the ranks in his company to team leader, and then he, along with his eight men, all specially selected by him, had served as guns for hire for the United Arab Emirates for the last year and a half.

But Hades had only seven men now.

Hulett rode in the backseat in silence for nearly thirty minutes before the BMW turned onto al Saada Street. This was downtown Dubai; luxury cars whizzed by as he and his luxury car turned into the Roda al Morooj, a five-star hotel.

Hades knew he wouldn't be overnighting here; it was just a convenient place for his employer to meet with him. He'd been here before, and he'd found the place stuffy and pretentious, but Hulett knew he was just a grunt working for a paycheck, so he figured the guy who signed the paycheck could meet him wherever he damn well pleased.

He was escorted directly past security in the lobby by a pair of well-dressed guards, caught a few looks from tourists who regarded his Hawaiian shirt, beard, bedhead, and flip-flops with more amusement than disdain, and soon he was in an express elevator, followed in by two additional security men. They traveled to the eighth floor, then walked together down a carpeted hallway to a set of hand-carved and gold-embossed double doors.

Hades had forgone the security protocols at the entrance to the hotel, but here at the front door of the suite he lifted his arms, and a new pair of men in suits frisked him from his ankles to the top of his head. One of the men pulled a penlight out of the breast pocket of his coat and shined it in Hulett's face. "Open," the man said, and Hulett opened his mouth.

The security man searched his mouth and throat for weapons; what kind, specifically, Hulett had no idea, but upon finding nothing but a few fillings, the Middle Eastern man allowed the American to pass.

Keith Hulett recognized the suite from his last visit to meet with his contact in the Signals Intelligence Agency.

He knew the man only as Tarik, which was a first name, and probably made-up. "Tarik" meant "conqueror" in Arabic, and Hulett only knew this because when he fought in Iraq, a corrupt police chief in some backwater shit hole outside Karbala had told him this, shortly before the man's corruption led to his death by the hands of a local businessman he'd been shaking down.

Hulett was by no means fluent in Arabic, but he'd picked up his fair share in his four deployments in Iraq, his three in Afghanistan, and then fighting for a paycheck in Yemen for Tarik.

Yemen had been fulfilling work for Hades and his team. They got the job done, no matter the mission, and of this they were proud. Their tactics and procedures would have put them in Fort Leavenworth if they were still in the U.S. military, so to Hulett's way of thinking, he had the best of both worlds. Flexible rules of engagement kept him and his men safer and the enemy deader, in a mission fully supported by the U.S. government.

A coalition of nine nations fought in Yemen, mostly through proxies and mercenaries, against Iranian-backed Houthi rebels. But while the United States was part of the coalition, and while they helped and supported the Emirates, the men in Hades's small team were not working for the USA.

The Middle Eastern monarchy hired these Americans to eliminate its enemies, but the CIA knew about it and didn't push back, and this gave Hulett more than enough justification to cash his check every month.

It was militarized contract killing, and Keith Hulett had been doing it for a year and a half under the cloak of authority of the UAE, an American ally and partner.

And although he did his job for money, he was technically not a mercenary, because the Emirates had given him an officer's rank. He found this mildly amusing; he'd never been an O. He'd spent thirteen years in U.S. special forces, worked his way up to master sergeant, but had been given the dreaded OTH, or other than honorable discharge, after members of his A-team accused him of killing an unarmed man in the Sangin Valley and then planting a walkie-talkie on the body to make him appear to be an enemy conspirator.

He was tossed from the military for that, but it didn't hurt him much in his subsequent private work. Hulett made over three hundred grand a year now, and he'd told himself there was nothing he wouldn't do if he was paid to do it.

All the men under him in his merc unit had had their own run-ins with the military judicial system and then fallen on hard times, each for a different offense, ranging from bad conduct discharges to dishonorable discharges.

These men entered the mercenary world already dirty, and that only helped them justify their actions. Still, the dirt had grown on them insidiously in the past eighteen months of increasingly violent, and morally questionable, operations, to the point where Hulett wondered sometimes if he was the only man on his team who wondered if he was going to hell for his actions.

He was certain he would never know, because he would never ask the guys if they had any reservations.

The other men made an average of one hundred twenty grand a year, a fact Hulett was thinking about at present because of Ronnie Blight. Ares's family would have to find another source of income, because the company they all worked for didn't pay death benefits.

The American steeled himself to speak with Tarik about what had gone down in Venezuela, and was certain that the death of his contractor was the reason he'd been brought to downtown Dubai straight off the aircraft.

Tarik entered in a crisp white button-down shirt, open at the collar, and a pair of designer blue jeans. He was probably about forty-five, Hulett thought, with silver sparkling in his short black hair and thin beard.

The men shook hands; neither of them was smiling.

Hulett said, "I apologize, sir."

"For what?" Tarik's English was impeccable.

"I should have probably cleaned up a little first. Just got off the transport."

The Emirati gave a slight look of offense. "You don't think I've been to war? You don't think I've lived in shit? I spent five years in and out of Yemen, started as a soldier, ended as a policy maker."

Hulett was sure Tarik had not been a soldier, and he was not a policy maker now. He was a spy.

He said, "I've spent my time in the ditches and in the streets. I don't care how I, or how my soldiers, look or smell. I only care about results."

The American said, "Well, sir, if you aren't offended by my odor and my dress, then I guess I won't bring it up again."

Tarik nodded, and the matter was settled. "You are probably wondering why I brought you here."

The two men sat down on comfortable chairs near the window.

"I assume it has to do with everything that happened in Venezuela."

Tarik shook his head. "No. I'm satisfied with that operation."

Hulett cocked his head now. "You're *satisfied*? One of my boys got killed."

The Middle Easterner seemed to think about this a moment before asking, "Have you ever lost a man before?"

"I've never been an officer before, so while men on my A-team died when I was in SF, I wasn't the OIC."

Tarik sat ramrod straight in his chair, his dark eyes boring holes into Hulett. "Yes. Well, I have been an officer in charge, and I have lost many men. As long as the mission is honorable, then there is nothing to worry about. You might not believe in the same God as I do, but I know that your man was martyred and valorous. What more can a soldier ever hope for?"

Hulett figured Ronnie Blight had probably hoped for something more than martyrdom via a bullet through his windpipe and a lonely unmarked grave in a foreign country for his charred corpse.

But he didn't argue the point. Instead, he said, "I get the fight we're waging in Yemen. But I don't get what the hell we were doing in South America. That dude we wasted was a middle-aged American. We're supposed to be over here fighting rebels working with Iran's Quds Force. You can't tell me he was working for Quds."

"He was not Iranian. But he was working in the furtherance of the aims of our common enemy."

"He was working for the Iranians?"

"Originally, in fact, he was working for me."

Hulett sat back in his chair. *"What?"*

"He was supporting my efforts in Europe. He ran with valuable information about our operation, then I found him, and I sent you."

"With orders to kill him?"

"Yes. He had intelligence that could have seriously degraded our abilities in Yemen. We don't think he told the Venezuelans, but if some other nation got to him, it could have made trouble for us."

"I'm not so sure someone else *didn't* get to him."

"Meaning?" Tarik asked with a raised eyebrow.

"We never saw anybody on site but the target, and four Venezuelan intel pukes. But I had one dead and two others hit, a third of my damn force. The Venezuelans had been drugged, that was for sure. They didn't do it, it was someone else." He paused. "And it wasn't Drummond. No way."

"Another gunman was present? What do you know about him?"

"They said he was good. Confident. They couldn't get a good look at him. Spoke English, but every dumbass on Earth speaks English these days."

Hulett noticed Tarik's normally confident mood falter a little; he looked out the window of the high-rise, silent for several seconds.

The American understood. "You know who it was, don't you?"

Tarik looked back to his mercenary again. "The data you transferred to me in the aircraft. I had my people look through it. It was a computer application and a database that Drummond took from us. A tool that helps us find the enemy before they find us."

Hulett sat up straighter. Tarik was about to tell him who killed Ronnie Blight.

"We decrypted the information, thinking Drummond might have used this program in Venezuela in an attempt to keep people away from him. He was an outlaw in America, after all; it stood to reason America would come after him."

"I'm listening," said Hulett.

"Our cyber staff linked into the entire network of cameras in northern Venezuela, in the hopes we could find out who Drummond met with, if someone from the USA had made contact with him. We didn't find any evidence that someone spoke with him before you killed him, but this morning an image was picked up many kilometers from Drummond's house."

Tarik nodded, then said, "The man recognized by the software is a former American CIA officer, but a man who has been disavowed by the

Americans. He's a rogue, a freelance assassin. One of the best, if not *the* best, in the business.

"We don't know for certain if he was involved in what happened to Drummond, but they call him the Gray Man."

Hulett sat up straighter. "Most folks I run with say there are about a dozen jokers out there calling themselves the Gray Man."

"Then most folks you know are wrong. There is one man. And I have his name."

Hulett's nostrils flared like a bull. "Who is this fucker?"

"Courtland Gentry. Several years ago the Americans came to me for help in finding him. I was unable to provide much assistance; the man never showed up on my radar. But I do have images of him, and it is clearly the same person."

Tarik thought for a while, then said, "We will have to keep an eye out for this man, and others like him. Our entire operation was almost compromised by Mr. Drummond, and I can't have that happen again."

Hulett shook his head. "This is getting a little too Jason Bourne for me. Look, Tarik, I'm a shooter. My guys are shooters. You give us a target, a clean target, and then we go and hit it. That's how this shit works."

Tarik countered. "That's how it is *supposed* to work. But you killed thirty people the other night in Aden. Most of them Sunni. Not very clean, was it?"

Hades made a face, surprised at the apparent admonishment. He didn't hide his anger now. "Sometimes we hit it clean. Sometimes, like in Aden the other night, some collateral catches it, but that's just war. It's precision counterterrorism, what we do for you. Bitch about me all you want, but this is a shit-ton cleaner than carpet-bombing cities, which is what you jokers would be doing if it weren't for us."

Tarik reached out and put a hand on Hulett's knee to calm him. "That is fair, Hades. Honestly, I don't care about the lives of some shopkeepers. We are fighting a cancer, and in so doing, some benign tissue is necessarily damaged.

"You and your small team are valuable additions to our fight in Yemen, but even so, the Emirates are struggling in that cesspool. Iran and its proxies are pushing not only there but in North Africa, in Syria. Their expansion around the world is shocking, and it is growing, and the UAE does not have the means to stop it. Our sometime partners in Saudi Arabia are helpless, as well."

Hulett said, "Well, maybe if you didn't have us off running errands in South America, we could help the cause."

Tarik shook his head. "Our footprint in Yemen has been shrinking. The Shias are dominating. We are pulling forces out immediately." He paused. With a pained expression he said, "That battle has been lost."

Hulett didn't know why he was getting this lesson, but he had a guess. "Are you firing us?"

Tarik shook his head. "Repositioning you."

This was a surprise. "*Repositioning* us? Where?"

"The battle for Yemen might be lost, but there is a way to win the war against Shia expansion. You'd like that, wouldn't you?"

The American shrugged. Shias, Sunnis, he didn't give a shit about any of that talk. He concerned himself with whomever the opposition in front of him was. He wasn't here to win any wider war. Still, he *was* here to get paid, and it sounded like the spigot of cash from Yemen was about to be shut off unless he was ready to pivot to whatever Tarik wanted him to do. "Where are you sending us?"

"I want you to go to Europe."

"I don't catch a lot of news, but I'm pretty sure Iran isn't using local rebel forces in Belgium to expand their territory like they're doing in Yemen. What the hell is over there for us?"

"We are running an operation against Quds Force terrorist cells active across the continent."

"Quds Force is planning attacks in Europe? Why don't you just communicate with the CIA about all that?"

"We are working in conjunction with the Agency, just as always. Our efforts in Europe are supported by them, just like our work here in the Middle East would have been impossible without our American partners."

This placated Keith Hulett, so he didn't question his mission anymore. "What do you need us to do?"

"I need you to go to a nice home in Berlin, a safe house we will acquire for you. My associates there will be looking at camera feeds, and if Court Gentry shows up through facial recognition in Germany, I will give you a target."

Hulett was skeptical. "So, we just sit and wait, hope you get lucky?"

Tarik shook his head. "I have other work for you. I need men eliminated. Easy targets, certainly not of Gentry's caliber. It should be quite simple for you. The targets will be Iranian nationals. Terrorists."

Hulett sat back in surprise. "You want us orchestrating kills on European soil? That's a damn sight different than waxing some fuckers in the middle of a war zone."

"Is it? Is it, really, if the . . . how did you put it? If the *fuckers* are cut from the same cloth, come from the same enemy, and your nation approves of the mission?

"You and your eight . . . apologies, *seven* men, will be paid two and a half times your current wage." Tarik smiled. "It will be easy work for you. You don't stand out in Europe the way I would, the way my case officers would."

Hulett wasn't buying this. "I've been to Europe. There are a lot of Arabs there."

"Who receive extra scrutiny from the authorities. I had operatives working there, doing the same work I am asking of you. They were good, but they were running greater and greater risk of compromise every day, due to the color of their skin, whereas you and your men will have unlimited freedom of movement."

This made sense to Hulett, more so because he wasn't one to challenge a new job opportunity falling into his lap just as another job was lost.

"When would we leave?"

"Take a day to rest. I've run you all hard. Grieve for your fallen comrade. Then I'll have you transported to Germany. We are already watching out for Gentry in case he shows up where he can cause us strife."

Keith Hulett liked the thought of getting out of Dubai and heading into the heart of Europe. He liked the thought of leaving the war behind for a while and working as a hit man for an intelligence service that had the full backing and confidence of the CIA. And he liked the idea of killing the son of a bitch who killed Ronnie.

This seemed like solid work for a man of his skill set.

In the back of his mind, though, he had suspicions and reservations about what this sneaky intelligence chief sitting in front of him would have him do down the road. But Hulett would go and be a good soldier, because even after everything he had done, that was the story that he told himself about himself.

SEVENTEEN

The woman calling herself Stephanie Arthur climbed the stairs out of the U-Bahn station at Dahlem-Dorf in southwestern Berlin just after one p.m., keeping pace with the crowds on their way back from their lunch breaks or hoofing it to class at the nearby Freie Universität Berlin. The sun shone hot, but a low rumble to the south gave her the impression the weather was about to change.

The university was to the right, but she made a left on Königin-Luise Strasse, careful to meticulously catalog the faces she saw around her without giving any hint that she was doing so. She glanced in shop windows, scanned patrons at a sidewalk café, eyed a young man on a motorized skateboard as he whizzed towards and then past her.

Normally an American intelligence analyst, formerly of the National Security Agency, would have no special concerns about walking through a European capital, but Stephanie Arthur was, in fact, Zoya Zakharova, and Zoya had more than enough reason to be on guard. She knew good and well the Russian government wanted her dead, and she knew her cover had been blown, at least to her employer. She didn't know if the Kremlin was aware she was here, but she had spent the last couple of weeks operating under the assumption that killers lurked around every corner.

She continued down Königin-Luise until she was flush on the sidewalk with Eis Zeit, an ice cream shop nestled on the tree-lined street between a perfumery and a hair salon. She didn't go into any of the shops; rather, she stepped out into the road and climbed into the back of a parked blue van with a collection of ladders attached to the roof and sides.

The van's engine wasn't running; consequently, neither was the AC. It was warm inside, even in the darkness that had Zoya ripping off her Tom Ford sunglasses and slipping them into her purse as soon as she sat down. And though it was hotter in here than on the sunlit street, that wasn't the only discomfort. Her left shoulder was pressed against the side of the van, and a low table lined with monitors and other equipment was wedged against her rib cage on the right side.

Two men were in there with her; they were all three packed so close she could smell the sweat under their armpits, mixing sickeningly with the scent of hair gel off one of their heads.

Both men were in their twenties; Moises was Israeli, a translator and technician for Shrike International Group who spoke fluent Farsi. Yanis, also a Shrike employee, was French Algerian, and Zoya could see he was the one with the gel spiking his short black hair.

These were the techs Stephanie had been assigned for her first operation with the company. Yanis drove the van and monitored equipment when not doing his main job, which was black-bag ops. He led the pair on clandestine break-ins and other operations where they would set microphones, photograph documents in buildings, and the like. But in the van, Moises was in charge of this operation.

And Stephanie Arthur, Shrike International's newest case officer, was in charge of them.

Zoya had met the two younger men on her first day on the job two weeks earlier, and they had worked together since as a small team, setting up surveillance on several Iranian embassy staffers. Yesterday, she received a new targeting order. She'd briefed Yanis and Moises, who had then gone directly to this neighborhood to the southwest to install listening devices in the man's roomy flat three stories above the ice cream shop.

Zoya hadn't joined them for the operation to emplace the bugs, but she'd spent the balance of the evening looking over her target's portfolio.

Javad Sasani was a thirty-six-year-old Iranian consular affairs officer here in Berlin, and Shrike Group had been hired by its mysterious customer to investigate the man to see if he was, in fact, an operative with VAJA, the Iranian Ministry of Intelligence and Security.

Zoya didn't know why Sasani was suspected of ties to Iranian intel, nor did she even care. Her real mission wasn't to out this one potential spy in an Iranian embassy that was surely bursting at the seams with spies. No, she was really here on a Poison Apple initiative to acquire intelligence about Shrike Group from the two men seated next to her.

In her short time at the company, she'd only met Ric Ennis, the man who hired her, and this pair of young men. Ennis was certainly a more prized target for her to plumb for intel relating to the corporate intelligence firm, but Moises and Yanis were here, with her, so she got right to work on them.

Just like she'd done most every day for the past two weeks.

She'd already placed a tracker on two of their vehicles, hoping to see if they did other work for Shrike that would help her understand the organization. So far she'd found nothing of interest, so today she was determined to attempt to socially engineer the two to get them to reveal information.

Zoya reached into her purse and pulled out a pair of cold Red Bulls she'd just bought at a market, then slid them down the little table to the two men. "I know you guys didn't get much sleep last night."

Both Moises and Yanis instantly popped their cans.

The Frenchman said, "Thanks. Actually, it wasn't too bad. He had an alarm system on his door, but the window just had a lock, with a glass break sensor on the ceiling of the living room. I defeated the old lock with a shim and slid it open in no time. The subject was out at dinner and we had a cam on him there, so we knew when he left and began heading back to his flat." With a self-assured tone he said, "In my world, this one was pretty easy."

Moises added, "Yeah, might be he's easy because he's not an intelligence officer. I've listened to him all day and he's just watching TV. No calls in or out, no visitors."

The woman the two men knew as Stephanie said, "Well, it's Sunday. I'll tail him tomorrow and see if anything shakes out."

Yanis nodded. "You know, you don't have to stay with us in the van. We'll let you know if—"

"Are you trying to get rid of me?" she interrupted, and the men looked at each other nervously. After a second she said, "I'm kidding. I'll stay. What else do I have to do? This might not feel like much to you, at all, but this van is the center of the action as far as I'm concerned."

Yanis drained the last of his Red Bull, then slipped the can into a garbage bag lying on the floor at his feet. "My colleague here insists we remain in the vehicle. Now that we have the bugs placed, we could monitor the subject just as well in a nice, comfortable flat in Charlottenburg or in your suite in the Adlon or—"

"No," Moises interjected. "You hear people say all the time that proximity doesn't matter anymore. They say with the Internet you can be in Canada and listen to someone in Istanbul, or you can be in California and track the computer of someone in Berlin."

"Yeah. People say that because it's true," Yanis replied.

"No, that's bullshit," the Israeli countered. "If you are conducting surveillance on someone worth conducting surveillance on, then *they* are going to be running some sort of a counter. And the easiest counters these days are on Internet and Wi-Fi. The only real advances in the past fifteen years have been cyber related. You're better off with regular short-range transmitters: easier to hide their signal in the digital background noise of coffeemakers, computer equipment, smart dishwashers, all that stuff. We have to be close to do this right."

Zoya said, "I'm with Moises on this one. It's harder this way, but it works better." She added, "And I'm new here, but I can tell Shrike Group prides itself on running an efficient operation."

"We try," Yanis said.

After a moment sitting quietly, Zoya pressed. "Tell me about yourselves. Do you two come from domestic or military intelligence in your home countries? Neither of you look like soldiers to me, so I'm guessing you're academics recruited directly by Shrike. Electrical engineering majors? Did I get that right?"

Neither of the men spoke for a moment, until Moises said, "One thing that's important at Shrike is that we don't talk about our previous work with the other employees we come in contact with. Operational security."

Yanis added, "Yeah, surely Mr. Ennis told you that."

"Yeah, I get it, but I'm trying to get a baseline for your capabilities. If we're going to be working with one another, we have to—"

Moises shook his head. "I was told when I was hired that my employment would be terminated if I discussed background beyond country of origin with any of my colleagues."

"Me, too," Yanis said. Neither of the men seemed put off by her question, but Zoya noted that these two took their pledges to keep their stories to themselves seriously.

"Understood, guys," she said. "I'm new. I've only met you and Ennis."

"That won't change much," Yanis said. "I've been here almost two years and I've only met six or seven other Shrike Group personnel other than you and Moises."

"I was told it was a horizontal structure."

"Yeah," Moises added. "We don't even know who the client is."

Zoya tried to think of her next line of questioning, but before she could come up with something, Yanis muttered under his breath, "I do."

This was too good an opportunity for her to pass up. "You do?"

"Yeah. It's obvious. It's the Mossad."

"Bullshit," Moises said. "Why do you say that?"

Zoya found herself in the enviable position of sitting quietly while someone else probed for the intelligence she sought.

"Look, man," Yanis said. "Sure, it's set up with a German front company. Some ex-Stasi character who is probably living in the south of France and has less to do with running this show than I do. But three of the four case officers I've met are Israeli. You're Israeli. I've met Ennis, a Dane, a guy from the UK, and Stephanie, but the rest of you guys are straight-up Mossad."

Moises shook his head. "I'm Israeli, but that doesn't mean I'm Mossad. Never was. We aren't supposed to say anything about our backgrounds, but I guess I can say what I *wasn't*."

Yanis said, "Okay, maybe you were recruited by Shrike, but what about Dan, Simon, and Miriam? All three case officers with clearly a ton of experience, and all three Israeli."

Moises shook his head. "I don't know Simon. Dan's from Tiberias, which is in Israel, and you're right, he's probably former Mossad. But Miriam isn't Israeli."

Yanis cocked his head at this. "She's not?"

"I've worked with her. She sounds German to me. She speaks Hebrew, but she has a little accent."

"Israeli or not, Miriam is hot," Yanis said, and Moises agreed, but added a caveat.

"Not as hot as you, Stephanie, if you don't mind my saying."

She was barely listening to him. "Maybe I'll work with Miriam soon."

Yanis shook his head. "You are a case officer, she is a case officer. Shrike keeps the officers compartmentalized. Us techs work with different officers, but you guys only work with us techs."

Yanis continued with his thought stream. "Still. I think this is a Mossad front, set up in the heart of Europe to tear into Iranian intelligence efforts here. What we are doing is good, and that's all I care about." He grinned. "We're gonna change the world. We've uncovered a Quds Force cell, and when the operation wraps up next week, our client is going to go to the German government and get those guys arrested."

Zoya was surprised at this news. "Quds Force? Here? In Berlin?"

Moises nodded. "Yeah, like a big-time commander of them, who has recruited his own cell of operatives. They are dormant now, anyway, working in the shipping and transportation industry."

Yanis said, "They're dormant because they're sleepers. But as soon as they get the go-ahead from Tehran, they're going to light this town up."

Zoya was astonished. "Why don't we notify the German government now? Why wait till the end of the contract?"

Yanis answered, "Because if we do that now, they'll just get deported. Germany has eased sanctions, moved towards normalized relations. They are basically trying to distance themselves from the U.S., Israel, and anyone else playing tough on Iran. But if we catch these assholes actually planning something, then the Germans will hold them, interrogate them, and hopefully find out who else is out there hiding."

The plan made sense to Zoya, unless, of course, the cell was able to pull off a terror attack before getting arrested.

Moises was obviously worrying about the same thing. "I don't think Shrike is a front for Mossad. Mossad wouldn't play on the knife's edge like this. Our surveillance screws up for one day, and Quds Force could blow up a restaurant or something."

Yanis thought this over, but before he could form a retort, Moises added, "Also, I don't see why Mossad would need to establish a front company like Shrike to do all the work Mossad is doing anyway."

But Zoya had a feeling she did know. If Shrike was secretly hiring the missing intelligence officers from around the world, men and women with state secrets from their home nations, then Israel would not want to be affiliated with the operation officially.

An hour later Zoya Zakharova climbed out of the van as a warm rain fell, opening her umbrella as she headed south. She was in a foul mood, because right in the middle of her social engineering experiment to glean information from the two young technicians in the van, Suzanne Brewer began blowing up her phone with cryptic texts demanding she check in. She'd ignored them at first, but finally relented and told Yanis and Moises she'd be back later in the afternoon.

Now, as she walked in the direction of the Freie Universität, she pulled out her phone and placed a call.

Her handler answered quickly.

"Brewer."

"Anthem. Iden Charlie, Mike, Golf, seven, one, Charlie."

"Iden confirmed."

Zoya said, "You need to stop reaching out to me. I'll come to you if I need you."

"I have intel for you. Hence the texts. First, what do you have to report?"

"Nothing to report. I'm just doing low-end surveillance."

"Who is the target?"

"A consular affairs staffer at the Iranian embassy. Seems like a nobody."

"What does Shrike Group suspect him of?"

"The usual. They think he's VAJA. Haven't seen any evidence of it yet, but we've only been on him for twelve hours or so."

"Why is this one potential spook so important to them?"

"Unknown. I was just given a portfolio of the man and his home and employment information, and ordered to work with a team to dig into him."

"So, you have created other contacts with Shrike Group?"

"Just a couple of young surveillance techs."

"That's it?" Brewer was displeased.

"I've been here two weeks, Suzanne. I haven't unraveled the mysteries of the universe just yet." After no response she said, "Something for you to work on, though. The techs are talking about another case officer at Shrike. She's using the name Miriam, which might be a pseudonym. She's posing as an Israeli, but I think she might actually be a German national."

"Age?"

"Thirties, and that's just a guess."

"Description?"

"Hot."

"I beg your pardon?"

"The boys said she was hot. That's all the description I have."

"So . . . what would you like me to do with that information?"

"I don't know what you do, Suzanne. I'm not sitting in an office at Langley, am I?"

Brewer answered back with, "Let me show you what I do. This mysterious Miriam you are looking for is named Annika Dittenhofer. She is thirty-six years old, and she has a flat in Kreuzberg, in the south of Berlin. She was born in Dresden, not too long before reunification, and then she served in the Bundeswehr—that's the German army. After that she was German foreign intelligence, but she's been out and working for Shrike for several years."

Zoya was listening, but her true focus was on the source of this intel. "How the hell do you already know all this? I was told by Hanley we had no other access points into Shrike."

"This is intelligence that came to us in the last twenty-four hours. That's all I can tell you."

Zoya didn't like being kept in the dark like this, but she let it go. "Anyway, I'm told she is a case officer, like me, and I will never meet her due to the firm's policies about internal security."

"Where there's a will, Anthem, there's a way. You might never work with her, but Ennis will know who she is. You're going to have to get closer to him. As close as is necessary to complete your assignment."

This angered Zoya. "Meaning what, Suzanne?"

"Didn't your nation have a very famous Sparrow school where the art of seduction was taught to pretty young recruits?"

Zoya wanted to reach through the phone and punch Suzanne Brewer in the jaw. But she forced calm into her voice and said, "We also had a very famous school where the art of lethal combat was taught. The kind where a student is trained to snap a neck without any real effort." After a beat she said, "I went to *that* school, not sex camp."

"That's too bad. Snapping Dittenhofer's neck will tell us nothing. I want you to keep working Ennis. Work the two techs, as well, for whatever good they may provide."

Zoya asked, "Have you picked up any hints that Moscow knows I'm here?"

"Nothing at all," Brewer replied. "Obviously I will make contact if that changes."

She muttered under her breath, "Obviously."

Minutes later she was back in the U-Bahn, heading home to her hotel.

EIGHTEEN

Russian assassin Maksim Akulov stepped out of central Warsaw's rainy noontime bustle and entered through the door of Alkohole Nonstop, a state-run liquor store on Widok Street. He was alone, but as he nodded to the old woman behind the counter, she gave him a sideways glance and a slight nod, indicating that those he'd come to meet had already arrived.

He let water drip from his black raincoat onto the floor as he headed towards the back in the direction of the woman's glance, then took a narrow staircase down into the basement and began moving past stacks of boxes of Irish whiskey, Polish vodka, and Hungarian wine. He made a left at a stored display advertising a popular local honey liqueur, then continued down a dark and narrow aisle. Passing a shelf of loose 1.5-liter bottles of various alcohols, he didn't break stride as he yanked a room-temperature bottle of Chopin vodka, then continued on into a back room, the booze now tucked under an arm.

Here, two women and a man sat at a small table, each with a paper cup of coffee from nearby Café Nero. A fourth cup sat on the table in front of the one empty chair.

Maksim took the remaining seat with his wet coat still on. He put the bottle down on the table and opened the lid of the coffee cup.

The man on his left was older, with gray hair and a thick midsection. One of the women was a little younger than Maksim at thirty-nine. She was dressed in a business suit and wore eyeglasses; her long blond hair was braided and a tablet computer rested in front of her. The other woman, still in her twenties, had dyed platinum blond hair, cut short, and she wore jeans and a tank top. At first glance, Maksim thought she was the most attentive of the bunch today, and he was proven right as soon as he sat down.

She spoke up brightly. *"Dobroye utro." Good morning.*

"Is it though?"

She motioned to the cup now in his hand. "Brought you some coffee, sir."

Maksim replied with a disinterested *"Spasibo,"* then took the coffee and poured it unceremoniously onto the concrete floor next to him while the younger woman looked on.

He unscrewed the lid off the Chopin now, poured himself a long shot into the still-hot cup, and then downed warm coffee-infused vodka in a single gulp.

Both women winced.

The other man at the table chuckled a little. "Polish vodka? Are you just keeping up your cover or do you really like it better than good Russian vodka?"

Akulov flinched a little with the bite of the drink going down, then recovered and poured himself another shot. While doing so he said, *"Nyet,* Semyon, it's not better than *good* Russian vodka, but it's better than *shit* Russian vodka, which is the only kind these idiots import into their country."

"They are used to shit," declared Semyon Pervak, making the statement as if it were common knowledge.

Inna Sorokina, the older of the two women, kept her eyes on Maksim as she took a careful sip of her hot brew, and then her eyes flashed over to the younger woman on her right.

Maksim caught the glance between Inna Sorokina and Anya Bolichova, knew he was being judged by his female subordinates for hitting the bottle before noon, but he didn't care. As far as he was concerned, his constitution could handle anything he could throw its way, at least until the next morning. Still, he told himself the sooner he started drinking each day, the sharper and smarter it made him and, more importantly, the sooner the day would be over.

He knew that Semyon Pervak, Anya Bolichova, and Inna Sorokina all looked down on his life choices, but they hadn't walked in his shoes. Despite their judgment, however, Maksim Akulov knew they would shut their mouths and do their jobs, just as soon as he gave them a job to do.

To that end, he ignored any further pleasantries, reached inside his coat, and pulled out a sheaf of papers in a manila folder. "Back to work, finally. A target in Berlin. We leave today."

"Berlin is boring," Bolichova declared.

"And Warsaw isn't?" Pervak asked.

Maksim downed the second shot before saying, "I'd love an assignment in Tahiti as much as the rest of you, but we go where they send us, don't we?"

It was a rhetorical question, and his team regarded it as such.

He put the folder down in the middle of the table and kept his hand on top of it. When Semyon reached for it, Maksim held it firm. He looked up at Sorokina instead. "Inna will see the assignment first."

The thirty-nine-year-old woman cocked her head in surprise. Semyon Pervak was second-in-command on this team, not her.

She pulled the folder to her and asked, "Why me?"

Maksim smiled; he was already reaching for the big bottle of Chopin again. "You'll see."

Inna opened the folder, and almost immediately she let out a little gasp. She then looked quietly through the five-page dossier, until finally she closed it.

Her gray eyes darted back up to Maksim. With a tone of wonderment, she uttered one word. "Sirena."

"Who the fuck is Sirena?" asked Semyon.

Maksim answered. "The target is Zakharova, Zoya F., former SVR officer. Her code name was *Sirena Vozdushnoy Trevogi*. Banshee, in English." His eyes were still on Sorokina's. "Inna, you knew her when you were with foreign intelligence, I presume."

The blonde took a slow, measured breath. "I knew her well. Trained with her. Worked with her in the field several times over the years."

Even through the haze of drink, Maksim had a sharp mind that he was able to focus like a laser, ready to pick up every microexpression on his female colleague's face when he asked the next question. "And"—his tone was slow and measured now—"how do you feel about targeting your old friend?"

But there was no mistaking how Inna felt because there *were* no microexpressions. Only macroexpressions, obvious to all. She scowled at Akulov. "I did not say she was a friend. In fact, she killed a friend of mine in Bangkok a few months ago." She took another sip of her coffee as she pushed the dossier back across the table. "I will very much enjoy watching her die."

Semyon Pervak felt ignored. He'd been at this a long time; he was usually the one who knew the target, not fucking Sorokina, the officious and buttoned-up ex-government spy. Pervak, in contrast, had been a street thug, a mob enforcer since the heyday of the Russian mafia in the nineties, and though he was well over a decade older than Maksim, he was still proud to be the former Spetsnaz soldier's number two.

But he wasn't about to take a backseat to a woman. "Who gives a shit if one of us knows the target? She'll go down like all the rest."

"No," Maksim corrected. "Not like all the rest. This one is different. Moscow wants us to give her a chance."

Anya Bolichova didn't understand. "A chance for . . . *what?*"

"A chance to come home. A chance to tell Yasenevo what she's been doing, who she's been doing it with, and who she's talked to."

Sorokina wasn't having it. "She's too smart for that. She'll know that no matter what she says, she'll end up with a bullet in the base of her skull and an unmarked grave."

Akulov smiled a little. "I'm banking on that. I'm banking on the fact that she'll know that her only chance is to run from us." He nodded, almost to himself. "That would be good. I need a hunt."

"Rules of engagement?" Pervak asked.

Akulov sighed at this. "Assuming she runs, they don't want attention on this one. We need her quietly dispatched if we are going to do it in the German capital. We'll have to make it look like an accident, or natural causes, or a suicide." He shrugged. "I'll slit her wrists, toss her in a bathtub, and the locals will forget about her in days. No comebacks on the Rodina."

Anya Bolichova spoke next. "How current is the intel?"

"Nearly real time," Maksim responded.

"What does that mean?"

"We have someone at her organization, apparently, who can notify us of her location. The intel goes through Moscow before it comes to us, but we should have excellent intelligence on our target's disposition." He readied the Chopin to pour himself a third shot. "Almost too easy."

Inna Sorokina surprised everyone when she all but lurched across the table, yanked the bottle away from her superior, and lobbed it into a plastic garbage can in the corner. "Listen to me, Maksim. *Nothing* with Sirena is easy. The SVR's most elite went after her in Asia. And now, some of them are dead. You get it? I've seen her in action. She was always a formidable ally. She will be a formidable foe. She is the best."

"I thought *you* were the best," Maksim chided.

"If I were the best, I wouldn't be working for you, you'd be working for me."

Pervak snorted out a little laugh. "You sound scared, Inna. I don't work with cowards."

"I'm not scared. I'm careful, and I'm knowledgeable about this target." She turned back to Akulov. "Trust me, Maksim, if you want to kill her, you can't just stagger off a train in Berlin, go to her flat, and slide a knife across her wrists. Not with Sirena. If you aren't at your best, then she'll either disappear from us completely or we'll lose her until she shows up behind you and slides a knife into *your* spine."

Bolichova's eyes were wide, but Maksim and Semyon were wholly unimpressed.

Sorokina ignored their annoyance as she looked slowly around the table at all three. "We might get her, but she'll get one of us, at least. I promise you that. Which one of you wants to die?"

Maksim raised his hand, and Anya took it as a joke and laughed.

Semyon shook his head. "You're being ridiculous, Inna. I've been doing this for a long time and—"

Now Sorokina yelled at the mafia enforcer. "You've been killing hapless fools who never saw you coming! Zoya knows there are teams like us out here, hunting her! She has her defenses up, and she is a hair trigger away from going on the offense at any time!"

Maksim rubbed his eyes like it was five a.m., then ran his fingers through his thick and unkempt reddish-brown hair. He took in Sorokina's words, then shrugged in acquiescence. "I don't need to be told that every good plan can go to shit. We hear you, Inna. We'll be extra diligent.

"Let's get back to the information we have. We build this operation like any other. Zakharova is in Berlin, posing as an American, using the name Stephanie Arthur. She's working in cover for a private intelligence firm; the Kremlin thinks it has Israeli ties, but she's essentially on her own. There will be no one watching her back."

"Bullshit," said Inna.

Maksim sighed now. "Are you suggesting our intel is wrong?"

"I'm suggesting we don't start complimenting ourselves on a job well done before we do the damn job. She knows Moscow is after her; if she is showing up on our radar like this, then there is a bigger game at play. Whatever she's doing, she will be ready for us."

Semyon Pervak leaned back in the metal chair, his cheap blue blazer open and his girthy midsection on display, covered by an off-white shirt that needed a wash and a press. "Dammit, Sorokina, this Zoya isn't the fucking Gray Man."

Bolichova laughed aloud. She knew the legend of the unkillable uber assassin the Gray Man, and she also knew it was nothing but a fantasy.

Akulov said, "No . . . she's not the Gray Man." He sighed wistfully. "But I wish she were."

The meeting adjourned after another half hour, with a game plan of moving the team and their equipment into a safe house in central Berlin having been established. Bolichova handled the team's logistics, so she left first to begin preparations. Pervak was "the Cleaner"; his task was to reconnoiter in advance of the hit, and then to come along behind the hit, before the first responders arrived, and make sure there was no evidence left behind that might incriminate the team.

Inna Sorokina served as the intelligence officer in the small unit. She orchestrated target acquisition, and she, along with Maksim, decided on the time and the place for the actual assassination.

Maksim Akulov was the trigger man, save for one time on the island of Crete where he had been too drunk to get out of the car to shoot a man in an outdoor café, so Pervak was forced to both do the deed and clean up any evidence from the scene.

No one in the unit talked about that night in the island town of Chania, and Maksim Akulov had made amends somewhat on the two jobs since, for which he had stayed off the bottle, at least for a few hours before conducting his kills.

After Semyon left the liquor store, Inna sat with Maksim, who gazed at the garbage can where his bottle of vodka had been tossed.

Inna saw the distant look in his eyes. "*Pazhalusta*, Maksim." *Please.* "Respect this woman as a competent foe."

"You think I won't?"

"I think that, if you want to survive, then this job has to be run like Minsk, like Ankara, like Long Island. It can't be another Crete."

Akulov pushed himself up from the table, slid the dossier into the small of his back. "Fine. You run the pre-workup to the target, and when the time comes to act, I'll be on my best behavior."

Inna was pleased. "Good. We go in with full stealth, she never sees or hears—"

Maksim raised a hand. "You read the brief. She has to get a chance to walk in."

"She won't do it. That's insanity."

"Yes, that's insanity. Do you know what else it is? It's an order. When we have her found and fixed, you, her old colleague, will contact her and tell her there is no escape except to face the music back in Moscow. I admit, it's a strange way to go about things, but there is someone very, very high up at SVR or in the Kremlin who is mandating this. They want to know where she's been and who she's been talking to."

"Why don't we *not* do this, and then just tell headquarters we *did* do this, and she said no?"

Maksim laughed at this. "Lie to HQ?"

"Why not? We lie to HQ every time we tell them you are operation-ally fit."

Maksim stopped laughing, but he kept a little smile. "A low blow, Inna. Ever since I got out of the asylum, I've kept my shit together, more or less."

Sorokina didn't miss a beat. "More or less? Yes, that's fair. More in Long Island. Less in Crete." Akulov didn't respond, so she added, "You are headed one of two places, Maksim. Either back to the loony bin or to the morgue. I can't stop you, but I don't want you taking me with you to either of these places."

The man with the reddish-brown hair laughed again; it was clear to Sorokina that Akulov didn't give a shit what she thought. Then his head seemed to clear a bit, and he said, "You will make contact with Zakharova just before we move on her. When she refuses to surrender, we kill her. That is final."

Sorokina didn't like this complication, but she wasn't going to fight Aku-lov. *"Ladno." All right.* "You take care of your part, I'll take care of mine. We'll wait for Anya to get the safe house arranged, then we get on a train. We can be in Berlin by tonight. Pervak can do his recon, I can conduct surveillance, and after a couple of days learning her pattern, we can act."

"Which means," Maksim said as he turned and headed for the door, "Zoya Zakharova has about seventy-two hours left on this miserable Earth." He drew a cigarette from a pack and lit it. "Lucky girl."

Inna did not respond. Her leader had a death wish, he was about to target an incredibly challenging opponent, and, the Russian intelligence specialist was certain, there was more to whatever Zoya was up to in Berlin that she needed to figure out before they went after her. She told herself she'd concentrate on the target profile, and she'd just hope like hell Mak-sim could keep his shit together long enough to make the kill.

She followed her trigger man out the door of Alkohole Nonstop and back into Warsaw's warm rain.

NINETEEN

TWELVE DAYS EARLIER

Sultan al-Habsi did not have to go personally to the factory in Karabük, Turkey, to see the shipment loaded into the tractor-trailer. But he was here this warm July morning because he wanted it to be known that he had orchestrated every single part of this operation. He wanted his fingerprints on everything. Figuratively, of course, not literally. He wanted—needed—this to be his operation, because there was one person Sultan wanted to prove himself to.

His father.

The crown prince.

He shook thoughts of his father's judgment from his head just as he had shaken out the thoughts of his brothers' deaths in Yemen, and then he climbed out of the armored car and followed an entourage of local men and women towards a sterile warehouse. At the door they had to don protective equipment so they would not contaminate the environment inside. Sultan pulled the white fabric over his suit, placed the plastic shoe covers over his feet, and shrouded his face and head in a full mask. Once everyone had done the same, they moved past the warehouse floor and into a large storage and loading area. Here there were several loading bays on the wall, but only one door was open. A tractor-trailer had been backed up to the bay, and armed security men, themselves dressed head to toe in white protective gear, stood by it.

In front of the truck, presented dramatically for al-Habsi's inspection, were the items he had traveled all the way from the UAE to inspect.

There were forty quadcopter drones, all arrayed on the floor in two arrow-shaped formations. Each of the forty devices was one meter wide and a half meter in height. Packaged together for shipping, he knew they would just fit into the sixteen-meter dry van trailer waiting for them, but first al-Habsi would sit through a lesson delivered by the president of the company.

In truth, he didn't need the lesson; the Emirati spy chief had read every single page of every single document about the drones. But Sultan al-Habsi wanted his father to learn, once the operation was complete, that his son had personally accompanied the quadcopters on the beginning of their journey, and personally met with the manufacturer after communicating with him for months online.

The Turkish technology company director spoke in Arabic with beaming pride. Less like a salesman and more like a proud parent. "The Kargus. It means 'hawk' in Turkish. Designed and made right here. Suicide drone quadcopters. Capable of operating in a swarm of up to twenty, and each unit is able to deliver a three-pound warhead. Top speed is one hundred forty-four kilometers per hour, and the range is ten kilometers on a single charge.

"They can be flown remotely, or they can hover and loiter, and choose their own targets, based on whatever parameters you set up for them."

He went on for a few minutes, then demonstrated a similar device by flying it off the warehouse floor and into the loading area, positioning it head high in front of the Emirati, its buzzing rotors furiously beating the air for lift.

Sultan stepped closer and put his face centimeters from the camera eye. The crowd laughed when a massive brown eyeball appeared on a screen against the wall.

The director of the company said, "Just as you are inspecting him, he is inspecting you."

Everyone laughed again.

The demonstration of the drone itself complete, al-Habsi started in with questions.

"The warheads are as we discussed?"

The Turk nodded. "Fifteen high-explosive, fifteen antipersonnel, and ten armor-piercing shaped charges. If your targeting data is good, then you will be able to fly these in any formation you want and deposit the loads within centimeters of your target."

"Very well."

More questions followed, questions al-Habsi had the answers to already, but questions that showed everyone in attendance that the Emirati spy chief was intimately well versed in UAV technology.

The payment had already taken place via secure wire transfers through multiple offshore accounts, so there was nothing left to do but watch while each unmanned vehicle was put in its own hard plastic crate, then loaded onto pallets by hand and into the truck by forklift.

Al-Habsi put his hand on the trailer after the doors were shut, and then he watched the vehicle roll off towards the highway.

He had only landed in Turkey an hour and a half earlier, and his private plane was ready to return him to Dubai. Once back in the armored car, he turned to Omar, his deputy director of operations. "Remind me of the route."

Omar answered back in a subordinate's voice. "Bulgaria, Serbia, Hungary, Slovakia, Czechia, Germany. Three days' transportation time, depending on the waits at the border crossings we've already cleared with bribes. We are sending two dummy trucks along the same route with the same arrangement. If we run into any trouble with one of those, we'll have to go to our backup route, but I am convinced the merchandise will be at its final destination in not longer than four days."

Sultan nodded. "Plenty of time. You will be there when it arrives?"

"Just as you arranged, sir."

Now Sultan looked out the thick window of the armored car, and he allowed himself a brief moment to think of family, of loss, and of valor.

It wouldn't be long now, he told himself. Almost everything was in motion, and he could hardly wait for the next phase. If all went according to plan, in just two weeks the lone surviving son of Rashid al-Habsi would, almost single-handedly, redesign the landscape of the Middle East, and he would do it in the heart of Europe.

TWENTY

PRESENT DAY

Just like most evenings, Dr. Azra Kaya exited the emergency room door of Franziskus-Krankenhaus on Budapester Strasse, and walked alone through the night. Her flat was in a building on Tiergarten Strasse, in the heart of Berlin, just fifteen minutes away at her typical brisk pace. She usually listened to music during the walk but she had forgotten to charge her headphones, so tonight she just leaned into a cool breeze and thought about her cases of the day.

She was completely oblivious to the man sixty meters behind her, moving along the opposite sidewalk in the same direction on Tiergarten Strasse.

Dr. Kaya was an internist, still with another year of residency to go, and she typically worked long, hard hours. Born in Turkey, she'd immigrated alone at eighteen, leaving her family behind. She now considered herself more German than Turk by a wide margin, a fact her parents, like many parents of first-generation immigrants, had mixed feelings about.

She'd gone to medical school in Heidelberg, graduated near the top of her class, and almost immediately began working in hospitals and clinics around Berlin. Single at thirty, like many Turkish women she had a modern view of her role in society and was in no rush to settle down. She lived for her work, and she worked a lot.

At 12:18 a.m. she entered her building, then made her way through the small and dark lobby to the tiny elevator. The trip to the fourth floor passed quickly, and she pulled out her keys as she walked halfway up the hall, finally stopping at number 403.

She was inside in an instant, locked the door behind her, and plopped her purse down on the kitchen island there. After grabbing a can of sparkling water from the fridge, she stepped into her bedroom to shower and change.

Tonight's shift hadn't been especially taxing, but still she was looking forward to watching a movie while eating popcorn, one of her favorite late-night pastimes and a habit that she'd found helped her fall asleep.

Twenty minutes later she'd changed into a black Puma tracksuit, and she'd removed her hair tie so her dark and curly wet locks fell down past her shoulders. She popped out her contacts and put on her eyeglasses, and then she picked up the nearly empty can of sparkling water and headed back towards the kitchen.

She entered her living room and was surprised by a slight breeze. Looking to her right, she saw that the window by the television was open. She pulled to a sudden stop, terror filling her chest, and her eyes then shot to the kitchen on her left.

There, just four meters away, a figure stood, leaning back against the kitchen island. She let out a meek gasp, but she did not scream, and she did not run.

Her voice was measured but calm, considering the circumstances. "Wer sind Sie?" Who are you?

In English the man replied, "I need help."

Azra took in a deep breath of air, then let it out slowly before switching to English. "You scared the shit out of me." And then, "I didn't get a text."

"I know."

The young doctor said, "And if I don't get a text first, I don't treat you."

"Come closer. Look at me. You know me."

Dr. Kaya was no longer uncomfortable with the stranger in her flat. She marched up to him, flipping a light switch on the way.

As soon as she did so, she examined the man's face carefully. "You," she said, a fresh tone of bewilderment in her voice.

"Yeah. Me." The man coughed.

"I know you. Three and a half years ago, you came to me."

The man smiled a little. Dr. Kaya thought he looked ill. He said, "You have a good memory."

"In your case, it's easy," Azra said. "You were my first. You always remember your first."

Court cleared his throat nervously. There was a joke to be made here, but he didn't feel like making it, and she looked at him like she had other things on her mind.

Then Dr. Kaya smiled a little. "Your arm had a serious gash. I asked you what cut you, and you told me it was broken glass." She paused, her eyes locked on him in the low light. "It was not glass."

Court confirmed the doctor's statement. "It was not glass."

"It was a knife," she said.

"It *was* a knife."

"You'd lost some blood, but you were incredibly fit. Stoic, too. You just sat patiently and bled while a twenty-six-year-old medical student desperately tried to treat you. My hands were shaking."

"You did great."

Court remembered it all as well as Azra. He had been hired by a Russian mafia concern to go to Berlin to assassinate a Chechen mobster who lived under heavy guard. Court had done the deed, but on the exfiltration he found himself on the wrong end of a knife, wielded by a bodyguard who'd run out of bullets.

Court killed the Chechen with the same blade an instant after it had slashed into his arm.

At the time Court worked as a hit man for hire for a British handler, who belonged to an underground resource network his contractors could call upon, all over the world, if they needed help. Among the resources were medical professionals for clandestine treatment. Court had used the service many times over the years while working for Sir Donald Fitzroy, but now, as a freelancer and sometimes off-book CIA contractor, he sought out members of the network for help on his own.

Dr. Kaya said, "Soon after you left, three thousand euros appeared in my bank account."

Court said, "I was surprised that someone like you would work in the network."

The young Turkish woman with the wet hair said, "I'll take that for a compliment." She looked him over. "You need medical assistance. But . . ." she repeated, "I did not receive a text."

"I'm working outside the organization that retains you to treat patients in the area. But I am here in town, and I needed your help, so I came." He added, "I can pay you. Cash, right now. Will you help me?"

"Come, sit."

Court moved to a small settee in her simple living room and sat down roughly, his knees almost giving out completely as he bent. She steadied him, then hurried to her bag on the kitchen island to get her stethoscope.

Court said, "I have an infection in my shoulder. In the bone. I think it's pretty bad."

"When did you contract it?"

"A month ago."

"How?"

He hesitated, and then said, "You know how it is. Broken glass."

She knelt on the floor in front of him. "Whatever you say." He took his shirt off and she looked at his bandages for the first time.

"Who dressed this wound? A monkey?"

He coughed again. "The monkey wasn't available, so I did it myself."

She laughed a little, and gently removed the dirty bandaging. Looking the surgical wound over, she put her hand on the skin near the cut and then on his forehead.

"A good surgeon." She held her hand on his forehead. "But you have a fever. How have you been treating it?"

"IV antibiotics. Three weeks or so. I stopped a few days ago, but am taking pills."

"You just ended your IVs?" She seemed surprised. "You need an infusion of Cipro for eight weeks, at a minimum. This is very serious." She looked around her flat a moment. "I can rebandage you for now, but I'll have to get the antibiotics, saline, and an IV pole and tubing. I'll need you to come back every night and I will administer—"

"I don't think I can do that."

She looked at him. "Right. I understand. That's a lot of coming and going. You can stay here. I have a guest room. It's a mess, but there is a bed. I can bring the medicine and saline when I get off shift and rig up—"

"I can't do that, either. I am here in town to work. Not to lie on a sofa."

"But you—"

"Pills. I need more pills. A lot of them."

"Oral antibiotics aren't strong enough to defeat a bone infection."

"They don't have to win the war; they only have to keep me in the fight."

"I don't understand."

"I need to keep going. A week would be my guess, but it could be longer. Once I'm done here, I have a place I can go and get IV antibiotics, as long as I need them. I just have to hang on until I'm done."

She put her head in her hands, a show of frustration. "What is it that you people do that makes you so . . ."

She seemed to be searching for the word, so Court tried to help. "Crazy?"

"I was going to say 'relentless.'"

"Yeah, well. I get myself into situations. Sometimes I need help getting out of them."

"I'll give you the pills, but you have to let me see you when you can. The infection can grow even with the Cipro. As long as you are in town, you'll need to try to come back regularly, and I will give you an infusion."

Court nodded. "Deal. I also need some other drugs."

"What other drugs?"

"Adderall to keep me on my feet. Something to help me sleep when I have time for rest. Klonopin works. And something for pain, for my shoulder, and for anything new that comes along."

"Anything *new*?"

"There is no shortage of *broken glass* here in Berlin."

Dr. Kaya looked him over again, and for the first time, he felt judged by her.

She said, "So, what you are telling me is you are falling apart and need drugs to keep it together."

Court shrugged. "I've got to keep moving. Whatever tools I can employ to stay in the fight are the tools I'm going to use."

The young resident nodded after a time. "I can get what I need at the clinic. I will secure IV equipment, as well. Will you return tomorrow night?"

"I think so."

She went to her purse and began digging through it. Court shifted his hand closer to his right hip, ready to pull the pistol in the small of his back if she brought anything out of the bag that could pose a threat to him. But instead she just took out a bottle of pills. "Lortab," she said. "It will help with the pain."

Court shook his head. "Tramadol. It's milder. I just need to take the edge off."

She threw the bottle to him and he caught it. "Break those in half. I had oral surgery some months ago. Only needed the pills a couple of days for the pain."

Court had dealt with painkiller addiction in his past, a shockingly common occurrence among military and intelligence paramilitary operatives. But he also knew his body, and he knew the drugs. If he took the opioid only when he was, indeed, in real pain, then there was less chance his addiction would fire back up.

And he was in pain now. "Thank you," he said as he put his shirt back on.

"Thank me by doing me one more favor."

"Sure." He broke one of the pills and downed it without water.

"You have a lot of bruises and scrapes. Contusions that are not three weeks old. Whatever you are doing, it still involves the risk of injury." She patted him on the arm. "Try not to get hurt any worse than you already are."

Court nodded, looked out the window to the street. "I've been trying and failing at that for twenty years." He looked at her now. "I'll try harder. Just so you don't stress."

He produced a wad of euros, and she looked at it, but did not take it. "Tonight was just a consultation. I'll take your money, but not tonight. You are an old friend, and it is good to see you."

Court had spent just a few hours in this young woman's care years earlier. He remembered little of their encounter. It spoke volumes about the other sons of bitches sent here for treatment that she remembered him so warmly.

Five minutes later he was out the door of Dr. Kaya's apartment. As he walked along Tiergarten Strasse, he looked in every dark alcove, noted every parked car, took stock of which lights were on in which apartments at one in the morning. His actions were automatic; he recorded mental notes so that he would understand the natural patterns in these surroundings, because he knew he'd be back again.

He also thought about Zoya.

He climbed into a taxi in front of the Swedish embassy, asking the driver in passable German to deliver him to the U-Bahn station at Rathaus Spandau. They drove west through the night for nearly fifteen minutes before the Mercedes pulled over and Court climbed out and began walking again, alone through the empty streets.

Ten minutes later he entered an all but darkened building and started up the stairs.

Court had rented a completely nondescript flat at Bismarckstrasse 64, not too far from the U-Bahn, just west of the Havel River in the Western Berlin district of Spandau. The small space was on the third floor next to a staircase that led down to a rear parking lot, and it had a dingy and unadorned yellow balcony that looked out over the main street. But other than a good rear exit and good sight lines on a forward approach, the flat had little going for it. Here Court was four miles away from the center of the city, the floors and bathroom were dusty and grimy, and the only neighbor on his floor seemed to be grilling some sort of sickly-sweet-smelling meat on the next balcony over, even now, well past one a.m., with the scent wafting into Court's shitty rental property.

He normally preferred sleeping in closets; he felt safer there than in a bed, because anyone sneaking up on him in the night would naturally expect to find him in bed. But here at Bismarckstrasse 64 he tossed his threadbare bedding onto the cold vinyl flooring of the bathroom, as there wasn't a single closet in the 450-square-foot flat, only a dresser with drawers that felt like they had been welded shut by time, humidity, and poor craftsmanship. He flipped off the lights, drew his HK VP9 pistol, and placed it next to him on the floor.

His fever had already broken due to the hydrocodone Dr. Kaya had given him, though he knew it would return by morning. His shoulder burned and stung, but not so bad now with the pain medication, and he didn't expect it to impede his sleep much at all.

He was too exhausted to worry much about pain. Tomorrow he'd be watching Zoya from afar, and he needed to get his head around that now.

He wasn't looking forward to his mission here, but he preferred it to Zoya being dangled out alone by the CIA.

He closed his eyes and willed himself to sleep.

TWENTY-ONE

NINE DAYS EARLIER

The *Remora Bay*, a midsized dry-goods freighter flying the flag of Singapore, had left Mumbai, India, four days earlier with a mixed load of patio furniture, glassware, and cutlery, and it then began its voyage west across the Arabian Sea. She anchored in Abu Dhabi, offloaded one half of her cargo, and then made her way around the Arabian Peninsula, where she again moored off Assab, Eritrea.

There, in the midnight hours of a moonless night, two small dhow craft approached the anchored freighter from the east, and four rope ladders were lowered from the *Remora Bay*'s deck. The crew of the freighter, having dropped their ladders, hurried to the galley, turning off the deck floodlights along the way as they had been warned not to set eyes on their new cargo.

Fifteen men made the three-story climb from the decks of the dhows to the railing of the freighter. Cool, salty breezes blew across lean, sinewy physiques as they ascended. Each man carried a small folding-stock, short-barreled Zastava Kalashnikov rifle and extra loaded magazines slung and fastened to their bodies, as well as a large Patagonia backpack containing rations, Western-style clothing, and other essentials.

The first man onto the *Remora Bay*'s deck was dressed in black and wore collar-length black hair and a short beard and mustache. His weapon and gear hung behind him as he adroitly scaled the rope ladder, rolled onto the deck, and landed silently on his feet with the dexterity of a cat. He immediately turned back to the ladder, pulled men up by their hands, and pointed them towards the entrance to a stairwell that led directly from the deck to the cargo hold.

He was Hasan, a Signals Intelligence Agency operative from the UAE, and Sultan al-Habsi's hand-picked operational commander for the mission in Europe. And the other fourteen were the Iranian prisoners of war released from the UAE black site in Yemen, just across the Bab al-Mandab Strait. While highly trained fighters, these men were slower, less healthy, but their fervent devotion to their mission was greater than Hasan's. He was being paid for leading this group to their final objective; their will alone drove them on.

And despite having less experience than their Sunni leader, all these men were steeped in urban warfare; they'd all carried guns since puberty.

Hasan was the last man off the deck of the *Remora Bay*. He stood at the doorway to the stairwell and turned, looking back across a ship he could barely see at an ocean invisible in the night. He took a deep breath of brackish air, because he knew it would be his last for many days. He thought about his mission, his chances for survival, and he told himself that if he did make it back home, the crown prince would reward him with praise, money, and prestige. And when Rashid died, his son Sultan, Hasan's boss, would be the leader of the nation, and he would make Hasan the new operational head of the SIA, while Sultan himself ascended to the throne.

There was much work to do between now and then; this, Hasan knew. But the incentive on the other side of this op was real, and it was incredibly enticing.

Hasan turned for the stairs, then descended into the belly of the hulking vessel.

TWENTY-TWO

PRESENT DAY

Court left his flat at six ten a.m., the weight of the hour wearing on him more than usual in his weakened state. He'd taken more tablets, but he hadn't reached for the heavier painkillers, preferring instead a small handful of anti-inflammatories he'd brought with him from Aruba. He'd get drugs from Dr. Kaya tonight, but for now he knew he just had to power through.

Tonight seemed like a long way off.

His HK VP9 was positioned inside his waistband, jammed into his appendix. Additionally, he carried a small and cheap black duffel bag he'd bought the evening before in a street-front shop, where he also bought a pair of *I ♥ Berlin* sweatshirts. The sweatshirts gave bulk to the otherwise empty bag, and now it swung over his shoulder along with his movements.

Soon he climbed aboard a train at the U-Bahn station in the Spandau Altstadt, destination east.

At seven Court was five miles from his apartment, sitting on a bench next to a pond in the Gardens of Charlottenburg Palace, eating a fluffy coffee cake and drinking a tall cup of black coffee. He checked his watch, took a few more bites, then tore the last third of the pastry into tiny pieces and tossed them to the ducks milling on the shoreline.

He stood, finished his coffee before throwing the cup into a bin nearby, and began walking along a narrow asphalt pathway, winding through statues and trees.

There was no one in sight at first, but soon he noticed a dark-skinned man heading in his direction.

Court eyed him for just an instant, then turned his gaze away, looking back out to the pond. He'd seen the stranger carrying a small black duffel bag over his shoulder; it was identical to Court's, and he appreciated the fact that the man's timing had been perfect.

The two neared each other, did not look at each other, nor did they slow or stop in the path. They merely passed, but while doing so both men let their duffels slip off their shoulders to their hands, then they reached across their bodies and took the duffel from the other man's hands, letting their own go.

An instant later Court had the new duffel on his right shoulder, just where the other one had been, and he had no doubt that the man behind him had done exactly the same.

The two-way brush pass had been executed flawlessly, and Court found himself impressed, if only mildly so, with the skill of this CIA Berlin station case officer.

Court had asked Hanley to have a list of items for him here in Berlin. He decided he'd risk the small chance of compromise by getting the items directly from the CIA, but he hadn't lived this long as an assassin by not being careful, so he did a thirty-minute surveillance detection route, climbing on and off streetcars and underground rail cars, even taking an Uber to the Reichstag, where he immediately bladed his body and moved through the day's first tourists clambering to get pictures of the German Bundestag building, and then he climbed into a taxi that whisked him away, towards the former East Berlin.

At a quarter till nine he pulled out his phone while walking through Alexanderplatz, having just completed his SDR. He opened Signal, his end-to-end encryption app, selected a preloaded number, and surveilled the area while he waited for the call to be answered.

Finally, he heard a familiar voice. "Brewer."

Court had spent the last couple of minutes mentally preparing himself for this call. He would rather not have been in comms with Suzanne Brewer at all, but since he needed information from her, it was necessary. His secondary intent, however, was to avoid giving Brewer any information about him and his whereabouts.

He answered with, "Violator. Iden code Lima, Yankee, Papa, fiver, one, Golf."

"Iden confirmed. I take it you got the package?"

"Affirmative. I need to know where Anthem is."

"I don't have a fix on her at present."

Court imagined that Suzanne Brewer had practically blown her top when Matt Hanley told her that he would be involved in this operation, even if only in a countersurveillance role. He'd expected her to be short and caustic with him—such was their relationship—but he didn't think she'd dare defy Hanley's order that she lead him to Anthem.

"Why don't you know?"

"She hasn't checked in since last night. I can vector you to where she is staying, or I can vector you to her target at Shrike International Group, but as far as where you will find her, well, I guess you'll just have to go looking for her."

"Who's the target?"

"Javad Sasani. He's suspected Iranian foreign intelligence, relatively midlevel, no personal security. A pretty easy mark. Boring work, from what she says."

"Then why does Shrike have Anthem following him?"

"She's only been with the company a couple of weeks. She figures they are just giving her something mundane at first." Brewer gave Court Sasani's address.

"Got it," he said, memorizing the information. And then, "Where is she staying?"

"She has a suite at the Adlon. 405."

"Near the Brandenburg Gate?"

"Yes. And that means it's also near the U.S. embassy. Don't show your face on the west side of the hotel; American cams might pick it up and ID you through facial recognition. Remember, the CIA is still officially hunting you."

"How could I forget?"

"Hanley did stress to you how important it is that no one suspects Anthem has people working with her, didn't he?"

"Nobody will know I'm there."

"Entire cities have burned down where you've said that before."

Court felt like this was a serious exaggeration, but the point was not without some validity. This time, he told himself, he would err on the side of his own operational security so that Zoya would not be outed as a supposedly solo act who, for some reason, possessed countersurveillance assets watching her back.

He was here to help her, not to get her killed.

Soon he was off the phone with Brewer and on his way to the home of Javad Sasani.

TWENTY-THREE

TWO DAYS EARLIER

After a seven-day voyage through the Mediterranean Sea, around the Iberian Peninsula, and north up the Atlantic past France, the cargo ship *Remora Bay* entered the English Channel on its way to port in Amsterdam.

It had been an uneventful journey for the crew, other than the fact that, every night, all except the captain at the helm were ordered into their cabins for ninety minutes, presumably so the human cargo stored on board could get some fresh sea air.

The channel was misty, with low clouds hanging over the water, but they broke back into sunlight as they passed Antwerp to the east, and by nightfall they had reached the North Sea. The faint glow of light from the Dutch coast at Den Hague was just visible to the crew in the distance off the starboard side, and became more so as the ship's course tracked ever closer to land. By the time they approached Amsterdam, the city lights were in full view.

At midnight they changed course, headed due east now through the Frisian Islands and the Wadden Sea, heading back on a southerly course, past the city of Harlingen and down towards Amsterdam.

At two a.m., the *Remora Bay* slowed to seven knots, and the crew retired to their cabins on orders. Only the captain was at the helm when a twenty-one-meter fishing trawler steamed into view, first on radar, and then visually as it turned on its spotlights.

A pair of large Zodiac skiffs were launched from the vessel; the captain had been instructed to pay no attention to the name of the ship, but its stern was visible in the deck lights and the name *Gerda* prominent in white on the dark blue hull.

As the captain watched, the Zodiacs came up alongside the *Remora Bay*, and on the deck men climbed out of the cargo hold, one by one, each carrying a heavy pack. A large climbing net was tossed over the side, and his human cargo began moving down it.

The captain couldn't see the Zodiacs abreast of his vessel, and this bothered him, because he had to continue making at least seven knots so as not to arouse the suspicions of anyone tracking the *Remora Bay* electronically.

The *Gerda* steamed along, just a few hundred meters to the east, at the same speed, which would have looked suspicious if the two vessels kept this up for long.

Minutes later, however, the Zodiacs pulled away; the captain could tell from a brief flash of the *Gerda*'s spotlights that both boats were laden with men and baggage, and the captain both increased his speed towards Amsterdam and sent word out through the intercom that the rest of the crew could come topside. It had been a stressful week, but it was over now, and the rest of this journey would be normal.

He looked forward to being relieved by his first mate and retiring to his quarters, where a bottle of scotch waited for just this moment.

His transport of fifteen men into Europe had earned him, if not an actual fortune, certainly a fortune to a forty-year-old cargo ship captain from Indonesia.

The two skiffs made landfall just north of Harlingen, and the fourteen Iranians and one Emirati climbed out of the boats, up a low stone dyke, and then down the other side. There was little moonlight; Hasan had planned his landing date with this in mind, so it took the men a moment to find the two work vans parked on a gravel access road through a field of sugar beets.

The sound of the Zodiacs racing back to the *Gerda* faded away slowly as the Emirati split the team of Iranians up into the vans, and soon they were all driving to the east.

They passed through the towns of Franeker, then Leeuwarden, still hours before sunrise. They were careful to keep some distance between the two nearly identical vehicles, and to keep their speed under the limit. Other than the drivers, the rest of the men held weapons at the low ready, prepared to kill any law enforcement who impeded their travel. Hasan was the only one among them who had ever been to Europe, and although some had been taught English in school, they wouldn't pass for anything other than foreigners without papers while carrying guns.

But they remained unmolested, and just as the orange hues of dawn began to fill the air, Hasan directed the lead van up the drive of a tree-shrouded farmhouse on Adelheiderstrasse, just outside Bremen, Germany. Here Hasan climbed out, scanned the area, then waved for the Iranians to follow him. The weary men climbed out, slung their packs and their weapons over their shoulders, and went inside.

Waiting for them there, wearing comfortable Western clothing, was another Emirati man they had seen at the prison in Yemen alongside the mastermind of this operation, the Sunni they knew only as Tarik.

He would be SIA, the Iranians knew, just like Hasan, and just like Tarik.

"Call me Mohammed," the man said after greeting Hasan with a warm hug. "Welcome, my brothers. You have arrived just in time for prayers."

TWENTY-FOUR

Rudolf Spangler, by any measure of justice, karma, or providence, should have been dead or in prison. He'd killed people, he'd had people killed, and he'd ripped untold numbers of lives apart with his actions. But here he was, sitting in a booth at the rear of Charlotte & Fritz, a restaurant in the five-star Regent Berlin hotel, sipping a glass of orange juice and reading a newspaper alone.

Not completely alone, actually, as his four-man security detail occupied the next table.

It was just before eight a.m., and Spangler looked ready for the day. His suit had been hand tailored in London, his eyeglasses crafted by masters in Milan and fitted to him perfectly. His mostly dark hair and his boyish face belied his sixty-six years on earth, and his urbane, almost effete mannerisms belied a heart so cold he could witness every man, woman, and child in sight die without losing his place in the article he was reading in *Die Zeit* on immigration policy.

East German by birth, he wasn't recognized by any of the twenty-five or so Berliners and foreigners seated around him outside his phalanx of unobtrusive-looking bodyguards, but he'd once been quite well-known, if only for a short time, and if only several years ago.

Spangler had begun his life in obscurity, a child of a midlevel government bureaucrat who managed collective potato farms around the village of Oehna, halfway between Leipzig and Berlin. Young Rudolf's brother and sister both went into agriculture, but he himself aspired to see the world. He went to university in the USSR, then took a job with state security, secured for him with the help of his father's middling connections.

He didn't see much of the world. He did, however, see anodyne border crossing stations all along the 850 miles of fence between East and West Germany, as well as prisons, interrogation facilities, and so many bland administration buildings he'd lost count by the age of twenty-five.

His fortunes changed a year later when he was promoted to Stasi headquarters in Berlin, where he began his meteoric ascension via a combination of sycophancy, intelligence, ruthlessness, and a strict adherence to the party doctrines of both his home nation and the masters of his home nation, the Soviet Union.

By twenty-eight he was conducting covert operations in West Germany and beyond, and by thirty-one he was second-in-command at the Main Directorate of Reconnaissance, the foreign intelligence apparatus of the agency. He carried the rank of colonel and was well regarded, respected, and always relied on by the few people in the building with higher rank than he.

There was no one in the vast Stasi HQ in Lichtenberg who would have bet against Rudolf Spangler taking over MDR, running the entire spy apparatus for East Germany, before his thirty-fifth birthday.

But then the wall came down, and it all went to hell for Rudy.

Almost overnight Spangler, young, powerful, and untouchable, became a recluse hiding out in a cheap apartment building in Dresden, waiting for the inevitable fallout when East German intelligence archives were cracked open and all the secrets of the Stasi were laid bare. And, just as he feared, it happened, and, just as he feared, he was forced to go on the run.

He made it to Poland, to Belarus, and then into Russia, but by then the Russians had their own problems, so he was carted back to Germany, where he spent four years in Landsberg Prison in Bavaria, before being released through a combination of old contacts and connections still in the reunified German government, and some luck that a few of the more incriminating files with his name on them had somehow disappeared.

Rudolf Spangler was still in his thirties when he moved to the Caribbean island of St. Maarten for a fresh start. He lived on the Dutch side and imported liquor for high-end resorts and restaurants. It was an eye-spinning fall from his former life, but he was, at least, alive, and after nearly a decade lying low, he again put the talents that made him a senior Stasi administrator to use.

As the world's problems shifted from the scourge of communism to the scourge of organized crime and Islamic terrorism, Spangler slowly renewed contacts with former colleagues, many of whom had done prison time themselves for their crimes against their countrymen. When he felt the coast to be reasonably clear, he flew to Berlin. A man returning, not triumphant, but seemingly cleansed of the fallout of his past.

There he fostered new relationships with those in corporate intelligence all over the world, and by the beginning of the new millennium he'd opened his own small shop, doing risk assessments and consulting for midsized companies all over Germany. Grocery store chains, freight hauling concerns, telecom start-ups. His client list grew and grew, and within a few years he was being paid by Daimler-Benz, Siemens, and even the governments of Moldova, Slovenia, and Hungary for his services. He recruited case officers and analysts to keep up with the demand, location experts and subject matter experts and criminal intelligence experts and lots and lots of technical support personnel.

The German government harassed him some at first; there was no hiding that he was a high-level ex-Stasi man, and though he'd served his time for his crimes against the nation, there were those in power who felt he got off too light. But nothing stuck, and eventually his firm, Shrike International Group, named after the predatory bird, grabbed a coveted contract with the German government itself. Spangler consulted with the Federal Republic of Germany's economic ministry, helping them gauge continued unrest in markets in the Middle East and Africa.

Shrike was growing and growing, and soon German intelligence operatives began leaving the BND, German foreign intelligence, as well as the BfV, German domestic intelligence, and joining the private firm.

And then the story broke.

The German magazine *Der Spiegel* found some papers, hidden by a

Stasi functionary who stole evidence from HQ in those fast-moving dying days of the DDR in hopes of using them as a bargaining chip if ever captured. The man died alone and forgotten in a run-down flat outside Cologne, and among his things, incriminating official documents revealed fresh secrets of a foul past.

And one of the documents was a glowing performance review of Rudolf Spangler.

Colonel Spangler has exceeded every measure of the agency and the party. His operations in West Berlin in May of 1988 led to the unmasking of four senior agents of the Federal Republic of Germany on DDR soil, three of whom were expatriated, where they were executed in East Berlin by the KGB, and one of whom Spangler himself killed in a shoot-out in West Berlin.

It went on from there, and though no charges were ever filed for these particular crimes from back in the Cold War, he made the news, and he lost every single client in Germany, and all but a few others around the world.

And then, for the second time in Spangler's life, he received a fresh start. He was asked to come to Dubai for a meeting, and there he was told a wealthy benefactor wanted to hire his European-based firm to keep tabs on the espionage activity of the Islamic Republic of Iran. The client, it was intimated, was the Israeli government, although there would be no official confirmation of this, ever. He was given what he assumed to be a cover story: a billionaire Israeli was worried that the world was too fixated on Sunni terror—Al Qaeda, the Palestinians, ISIS, and the like—and insufficient attention was being paid to the expansion of Shia influence around the world.

Spangler agreed to publicly resign from his own company, though in truth he would retain control of everything. For two years, the agreement went, Shrike would have only one client, and Spangler would recruit a special team to fulfill the client's demands.

The work came with an incredible payout for Shrike International, enough for Spangler to not only get back on his feet but hire the best of the best throughout the world.

And the client was as good as his word. Over the next two years Spangler built a network all over Western and Central Europe to monitor known and presumed Iranian spies and to track Iranian nationals, no matter if they worked in a pizzeria in Belgium, a kindergarten in Germany, or an auto parts manufacturer in Italy.

Over time it became clear to Spangler that his mission was more than he'd been told. Many of the names his client gave him to surveil were actually anti-Iranian regime activists, groups of expatriates who wanted to overthrow the nation of Iran. He assumed the Israeli government was looking to recruit these Iranians as spies, but he also knew this skirted the law that private intelligence organizations were sworn to follow, that they could not themselves be involved in recruiting agents for a foreign power.

Spangler hid the aims of his clients, even from his employees. He kept senior Shrike Group operations officers apart, gave each one just a tiny soda-straw view of the overall mission, and endeavored to hire more employees from intelligence agencies around the world, specifically those who he felt would work on operations that were, to put it mildly, morally ambiguous.

This worked for a while, until his client upped the ante again and ordered Shrike to run operations against Western nations, not solely Iran itself. The rationale was not without merit, as far as Spangler was concerned. The EU had recently lifted many sanctions on Iran, giving the regime in Tehran the cash it needed to buy and build weapons, and that, in effect, made the EU Israel's enemy.

But still, it was dirty work, a German spying on Germany, on Belgium, on France. But by now Spangler was in too deep to question the wishes of the one entity that had rebuilt him from the ground up for the second time in his life. He hired denied assets, kept them hidden from Shrike itself, and used them around Europe to do the dirtiest work.

He told himself he would do whatever his client wanted. Spangler was a former operative in the Stasi, responsible for death and misery to many; he had no personal qualms about being a spy against his own nation, against his own people.

He'd done it before, after all.

He only had to find employees who would do the same.

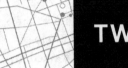

TWENTY-FIVE

One of these employees walked through the door of Charlotte & Fritz promptly at eight and began heading over in his direction.

Annika Dittenhofer was only thirty-six years old, but she had been one of Spangler's most trusted employees for well over a decade. She was in charge of Section Four at Shrike Group, where she recruited and ran spies and analysts and technical support staff on behalf of Shrike, men and women who were kept away from the company itself for operational security concerns. They were intelligence officers, analysts, and technical support personnel who had stolen secrets from their former employers, had violated noncompete clauses with their former employers, or were on the run from someone or something and needed to stay in the shadows.

Her employees all assumed they were working for the Mossad, as Annika had been raised in Israel and could speak Hebrew almost like a native. She used the name Miriam in the field, but since Spangler had first met her himself when she was a twenty-four-year-old army sergeant in Department III (counterespionage) of the Military Counterintelligence Agency, he knew her as, and still referred to her as, Annika.

Annika had recruited Ric Ennis, an American former CIA officer, a year prior. He conducted human intelligence operations, as did "Miriam," but she wasn't privy to his tasks and targeting lists. The "need-to-know" culture Rudolf Spangler had instilled in his company was extraordinary.

Spangler gave assignments to his senior employees, and they carried them out, reporting back only to Spangler, who then, in turn, reported to the customer.

Ennis had also done some recruiting of his own recently. He'd hired Zoya Zakharova into the denied division when she applied for a job under an alias on the white side of Shrike. Spangler had approved the hire, saying that within a few weeks the company would finish its contract with its only client, and at that time they would be looking to expand more widely into the corporate intelligence landscape.

Annika didn't like Ennis; he was a misogynist and a lout as far as she was concerned, but today she had other, much more important problems on her mind.

She sat with Spangler and ordered a cup of coffee, then turned to her boss. "Did you see the news from Venezuela?"

"That Clark Drummond was killed in a robbery the other night? Terrible thing. Obviously, I don't have a high opinion of the man, but I certainly didn't want *that* for him."

"A *robbery*? Like what happened to Gretchen here in Berlin?"

Spangler shrugged dramatically. "It appears so."

"And Tony Hutchens's heart attack?"

"What is it you are getting at, Annika?"

"What's going on, Rudy? What are we doing?"

"The same as ever. We are building a private intelligence empire."

"Our people are dying. You see that, don't you?"

Spangler nodded solemnly. "We have one hundred thirty employees throughout Europe, and three of them have died in the past few weeks. Statistically improbable, but not beyond the realm of possibility, especially in the case of Clark Drummond. Crime in Venezuela is quite high, I hear."

She shook her head. "We have turned into something dangerous."

"*Nein.* We did not kill anyone. That's not who we are. We are a force for good. It is difficult work, but we must do what we have to do to achieve the aims of our company, and our client." Now Spangler leaned forward, put his forearms on the table. "No matter where this road leads."

Annika looked at her boss for a long moment, then said, "Do you know something about where this road leads that you are not telling me?"

He glanced around the room; there was no one in earshot save for his four bodyguards. Spangler said, "What do you think about our mission?"

"Lately I find myself trying not to."

"I'm asking you for your opinion on what is going on."

Annika Dittenhofer considered this a moment, then spoke with carefully curated words. "I think our client had us spend two years investigating Quds Force and the Iranian Ministry of Intelligence and Security as we grew and grew as a company, thanks wholly to their unlimited resources. We built profiles of many of the Iranian intelligence actors all over Europe, and we identified a sleeper cell right here in the capital. And then, for the past few months, the client has changed our mandate, and now they have us spying on Germany, on Belgium, on other benevolent nations, trying to find out what they know about Iranian intelligence activities in the EU.

"Two of our staff expressed doubt in our mission, and another ran from us with information about our activities." She bit her lip before saying, "And all three of them are now dead.

"You asked me what I think? I think that, whatever it is that we are actually doing, we could all end up in prison. You, for the second time." She sniffed. "And *this* time, Rudy, they will not let you out."

Spangler gave her nothing. No denial of her assumptions, no confirmation. "I follow orders. I followed governmental orders when I was employed by state security, and now I follow the orders of my client. It is who I am. We have our assignments, and we are carrying them out. Our benefactor is pleased overall with the work we are doing. Everything is going—"

"What *is* the work we are doing, exactly?" she interjected. "A year ago I thought I was outing Iranian spies for the good of the free world. And now, in just the last month, I've spied on an anti-regime activist, pretty much the opposite of an Iranian military intelligence terrorist. I've spied on my home nation of Germany, I've spied on the French and on the Americans."

She took another sip and put the cup back on the saucer in front of her. "I have only one question, Rudy. When did *we* become the bad guys?"

Spangler chuckled. "I've known you ten years. We've been through a lot together. This is an odd time for you to grow a conscience."

"No one ever died before." She sighed. "And I never felt you were keeping things from me. Now I know you are." She looked at him a long moment, then said, "What is Ennis doing?"

"You know I don't talk about other officers' operations."

"I don't trust him," she said flatly.

Spangler smiled, then finished the last of his orange juice. "Well then, it's a good thing you aren't working with him, isn't it? He's doing what I am telling him to do. Just like you." He paused, put a gentle hand on her forearm. "Look, we are survivors, you and I. *Ja,* our mission is dirty, so true. But so what? When we fulfill our contract to the client, then we will have helped create a marginalized Iran in the EU." He put his glass on the table. "Our client knows what he is doing."

She sipped her coffee in silence.

Spangler said, "Now. Let's discuss recent events. Potential comebacks on Shrike Group after Drummond went to the Venezuelans."

Annika waved a hand in the air. "Shrike is in the clear."

Rudolf smiled, motioned to the waiter for a refill on Annika's coffee and another OJ for himself. "You'll have to indulge me a little. How do you know that? How do you know if Drummond told Venezuelan authorities about his actions here?"

"It wouldn't have served his interests to do so, but even if he told them every single thing about his time in Berlin, what could he say? He thought he was working for the Mossad. He had no connection to Shrike Group whatsoever."

Spangler was, if not satisfied, at least somewhat placated. But then he said, "What about the Russian woman who was brought in by Ric? She knows she's with Shrike."

"She will keep her mouth shut and do whatever we want. And she won't talk because she's a hunted woman, Rudolf. She needs us more than we need her, and we do absolutely need someone like her assisting with ops, especially when we attract new clients." When Spangler seemed unconvinced, she added, "We have handed her a lifeline; she won't betray us. If she does, she knows we only have to pick up the phone and the Russians will come for her." With a shrug she said, "She's as safe a bet as they come."

The next round came, but neither reached for their beverage. Annika said, "Drink up, Rudy. I'll pass. I have two techs in the field I have to supervise. Both of them are tracking MeK-affiliated students here in town." Sarcastically, she said, "We're tailing anti-regime Iranian college students so that we can help end the Iranian regime?" Then her sarcastic tone faded away. "What the fuck are we even doing?"

Spangler stood and motioned for the check. "Our jobs. That is all. Be safe, Annika."

She softened a little, then kissed him on the cheek, the actions of a daughter towards an older man she considered a father figure. And then she turned for the door.

Rudy Spangler's eyes tracked his star intelligence officer as she departed through the restaurant, or more accurately, his eyes skimmed back and forth around her, checking to make sure she hadn't picked up a tail while they were sitting here talking. It came from over a generation in the intelligence game, and Spangler was as good at it as he'd ever been, as far as he was concerned.

Annika left the Regent without generating any obvious interest, so Spangler turned away, pulled his phone from his pocket, and dialed a preset number. He ran a fingertip around the lip of his juice glass while he waited for the international connection.

He didn't have to wait long at all for an answer on the other end. "Hello, Rudy, my friend. How are you?"

"I'm concerned, Tarik. Very concerned. The quickening of events has me, and more importantly, my staff, troubled." He was normally agreeable with his benefactor, but the recent spate of killings had him spooked to the point where he wasn't concerned with demonstrating an annoyed tone.

"I understand. Of course, I understand." He paused, then said, "We should talk."

"Yes, let's," Spangler said.

Tarik surprised him with his next comment, though. "How about I meet with you the day after tomorrow? Lunch?"

The German cocked his head, the phone held tight against his ear. Tarik had never come to Berlin to speak with him. "Lunch? In Berlin?"

"I'm on my way to Qatar at the moment, but I'll be in Berlin by the end of the day tomorrow."

"You had some other business to attend to here?"

"No. Just you."

Spangler was pleased. "I think that would be very useful, Tarik. Thank you."

"Of course. As you said, our contract is near completion, and as you and your staff have detected, there is a quickening of events. I want to ease your concerns."

Spangler was happy that he was going to get some face time with his benefactor. They had only met twice before, both times in Dubai. He said, "Very well, I'll look forward to having my worries allayed."

"I'll contact you when I land," Tarik said, and then the line went dead.

Rudolf Spangler was no fool; he had worked out the fact that his benefactor was from the United Arab Emirates and not Israel. He was likely a Muslim, a Sunni, and no doubt the man had some relationship with the Signals Intelligence Agency, UAE's American-supported spy shop. The UAE would be just one of many Sunni countries terrified of Shia expansion around the world, and it was one of only a few nations with the assets to try to do something about it.

He could have made some inquiries, but he knew better than to look a gift horse in the mouth. If Tarik wanted to play his cards close to his vest, that was fine with Spangler, as long as the wire transfers came in on time.

The sixty-six-year-old German swigged the last of his orange juice and rushed for the door of Charlotte & Fritz, his four Israeli security men racing to get into position around him.

TWENTY-SIX

The man who had adopted the code name Tarik landed at Hamad International Airport in Doha, Qatar, just west of his own homeland of the UAE, on an Airbus Citation executive jet owned by his father. He and his four personal security men, all men with significant combat experience, easily passed through customs on a diplomatic passport, and then they were met by a driver outside the VIP arrivals lounge.

The doors to the silver Bentley were open, and the five men climbed in, along with the driver.

The Bentley rolled down B Ring Road, its chrome radiating the noonday Doha sun. The temperature was already one hundred six degrees, and not a single cloud provided any coverage over the city.

Sultan al-Habsi rode in the backseat, his mind shifting between his operation in Berlin and the events that would transpire here in the next hour. If he was honest with himself, he would have to admit that, with all the dangers and risk of failure and the ticking clocks of Berlin, he was more frightened about Doha right now.

His trepidation only increased when the Bentley made a right off B Ring, and more so when it made another right onto Al Khudri Street. And by the time the sleek silver vehicle pulled into the parking garage of the Apollo Cancer Center, Doha, al-Habsi could feel his heart pound while rivulets of perspiration ran down his temples past his ears.

He was led into a private VIP hospital entrance by doctors who met the Bentley in the garage, and then he was taken, surrounded by the doctors and his assemblage of bodyguards, directly to the sixth floor, where he was express-laned past two dozen other people waiting to see patients in the ICU.

Outside a door he was handed a mask and given brief but detailed instructions, going over what was about to happen. He listened distractedly, took slow and measured breaths to control his anxiety, and then closed his eyes to steady his brain an instant.

He opened them, nodded resolutely to the doctors, and a door slid open. The small entourage walked down a hall, past examination rooms, and then finally to the door of the cancer ward's ICU.

Al-Habsi moved more slowly with each step; he had to will himself into the room indicated by the doctor with the mask over his face.

Inside, an old man lay on a hospital bed, a catheter reservoir hanging from the side. There was an oxygen tube in his nose, an IV PICC line in his arm, and various medicines and other chemicals dripping into him. His eyes were open and alert; he looked towards Sultan, but no expression could be discerned from the white-bearded man's face.

Sultan stepped in closer, all the doctors and bodyguards waited outside, and the door was pulled shut behind him.

The younger man spoke first. *"Waladi." My father.*

The old man regarded him for a time, no real excitement or emotion to speak of, and then he said, "My son."

"How are they treating you?"

Sultan's father coughed, and heavy congestion was evident in his chest. When he recovered, he just shrugged a little and said, "They're Qataris," as if that said it all.

The son came closer still, marveling that all the color had left his father's face, and his previously jaundiced eyes were now even more yellow. He said, "This hospital, these doctors, they are the best in the region. We could have gone to the U.S. and perhaps your care would have been even—"

"I'll happily die in Qatar before I go to the Americans."

Sultan held in a sigh; he never showed frustration with his father. He pivoted and said, "No one is going to die anytime soon."

The father looked away. "I thought you were an intelligence officer. Surely you can pick up some intel from everything you see around you."

"Well, I spoke with the doctors, and the chemotherapy is—"

"Enough!" The old man, even racked with cancer and on his deathbed, remained psychologically stronger willed than his younger, robust son, and both men knew it.

Sheikh Rashid al-Habsi was the crown prince of all the United Arab Emirates and the ruler of the Emirate of Dubai. He'd not made it to where he was by closing his eyes to reality. And he'd not raised a son and placed him, covertly, high in the nation's intelligence services, only to have him come see him on his deathbed and spew worthless lies about his condition.

Before Sultan could speak, Sheikh Rashid said, "I wanted one thing from you when you were a child. I wanted you to become a religious scholar." He licked his dry lips. "And you failed me."

Sultan nodded with his eyes lowered. He'd heard this before. He said, "But I felt—"

His father interrupted him. "And then, when you were grown, I wanted one thing from you again. I made you a deputy of my nation's intelligence apparatus with one mission, one mission only." The man's hazy eyes cleared a little. "To protect our people."

The father sighed now. "And you have failed me again."

"No, I have not. I'm on the cusp of success. I just need—"

"What was it I told you I wanted to see in my lifetime?"

"You wanted to see the overthrow of the mullahs in Iran."

Rashid nodded; it looked like it took significant strength to do so. "A lofty wish, I know, but I put my own trusted son in a position where he could make that happen. You were the one who went to America, you were the one the CIA and the president trusted, you were the one given the training, the inside contacts, the resources, the funds."

"*Sahih.*" *True,* allowed Sultan.

"And what did you do with everything bestowed on you, with one mission to accomplish? You fought Iranian proxies in Yemen, along with your two brothers. Yemen! Houthi rebel savages doing the bidding of Tehran, but so far removed from Tehran that you could slay every single one of them and not damage the mullahs in the least."

Sultan was about to respond to this when his father said, "And when your two brave brothers came home in bags, you shifted your focus to fucking *European sanctions*. *You*, Sultan, are a fool. I had three sons. Two are dead, martyred, and one is a disappointment and a failure."

Sultan hated his father. Sultan loved his father.

He tried to get through to him. "What I am doing has nothing to do with sanctions."

Sheikh Rashid sniffed. "You don't think I have my own people still? You don't think I can't simply lift this phone by the bed and know exactly what you are doing? All those people at SIA who swear allegiance to you only do so because they have sworn allegiance to me. Are you too thick to see that?"

"No. But I have hidden my aims from everyone in SIA. I am working with my partners in Europe to achieve my objective, but even they do not grasp what is in store."

"Your partners in Europe?"

"Nem." Yes.

The milky eyes of the man lying in bed narrowed a bit. For the first moment since Sultan al-Habsi's arrival, he felt like his father was actually listening to him.

Then the old man turned his head away again. "Your plan, no matter how good you say it is, is irrelevant to me, as I will not live to see it."

"You will, Father. I promise you will. You can see all my . . . *our* hard work come to fruition."

"When?"

Sultan smiled now. "Tomorrow night, it begins, I swear it."

Sheikh Rashid al-Habsi, prime minister of the UAE, gave off no obvious emotion, but Sultan had become an expert at reading his father's subtle signs.

There was hope in him. Mistrust of his son's abilities, but hope that he was wrong, and Sultan left his meeting ebullient.

Minutes later al-Habsi passed his father's guards and minders, passed the doctors, without speaking to them. There was an intense spring in his step, and even his own personal protection detail had to struggle to keep up with him.

As they all stepped into the elevator, he said one word to his entourage, though that one word was packed with purpose, determination, and satisfaction.

"Berlin."

TWENTY-SEVEN

Keith Hulett, call sign Hades, had only been in Europe for two days, but he was already getting the feeling he was going to very much enjoy living the life of an international hit man.

He'd never considered himself as such when working in the private military field. Even when he and his men went out to eliminate a bad actor behind the lines, he saw it as war, not assassination.

But right now he took stock of his situation. He walked through Alexanderplatz, the center of the former East Berlin, and the mild midmorning sun beamed against his face, a covert earpiece rested in his ear, and comfortable Western clothes adorned his body. An hour and a half earlier he'd eaten a good breakfast at a café near his safe house in Reuterkiez, just north of the old Tempelhof Airport, and then he'd climbed into a rented Mercedes with three of his teammates and driven to his target's home, a small flat next to Humboldt University's school of business and economics.

The target was a twenty-four-year-old student at Humboldt named Kamran Iravani. Tarik had given Hades the name, along with an address and a photo, and he'd told him his target was an Iranian Quds Force sleeper operative.

So Hulett and his second-in-command, Atlas, now sat at an outdoor café and had coffee and strudel while waiting for this Iranian sleeper agent to leave for school.

And this, like everything else they'd done this morning, they'd also done yesterday. Yesterday had been recon; today would be "wait and see." They didn't have to act immediately, but they were most definitely looking for an opportunity.

The past two mornings hadn't exactly been typical for Hulett, an American who had been fighting in the Middle East, virtually nonstop, for many years. It seemed like no matter where he was in the sandbox, Hulett rose from a tiny bunk each morning, already stinking from the heat, ate breakfast out of a plastic bag, pressure-washed blood and grime off his equipment from the night before, and faced the prospect of death anew.

Berlin couldn't have been more different. There was abundant food, abundant showers, an overabundance of beautiful women, and fucking air conditioning.

Hulett told himself he could get used to this, and he hoped like hell Tarik had plenty of targets for him, so he could milk this gig for a while.

While Hades had jumped on board the hit man express quickly and with little reflection, his men had needed some talking into it. Of course, everyone was worried about getting picked up by the local police here in Berlin. This wasn't like Yemen, where they would, at least, have a chance to bust out of any Houthi-run holding facility were they to be captured by the enemy. Arrest here, whether for murder, attempted murder, or even carrying a pistol, would mean incarceration for a very long time.

But the money offered by Tarik helped mitigate the men's fears, and ultimately, Hades had all his boys on board on this op before they touched down at Tegel.

Their target had left his building that morning at eleven a.m., same as yesterday, then headed in the direction of his university. The young man wore knockoff Beats by Dr. Dre headphones, and he did not check behind him at all. He just plowed ahead, as if he were going to class. The two Americans had already paid their check at the café, so they simply rose to their feet and followed along behind him, just as they'd done the day before. Their eyes were hidden behind shades so they could lock them on the back of the young man with short black hair, a long beard with no mustache, as he walked just fifty feet ahead of them.

Tarik had told Hades it was important that Kamran Iravani was taken off the table in a manner that didn't draw too much attention to the act. No shoot-outs in the street. No sniper shots from across a park and, Tarik had been quite clear, no fucking *bombs*.

Make it look like an accident, or natural causes, Tarik had suggested to Hades.

Whatever, Hades had told himself at the time. He didn't have a clue how to kill someone to make it look like they'd died of natural causes. No, the best thing he could pull off, maybe, would be something that looked like an accident.

They'd followed him into his school the day before, where he'd spent several hours, before leaving to go to a mosque, and then home. He'd stayed in all night, and Hades had seen no opportunity to go after him inside his residence, considering the cameras placed everywhere around the school.

His plan today was to do another follow, to maybe come up with some sort of idea of how to take him without being seen, and then to kill him by kidnapping and throwing him off a building, in the hopes it would look like suicide.

Hades and his team weren't real assassins or surveillance experts. No, they were ex–special operations soldiers and mercenaries. They'd had some tradecraft training, and they'd followed targets in the Middle East a few times, when the intel provided to them had not been actionable without further reconnoitering. But still, he and his men were not a team of spooks. This was going to be new to them, tough for them, but for what Tarik was paying, Keith Hulett told himself he'd figure out how to make this work.

This morning their target revealed himself to be a creature of habit. He'd left his flat at the same time and walked the same route, more or less. Hulett had sent two men ahead to walk the path he'd taken yesterday, looking for cameras and dead areas where cameras couldn't reach. A further pair were in a chase car, moving slowly through traffic a few blocks to the south.

And the last two men on the team were also on foot, also looking for cameras, but on nearby streets, in case Hades and Atlas had to make a quick getaway. These men had a car of their own, parked in a garage near the old, East German, spire-like TV tower.

Fifty feet in front of Hades and Atlas, their target passed a tram stop on Alexanderplatz, and a long yellow streetcar heading in the opposite direction pulled up to a stop next to him. He did not board, he only kept walking, and soon enough the streetcar rumbled off.

Atlas leaned a little closer to Hades and said, "We could knock his ass in front of one of those?"

"Maybe," Hades replied softly. They closed on him, then held back to about twenty feet.

His route took him right alongside the tramway, and another big yellow streetcar approached in the distance. Thor said, "Say the word, boss. I'll do it."

But Hades replied softly. "No way to do this here without cameras catching it."

"Probably right about that. Do we abort?"

"Let's just keep following him, see what we see."

They continued on another ten minutes, crossing a bridge over the Spree River, remaining behind their quarry while he talked on his phone, listened to his headphones, and seemed to be in no special hurry.

Soon they began trailing their man through the urban maze of Humboldt University, down Kronenstrasse. There wasn't much foot traffic here, but a lot of cars and trucks and buses rumbled by at speed.

A large double-decker bus appeared ahead, moving towards them, and both Atlas and Hades picked up the pace to close on Iravani.

As they moved forward, Hades spoke softly for his ear mic. "Hades for Thor, how copy?"

"Five by five."

Thor was on the advance team looking for cameras; he should have been just a block or two ahead. "You have five seconds to tell me if I'm clear to execute on the corner of Kronen and Charlotten."

"South side has a cam at the Avis, but it doesn't look like it's hitting the street. North side has multiple angles of the sidewalk covered. Middle of the street is clear."

They were on the north side; Hades muttered "shit," but then, just twenty feet in front of him, Iravani turned to his left, moved between a pair of parked cars, and then stopped to let the bus pass before continuing across the street.

Hades saw a Starbucks a half block ahead on the other side, and wondered if the young Iranian sleeper agent had decided to get a cup of coffee before class.

Atlas and Hades picked up the pace and moved between the parked cars behind their target.

Thor came over both men's headsets. "That bus will cover the Avis camera, and the cams on the north side of the street can't see you off the sidewalk."

Hades replied. "Roger."

Atlas said, "I've got this, boss."

"He's yours."

When the big red double-decker bus was less than ten feet away, Atlas shouldered hard into the smaller man, sending him stumbling forward, out into the street.

The bus slammed into him at thirty-five kilometers an hour, killing Kamran Iravani instantly and then running over his body. It slammed to a halt, tires screeching and smoke billowing from them.

Both Atlas and Hades turned away, walked back onto the sidewalk on the northern side of Kronenstrasse, then headed east.

Forty-five seconds later they were picked up by Mercury and Mars, heading south, back in the direction of their safe house. Their chase car picked up the other men and then stayed back behind Hades's vehicle to make sure no one was following them.

By one p.m. the eight men sat in the tiny walled-in backyard of their safe house on Albertstrasse, drinking Berliner Kindl pilsners and complimenting one another on a job well done. Hades had already called it in to Tarik, and much to his pleasure, Tarik told him he'd have a new target for him shortly.

The men were proud of themselves. They'd killed a piece-of-shit terrorist on the streets of Europe, a dream mission for them all, and they couldn't fucking wait to do it again.

TWENTY-EIGHT

Court Gentry found himself walking down narrow, tree-lined Archivstrasse at one p.m., one block away from the Iranian intelligence agent's flat and, he hoped, the woman who was here in town spying on him. He had no idea if Zoya herself would be at this location, or if she had an array of remote cameras and mics, or even a team of surveillance personnel here instead. But this address was all he had to go on at present, and he told himself even if he couldn't get eyes on his target, then he could at least get a proper lay of the land here, to identify the normal patterns of life in the Dahlem-Dorf neighborhood, and thus be better prepared to identify risks and abnormalities on subsequent surveillance sessions.

This kind of tradecraft was not an especially exciting way of life. For every moment of action or intrigue there were hours, days, years, of sitting, waiting, looking, watching other people live lives that seemed altogether more enjoyable.

Court found himself here, sick and down, his low mood only overcome by his intense discipline and his will to help out Zoya, even if he wasn't allowed to communicate with her.

He told himself he'd get meds from Dr. Kaya tonight, but for now he just had to tough it out for ten more hours.

He turned on Königin-Luise Strasse, crossed to the far side of the road from Javad Sasani's apartment, and walked on, his hands in his pockets, his small gym duffel hanging off his shoulder and his head hunched down, eyes on the sidewalk ten feet in front of him. There wasn't a lot of pedestrian traffic at the moment, but Court had made his living slipping through scenes around the world without anyone ever seeing him, and he was more than confident he could do that now.

He was not without worry, however. He had no concerns Sasani would detect his presence. It was a workday, and he doubted the man would even be home, but even if he were, Court didn't place too much respect on an embassy-based case officer. No, Court had learned over the years that the real spooks to respect when it came to countersurveillance were the NOCs. Intelligence officers working under non-official cover. NOCs knew they were operating without a net, and their personal security usually reflected this in the form of high tradecraft skills and an almost paranoid demeanor that came from years existing under the assumption that any mistake, no matter how small and inconsequential it seemed, could lead to capture, years and years of incarceration, or even death.

Sasani was no NOC; according to Brewer he was a straight-up official cover employee of the Iranian embassy, so Court doubted he'd have his senses tuned to a high degree when it came to threats to his person.

Court was similarly unconcerned with the two-man team Brewer had mentioned Zoya had working under her. These would be audio techs, entry specialists, black-bag guys, bug planters, and bug monitors. They would have received plenty of training about remaining undetected while they worked, perhaps even a little countersurveillance training, as well, but Court suspected that these guys, like most doing that line of intelligence work, saw themselves as offense, and spent considerably less of their focus on defense. If Shrike Group was, indeed, privately run, then Court suspected Zoya's team would be even less likely to be on the lookout for threats.

They would not, Court felt sure, scrutinize everyone in their area as a potential threat.

The street was lined with parked cars, each pulled up to the curb at an angle, and he scanned the makes and models, looking for obvious covert vehicles.

He'd gone a full block before he noticed a blue panel truck with ladders on the sides. There were no markings as to what sort of service the company that owned the vehicle offered, but it was clearly either a painter's truck or a vehicle designed to look like a painter's truck. He flashed a quick and covert second glance at it as he passed. It rode low on its suspension, indicating there was some weight inside, and he deemed this location to be perfect, a block away from the target, just out of the field of view from the windows of Sasani's first-floor apartment, and tucked in tight between other parked cars.

If he had been running a surveillance van, he'd park it right here.

A bakery sat just ahead, twenty yards down from the van, so he stepped inside for a coffee and a secure vantage point.

The Kornfeld Dahlem Café had both indoor and outdoor seating, but Court chose a small two-top inside, against the window. The sun against the window would obstruct anyone's view inside, but he could see the front of the panel truck from here. He couldn't see inside due to reflection on the glass, but nevertheless, he had an objective so he got down to work.

As he sat with his steaming coffee in front of him, he pulled a small wireless camera no larger than a pair of sugar cubes out of his duffel and flipped it on. He placed it in a tiny flower arrangement on the table by the window, facing in the direction of the painter's truck. He then pulled out his phone, opened a hidden app, and on his screen he saw a closeup view of the white bloom on a Gerber daisy. He reached down to the little vase in front of him, careful to remain nonchalant, and he adjusted the angle of the tiny camera until he had an unobstructed view of his target.

On his app he zoomed; the entire screen was filled by the front grille of the vehicle twenty-five yards away, and he tapped the record button on the phone.

Then Court put the phone down and enjoyed a leisurely coffee while appearing to idly look at his phone.

Twenty minutes later he was back on the street. It had only taken him a few minutes to see what he needed to see. By focusing on the front grille, rendered just feet away with the camera's zoom feature, he had recognized obvious movement. It wasn't much, but at this level of detail it was unmistakable.

It had been abundantly clear to Court that there were occupants sitting in the van, and occasionally moving around.

This was the Shrike Group vehicle. He caught himself wondering if

Zoya was inside, or if it was just members of her team. He had a small magnetic GPS tracker that, in normal circumstances, he would put on the van, but he knew it was too risky to chance getting closer to the vehicle if Zoya was inside.

He had to conduct his surveillance from standoff distance—the old-fashioned way. He would rent a motorcycle and try to be back in time to follow the van when it left. If he missed it, it was no great loss. Brewer had told him Zoya was staying at the Adlon Kempinski. He could find her there, eventually, but he knew that would entail buying some halfway decent clothing so he could blend in around the five-star property.

The backpack of clothes Court had brought with him to Europe consisted of two different colors of jeans, four T-shirts, a long-sleeve pullover, a hoodie, and some toiletries. He'd fit in in the more urban or industrial areas, a construction worker leaving his shift, a cargo delivery driver heading back to his car from his truck, or he could even pull off a college student with his relatively long hair and a beard that made his age all but indeterminate.

But he had nothing with him that would help him blend in at the nicest hotel in the German capital.

As he walked to the streetcar stop to catch a train to the motorcycle rental shop, he pictured Zoya walking around the Adlon, looking amazing, and it made him long for her even more.

He couldn't help it. This wasn't just about keeping a colleague safe while she completed her mission. This was about love, and it pissed him off every single time he allowed himself to admit it.

He kept walking, doing his best to push his thoughts of Zoya away so that he could stay on the mission, the mission with Zoya at its center.

As he walked, he kept his eyes out for security cameras of every type. He had known from the beginning that there was no way to keep himself out of the lens of every camera in Berlin. But he did his best, and avoided the vast majority of them.

But he never saw the traffic camera on Archivstrasse. His image was recorded, and it was automatically fed through the PowerSlave database built by Clark Drummond, which now resided on a computer at Shrike International Group.

A computer analyst for Shrike clicked on the ping and saw that a former CIA Special Activities Division operative named Courtland Gentry was walking a few blocks from an active Shrike surveillance operation.

There was not much data about Gentry, but the analyst had gotten an e-mail from Rudy Spangler the day before instructing him to pass all PowerSlave positive sightings directly up to him, because the client had requested the information.

With a few clicks of the keyboard, the young woman sent on the positive sighting to the owner of the company, and then she went back to work without thinking of it again.

Court was made in Berlin, and he had no idea.

TWENTY-NINE

Zoya yawned and did a couple of neck rolls in the rear of the surveillance vehicle. She'd gotten nowhere with Sasani today; he was home from work sick, and from the audio, he had been either in bed or on the toilet all morning. She'd not had much luck with her two assistants, either. Both Moises and Yanis seemed a little more tight-lipped today than the previous times they'd been together, at least as far as anything to do with Shrike.

She was about to start a new probing operation to get the boys to talk when she heard her phone chirping in her purse. She pulled it and looked at the incoming number. It was Ennis, her supervisor.

She answered with a light, "Hi, Ric."

But the normally confident man's reply seemed surprisingly clipped and serious to her. "Anything going on over there?"

"No, except the target didn't go into work today."

"Why not?"

"He's sick. We can hear a lot of coughing and nose blowing. Sounds like he's got diarrhea, too. Mercifully, Yanis didn't put an omnidirectional mic in the bathroom."

The two younger men laughed at this.

"Has he been on the phone? On his laptop?"

Zoya could detect an anxiety in Ennis's voice that confused her.

She said, "He . . . he called in sick to work, early. That's it. Why the sudden interest in this guy?"

"Look," Ennis said. "We need to . . . we need to abort. Break down surveillance right now. Leave all devices in place but shut them down. Get yourself, and your people, out of there."

"What's going on?"

He took a few labored breaths. There was more than anxiety on the part of Ennis, Zoya recognized. This was fear. "Look, someone we have been monitoring in the past, another officer's target. He . . ."

"He *what*?"

"He died. Less than an hour ago."

"Here? In Berlin?"

"Yes. Hit by a bus. Police have *not* ruled out foul play."

"Who was he?"

"He . . . that's not important. He was a foreign national, I can say that. We'd been asked to investigate him for our client. We had completed our investigation and no Shrike personnel were at the scene of his death, thank God. That's about all I know, but I *don't* yet know if there are going to be any comebacks on any of our operations, so it's best we just give it a couple of days."

Ennis's voice displayed none of the bluster or assertiveness she'd known him to possess. He sounded like a terrified kid, and this told Zoya there was more to this story than she was hearing.

"The deceased. He was Iranian, I take it?"

"Yes."

"An IO? Another VAJA man from the embassy?"

"No. I am not prepared to say who he was affiliated with, but we are pulling all our local operatives out of the field until we see how local authorities react. I've got a couple more calls to make, Stephanie, so I have to go." He switched gears suddenly. "How about we talk more about this over dinner? The Lorenz in the Adlon? It's very nice."

And it was also in her hotel. Ennis knew this, and Zoya took this to mean he would be looking for an invitation upstairs after the meal. He wouldn't get it, but he would get dinner with her. It was her job to learn whatever she could, and this sounded like a perfect opportunity to do so.

"That will be fine," she said, playing it cool.

He was still distracted, still stressed. "Meet you there at eight thirty."

Zoya looked at her two techs, who both stared back at her. "Pull the plug," she said, then turned her attention once again to Ennis's call. "We are shutting down right now. I'll await further instructions."

"See you tonight."

Zoya hung up the phone, started to reach over to flip off the master control switch to the microphones in the house. She did this just as Yanis began taking his headphones off.

Moises was closest to the front of the van, so he started to move towards the driver's seat.

Zoya scooted her little stool to the computer terminal and reached to flip the switch that operated the microphone in Sasani's mobile phone, but just as she did this, Yanis put his headphones back over his ears, fired out a hand, and grabbed her by the wrist. "Call coming in. Do we shut down, or do we listen to it?"

She said, "We listen, of course." She pulled her own headphones on now, as well. Zoya didn't speak a word of Farsi, but she wanted to hear her target's voice nonetheless.

Moises hurried back to his computer to work on squelching any background noise.

Sasani answered after several rings. Zoya could hear both fatigue and congestion in his voice. He sounded like the last thing he wanted to do right now was talk on the phone, so she wondered if the caller might be someone important.

The caller's voice spoke up, his cadence fast and intense. Zoya turned to Yanis, who began a running translation of both sides of the conversation.

"Where are you?"

"I'm at home. I called out sick four hours ago."

"Did you hear the news?"

"I haven't heard anything, brother. I'm in bed."

The rapid-fire voice coming from the apartment shot out a string of vowels and consonants that impressed even polyglot Zoya Zakharova. Yanis waited for him to finish before translating. "That student with MeK, the one working for German intelligence at the mosque. You know the one?"

"Yeah. Iravani. What about him?"

"Fucking murdered, brother. Just this morning. Witnesses told the *polizei* that two big white guys knocked him in front of a bus. Definitely an assassination."

Sasani's fatigue seemed to dissipate quickly. "We've monitored him, but cyber only. We never put men on him. We picked up no signs of anyone else targeting him. Listen, Ali, we definitely didn't have *anything* to do with it."

"It doesn't matter if we did or not. If the *polizei* find out he's MeK, then they are going to point the finger at us. We need to be careful, Javad."

There was more back-and-forth to the conversation; Yanis relayed it all to the case officer he knew as Stephanie Arthur, but she was barely listening now. Instead she thought about what this all meant. If Shrike Group had been gaining intelligence on a member of the MeK, the Mujahedin-e Khalq, that meant that along with the Iranian government spy she had been surveilling, and the Iranian military operatives that Moises and Yanis had mentioned were also being monitored, it now appeared Shrike was surveilling *anti*-regime operatives.

The MeK were one of just a few groups of Iranians actively trying to overthrow the government in Tehran. They weren't one one-thousandth as strong as they needed to be to do so, but they were definitely enemies of the ayatollah and mullahs who ran the nation presently.

And one of these anti-regime people, one who had been under surveillance by Shrike Group, had just been murdered on the streets of Berlin.

Finally, Zoya said to herself. *This is getting interesting.*

As soon as Javad Sasani hung up the phone, sounding to Zoya almost exactly as worried as Ric Ennis had been about this apparent assassination of someone both VAJA and Shrike had been monitoring, she ordered Yanis to power down the equipment and Moises to drive them out of the area. She didn't know if German internal security were aware that Javad Sasani was, indeed, an Iranian intel officer, but if they had been aware, then it wouldn't be a great stretch of the imagination to assume the BfV might come here to talk to him.

And she didn't want to be anywhere around when that happened.

THIRTY

Rudolf Spangler sat in his office in the unassuming Potsdam headquarters of Shrike International, drinking coffee and scrolling up and down his offshore accounts on his computer. His organization was flush with money for operational expenses, flush with profits even after paying all their people, both on the white side and on the black, and for a brief moment, the man was without worry.

Worry came seconds later, however, with the ringing of the phone.

"Spangler," he said.

"Rudy, it's Miriam," she said in English, using her code name as a matter of personal security. "Kamran Iravani was murdered this morning at Humboldt."

Spangler's eyes narrowed as he took this in. "Iravani. He was a target of yours, correct?"

Miriam said, "Up until three weeks ago. Now he's dead."

Spangler said, "Well . . . it doesn't involve us."

But Annika Dittenhofer wasn't listening. "Iravani was MeK. And he was spying for the Germans against Iran here in the city."

"If he was actively spying against Tehran, obviously Iranian assassins killed him."

"*Nein*, Rudy. We've seen no action at all from the Quds Force personnel we're monitoring, no chatter from the Iranian spooks in town we know of. Someone else killed this kid. Someone who is protecting the Iranian regime for some reason."

Spangler breathed heavily into the phone as her information began to weigh on him.

"Say something, Rudy!" Annika shouted.

"I . . . We didn't do it! That's all I know."

"But our client? Did *he* do it? We obtained the intel on Kamran Iravani, we sent it off to our mystery client, and now the kid is dead." Spangler did not respond to this, so Annika said, "Rudy, did you tell our client about Drummond, about Hutchens, and about Brust, too?"

Again, Spangler said nothing, but this told Annika everything.

"Well, then." Her voice was lower and graver than Spangler had ever heard it. "Now we know. Don't we?"

Spangler said, "I will bring up your concerns when I speak with the client."

Annika replied, "*Concerns?* Do I sound concerned to you, or do I sound fucking horrified?"

"Very much the latter."

"Iravani was an informant for the BfV. German intelligence is going to look very hard into what happened to him. If our client was involved, Rudy, then we are going to be in the bull's-eye."

"I don't know if the client was involved or not. I'll speak with him. What else can I do?"

Annika paused before saying, "Be careful, Rudy. You know what happens to people who ask too many questions these days."

"That's ridiculous. I run Shrike Group. I am not afraid of—"

"Do you, Rudy? Do you run Shrike Group? Or is our one client, the man keeping us afloat, is *he* actually the one in charge?"

Annika Dittenhofer ended the call, and Spangler put down the phone and rubbed the back of his thick neck.

Keith Hulett and his team were enjoying their afternoon, celebrating their successful antiterror operation.

Thor said, "That shit was almost too easy. We walked out of there totally invisible. Nobody looked at us twice."

Hulett remembered Tarik telling him that as white Westerners, he and his team would be exceptionally suited to this type of work. He wondered if the previous team of hit men Tarik had mentioned had come to some misfortune, either from the Quds Force members they were targeting or from the local police.

Either way, he endeavored to make certain he and his men didn't run into any similar trouble. They'd take the time to execute all of their hits just as cleanly and quietly as they had this morning.

Hulett's phone sat on the coffee table around which he and his men sat. It began ringing, so he snatched it up and looked at the number. Instantly he was on his feet, heading down a back hallway to his bunk for some privacy.

"Go for Hades," he said, because he knew who was calling.

"Hades, this is Omar." Omar was one of Tarik's top lieutenants.

"Yes, sir. The operation was successful. Scratch off one bad guy." Hulett was still basking in the afterglow of his success, as he assumed the call from the UAE was simply to praise him and his men.

But Omar wasn't praising anyone. He held tension in his voice. "I don't care about that. We need you back out. There is a man who arrived in Berlin who is threatening our operation."

Cool, Hulett thought. *More work.* "Who is he?"

"We think he is the man you encountered in Caracas the other night. I'm texting you his picture."

And now the American mercenary stood straighter, began walking back up the hall to his men in the great room.

"Roger that. *Where* is he?"

"He was picked up on a camera near an operation our European partners are running, just thirty minutes ago. And then, two minutes ago, he was seen again, renting a motorcycle. He then went back in the direction of the operation."

"Copy all. Tell me where the op is, and give me the description of the man and his bike."

Omar directed him to Sasani's neighborhood, Dahlem-Dorf, and gave the make and model of the bike. He then sent a secure text with two pictures of a man in his thirties with shoulder-length hair and a short beard wearing a dark T-shirt and jeans.

"This fucker? *This* nothing joker is the one who killed my man the other night?"

"Affirmative. We have information that this man is operating alone, but he has extraordinary skill. Use caution."

"Yeah, well, I've got some skill myself, and I'm *not* operating alone. I'll take care of this little bitch."

As soon as he hung up his phone, he rushed back into the living room of the safe house. "Everybody saddle up! We're about to go get us some payback for Ronnie!"

The thirty-nine-year-old blonde checked into the Adlon Kempinski just after three p.m. A corner suite on the fourth floor had been reserved for Xristina Dolyna by her company, a Danish housewares manufacturer, and her Ukrainian passport was in order, so she was quickly handed room keys and escorted to the elevator, while her Gucci bags were loaded onto a luggage cart.

She entered her suite and opened the double windows in the living room. The view of the Brandenburg Gate was spectacular, and she imagined it would only be more majestic at night. In front of the gate, still to her right, the Pariser Platz was an open city block with both concrete and grassy spaces, with the U.S. embassy on her side of the square and the French embassy across the wide concrete plaza.

She looked down on Unter den Linden, lined with taxis in front of the hotel, tables sitting at outside cafés, and restaurants and bars in both directions.

The woman stepped back inside when the bellman knocked. He gently put her two suitcases on racks in the living room of the suite as directed by the Ukrainian guest.

Another knock came minutes after the bellman left. The blonde looked through the peephole, then opened the door.

Russian assassin Semyon Pervak stood in the hall. He wore a camel sport coat and white designer jeans, neither particularly flattering on his bulky frame.

He entered the foyer of the suite, giving barely a glance towards the woman as he passed by, though he did speak to her.

"I can't find Maksim. He's not answering his mobile."

Ukrainian Xristina Dolyna was, in fact, Russian Inna Sorokina, the intelligence officer for the four-man hit squad sent to hunt down Zoya Zakharova.

Sorokina shut the door and followed Pervak inside. She displayed no surprise at Pervak's inability to track down her team leader; this was par for the course.

Matter-of-factly, she said, "If he is not answering at three in the afternoon, then he is drunk in a bar."

Pervak said, "I have Anya checking the pub near the safe house, but he could be anywhere." He shrugged, then pulled off his coat. "Doesn't matter, we won't need him till tonight at the earliest."

"Yes, but when we need him, we *will* need him sober."

"Whatever. We will make do."

Sorokina bit her lip for an instant, then said, "He might not be out drinking at all."

The middle-aged man looked back at her. Soon he shook his head. "No, Inna. If Maksim is going to kill himself, he won't do it while on mission. He likes this part of the life. It will be during the downtime when he puts his gun in his mouth. We go another six weeks without a job after this, and we'll find him floating in a river, but as long as there is work, there will be Maksim."

Pervak turned away from her, looked out at the view from the windows of the living room.

He wanted to drop the subject, it was clear, but Inna said, "You *do* know how this ends, don't you? Maksim gets one of us, or all of us, killed."

The big Russian mob hit man sniffed loudly. "As long as Moscow says Maksim is in charge, then that's good enough for me."

"In charge?" Sorokina snapped. "Has he been taking charge of late?"

Pervak turned from the view and squared his body off towards her. "I might have to tell our team leader that his third-in-command is attempting to undermine his authority."

Inna laughed at this. "If you told him right now, while he's slumped over a bar stool, I doubt he would hear you, and I am certain he wouldn't care."

Pervak shrugged again, but his attention was on the luggage in the living room now. "You've got to be kidding me. Gucci? Headquarters okayed that purchase?"

Sorokina unzipped the first bag. "Reproductions. Picked them up in New York when we were there. Seventy-five dollars, U.S." From it she pulled a laptop and some cables, and she began setting it all up on the bar area in the kitchen, while Pervak opened the other bag and began removing cameras and listening devices.

There was another knock at the door a minute later; Semyon headed for it, but while doing so he reached into his jacket at the waistband and put his hand on the butt of his CZ P-01 Omega pistol. He looked through the peephole, just as Inna had done a minute before, and then he relaxed his gun arm and opened the door.

Anya Bolichova wore a yellow and red sundress, large-framed mirrored glasses on the top of her head, and wedge heels. She carried nothing other than a small handbag over her shoulder.

Her mood was not as sunny as her outfit, however.

"I couldn't find Maksim. I guess he's out on another bender."

Pervak said, "I hope it's German beer he's drinking. Better that than the vodka."

Bolichova looked past Pervak, at Sorokina. "Okay, Inna. We don't need our shooter now, anyway. What can I do?"

Inna said, "Can you get into the hotel guest list?"

"*Da*. Of course. Don't need to be in the building to do it." She looked out the massive floor-to-ceiling window a moment, past the railing and down to Unter den Linden. "But it's nice here, so I'm not complaining."

"I want to look at all the names, all the companies who have reserved rooms here, run it all against known actors. I have a hard time believing Sirena is what she claims to be. Her cover is too thin; she should be hiding under a rock right now, not working for an intelligence firm in Western

Europe. If we are lucky, we might find out she has confederates, and they might be staying here so they can watch out for her."

Anya Bolichova got to work. She hacked into the hotel's servers in a matter of minutes, which gave her access to all the cameras, the guest list, the employee schedules; she could even see reservations in the cafés and restaurants on the property.

As they had been told by their handlers in Moscow, a woman using Zakharova's alias, Stephanie Arthur, was staying at the far end of the long hallway here in room 405.

Inna couldn't help but wonder if she was only thirty meters from Sirena right now.

Bolichova did more digging into the other guests, running names against known intelligence officers kept in a database, she assumed, at Russian Foreign Intelligence, but processed through her handler in Moscow.

When she had all the data, she summarized to Inna and Semyon. "Over two dozen people from the intelligence services, representing nine different nations, are staying here at the hotel. But that's to be expected. We are near many embassies and consulates, after all. And the Reichstag is only a couple kilometers away."

Sorokina looked over the list. Evaluated what was known about each of these players her colleague had identified. Finally, she said, "This name at the bottom."

"That's Ric Ennis. American. He used to be a case officer with CIA, but now he works for Shrike Group, Zakharova's firm, here in Berlin."

"And he is staying in the hotel?"

"No, but he has a dinner reservation for two tonight at eight thirty. Downstairs in Lorenz."

This wasn't what Sorokina was looking for, but it was something. She said, "Semyon, you go to the bar at Lorenz at eight fifteen. Be in position. Let's see if darling Zoya makes an appearance with Mr. Ennis."

Semyon didn't like Sorokina telling him what to do. He was technically over her. But she was the intelligence officer, and ultimately these were her calls to make. He looked down at his watch. "That gives us five hours to find Maksim."

Sorokina said, "When it comes time, you might have to do this your-self. There is no way she will come back with us to Moscow."

This was, Semyon knew, *not* her call to make. "I agree that she will not surrender. The only way she's leaving here is in a body bag. But Maksim is in charge. If he tells me he needs me to stand in, I will stand in. Otherwise, we will wait and watch the target."

Pervak was right. The restaurant wasn't the right time or location for this. Inna had another idea. She looked over Anya's shoulder at the data for a moment. "Can we see room service orders?"

"Of course."

"Has she ordered anything so far?"

Anya pulled it up. "Yes. She's been here two weeks, and she's ordered breakfast every single morning, lunch once, and dinner twice. She's not just sleeping here; apparently she's spending most of her time working from her suite. Some of these breakfast orders make it look like she's meet-ing with others here. Multiple pots of coffee, lots of food for one woman."

Sorokina nodded. "Okay. We can do this just like D.C."

"What happened in D.C.?" Anya asked. It was before her time with the unit.

Pervak said, "The Dupont Circle Hotel. A year and a half ago we elim-inated a Russian-born reporter who had been filing some embarrassing and completely untrue stories about our dear president. Maksim wore a room service attendant's uniform, made entry on the man's hotel room, and I came in behind him. He was drunk, we got him drunker, bashed his face in with a bedpost. We got away, the death was listed as natural causes, a drunk who fell and hit his head, and no one ever knew we were there."

Inna said, "I want a camera in her room. We need her to be alone, and we need to be absolutely assured of this."

Bolichova said, "I can open her lock, but I have to physically go down to her door with a computer and plug in to the battery port on the bottom of the latch."

"Is that a problem?"

She smiled. "No. I'll play a recorded loop of the hallway cameras, won't take me a minute once I'm there."

Semyon looked around Inna's suite, assessing the ceiling, the fixtures, the layout. "I'll take two cams, put them high on the walls in the living room and bedroom." He turned to Inna. "Bathroom, too? Just to be sure?"

Sorokina replied with, "Grow up." And then, "Watch out for telltales, look for other cams or recording devices. This isn't like any other operation you've ever been on."

Semyon loomed over Sorokina, brought a finger up to her face. "It's exactly like every operation I've ever been on. I'm a fucking professional, too."

Inna let it go. She knew Semyon was good at his job, and she had done all she could to plant the seed that his best efforts would be required for this mission.

If he fucked this up . . . well, she told herself, then that was on him.

THIRTY-ONE

Anya Bolichova disengaged the electronic lock with her handheld computer, then quickly pulled the wires out of the latch. Semyon stood over her and moved past her to enter the room.

He instantly brought a device to his eye that he could look through, and he began walking the suite, focusing on all the places cameras were usually secreted by professionals. The computer on the small device checked for reflections coming off the lenses of cameras, even ones no larger than a few millimeters, while at the same time searching for radio frequency transmissions given off by most remote cameras.

While he searched, Anya Bolichova took photos inside the living room, the bedroom, and the bathroom, and then she moved a chair over to the door to the suite. She climbed on top of it, pulled out a tiny pinhole camera with a fish-eye lens, and affixed it by pressing the removable epoxy on the back of the device to the wall.

The cams didn't have microphones; that would entail a much larger device, and keeping these cams hidden from a woman trained to look for them meant using the smallest devices for the job. They just needed to know she was in her room, and she was alone. This was an assassination, not a surveillance operation.

In her earpiece she heard Inna's voice. "Survey One is operational. Image nominal."

"Roger," she whispered back, and then, "Hallway still clear?"

"*Da.*"

Semyon finished his scan, finding nothing out of the ordinary in the suite, shortly before Anya placed the second camera low in the corner by the window in the bedroom. Neither of the operatives opened Zakharova's luggage, looked through drawers or closets, or touched any of her belongings, knowing full well that their target had all the training she needed to detect any sort of intrusion or insult to her things. A single strand of hair tied between two zippers on her suitcase, a hairbrush oddly askew next to other items left orderly, furniture slightly moved that a less-than-careful infiltrator would feel the need to put back in place.

Zoya might not have cams set up in her place, but she sure as hell would know someone had paid her a visit if Bolichova and Pervak weren't extra careful.

Six minutes after leaving suite 405, the two Russians returned to 401. Inna had been watching hotel cameras the entire time, even the ones in the lobby, with the worry that Zoya might be making an early return from her workday.

Soon, though, the team began talking about a plan of attack. Normally Maksim would be involved, but Inna was the intel officer, so this part of the mission was usually hers to run as she saw fit.

"Semyon, we need a room service attendant's uniform and a cart. We will have it ready for Maksim."

"Remember," Pervak replied, "HQ wants you to give her a chance to surrender herself first."

"I'll look for an opportunity to confront her. With luck I can speak with her tonight." She thought a moment. "She will refuse to return to Russia, of course. After that, we'll need to act quickly. If I can do that, Maksim can do his work tomorrow morning."

Bolichova looked at the time on the laptop, then said, "So about fourteen hours to find Maksim and sober him up."

Semyon Pervak ran his fingers through his white hair. "We've done it in half the time, haven't we?"

"True," Sorokina agreed. "But he's sunken lower than ever now."

. . .

Court Gentry had rented a silver BMW G 310 GS motorcycle, and although by the time he returned to Sasani's neighborhood the painter's truck had left, he caught a glimpse of it far ahead of him in traffic as he raced towards the Adlon Kempinski. He'd hoped to see it stop in front of the hotel, but he had been in the process of making a U-turn near the Brandenburg Gate when a bus cut off his view of the hotel's entrance. As soon as the bus rolled out of the way, the blue truck was pulling off from the canopied entrance of the hotel, and Court assumed Zoya had been delivered back to her suite by members of her surveillance team.

This all happened just after two p.m., and Court wondered why she wrapped up surveillance of her target so early, but it was good news for him. He knew she was using the cover identity Stephanie Arthur, and she was in suite 405, so all he had to do now, he told himself, was keep his eyes open for Russian assassins in the area.

This wasn't technically true, of course. He motored his BMW past the U.S. embassy, directly next door to the Adlon Kempinski, and he knew he had to keep away from the array of cameras on the grounds of the building. He wore a black motorcycle helmet, so he knew he was safe for now, but he also knew he'd have to find a place to conduct a longer-term surveillance operation.

There were no two ways about it. Since Court had no idea if Russian hit men were already in the Adlon, he knew at some point he'd have to go in himself.

Which meant part of this afternoon would be spent racing through a clothing store and grabbing shit that looked like it would fit in inside one of the nicest hotels in Europe.

Court groaned in his helmet at the prospect of spending this kind of time away from his coverage of her, but good cover was crucial to his tradecraft, and more crucial now than ever. Remaining covert wasn't just for his own safety; it was also for Zoya's.

Keith "Hades" Hulett and his team tracked down the silver BMW bike, having been told by a contact at the SIA that the motorcycle and driver had been picked up on a camera just outside Hellman Mens Wear on Kurfürs-tendamm.

He didn't know much about facial recognition, but he was surprised this supposedly badass killer had managed to get himself fixed three different times today, and he wondered if either Tarik had access to connections in the German government, or the SIA was simply that good.

Either way, the American mercenary didn't care. Killing a terrorist and executing a retributive strike on the bastard who'd killed one of Hulett's men would make this day both a personal and a professional high point.

The two sedans parked in an hourly lot two blocks away from the last known location of their target, and then the men broke off into four teams of two, with three teams fanning out to check all the shops and eateries in the area, while Atlas and Mercury went hunting for the motorcycle to keep an eye on it in case Gentry tried to leave the scene.

They checked a couple of street-level lots before entering an underground parking garage a few blocks away from their target's last known location.

On level P3 the two Americans found the silver BMW parked in a corner not far from the stairs, and though they were too far underground to get cell phone signal to notify Hades of their discovery, they'd expected this to happen, so they'd been given instructions to find a place to lie low and cut off any possible getaway for Gentry. The men decided to split up, with one moving just outside the stairwell door to wait in the dark, and the other positioning himself between a pair of compact cars parked directly next to the bike.

Once in position, both men opened their backpacks and pulled out Stribog SP9A1s, compact Slovakian-made 9-millimeter submachine guns. Each weapon had a silencer and a folding stock, and would be ideal for the close-in work needed to dispatch the man who killed Ronnie.

Once their safeties were off and their weapons were on their shoulders, all that was left to do was wait in the dusty garage.

Hades and Thor stepped into Hellman Mens Wear at 3:40 p.m., doing their best to look like casual shoppers. Men more highly trained in tradecraft might have known better than to enter the store itself; there was more chance of them compromising themselves to their target if they left the street and the crowds and began browsing the shop. But Hades told himself they were just going in to see if the man was still there, and if they identified him, they would leave and lie in wait outside.

They gave the sales floor a quick glance upon entering, then went over to a wall and began going through a rack of dress shirts. A clerk asked them if they needed help, speaking in English because the men didn't look like they could possibly be anything else but American, but Hades sent him away.

They spent the next minute making their way slowly towards the back, glancing up from time to time to see if they saw their target, and then, without discussing it, the two men split up to check out the store more carefully. They worried he'd left the shop and headed somewhere else on Ku'damm, even though they could hear the two other teams reporting in one dry hole after another.

The men at street level had lost comms with Mercury and Atlas, but they attributed that to the fact that they'd most likely gone down into an underground garage.

Hades turned to look at a rack of merino wool sweaters while, just ten yards or so away, Thor checked out a pair of slacks on a mannequin.

Court Gentry stepped out of his dressing room with the dark blue suit and collared shirt he'd tried on in his arms, and he headed towards a rack of shoes. His plan was to grab a pair, check out, and then head back to his flat to change before racing back to the Adlon.

He was fighting off the exhaustion that seemed to increase every minute, but he told himself once he'd reconnoitered Zoya's hotel he'd find some coffee and that would get him through the evening until he could make his way to Dr. Kaya.

He stepped back onto the sales floor of the clothing store, but before he made it halfway to the shoes, he stopped in his tracks, turned, and retreated back into the changing rooms.

He'd seen the two men, one from the back, one from the side. They were dressed casually, with both of their short-sleeved shirts untucked. The man who had his back to him had massive shoulders, and the one he'd seen from the side possessed bulging biceps and triceps that Court could discern from across the room.

This man wore a pair of sunglasses high on his head. Both men were bearded, and both men were what Court and people in his world referred to as FAMs.

Fighting-aged males.

They were American operators, this was obvious. And he had little doubt that they'd be armed.

Court stood in the dressing room, thought over his options.

He was of two minds. He needed the clothes he had chosen, otherwise he'd have a very difficult time tailing Zoya. But he also needed to get the fuck out of here, because these two dudes had come for him, he had no doubt in his mind.

He didn't waste much time trying to figure out who the hell they were, who the hell had sent them, and how the hell he'd been discovered. None of that mattered at present. No, the only thing Court concerned himself with was how to get past these two, as well as any confederates they had outside.

And to make it out of here with the clothes.

He had two options. He could shoot it out with these two jacked-up shooters by the checkout desk, or he could shoplift.

Quickly he searched the clothing, looking for any sensor tags that would set the alarm off when he left. Finding none, he ripped off his T-shirt and jeans and changed into his new blue suit and white shirt. He didn't have dress shoes, so he slipped his dark brown Merrells back on.

In seconds he stood in the threshold of the fitting room and looked back into the store. Both bearded men were there, facing away, so he took off at a run.

A sales representative for the store cried out at the customer as he rushed by, but made no attempt to stop him. As the man in the suit raced across the sales floor, shouldered into the glass door, and then stumbled out onto the street, the clerk just stood in the middle of the floor with his mouth agape.

The clerk then took a single step closer to the door, but only a step, because he was instantly waylaid by a large man who crashed into and then over him, desperately chasing after the fleeing shoplifter.

The young man pushed himself up to his knees, watched the second man slam open the door and run through it, then heard loud slapping footsteps behind him. He ducked down to the floor just as a third man passed, this one leaping over him, following the other two out onto the sunny street.

THIRTY-TWO

Court didn't have a lot of sprint in him, this he knew, but he had a little, and he'd give it everything he could before he collapsed.

Whereas before it hadn't mattered to him how he'd been compromised and who these people were, now it was at the forefront of his mind. He needed to ascertain if there were others, and he needed to learn their rules of engagement. Would he actually be shot in the back in central Berlin? He knew it all depended on the identities of the men on his ass and the mandate they'd been given by their masters.

Court assumed that the two immediate threats behind him weren't the full measure of the threats against him. He didn't know if others had discovered his bike, or if they were even aware of it, but, he told himself, he had to expect men lying in wait for him down in the parking garage.

But he had no choice. He'd dismantle anyone who got between him and the BMW and then he'd blast his way out of here on two wheels.

He raced across the street on Welandstrasse, running right in front of a large blue tour bus that was already slowing to a stop, and then he entered Walter-Benjamin-Platz, a paved pedestrian-only square lined with high-end shops and elegant cafés.

And though he could feel himself slowing and hear himself gasping for air, he kept pounding his feet against the pavement and pumping his arms up and down, leaning forward as he did so, desperate to get away from his pursuers.

Keith Hulett was forty yards behind his prey and closing when Gentry darted into traffic, right in front of a tour bus, before disappearing on the other side. By the time Hulett neared the bus, the door had opened between himself and his quarry, and it had begun disgorging elementary-school-aged kids on their way for a tour of the historic Kurfürstendamm boulevard.

The children moved single file, and Hulett was going to just plow on through them until he noticed they were all holding a rope to keep them in line for their teachers.

Hulett skidded to a stop, then turned and ran up the sidewalk to the rear end of the bus, only then darting out into the street after Gentry.

A DHL truck raced by, and to avoid getting run down, Hulett dove onto the hood of a parked Maserati and then rolled over the top, then down onto the sidewalk on the far side of the street from the schoolkids.

He struggled back to his feet and started forward again, checking behind him as he did so. He saw that Thor had gotten himself wrapped up in the children and their rope and was falling farther behind.

Once he reached the large square, Hulett could see that Gentry had increased his lead greatly. He wasn't running as fast as before, but still Hulett doubted he would catch up to him before he rounded a corner on the next block, ran to his bike parked in some lot somewhere nearby, and escaped.

He couldn't count on the fact that Mercury and Atlas would take him; he had to stay on the man's tail.

Hulett pulled his gun, thinking he had one last look at Gentry before he lost sight of him. One opportunity to get payback for Ronnie Blight. He held the weapon out in front of him and slowed, lining up on the tiny target, now over sixty yards away.

But he stopped himself before pressing the trigger.

This wasn't a run-down apartment block in Yemen. This wasn't an out-of-the-way dilapidated mansion outside Caracas. This was the very center of the very heart of Europe. Cafés spilled out into the square, and Hulett immediately realized he was likely being watched by many eyes.

He holstered his pistol and slowed, continuing at a brisk pace, but nothing like the speed of the man running away at the far end of the square.

Thor had broken free of the kids from the tour bus and now entered the square, as well. Following his leader, he slowed to a brisk walk, thirty yards back from Hades and nearly one hundred from Gentry, who disappeared around the side of a bakery.

Court felt like he was going to vomit, but he wouldn't let himself slow down to do so. He couldn't remember a single situation in his life where he literally didn't have time to puke, but that was where he found himself as he ran past a bakery and then down the single-lane entrance for the underground garage where he'd parked his bike. His run had slowed to a jog, and he had no idea how far back the pair that had been in foot pursuit were, but now he told himself to forget about them, and to instead focus on the unknowns ahead.

He gasped for air, his lungs straining as he left the entrance ramp and ran into the stairwell, then began descending to level P3, all the while acutely aware that he might not be alone down here.

Officer Jürgen Reichert exited Bäcker Wiedemann, a bakery on the corner of Walter-Benjamin and Leibnizstrasse, after witnessing a bearded man in a business suit racing past the window. It was a strange enough occurrence for him to step out of line and go outside to the sidewalk to investigate, but by the time he looked in the direction the man had run, he saw nothing.

He assumed the man had gone into some shop, or perhaps the underground garage entrance two doors down.

He shrugged, turned to head back into the bakery, then saw a man rounding the corner in the opposite direction. This individual broke into a sprint right as he made it onto Leibnizstrasse, running in the direction of the officer.

"Halt!" Reichert shouted, and he put a hand up, thinking the first man

was being chased by the second. When the big muscular man did not stop, he pulled a baton from his utility belt, held it out in front of him, and pointed it at the onrushing bearded man.

"*Polizei!*"

He wore a Heckler & Koch SFP9 in a holster on his hip, but he'd never drawn it while on duty, and it didn't even occur to him now to do so.

Keith Hulett had just started running again when he noticed the cop in his way. He slowed a little, unsure, but once he saw the man pulling his baton, he charged forward again. He couldn't see Gentry any longer and assumed he'd already made it up to the next block.

The cop tried to get in his way, and Hulett picked up more speed, running right for him. The young man raised his weapon as if to strike, but the American swatted the baton away, knocking it into the street as he continued sprinting up Leibnizstrasse, desperate to get to the next intersection before his target managed to evade him.

Thor rounded the corner, turning off the pedestrian-only Walter-Benjamin-Platz and onto Leibnizstrasse, running as fast as his team leader now. He saw the police officer dead ahead, standing there, flat-footed, facing away and watching Hades sprint up to the next intersection. When he was just twenty yards away from him, Thor saw the cop reach down to his utility belt. He first assumed the man was going for a radio to call it in, but was instead surprised to see the young cop drawing his Heckler & Koch pistol with an uncertain draw.

Thor figured the only reason this young cop would be pulling his side-arm was that he'd caught a glimpse of Hades's pistol under his shirt, and the officer was slowly coming to the dramatic realization that he was in the middle of some sort of life-or-death encounter.

The cop's movements showed he wasn't ready for a fight. But Thor, for his part, knew exactly what he had to do. He picked up the pace even more, tried to lighten his step as he ran to minimize the chance the cop would hear him barreling down from behind, and then, just as the police officer raised his weapon and shouted at Hades to *"halt,"* Thor charged into him from behind, ambushing him with a shoulder to his back.

The pistol cracked, the man lurched forward and fell in a crumpled heap, and Thor tumbled over the top of him and fell to the sidewalk.

The American came to rest on his back; the cop's pistol was feet away, so he reached over, grabbed it, and pulled himself back to his feet.

He took off again at a sprint, following after his TL while deftly disassembling the weapon and throwing the component parts on the ground.

Behind him, the officer writhed in pain on the pavement as passersby rushed to his aid.

Hades had run right past the sign that read *Einfahrt Öffentliche Parkgarage*; the single-lane entrance to the underground lot was so nondescript he missed it, and he made it all the way to Mommsenstrasse before slowing and looking around.

Thor finally caught up, and he pulled to a stop next to him. Breathlessly he said, "Where the hell is he?"

Hades realized it was up to Atlas and Mercury now, so he said, "Let's get the vic. Be back here to support the other guys. It's gonna be crawling with five-oh in a minute."

The two of them ran off to the east, heading the two blocks to their vehicle at nearly the same speed they'd chased after their elusive prey.

THIRTY-THREE

Court didn't draw his HK pistol as he neared the metal door to the level P3 garage, but his hand hovered near it, ready to pull if he encountered any threats.

He'd heard a gunshot above him as he descended; he had no idea what that was all about, but he didn't want to open fire down here unless he was absolutely forced to. If both the bad guys and the cops were up at street level searching the area, he didn't want to do anything to draw attention to this garage before he could unass it.

He opened the door with a loud metal creak, then moved around the corner in the direction of his BMW.

He scanned the mid-distance of the well-lit and nearly packed garage, but then, right in front of his face, a submachine gun spun around in his direction. A man held it, the weapon was slung around his head and neck, and he'd apparently been as surprised by Court as Court was by him. He tried to get his weapon up and aimed, but Court fired out his left hand and grabbed the subgun by its suppressor.

The man yelled something, but Court wasn't listening. Instead he locked his hand down harder on the cylinder of the suppressor—he'd ID'd the weapon in an instant as a Stribog—then pushed the muzzle of the weapon away from him while simultaneously kicking out, striking the man in the chest.

The stunned operator fell to his knees, but he didn't go down because Court still held the business end of the rifle, and the rifle sling was wrapped around the back of the man's neck.

Court kicked at the man's face now, hit him with a glancing blow to his jaw, and then brought his foot back and kicked again, this time slamming the tip of his Merrell shoe into the rifle's receiver. He was aiming for a particular part of the gun, but he missed his target, so he fired his foot out a fourth time while still controlling the muzzle of the gun with his left hand.

And this time he did it. His boot kicked the magazine release of the weapon. The mag dropped out of the mag well and onto the parking lot, and then Court used the bottom of his foot to push the weapon's pronounced charging handle all the way back, ejecting the shell from the chamber in the same process.

The rifle was empty, so Court let it go.

But the man on his knees had recovered, and now he drew a pistol from his right side and began swinging that up and into play.

Court spun on his left foot, around the rifle held between himself and the enemy on his knees, and he executed a reverse roundhouse kick with his right foot.

His heel struck the gun just as the man raised it, knocking it away, and Court followed up with a kick to the man's head, snapping it to the side.

The unconscious operator crumpled onto the dusty pavement.

And then a gunshot boomed in the enclosed space. Concrete exploded off the wall next to the metal door, and Court dropped to his knees, drawing his HK as he did so.

A second shot, then a third, both struck the wall near the first, but Court wasn't concerned with the impact points of the rounds; he was concerned with the origin of the fire.

And then he saw it. A weapon's flash all the way at the end of the row of vehicles, right where Court had parked his motorcycle.

He tucked lower, then moved behind a VW Golf parked near the stairs, hunting for concealment from the shooter thirty yards away.

And then, for the first time while in action, he felt his body failing him. Even with all the adrenaline in his system he could tell he was weakening considerably. His stomach retched, and he vomited against the passenger-side door of the Golf, then recovered, spit on the ground, and scrambled one vehicle closer.

He didn't love the idea of attacking the man who had a better defensive position and a better weapon, but he knew with the shooting down here it wouldn't be long before the lot was full of armed men, be they police or enemy.

He had to assault the man's position now.

He moved between the wall and the grille of a Mercedes. He was still low, and he fought off another wave of nausea before he heard scuffling sounds near his bike ahead. This indicated to him that his adversary was repositioning. He was probably trying to find his target, unaware Court was working on a flanking maneuver.

When there were only two vehicles separating the two men, Court saw his enemy again. He was crouched behind the rear end of an Opel four-door that had backed into its parking space.

Court himself was knelt down behind the engine block of a little Fiat 500. He knew he could rise and get an angle on the man, but he also knew the man might have a subgun like his partner, and if Court exposed himself, he could have thirty bullets coming his way faster than he could fire four or five from his pistol.

He began to raise his weapon to try to shoot through the windows of both vehicles, when he saw the man's head appear behind his suppressed weapon. The man fired first, bursting the window of the Fiat and narrowly missing Court.

Court dropped down hard onto his left shoulder, not just to avoid the gunfire but to also get a different sight line on his target.

The wound below his left collarbone spiked with fresh torment, but he remained in the fight.

Looking under the Fiat he could see the boots of the man just fifteen feet away, and Court aimed and fired, striking the man in the right ankle.

The operator fell to his knees; Court shot his left thigh, and then when the man tumbled down to his side, Court fired a fifth round, hitting the man in the neck and finally killing him.

Court pulled himself back up to his feet, using the Fiat to do so, and then he staggered around the Opel, his pistol leveled at the dead man lying next to it.

He climbed onto his bike and fired it up in one motion, then lurched forward in the parking lot, squealing his tires as he shot towards the ramp back by the stairs.

He fought to get his helmet on, using his right hand to do so because his left shoulder was killing him. The helmet wasn't just to protect his head; he was certain he'd been picked up on cameras somewhere, probably at the bike shop and again at the men's store, so he wanted to get out of there without any more exposure.

He rode off, out of the area, keeping pace with the traffic so as not to draw attention to himself.

Court had learned several things from the encounters of the past few minutes. For one, his data was on PowerSlave, despite Drummond's assurances it was not. Also, whoever it was he'd just confronted had been well trained, perhaps not in spycraft but at least in combat arms. He thought about the men he'd run across in Caracas a couple of days earlier, the team of operators who killed Clark Drummond.

These guys might well be from the same crew.

He fought nausea again but he kept it down, tried to control his breathing to slow his heart rate, and felt a trickle of blood down the left side of his chest. But he drove on, heading east, beginning an SDR that would eventually lead him back to his apartment in Spandau.

Hades and Thor stood over Mercury, clearly dead with gunshots to his neck and legs. They'd already scooped up Atlas, who'd been unconscious and bloody when they found him, and put him in the backseat of the BMW.

Thor said, "Just like Caracas."

Hades said, "Of course, it's just like Caracas. It's the same dude."

"Yeah . . . but . . . Ronnie, and now Scott? Both them boys were solid. This guy who did this . . . this *ain't* luck."

Hades finished Thor's thought as he turned to head back to the car. "It's skill. He's good, I'll give him that. But I want another shot."

"Same here."

"Get in the car, call the others, and tell them to stand down. When Atlas comes around, we'll find out what we can about this Gentry bastard."

The men climbed into the Mercedes and headed for the exit ramp as sirens blared at street level.

THIRTY-FOUR

Zoya Zakharova stepped off the elevator and into the lobby of the Adlon at eight thirty in the evening, dressed in an attractive blue dress and low heels. She carried a small purse over her shoulder, and her dark hair was down and flowing.

She moved through the light crowd with a pleasant smile on her face, but it was a ruse; her eyes darted left and right, worry filled her mind, and she was wholly unable to enjoy the beautiful surroundings because of the possibility that guns were pointed at her face right now.

She knew where to find Ennis. He'd called her from the lobby bar a half hour earlier, inviting her for a drink before dinner. She'd declined, said she was getting herself ready, but she imagined that although she'd forced him to drink alone, he would be drinking nonetheless.

He stood from the bar, a three-quarters-empty glass of beer in front of him, and greeted her warmly with a kiss on each cheek.

His tie was off, his collar open, and his light blue sport coat looked good on his fit frame. Zoya had examined his face carefully before they'd even greeted each other, searching for any hint of danger, but he looked like a man in control, like he'd regained some of the swagger he'd lost before his call earlier in the afternoon.

"Everything all right?" she asked.

He nodded. "For now I think we're in the clear about all that earlier today. No word of extra monitoring on us from BfV." He motioned towards the restaurant. "It's a nice evening, I've asked for a table outside."

Der'mo, she said to herself in Russian.

Shit.

Zoya hated eating dinner outdoors in busy areas; she always felt exposed doing so, but never more so than right now. But Ennis was insistent, and she knew that the way to play him for intel tonight without him realizing he was getting played was to allow him to think he was taking the lead, so she went where he led her, allowed him to pull out her chair for her and to even order a bottle of wine to share, a 2016 Pape Clément white from Bordeaux.

But before the waiter could leave to retrieve the wine, Zoya said, "Two glasses of vodka, on ice, please. A twist for the gentleman. Beluga Gold Line if you have it."

"Very well, madam."

Ennis smiled, gave a little whistle and a wink. "It's been a rough day, but tonight is definitely looking up."

Zoya smiled back at him. She had used alcohol to loosen tongues in the past, and as she had an ironclad constitution when it came to booze, she felt it was worth a shot to try to ply Ennis with a drink or two more before they even started on the bottle of wine.

He'd been nervous earlier in the day, but she could read him now. He was confident, content. The liquor and the beautiful surroundings and the company would open him up, she was certain.

While they waited for their drinks, Ennis talked about Berlin a moment, and she listened politely before finally interrupting. She was playing a role tonight, something she could do as well as any actress on any stage, and right now she wanted to convey vulnerability to Ennis, because she had the impression he got off on it.

"I have to ask, Ric." She looked around, her trepidation *not* part of the act. "You're certain no one from Shrike has been in touch with Russian authorities about me?"

He shook his head emphatically. "Absolutely not. You are totally safe."

He leaned forward now, their shoulders almost touching. "Trust me. I wouldn't let anything happen to you."

Zoya affected a little smile while the waiter put down the two drinks. She fought like hell to keep from swiveling her head in all directions, or diving under the table.

Somebody was out here, watching her, right now.

She could feel it.

Court Gentry sat on a bench in front of the Dunkin' Donuts on Unter den Linden and drank black coffee. The two donuts he'd downed for added quick energy were already rumbling in his stomach; he regretted eating them, but that was not where his focus lay at present.

His eyes were locked on a café across the street, some forty yards away. More specifically, they were locked on Zoya Zakharova, except when he surveyed his surroundings to make sure no one was taking an interest in him, or when sweat from his forehead dripped down into his eyes.

The man she was with was good-looking; he appeared confident by his mannerisms, and though Court was no expert on romance, he *was* an expert on body language, and it was clear enough the man was totally captivated by his dinner companion.

The man Brewer had identified as Ric Ennis leaned in her direction; his legs were pointed towards her under the table. Zoya did have her face and upper torso turned toward him, but under the table Court saw that her legs were directed straight ahead and not at Ennis at her left. This was a cue that he was more in tune with her than she was with him.

Still, Court watched her smile and nod passionately at the American man's long oratories, touch her hand to her chest a few times as she seemed to laugh.

He turned away from the scene. He had a job to do, and it didn't involve watching the woman he loved out on a date. It involved watching for anyone *else* watching her. He told himself the woman across the street wasn't Zoya; she was Anthem, a Poison Apple asset in the field who needed a first-rate countersurveillance operative keeping watch over her, because there were credible—no, almost certain—threats against her.

It was still early dusk; full darkness wouldn't take place until around ten fifteen p.m. Court had binoculars in his backpack, but he wasn't going to pull them here. He was in the process of running countersurveillance for someone else; he didn't have the ability to do much countersurveillance for himself, but he could, at the very least, try to avoid sticking out like a sore thumb.

He was dressed in jeans and a black T-shirt, but inside the backpack was his dark blue business suit, carefully folded. Court figured there was a chance he'd need to make entry on the hotel tonight, but he liked the casual clothing he was wearing because he felt it helped him fit in better sitting on a street corner bench.

He'd picked up a pair of dress shoes and some other odds and ends at a used clothing store west of Spandau during his SDR earlier in the day, and then he'd returned to his flat and slept like the dead for forty-five minutes before waking to prepare for this evening.

For now, though, he sat, watched, and fumed. He found himself angry at Zoya for a multitude of reasons. Angry that she sat outside tonight. This was a defensive logistical nightmare; there were vehicles and pedestrians and windows and rooftops and no way in hell to stop a determined attack on her.

The one thing he did have going for him, however, was that the crowd was large enough that anyone who acted would be doing so in front of hundreds of people, so if a potential murderer wanted to save his own skin, then this wouldn't be the time to act.

But it *would* be the time to ID Anthem as their target, and a good time to begin surveillance on her that would lead, inevitably, to an assassination attempt.

He was angry that she downed her vodka in a single swig and called the waiter over again, apparently ordering another round for them both, and that she smiled and laughed while the man in the light blue sport coat gesticulated wildly, telling some story about something that pissed Court off even though he didn't know this asshole and he didn't have a clue about what he was saying.

Court rubbed more sweat off his face. He was sick, he was tired, his stomach hurt, and he was pissed off that he'd eaten dinner at Dunkin' Donuts while the only other person on this earth who mattered to him was across the street having the time of her life.

He forced his eyes away from her and rescanned the entire street, almost willing that some asshole try him tonight, because he desperately wanted to punch somebody in the face.

THIRTY-FIVE

The knock at the door of suite 401 came just after nine. Anya and Inna both stood up from the table next to the kitchen island where they had been working at their laptops, and they both pulled pistols from their purses: a Heckler & Koch VP9SK subcompact for Anya, and a not dissimilar HK P30SK for Inna.

Before they went to the door, Anya tapped a button on her computer that showed her the hotel camera view from right outside her door.

A second later both women sighed and resecured their firearms, and Inna headed to let her team leader in.

Anya kept looking at the real-time image on her screen. "He can barely stand."

When Maksim Akulov entered a moment later, he walked utterly erect, his chin up, the knot of his blue tie only a touch off-kilter.

It was a put-on, Inna could tell. Maksim couldn't hide his drunken stagger from her, even if Anya hadn't already seen it for herself on the screen.

Inna had been through this so many times before.

The smell of vodka came through his skin as he passed by her. Anya Bolichova pulled a chair out for him at the table where she was working, but he passed this up, as well, in favor of the ornate couch against the wall. Here he plopped down heavily, then made a show of smoothing the part in his bushy reddish-brown hair.

"Where's Sem?"

"He has the eye," Sorokina answered.

Maksim acted like he was taking in this information, but Inna figured he was just fighting a little dizzy spell, hoping to keep down everything he'd consumed in the hours he'd been missing. Finally, he righted himself and asked, "Target disposition?"

"She's having dinner with another employee of the company she works for. Downstairs, outdoor café. Semyon is at the bar inside, but he's got an angle."

Maksim pulled himself back up to his feet, surprising both women in the room. *"Ponial."* Got it, he said, and he started for the door.

Both Bolichova and Sorokina grabbed him by the arms, and they led him back to the sofa. He didn't fight them. "Not tonight," Sorokina said as he sat back down.

She knew Maksim would become especially volatile if she didn't phrase her next words carefully. "We see a much better opportunity ahead. I hope you will agree."

He put his elbows on the back of the sofa. "Okay, what's the plan?"

Inna said, "Tonight, once she returns to her room. I will go speak with her. I'll be unarmed, she'll have a weapon, but she won't shoot me. Not here."

Maksim leaned his head back on the cushions. "Fine. It's your neck. And when she refuses your offer of surrender?"

"I tell her she has forty-eight hours to reconsider."

"We aren't giving her forty-eight—"

Inna interrupted. "Of course we aren't. I just don't want her running out the door five minutes after I leave. My plan is room service, tomorrow morning. Like we did in D.C."

The Russian assassin seemed to take this all in, but he did not respond. Sorokina thought that this might be among the top five drunken episodes she'd ever witnessed. It was certainly no Crete. At least tonight Maksim had been able to stagger into the room and ask a couple of questions; in Crete they'd moved him as if they were transporting a body for most of a morning until he could be roused.

Nevertheless, right now, he was filthy, stinking drunk.

With a flash of her eyes to her young subordinate, Inna passed along a message to Anya that said, *Give us a minute.*

Anya understood; she walked to the table and grabbed her purse. "I'm going downstairs to give Semyon some arm candy."

When Bolichova was gone, he turned his face to Inna. *"Shto?" What?* He could tell she wanted to talk in private.

"You are a disgrace."

"I can go tonight. When she returns to her room, after you make contact. Anya can pop the lock and I can—"

"Nyet, Maksim. You can kick off your shoes and lie there on the couch. That's all you can do. Anything else, and you'll fuck it up."

Akulov raised his eyebrows. After a long staring contest, he said, "You've no right to speak to me like—"

"I told you we needed to take care on this one. But you are circling the drain so fast you can't even listen to me. Zoya, or her people, whoever they are, will kill you. And though that might please you greatly, Anya, Semyon, and I don't want to be part of the collateral damage."

He leaned forward and rubbed his face in his hands for several seconds, a feeble attempt to recover enough to have this conversation. "What do you want me to say?" His chest heaved a dramatic sigh. "I thought I just needed a job to get my mind right. That's always worked in the past. But not anymore." He shrugged. "Now . . . I just don't give a shit."

"Then tell headquarters. There is no shame in arriving at the sunset of your career. It's coming for us all."

"There is nothing beyond this!" he shouted. "As you say, I am circling the drain. Going faster and faster." He rubbed his hands through his hair and fished for a cigarette in his jacket. "But I don't know what happens when I actually get flushed."

He looked, to Inna Sorokina, like an utterly beaten man. His eyes welled up, from either tears or whatever ungodly amount of drink he'd consumed that afternoon and evening. She sat down in front of him, prepared to speak to him in a tender voice, to tell him he had a future after he left his work behind. He could become an artist or a mailman or anything he set his damaged and twisted mind to.

But then she stopped herself. *No.* Inna was here to do a job, and she couldn't do it alone. Maksim, when fit, was one of the best in the world at this. She had to find a way to rally him, one last time, to deal with Zoya Zakharova.

She slapped him hard on the face, knocking the unlit cigarette from his mouth. "You are an embarrassment to Russia! You are an embarrassment to the Bratva."

His face contorted in fury. "I could have you arrested for—"

"You aren't going to do anything! You won't even remember this in the morning! You have become less than worthless; you have become a liability. Go to sleep, fool, we don't need you."

She stood and turned away, walked past the dining room table.

He called out after her. He had, finally, a hint of passion in his voice. "You don't think I can do it anymore? Is that it?"

She sniffed out an angry laugh. "Just look at you."

Maksim stood slowly, rubbed his eyes again. Finally he said, "Where, in this suite, is our target?"

The blonde did not understand. *"Shto?"*

"Point me to my target." When she looked at him uncomprehendingly, he said, "Something over there in the kitchen, maybe? On the other side of the room. Is that her?" He pointed to a large basket of fruit left by management on the kitchen island. Beyond it on the counter was a coffee maker, next to which a kilo bag of ground espresso sat.

"There she is."

Maksim turned away on his heel dramatically, facing the balcony, and then he wobbled a little from the momentum of his spin.

"What are you going to—" Sorokina began to ask, but Maksim spoke over her.

"The grapefruit on top. *That* is Sirena's head."

Inna was positioned between her assassin and the fruit behind her. Quickly, she understood; she took a step to the right as Akulov spun back around, his coat flying up in the process. Almost too fast for her to see the movement, he reached into his belt on his hip, drew a flat-black metal knife, and flung it hard underhanded with a snap of both his wrist and his elbow. It sailed half a meter to the left of Inna's chest and over to the island with such momentum she couldn't track it, then sliced into the large pink grapefruit in the basket.

But the knife wasn't finished. It didn't come to rest in the fruit, it simply gouged it, then tumbled wildly across the kitchen, juice and pulp exploding into the air in its wake, until the knife finally buried itself into the bag of espresso grounds, bursting the bag and sending a black haze all over the kitchen.

Maksim fought obvious dizziness; he held his hands out away from his body to steady himself, then sat back on the couch, a look of smug satisfaction behind his bleary eyes.

Inna glared at him.

He found his cigarette and lit it. "Target destroyed."

"Along with the collateral damage," Sorokina replied softly. "Go to sleep. I will wake you at five a.m. and start pouring whatever's left of that espresso down your throat."

He kicked his feet up on the couch and closed his eyes; he hadn't even taken off his crumpled jacket or removed his tie. "Fine. No one moves without me. You understand that, right?"

"*Ya ponimayu.*" *I understand.*

She began turning off lights in the living room. She started to leave, but then she stepped back to him. "Give us the old Maksim, just one last time. When Sirena is gone, you can kill yourself with booze and pills, just don't kill yourself by doing a poor job here in Berlin. Your nation is counting on you."

He didn't respond, and after a few seconds she could hear him snoring.

THIRTY-SIX

Downstairs at Lorenz, Zoya's and Ric's food came, and across the street, through the trees lining the stretch of concrete running between the eastbound and westbound lanes of Unter den Linden, Court looked away. Fighting his infection, fighting the pain he felt in his heart. He knew Zoya was working, knew she wasn't really out with this man by choice, but he couldn't help himself. He was all alone, hiding in the shadows, and she was over there among the beautiful people.

Hanley hadn't wanted him to come here, and he now wondered if this was why. Perhaps Matt had suspected that Court watching out for Zoya would entail him seeing things he wouldn't want to see.

He asked himself if she would sleep with Ennis to gain intelligence for her operation, and he was immediately angry with himself for this train of thought. Still, in the back of his mind, he had to admit he didn't know what she did in the field.

Court looked back to see Ennis place his hand over Zoya's hand resting on the table. He smiled and kept talking, until she looked down at his hand, and he moved it away.

Court didn't like it. He squeezed his own hands together; his left tingled from the assault to the nerves in his shoulder a month ago. He fantasized about standing up right now, storming over to the shithead trying to hold Zoya's hand, and throwing his ass into the Spree River.

But he remained there, leaning back on the bench, trying to stay awake and on task.

He tried to push the thoughts from his head by making another scan of the street, all the way over to Pariser Platz, and the Brandenburg Gate to his right, to the traffic on Unter den Linden in front of him and to the left. Court was one man, and he knew one man couldn't cover all this territory with his eyes and hope to keep someone safe from harm, but he did his best.

He shook his head of the haze of his constant fatigue, heightened his focus, and pushed the idea out of his mind that he needed to go to Dr. Kaya right now and pick up the "go" pills he needed to reenergize him.

But that would have to wait, because Zoya had felt the need to dine al fresco in a European capital while Russian assassins hunted her down.

Fuck! he said to himself.

And then he stood, rushed back into the Dunkin' Donuts, and headed for the bathroom.

He'd just made it inside when he lurched over a large open rubber garbage can and vomited into it.

When he was finished he went to the sink, washed out his mouth, and threw some cold water on his face, and then headed back outside.

As he came out the door his head swiveled, on autopilot, but then it stopped suddenly. He wiped fresh perspiration off his eyelashes so he could see better. Two men, both in their forties, stepped out of the door to a Starbucks just a few doors down from Dunkin' Donuts. As he watched, they headed to a darkened alcove one building closer to him, then stood there, half-hidden in the dark.

They wore jeans and collared shirts, and comfortable black leather walking shoes. Neither had a beverage in his hand, but one faced towards the building while the other faced across the street, over towards the Adlon Kempinski Hotel and Restaurant Lorenz.

Court continued his scan, searched for anyone looking his way, then settled back on this pair, only one hundred or so feet distant.

He realized they might have just been a couple of guys meeting up for coffee at nine p.m. on a Monday; they certainly didn't scream "threat" by their dress or their actions. He kept his eyes tracking back to them for a couple of minutes, hoping one spoke into a cuff mic or another pulled out night vision goggles, both ridiculous breaches of tradecraft and something Court really didn't expect to happen.

He wondered what had drawn his attention to them in the first place, and when he spent a few more seconds looking, he realized what it was. While the man facing the Lorenz was leaning back against the wall of a souvenir shop, the one who faced the building stood straight. But Court saw that the man's feet were shoulder width apart, his knees soft and not locked, and he did not sway or change the weight of his body from one foot to the other. His hands were clasped behind his back for a moment, then released.

It looked like this guy was standing at parade rest—which meant he was likely military, or former military.

Spetsnaz? Russian special forces? Court couldn't be sure, but the man, while not huge, did have broad shoulders and a square jaw. He appeared possibly Slavic once Court focused on his face, and soon enough he found himself sufficiently suspicious that he might be looking at a pair of hit men from Moscow.

They also could simply be former German military, now working as carpenters or accountants or *anything* ordinary, so he knew better than to prejudge.

But when both men scanned around, as if checking for any surveillance on them, Court felt surer of himself.

Shit. He had a gun in his pants, but he really didn't feel like shooting it out with two GRU assassins in the busiest part of one of Europe's busiest capitals.

Thanks, Zoya, he said to himself, only partially recognizing that he was angry at her because she appeared to be having a nice evening and he, in contrast, most definitely was not.

Zoya took another bite of her Norwegian salmon, finding it to be perfectly cooked and seasoned. Ennis was enjoying his lobster; he made a show of cracking the claws and dipping the meat into the butter.

For practically the first time in the ninety minutes they'd been dining, Ennis stopped talking about himself, if only for an instant, so she decided to jump in.

"Ric . . . who is Haz Mirza?" Zoya asked.

Ennis looked up as he chewed the buttered lobster. He appeared surprised, but not concerned. After he swallowed, he asked, "Where did that name come up?"

"Sasani said the man killed today had hacked into Haz Mirza's computer."

Ennis nodded at this, looked out at the Brandenburg Gate over Zoya's shoulder. The massive structure was illuminated by blue spotlights in the fading light of dusk. She worried Ennis was going to clam up, but instead he took a long swig of his wine and said, "So, the guy who was killed today. Kamran Iravani. We found him a few months ago. We were tailing the leader of one of the Quds Force cells here in town. That was this Mirza joker. Anyway, our cyber team got to work on him, but we didn't find anything incriminating. Mirza had come from Iran as a sleeper a few years ago. He'd fought in Libya and Yemen and God knows where else; his Quds credentials are legit. But his cell here appears dormant. Our working theory was that he came, recruited his guys, and then they all got jobs at a trucking firm. They liked their lives here in Germany too much to start running around blowing shit up like any self-respecting terrorist would. Mirza's pissed about it; he's a true believer, but he's still here, so we wonder if he's slowly acclimating to life in the West himself."

Zoya countered, "Just because you don't pick up incriminating evidence on phone chatter doesn't mean they are inactive. They can use burners, Ric."

"Of course they can. We're inside their burners."

"Really?"

Ennis smiled. "You didn't hear that from me. Anyway, even with ears on them, we haven't picked up anything." He shrugged a little. "All this work against Iran . . . Honestly, I don't get the point."

"What do you mean?"

"No way Quds would act in Europe right now. The EU has thrown Iran a lifeline by lessening sanctions. Tehran's not going to fuck that up by blowing up a bus in Berlin."

"What was Iravani's connection to Quds Force?"

"Kamran Iravani had no connection to Quds Force. In fact, he played for the other team. He was MeK. You know who they are, right?"

Zoya found the question patronizing. "Of course, I do. Mujahedin-e Khalq. They want to overthrow the government in Tehran."

"Yeah. They're the opposite of Quds Force, if you like. Iranians, but anti-regime. Anyway, we were surveilling Mirza and didn't find what we were looking for, but we realized someone else had installed another back door into his computer and phone. It took our cyber team a few days, but they tracked it back to a server at Humboldt University, and that led us to Iravani. We put a physical team on him. He's straight-up MeK, goes to meetings and all that. He has associations with known People's Mujahedin leadership in exile. He was also a hacker. Nothing too sophisticated, mostly off-the-shelf attacks. The guy is basically just a cyberpunk, but he was watching everything Mirza's cell was doing. He'd cracked into some of their phones, too. No longer; they change out their burners every couple of months." He added, "And, yeah, Iravani's dead, so there's that."

"How many operatives does Mirza have?"

"We've ID'd ten. But, like I said, they all seem to be just regular working stiffs here in the capital."

Zoya thought this over. "So the only reason you were watching the anti-regime activist Iravani was to find the pro-regime people he was uncovering?"

Ennis nodded, chewed his lobster a moment, and sipped his white wine. He then said, "I guess so. Our client tells us what to do. We don't always know why."

Ennis gave her a wink now. "I wouldn't worry too much about Iran. We'll be off them in a few days."

Zoya nodded at this. "You told me when you hired me, the contract with this client was almost complete."

He nodded. "The client is about to go to the Germans with enough intel to get these bastards pulled into an American black site. The goal is to implicate the Iranians in some sort of impending terrorist act, something bad enough for the entire EU to put the sanctions squeeze back on."

Zoya thought of something he'd mentioned on the phone earlier. "You said we pulled coverage of Iravani before he was killed. Why?"

"Because we realized we weren't the only ones on his ass. BfV had a physical and cyber tail on him. They had his shitty apartment miked up, just like we did. We aren't supposed to be watching foreign nationals in Berlin, so we left our equipment in place and backed away before the federal intelligence service here found out what we were doing. Kind of like what you did with Sasani today."

"Do you think Shrike was exposed to BfV?"

The waiter appeared and poured more wine, and Zoya could tell Ennis was using the opportunity to weigh his options for answering. When they were alone again, he said, "Normally I would say yes. It would be hard as hell for Shrike to do all that we did to track Iravani and not be compromised by German intelligence doing the exact same thing. But in this case, I feel pretty confident we were in the clear."

"And why is that?"

Zoya realized now that Ennis actually liked talking about work; he was the authority, letting the "new girl" in on the gossip.

"Because the Shrike officer who had been running the op on Iravani is our best." He flashed a toothy grin. "No offense to you. She's been working for the company from the beginning, and she knows her shit."

"She?" Zoya said. "You must be talking about Miriam."

Ennis stopped eating, put his fork and knife down. With mild annoyance he said, "Moises or Yanis? Which one told you about Miriam?"

Ric Ennis had already freely doled out more intelligence than either of the two men on Zoya's team had, so she found it ironic that he seemed bothered by their relatively minor breach.

She said, "Her name came up in conversation. All I know is that she's good at her job, and she's attractive." Zoya didn't mention that Moises had said she wasn't really Israeli; she wanted to see what Ennis might say on his own.

Ennis seemed to let it go. Zoya knew he'd already consumed an impressive amount of alcohol, and it was showing its effects in his actions.

She didn't know if this was what was loosening his lips, but she also knew better than to look a gift horse in the mouth.

"She's very attractive. She is not as attractive as you." The Russian woman groaned inwardly, but she made herself blush slightly as she reached for her own glass.

THIRTY-SEVEN

Court moved a few feet closer to the two men watching Zoya across the street from the Adlon. He stopped just in the periphery of a cluster of young people both sitting at tables and standing around talking to one another on the sidewalk. He would be invisible to the men now, just another faceless body in the crowd. Court couldn't see Zoya as well now, but he was able to lock onto the pair of men without them noticing him doing so.

Finally, after five more minutes, Court noticed that the two men in the alcove finally stopped their chatting. The one against the wall pushed off and stood upright, while the man facing him stiffened somewhat.

Court read the signs. These weren't two guys about to say good night. These were two guys with a job to do, and they'd just decided it was time to get started.

The man who had been leaning against the wall reached into a pocket, pulled out something small, and pressed it into his right ear.

The other man did the same, then turned away, towards the Adlon, and began heading for the crosswalk that would help him navigate the evening Unter den Linden traffic.

Court's illness and lethargy seemed to slip away—momentarily, at least—as fresh adrenaline pumped into him. He dropped his empty cup into the trash and opened his backpack. He left the suit pants inside, put his dark jacket on over his black T-shirt, then slipped on the dress shoes. He shouldered the bag as he moved east on the sidewalk, in the opposite direction, to cross the street there.

Semyon Pervak received a text from Inna Sorokina telling him to halt coverage of the target for the evening, but he'd just ordered a second scotch, and Anya Bolichova had ordered a second cosmopolitan. Pervak acknowledged Sorokina's message, but he kept his seat and continued nursing his drink, although he did stop looking into the reflection in the mirror at the distant image of Zakharova and her colleague eating out on the sidewalk.

He and Bolichova had little to talk about that wasn't work related, and there were too many people around for that, so instead they just sat there until they finished. They looked like father and daughter, and they played that role well, both keeping their faces in their phones and all but ignoring each other.

When they were finished, Pervak paid the tab and the pair began walking back to the elevator. Neither was staying here at the hotel, but they wanted to speak with Inna about the operation the next morning and to figure out what to do about Maksim Akulov.

They were halfway across the lobby, moving together but not closely, when Pervak eyed a man coming into the hotel from a door on the eastern side. He had been sizing up people as potential threats for thirty-five years, and something about the man piqued his senses. His age, his fitness, his bearing. He was dressed in less expensive-looking clothing than most other people here in the lobby, and it all came together to ring alarm bells in the fifty-three-year-old Russian's brain.

Semyon didn't know who he was or what he was doing here, but he tracked the man with his eyes as he headed over to the bar, near the seat Pervak himself had taken to give him an angle on Zakharova. Once settled, the stranger looked up into the mirror, back in the direction of Pervak's own target.

Sorokina had insisted Zakharova knew better than to take this job with Shrike Group under thin cover. She felt certain their target had some sort of backup, or was part of a larger operation.

Semyon had discounted it at the time. He wasn't half as impressed with the target's dossier as was Sorokina, but now he did wonder if this lone man was here in some capacity to benefit her.

He couldn't think of any other reason she would have a tail. There was nothing in her file that suggested German or U.S. intelligence knew about her presence here, and there was no way in hell SVR or GRU would send two teams after the same target at the same time.

This odd man out was interesting to him, so he sent Bolichova into the elevator alone, telling her he was going to check something out before heading upstairs.

Pervak crossed the lobby and took a seat where he could see both Zakharova out the window on his left, and the mystery man alone at the bar.

Zoya was disappointed she had not learned more from Ennis during their nearly two-hour dinner. She did get the scoop on Mirza and Iravani, but once she'd brought up Miriam, the American had clammed up. She couldn't tell for certain if he stopped spilling the beans simply because he was worried about Shrike Group's veil of secrecy, or if it had to do instead with the fact that he'd shifted into brazenly making passes, and he treated all talk of work with complete disinterest.

As the evening wore on, he had seemed less inclined to pass out more intel, and more inclined to talk about his football days at San Diego State, and his travel and intrigue with the CIA. He talked about his divorce, about the loneliness of a bachelor on a long-term work assignment, and, after a second bottle of wine had been consumed, after they were halfway through their after-dinner drinks, he asked her to think of him not as a boss but as a close friend, a confidant, and whatever else she needed him to be.

Zoya thought him to be a self-absorbed prick, and never more so than when he spoke again.

"Your secrets, Zoya, *all* your secrets, I want you to know they are safe with me."

Ennis had the power to have Zoya killed by Moscow. He knew it, she knew it, and he knew that she knew it. Alluding to the danger while aggressively showing his interest in her was, as far as she was concerned, reprehensible.

The thought of grabbing her knife and plunging it into Ennis's carotid appealed to her, but she simply thanked him, and then she did her best again to steer him back to important matters. She couldn't be overt about it, she had to keep him comfortable talking around her, even if she didn't learn all she needed to know tonight.

But she pressed one last time. "You said we were tracking Haz Mirza."

He nodded.

"Are you the one on him?"

"Why do you ask?"

She shrugged, portraying nonchalance. "His name came up in my investigation today. Even if we have a horizontal structure at Shrike, it seems like I should be coordinating with whoever it is who has him under surveillance."

Ennis pounded his old-fashioned, sucked on the orange peel for a moment, then spit it back into the glass. "Forget about the way you used to work. We're different." She thought he was about to clam up for good, but instead he said, "Miriam is running the Mirza surveillance operation. Just telephonic conversations. She's not physically on his ass. If she learns anything relevant to your work with Sasani, I'm sure she'll communicate that to you." He smiled. "Through me."

"Good," Zoya said. "That's all I ask."

Finally, Ennis put the bill on his corporate card, and they stood and headed back into the lobby of the hotel.

Ennis had told her that his apartment was in Potsdam, but he had taken a room at the nearby Hilton for the last couple weeks of the Iran contract to avoid the daily commute into Berlin. It was just a few blocks' walk away, but he was following her back into the Adlon lobby, and not in the direction of his own hotel.

Zoya knew what his plan was.

On cue he said, "How about a nightcap upstairs?"

It was after ten p.m.; Zoya didn't know what tomorrow would bring, except for the fact that Ennis said Moises and Yanis would meet her in her room at ten a.m. for a breakfast meeting.

But it didn't matter what came tomorrow; even if she knew she had the entire day off, she didn't want to spend any more of tonight on Ric Ennis.

She shook her head politely. "I've got an early morning, sorry. Good night."

She turned for the elevator but made it just a couple of steps before Ennis took her by her upper arm. She spun back and looked at him, ready to tell him to take his fucking hand off her, but instantly something behind him drew her attention away from her creepy supervisor. A man strolling across the lobby fifty feet away stopped abruptly when she'd turned. Now the man walked over to some sofas, making a forty-five-degree adjustment to his earlier direction. Zoya had been trained to pick up on the movements and patterns of those around her, and in her heightened state now, this tell had not been difficult to detect. She had no idea if this was a Russian hit man sent after her, something else that posed a danger to her or her operation, or nothing more than a man who changed his mind about going to the elevators at the same time she turned around.

Ennis was unaware of all these thoughts going through Zoya's mind. "One drink," he pleaded. "Upstairs. Then I'll go." The man was clearly somewhat inebriated from the alcohol, but more than this, Zoya determined, he was drunk on his own confidence, certain he could cajole the vulnerable Russian woman into sleeping with him.

She looked back down at his hand. It lingered on her arm. "Ric. No." Her voice was strong, emphatic, but not angry.

Ennis released his grip slowly. When she looked up to his face, he held her gaze for several seconds, then gave a little smile. "Next time, maybe."

She wasn't thinking about next time. She wasn't thinking about Ennis at all.

She was thinking about the man on the sofa. His back was to her, but he would be able to see her in the window's reflection.

To Ennis she said, "Thank you for a pleasant evening." And then she turned toward the elevator.

This time Ennis let her go, and he spun away, began walking back to the restaurant and the exit to Unter den Linden there.

. . .

Court stood in the dark shadow of the grandfather clock in the lobby, some sixty feet from Zoya, as he watched her press the button for the elevator. He'd seen the slight altercation between her and Ennis, but as he was on the far side of the clock, he'd not seen what Zoya had seen, a potential follower caught in the open.

Court leaned back a couple of inches as Zoya scanned the room while waiting for her elevator, shielding him from her, but a moment later he heard the car arrive and the doors open. He waited an instant, leaned forward again, and saw the door as it closed.

Zoya was gone. This pleased him. He had no doubt but that she would be in for the night, and a five-star hotel like this would have decent security and an excellent camera system.

The Russians wouldn't stage a hit here in the hotel, of this he was reasonably certain. She was operating in the field, after all; there were too many opportunities for a successful hit and a quick getaway on the street, in the U-Bahn, on a streetcar, or in a café. To Court, the hotel would be the worst possible location for any assassin to act.

She was safe for now, as far as Court was concerned.

He stepped out from his spot near the grandfather clock, then turned his head to see Ennis leaving the hotel through the restaurant.

And then he saw something else. Ennis had a tail.

One of the men Court had recognized from the Starbucks across the street slid off a bar stool and headed after Zoya's dining companion as he left the restaurant.

Interesting, Court thought. It occurred to him he might not be tracking Russian hit men tonight, after all, unless the Russians also happened to have a tail on Ennis for some reason.

Doubtful, but possible. Perhaps their target was Zoya, but they wanted to understand Ennis's role before acting.

Court wanted to know where the other man in the duo had gone when the two split up, and since Zoya would likely lock herself in her suite for the rest of the night, he decided to terminate his coverage of her and shadow this unknown subject.

Court exited through the main door of the Adlon and then made a right, heading off in the direction Ennis and his follower had gone.

Zoya Zakharova exited the lobby of the Adlon via the western side door, moving along casually, but well aware there were likely eyes boring into the back of her neck even now.

She'd not climbed into the elevator, had not gone up to her room, but instead she'd shot across the lobby and headed back out into the night.

Zoya hadn't had much time to think through the best course of action, and she'd only come to this decision reluctantly. She told herself she needed to know if she did, in fact, have a shadow on her, and decided she'd run an SDR through nighttime Berlin to find out. It was an incredibly risky move; if this was, in fact, a hit man, her strolling through the darkness would give him an open target.

At the very least she would be giving him an opportunity to act.

But Zoya didn't like the idea of having this watcher in pocket right now and not exploiting the opportunity to learn something about the opposition. Who knew if she'd be able to find this guy, or one of his colleagues, in a crowd tomorrow before they shot her with a poison dart? He was on her now, and she needed to know his intentions *now*.

She carried a 9-millimeter SIG Sauer pistol in her purse, and this gave her the confidence she needed to take this dangerous stroll. She told herself she'd move through the neighborhood on foot for a half hour to an hour, to monitor the disposition of anyone following her, to look for handoffs of the surveillance to other shadows so she could identify them, to ID vehicles involved in the tail, and then she would adjust her own operational security accordingly.

If this was just one asshole sent to keep tabs on her movements, she'd continue with her assignment here in Berlin for CIA; if it was a well-trained team of Russian hitters, she'd call Brewer from a boarding gate at Tegel Airport before jumping on the next plane out of the capital.

Zoya was a professional; her mission was important to her, but she also knew how to look out for number one.

She walked under the Brandenburg Gate, passing people strolling along on a calm August evening, and then she turned to the left. As a bus rolled by she scanned its windows for a reflection showing any hint of someone tailing her.

She saw one person, too distant to know if it was the man she'd seen in the hotel after her spin back around caused him to fumble his surveillance of her. But it was definitely a lone figure in the dark, walking from the direction of the hotel, and Zoya had been doing this long enough to know she most likely had a tail.

She quickened her pace, nonchalantly tugging open the zipper of her purse as she did so.

Semyon Pervak followed the man who followed Zakharova, right in front of the U.S. embassy on Pariser Platz and in the direction of the Brandenburg Gate. He didn't know what the man had in store, nor did he know where the hell Zakharova was going, but he did know that he needed to call this in.

As he walked through the night he held his phone to his ear, waiting for his team's intel officer to pick up.

A second later he heard Inna say, "Anya says you were checking something out. I'm in the stairwell heading down now to back you up. You do *not* operate alone."

Sorokina sounded annoyed that he hadn't followed her instructions to return to the hotel room. He wanted to show her he knew his job better than she knew hers.

Pervak said, "Target is on foot, leaving hotel."

Sorokina was surprised by this. "What? Where is she going?"

"I don't know." Then Pervak tossed in, "She has a shadow."

Sorokina answered quickly. "A shadow? Who is this shadow?"

"Want me to go ask him?"

Sorokina snapped back. "I want you to follow him." She was clearly intrigued, though. "What are the chances they are together? That he's watching out for her?"

"Unknown," Pervak said, and then, "It looks like a standard foot-follow. I don't think he's working with her."

"I've been telling you for days that she is the best. She's ID'd her follower and she's running an SDR to see how many are on the team and to try to judge their skill. If they aren't with her, then they could be German or American intelligence, or . . . anybody else she's pissed off. Trust me, Sirena has enemies other than us."

This Pervak had worked out on his own, so he just kept walking, keeping himself at least fifty meters back from the man who was fifty meters behind Zoya.

Sorokina said, "Listen carefully, Semyon. Direct me to her, and I'll fulfill my obligation to give her a chance to surrender herself tonight."

"But the follower?"

"We need her to lose the tail before I get there. You can help with that."

Pervak nodded into the phone. "Kill him?"

"No. A mugging, something like that. Just take him off the chessboard. He might be armed, so watch yourself." She sounded to Semyon as if she were running down the stairs now. "Stay on the line and direct me."

"Passing under the Brandenburg Gate, making a left on Ebertstrasse. Come out the south side of the hotel and you can get in front of her."

"Copy," she said before hanging up.

Pervak adjusted his ill-fitting sport coat as he walked on, passing men and women here and there, but keeping his eyes on the man who had his eyes on Russia's public enemy number one.

THIRTY-EIGHT

Court moved east on Behrenstrasse, a block and a half southeast of the Kempinski hotel, tailing a man who was tailing a man who had just finished dinner with the woman he loved. His only plan was to try to get a fix on who this follower was, to make certain he wasn't part of a Russian kill team, and if he was, to somehow neutralize the threat.

The pain meds and the infection were going to make that already daunting task even more so, but he pushed himself forward, every step a chore, every block covered a sap to his already minimal energy and focus.

Far ahead, Ennis made a right on Mohrenstrasse, and his shadow, who had been walking on the opposite side of the street and behind him, crossed quickly and remained in pursuit, probably forty yards back.

Ennis turned suddenly, crossed Mohrenstrasse again, and stepped into the lobby of the Hilton Berlin. His shadow entered through a door on the west side.

Court stopped his advance now and stood alone in the darkened street, his legs more unsteady than ever. Ennis was going back to his hotel room, this seemed obvious enough. The tail would be heading in to surreptitiously get a look at what elevator floor he stopped on.

Could this be a hit? There had been opportunities to close on the target on the street if the man had wanted to do that. Walking into a four-star hotel to frag Ennis in front of cameras and witnesses would have been the wrong play. No, Court decided, this was just one of the two shadows he had detected earlier watching Zoya, and this one had branched off to follow her companion to learn more about him.

Just as Court himself now had done with Ennis's shadow.

Even through the fog threatening to overtake his brain, he'd been careful along the short stroll to keep one eye open for the other man he'd first seen outside the Starbucks. Now he was less worried about seeing two men, because if they had been working in a duo on the Ennis tail, then it would have been the other follower who actually went inside the building, and not the man who'd been directly on the target's ass for the entire walk.

Court knew this job, he understood the intricacies of the tradecraft better than almost anyone, and he was confident the show was over for tonight.

Unless, he realized, he could wait out here until the man learned what he needed to learn about Ennis and then went and met back up with his partner.

All Court wanted to do was to go see Dr. Kaya and get some pills that would make him feel like he wasn't trudging through chest-high molasses. He felt his body weakening by the minute, sleep fighting its way from his eyes, to his temples, and up into his frontal cortex.

And it was only ten thirty p.m.

But the mission came first, especially when the mission meant keeping Zoya alive.

He squatted down slowly on his haunches next to the revolving-door entrance to a bank that was long closed for the day. He sat back roughly against the window of the darkened space, then scooted his body deeper into the shadow of the corner of the doorway. If Ennis's tail came out the same door of the Hilton that he'd entered, Court would see him easily, but if he exited another door and headed back in the direction of the Adlon, Court would also have a view of him as he crossed Charlottenstrasse.

He closed his eyes a moment, thought of sleep again, then shook his head as he reopened them. An hour, no more, he told himself, and he'd be back at the Turkish doctor's flat, being pumped full of antibiotics and energy.

He also told himself he could tolerate the discomfort as long as he needed to in the interim. Tolerating discomfort, both physically and psychologically, was, in essence, his life.

But this time, he was wrong.

After less than ninety seconds his eyes closed and they did not reopen, and soon after his head lolled to the side.

Zoya's heart felt like a clenched fist, and her mouth was dry. She'd been in combat before, more times than she'd like to remember, and she'd faced death with regularity, both when she was SVR and then, in the past few months, as an operative in the CIA's ultra-black Poison Apple program.

But now she felt naked, unsure of the threats, unsure of what actions she should take to minimize them.

She just kept walking, all her senses roaring fires as she tried to discern the motivations of everyone in sight, tried to see into each dark window, divine the objective of the occupants of all the vehicles that passed her by.

She came to the Memorial to the Murdered Jews of Europe, a city-block maze of thousands of individual stone columns, lined by trees on the western side but otherwise open. During the day it would normally be covered in tourists, but tonight it looked like that which it was meant to represent, a graveyard. Many of the columns were no more than a meter high, some less, but as one traveled deeper into the maze, the stone monuments rose to several meters.

Zoya had originally intended to stay on the street, to make a left at the intersection ahead, perhaps to find her way back to the Unter den Linden U-Bahn or to climb aboard a streetcar, all part of her surveillance detection route to see if her tail would either follow or pass her off to others.

There was artificial lighting all around the monuments, but each of the 2,711 columns casts a shadow, so she knew that moving through them, as opposed to just remaining on the street, would be a labyrinthine haunted house for a woman nearly certain she was being followed by a man who aimed to do her harm. Still, she felt so exposed walking down the sidewalk, this actually seemed like the safer alternative.

She decided to use this danger as an opportunity. She turned suddenly and began heading into the columns, passing the low ones slowly, making sure she could be seen by whomever was on her tail.

Anyone who came in here after her, she decided, was a threat.

"Let's get on with it," she muttered to herself as she disappeared into the labyrinth.

Semyon Pervak walked on the far side of the street on the west side of Ebertstrasse, pangs of uncertainty creeping into his normally calm and confident tactical brain. He'd seen Zoya turn into the big, dark, and deserted memorial on the east side of the street, but in following her through the maze with his eyes from a distance, he'd managed to lose the man he was really tracking tonight, who had been walking well in front of him on the same side of Ebertstrasse.

Zoya's shadow, as far as Pervak could conclude, had ducked into the trees here lining the west side of the street, perhaps because he was worried his target was trying to lead him into a trap in the warren of monuments. The big Russian stepped into the trees now himself, began walking slowly and carefully, expecting to come up behind some crouching man peering across towards the east, weighing the danger of continuing the foot-follow against the desire of his superiors, whomever they were, for him to get the intel they wanted.

Semyon himself had lived through many moments like this while working surveillance.

The big Russian did not draw his pistol from its shoulder holster; he wasn't going to get into a gunfight tonight, but he did have a hooked-blade knife in a sheath behind his belt buckle, and his left hand hovered close to it while he spoke softly into his phone.

"Target has turned in to that monument thing."

"What monument thing?" Inna asked, her voice still breathless as she rushed to move into a position to intersect Zakharova.

"For the dead Jews."

Inna answered back quickly. "I'm passing it on the south side now. I'll go in and cut her off. Have you taken care of the shadow yet?"

As she asked the question, Pervak saw the man he'd been tailing. He was dead ahead, standing still and staring towards the memorial across the street through the trees. It was almost completely dark here, and the Russian knew that with the man's attention focused elsewhere, he would be able to close on him easily.

"Consider it done." He tapped his earpiece to end the call, and he slowed his advance, hunting Zakharova's shadow by moving slowly through the shadows himself.

Zoya Zakharova ventured deeper into the intricate memorial; her hand was shoved inside her purse, her fingers folded loosely on the grip and trigger guard of the little SIG Sauer P365 that she had already drawn from its pocket holster.

If this was, in fact, a Russian assassin behind her, the only thing that would stop him from acting right now was the very real possibility that he would suspect he was being led into a trap. Even so, a hitter sent after her would not be sent alone, so she knew to be on the lookout for others moving in from the street on her right, or hiding somewhere ahead.

That seemed unlikely to her, because no one would have been able to predict she would pass through the center of this thick maze of columns, so no one would know to lie in wait here in the middle of the all-but-abandoned memorial.

Not long after she considered this possibility, she walked by monuments one, two, even three meters over her head. It was nearly dark here, and she felt she was coming to the end of the block. She turned to the right, hoping to make her way out onto Hannah-Arendt-Strasse, just to the south.

But as soon as she turned, she saw a silhouette of a woman standing just meters ahead of her in front of a tall column, her arms raised.

A feminine voice spoke Russian. *"Ne strelyay."* Don't shoot.

Zoya pulled the pistol out of her purse, aimed at the woman's chest, then spun a quick glance over her shoulder to make certain the man she'd seen wasn't slipping up behind her. After a moment, fighting a jaw that wanted to clench from terror, she said, "Who are you?"

The woman slowly began lowering her hands, and Zoya pushed her arms out straighter, aiming the pistol between the woman's eyes now.

The woman's hands went back up as she spoke.

In Russian she said, "I'm an old friend, Sirena."

And just like that, Zoya knew without any lingering shred of doubt that the Kremlin had tracked her down.

THIRTY-NINE

Zoya kept her weapon on the mysterious Russian woman in front of her, but again she spun her head left and right, still worried about the tracker from the street.

She moved closer to the woman, both to get a better look at her face in the horrible light and to put some distance between her and anyone who might show up behind her in the columns.

At only four paces away, the face in front of Zoya became distinct.

She knew who this was, and she also knew it meant nothing good.

The woman said, *"Prevet, Zoya." Hello, Zoya.*

Zoya kept her gunsight on the woman's throat. *"Prevet, Inna. Kak zhizn?" How's life?*

Sorokina shrugged now, her hands still raised. "You know, the usual. Take a train to some town, eliminate a target, take a train out of town and on to the next."

"That doesn't sound much like the SVR I remember."

"I'm not SVR any longer."

Zoya nodded. She had suspected this the instant she recognized Sorokina. It would be strange to have a highly trained intelligence officer from the Russian security services involved in a direct hit in a European capital city. She said, *"Solntsevskaya Bratva? Da?* That does sound like them. Of course, you are doing the bidding of the Kremlin, just the same. You know that, right?"

"And who are you doing the bidding of, Sirena?"

"I'm just a woman trying to live her life in peace."

"I want the same. May I lower my hands so we can talk about peace?"

"Do you have a weapon?"

"Grach. In my backpack."

Zoya moved quickly to her, pushed her up against one of the taller concrete monuments, and frisked her quickly. She pulled out the Grach 9-millimeter, shoved it into her purse, then fished out a phone from Sorokina's bag and tossed it onto the ground. There was nothing else. She spun Sorokina back around, then quickly aimed her weapon both to her left and right, still searching for more members of the hit team.

"You're not here alone," she said as she scanned.

"Of course, I'm not. You are a scary girl; I wouldn't dare come by myself." She smiled. "Relax. There *was* someone following you. He wasn't one of mine, but I have one of mine taking him out of the picture."

"Who was following me?"

Inna shrugged, then lowered her hands finally, although Zoya hadn't told her she could. "I thought maybe you could help me figure that out. My guess is that someone is helping you, keeping tabs on you. Trying to keep you safe."

"Why would anyone do that?"

"You tell me, girl. I don't believe your story about working here for Shrike Group, unaffiliated with anyone else. Who is your master? Germany? America?" She said "America" as if the word repulsed her.

Zoya said, "Anyone who is on my tail is *definitely* not on my side." But, deep inside, she caught herself thinking about Court.

Could he be here, protecting her?

With a jolt of emotion, Zoya said, "Your goon. What did he do to the man following me?"

With an unconcerned shrug she said, "I told him not to kill him." She smiled a little. "We don't want to make the news, do we?"

Zoya let it go. It wouldn't be Court. It *couldn't* be. She lowered her gun a little but kept all senses alert, either for threats from Inna or for threats from others. "Why are you talking to me? Shouldn't you be slipping up beside me and poking me in the ass with a poisoned umbrella?"

Sorokina smiled more broadly now. Zoya saw it as a put-on. She wasn't feeling any levity. Still, she answered with, "It wasn't raining."

Zoya remembered Sorokina from SVR. The blonde was several years older, much more serious, focused on her work to the point where Zoya found her difficult to interact with.

Inna continued, "I have been sent with a message. Yasenevo wants you back."

"Really?" Zoya's tone was, to say the least, dubious.

"*Da.* I will not tell you all is forgiven. That would be a lie, and you would see it as such. But I *will* say you have assurances from men higher up on the food chain than you will ever know that you will not be harmed, and you will not be held captive beyond the debriefing period."

"That is so incredibly gracious of them," Zoya said, unsure if straitlaced Inna would even pick up on her sarcasm.

But, to her credit, Sorokina knew she had some more selling to do. "Your late father was a legend. An institution. No one wants to kill the daughter of General Feodor Zakharov." Zoya's father had been head of the GRU, Russian military intelligence.

In response, she said, "And if I refuse?"

"Tonight, me coming to speak with you? This is our passive measure. If you refuse to return to Moscow with us, we will have no choice but to resort to active measures."

Zoya said nothing.

"We will give you forty-eight hours to decide. And then we will find you, and we will kill you."

"Why would you do that? You've already found me."

"I expect you to run now. I would. But we will catch you in the open. Wherever you go."

Zoya spun her head to the left and right again. The two of them remained all alone. Then she said, "Just don't forget, finding me is the easy part. Killing me won't be quite so simple."

"Then it's a good thing I won't have to."

Zoya waited quietly. Inna was about to tell her who else was on the team sent by Moscow.

"You know me," the blonde continued. "Would they send me to pull the trigger? No. I was good, but I was no Zakharova. I am the brains. Not the brawn."

"The man back there, then? Is he the brawn?" She motioned back in the direction of Ebertstrasse, where the man who had been following her had presumably been neutralized by one of Sorokina's confederates.

But Sorokina shook her head. "He's something, a *mafia* hit man, reputable, reliable. But not our chief weapon. No, Sirena, Yasenevo has sent the very best along with me, because if you won't come peacefully, you will die violently."

Zoya said, "I could shoot you right now, deplete your team by one."

Inna smiled now. "But I'm not the one to fear, darling."

Zoya saw something in the smile; it was real, it was confident. Satisfied.

"Who is it?" she asked, unsure whether Sorokina would give up this information.

But she answered with a single word. "Maksim."

Zoya stared Inna down for several seconds before speaking again. Her response was delivered with calm. "You missed an opportunity to frighten me. I haven't been gone from the service so long not to know that Maksim Akulov was sent to a mental institution, quite against his will, a couple of years ago. The Kremlin is farming out its wet operations to washed-up old soldiers pulled out of the nut house?"

But Inna didn't smile back. She only said, "*Da*. They have done just that, exactly."

Zoya could see it on the woman's face, even in the low light. She wasn't lying. Softly, and in English, Zoya said, "Oh my God."

She knew the legend of the great Maksim Akulov, and her terror grew to unimaginable heights.

Court jolted upright, banging his head on the windowpane of the bank behind him. He realized quickly he'd been sleeping. He also realized, a little less quickly, that standing over him and looking down on him was the unknown subject he'd been tailing.

In English the man asked, "Who are you?"

Court couldn't detect an accent; his brain was still coming out of the haze of sleep. He started to pull himself upright with the help of the window, and the man even helped lift him to his feet by taking an arm.

Court recognized what probably had happened. Ennis's tail had come out the same door he'd entered, crossed the street here to head back towards his partner, no doubt somewhere back at the Adlon. And this put him close enough to see a man sleeping in the shadows. Any closer inspection of Court would make it obvious he was no vagrant. He'd been dressed to fit in inside a five-star hotel, after all; he couldn't fool anyone for a second that he was a homeless person seeking shelter for the night.

Nope, Court had been compromised, and he'd been compromised simply because he couldn't keep his infection-racked body functional.

And now his infection-racked body was going to have to deal with a much healthier man who had the drop on him.

Court spoke to him in Russian. He had no idea if the man was one of the hitters he assumed would be in the area hunting Zoya, but he was looking for a clue, a tell in the man's eyes that he knew Court wasn't who he claimed to be. Plus, if the man was German or American or any other nationality, Court's Russian would give him pause, and help misidentify the mystery man when Court got away.

If Court got away.

"Sorry. I'm drunk. Fell asleep. You are police?"

The man cocked his head; it told Court nothing specific. Still in English, he said, "Let's look in that rucksack of yours."

Court leaned back against the window, and his eyelids drooped but didn't drop fully. He kept his pack where it was on his back.

He wasn't in the mood for this bullshit.

"Hey." The man was louder now. "Your ruck. Hand it to me." He then switched to German and spoke not to Court but apparently to someone on the other end of a call through his Bluetooth earpiece.

Court's German wasn't great, but he understood. "I think I had somebody following me. Be on the lookout. Over?"

. . .

Semyon Pervak was five steps from the man kneeling in the woods when the dark figure stood and spun around suddenly, reaching for a pistol on his hip as he did so. The Russian was surprised by the movement; Pervak was certain he'd made no sound, but he hadn't survived the nineties on the mean streets of Moscow without knowing a thing or two about adapting to sudden threats. He wasn't in knife range, so he yanked his CZ 75 pistol out of its holster and raised it in the man's direction.

The shadow moved his hand away from his gun and raised his hands.

Softly, and in thickly accented English, Pervak said, "Give me your money."

"My money?" came the reply, also in English. The man seemed confused, and it didn't look like he was about to comply.

"Yes. Money."

The man looked at the weapon with more fascination than fear, then shrugged, and slowly began reaching for his wallet in his pocket.

Pervak closed on him quickly, planning on pistol-whipping the man across the temple to knock him out, but as he neared, the man dropped his wallet on the ground and used the distraction to try again for his gun. The big Russian lunged forward even faster, knocked the man's gun hand away, and crashed with him to the ground, jolting the man's earpiece from his ear as they began to fight on the pathway in the trees.

Zoya Zakharova did not know Maksim Akulov, save for his reputation. He'd been a Spetsnaz operator for the GRU, then a behind-the-lines Vympel assassin for the Russian government in Chechnya, Ukraine, and Afghanistan. He'd done hits for the SVR, as well, killings in America and the UK and Lithuania and Hungary, and these were just the ones Zoya had heard about.

She'd never even seen a picture of him.

The word was the man was off his rocker, had been since his twenties, but a couple of years ago she'd heard through the grapevine he was finished. He'd seen too much, done too much, to function in normal society in any capacity. Hell, if he was too crazy to kill people for a living, then Zoya figured he should probably spend the rest of his days chained to a wall in a padded cell.

But now, if Sorokina was to be believed, he was here, in Berlin, and Zoya was his target.

With a voice remarkably weak for a woman who held another woman at gunpoint, she said, "Why would they put him back in the field?"

Inna said, "Maksim has run this team for the past year, after being pulled out of Mental Hospital Number Fourteen, quite covertly." Inna kept talking. "You come with me now, Sirena, or Maksim appears by your side while you're eating dinner one night. Slices your sweet throat as you swallow a sweet bite of strudel."

Zoya went cold. She suddenly felt more alone and vulnerable than she'd ever felt in her life. She began moving to the right, towards the street to the south, but she kept the gun on Inna Sorokina.

"I am the last friendly face you will ever see," Sorokina said.

Zoya didn't find her face friendly at all. The gun quivered, and Inna saw this.

The older woman smiled a little. "You understand. There is only one chance for you. Come home, and talk to us."

The man pressing his hand into Court's chest, holding him upright against the window of the bank, had been trying to raise his partner over his earpiece, obviously without result. Court was hoping this guy would just take off to go check on his friend, who was probably just having regular comms trouble, the kind Court had dealt with countless times before.

Court spoke English now, with a fake Russian accent. "I go back to hotel. I no trouble, sir."

The man wasn't listening to him. He held his free hand to his earpiece, said, "Noah? Noah?"

Court saw an opportunity to sweep the man's hand off him, to spin him away forty-five degrees with the movement, and then to slam a left jab into his jaw, hopefully dropping him outright or at least stunning him enough for Court to get away. This he could all do easily if he were healthy, but at the moment it would take more speed, strength, and dexterity than he'd exhibited in many weeks.

So he stood there, pressed back against the window, and hoped that whatever glitch was preventing this asshole from communicating with his teammate would take precedence over the drunk Russian, and this man holding him would just run off into the night.

But Court's slim hope evaporated in an instant as a gunshot cracked, the sound rolling across the empty street from the west. It came from several blocks away, but the sound was unmistakable to a trained ear. It was clearly pistol fire.

Court had been as surprised at the sound as the man holding him obviously was, but Court didn't wait around to see how this man responded to the gunfire. He swept his right arm up, broke the man's grip on his shirt, then threw a punch at the side of the man's head that did nothing more than knock out his earpiece. The man bent forward and charged him, slamming Court into and then through the bank window, and both men flew inside, Court landing on his back and his opponent crashing down upon him amid a shower of glass.

Zoya spun to the sound of the gunshot behind her, then trained her weapon back on Inna. Even in the darkness Zoya could see that her former colleague at SVR had been as surprised at the sound as she had been.

Just as she turned away to move off into the dark, Zoya heard the woman call out to her in Russian. "Last chance, Sirena. The faster you run, the quicker we'll finish you."

Both women then heard the sound of a large pane of glass breaking in the distance, from the opposite direction as the gunshot. Sorokina turned to look that way, and Zoya used the opportunity to lower her pistol and take off through the monuments.

Every one of the simple polished concrete statues around her—and there were thousands—felt like a threat, a watcher in the night, an assassin breathing down her neck. She felt claustrophobic, near panic as she fled, desperate to get back to the relative safety of her hotel room and to call in to Brewer, because at this point she didn't know what else to do.

. . .

Court shook broken glass off his face before it dropped into his eyes and created even more problems. The man above him had his arms pinned, and though Court practiced judo and Krav Maga, he was too weak to get the man off him through any of the standard moves he would normally use in this situation.

Sirens clanged all over the small bank, echoed into the night, and Court knew that in seconds this now-empty street would be full of onlookers and police.

He stopped trying to pull away, and he went limp. The man above him sensed the unstated surrender, and then he looked around for his weapon, which had fallen free when they'd slammed into the tile flooring of the bank. He saw it a half meter beyond Court's head where he lay back on the floor, and the man started to reach forward for it.

And with this Court found an opportunity, though he groaned inwardly with the realization of what was about to happen.

As the man straddling Court leaned forward to scoop up his pistol, Court launched his head upward with all his might. With a sickening crack his forehead met the bridge of the man's nose, breaking it, stunning him, and causing him to slump over onto his side and off Court.

The American pulled himself to his feet with the last of his strength, rubbed the already swollen goose egg on his forehead, and climbed back out through the window as men and women began streaming out of the hotel across the street.

He staggered off in a daze, unsure about anything that had just happened, but keenly aware that his only objective right now was escape.

Semyon Pervak pulled the wallet off the ground next to the dead man, and then he climbed off him, his ears ringing from the gunshot he'd fired moments earlier. He put his hand on the trunk of a tree to steady himself, reholstered his weapon under his shoulder, and then turned to the west.

He was on the eastern edge of the massive Berlin Tiergarten, a 520-acre wooded park in the center of Berlin, through the middle of which ran the wide boulevard Strasse des 17. Juni.

Pervak knew the Adlon was to the east, as was the closest U-Bahn station that would take him out of the area, but the darkened tree-lined pathway to the west afforded him his best chance of escape. Were it not for the thin line of maple and oak between himself and the street, he would be in full view of the rear of the U.S. embassy right now, and he had no doubt that there would be cameras there that would have caught this entire event.

He jogged through the darkness and thought about what had just happened. He hadn't intended to kill the man; he'd been certain that he could have remained stealthy all the way up to when he would have clocked him with his pistol and temporarily taken him out of the equation, as Sorokina had requested.

But the man had turned suddenly in Pervak's direction, almost as if he'd received warning that someone was creeping up behind him. The man was fast and strong, and the instant he saw the man try to draw his gun, the big Russian realized he'd have to stop him from doing so, by either nonlethal or lethal means.

And when the man in the dark got his hand on the weapon, Pervak went lethal.

One shot into the upper chest, from a range of less than two inches, and the shadow dropped his weapon and went still.

Semyon trained his CZ on his victim's forehead, and he stood and kicked the man's HK pistol out of reach. He quickly knelt down, fished through the man's clothing, and finally pulled his wallet off the ground where he'd dropped it.

As he raced through the park now he thought of the wallet, still in his left hand. He'd just slowed and begun looking through it when his phone began to ring.

"Yeah?"

"What happened?"

"I killed him."

"I told you to—"

"Yeah, well, he went for his gun. He was in comms with someone else, I think. Maybe Zakharova? She warned him."

Sorokina was clearly hoofing it, as well; her voice was breathless as she spoke. "I was with Zakharova. She didn't communicate with anyone." Then she asked, "Did you hear the glass smashing to the east?"

"I can barely hear *you*. Did you forget I just fired a pistol?"

"Are you clear?" she asked, and Pervak had had enough of Inna Sorokina.

"You take care of you, I'll take care of me. I'll be back at the Adlon in the morning. Have Maksim ready. Zakharova won't be sticking around long after tonight." And then he hung up, focusing his attention on the wallet in his hands, hoping to get some idea who he had just killed.

He pulled the German license from the closed billfold and saw that the man's name was Noah Fischer. Then he opened the billfold fully, and saw credentials identifying Noah Fischer as an officer in the Bundesamt für Verfassungsschutz. The BfV. German domestic intelligence.

Shit, Pervak thought.

The Krauts are after Zakharova, as well.

FORTY

Court made it to Dr. Kaya's flat just after eleven, and he rang her call button, then waited for her to buzz him in. After a minute he buzzed again, but she appeared in the darkened lobby and unlocked the door herself. As soon as she saw him, she took him by the arm without speaking. There were other residents returning home at the same time, but she put him in an empty elevator and stepped in behind him before anyone saw him.

When they began their ascent, she said, "I won't ask you what happened to your forehead. That, I can treat with ice. But you have a fever, a bad one, I can tell by looking at you."

With discomfort in his voice, he said, "I can tell by *being* me."

"As soon as we get into my flat, I want you to lie on the settee."

"What's a settee?"

"It's the couch you used three years ago."

"Right."

"I'm going to give you a course of IV antibiotics and some pain meds. I also have something for energy, but you'll want to wait till morning to take—"

"First I need a place to make a phone call. In private."

"Look at you, you're about to pass out."

"I already did pass out, so I guess I'm well rested."

She looked at him like he was insane. "You're anything but well—"

"It's a joke. Please, a five-minute phone call and then I'm all yours."

When they got off on her floor she led him up a flight of wooden stairs, and then onto the roof of the building. There were a few plants and chairs there for the residents, but this late at night, it was empty and quiet.

The young woman left him alone, and he called Brewer using his Signal encryption app.

She answered, he gave her his ID credentials, and then he said, "Zoya and Ennis had a two-man team on them tonight. She went to her room, so I followed one of the men when he started a tail on Ennis. He made me, we got into it, and I—"

"Were you two blocks away from the Adlon?"

Court replied, "Yeah, more or less. Anyway, I—"

"You killed him," Brewer said.

"No, I didn't kill him. I rang his bell, busted his nose, maybe, but he'll be fine. He could have been Russian, but he also could have been—"

Brewer interrupted. "Less than ninety minutes ago, two blocks away from the Adlon Kempinski, a man was killed. He was an officer in the BfV. Are you going to tell me you didn't do it?"

"BfV?" *Shit.* He thought back to his encounter outside the Hilton. After a moment, he said, "There was a gunshot. The man I fought had a partner. He couldn't raise him. Somebody must have—"

"*Somebody?* Even if it wasn't you, if you got your face on any cameras in the area, it's not going to look good."

"Maybe they were going after Anthem," Court said. "Has she checked in?"

Brewer did not hesitate an instant. "I just spoke with her. She's fine. She heard the gunshot, too, but says she was in her suite with the door locked when it happened."

Thank God, Court thought.

Now Brewer said, "Listen very carefully, Violator. Security is going to be even tighter around Anthem's hotel. Around the embassy, too."

"Because the murder happened near the U.S. embassy?"

"That, and . . . and other reasons."

Court understood. "Yeah, the thing Hanley keeps hinting at. Are we nuking Iran or something?" It was a joke, generated by a brain that was barely conscious and told by a man who wasn't in a good mood.

But Brewer didn't seem to take it as a joke at all. "Something," she said.

"Seriously?"

"I want you to cease your surveillance of Anthem and find Annika Dittenhofer," Brewer said next.

"Anthem is the only reason I'm here."

"Anthem is safe. She'll be in her hotel tomorrow, not in the field."

"All right," he said. "If you can assure me Anthem is secure, that the Russians don't know about her being in Berlin, and that she's going to remain in place for the next day, I'll go after Dittenhofer."

"I can assure you of all these things. Get back to work."

Court hung up, slipped his phone into a pocket, and sat there in the warm evening. He had not told Brewer the complete truth, and he imagined she hadn't told him the complete truth, either. He would comply with her request that he find Annika Dittenhofer—eventually. But the right play for him, right now, was to somehow make contact with Zoya. They could work this together, he just had to find a way to do it where he didn't blow her cover.

He shook his head to wake himself fully, then stood up on shaky legs. First things first, he told himself. He headed downstairs to Dr. Kaya's apartment, steadying himself on the stairs as he descended by dragging a shoulder along the wall.

Suzanne Brewer hung up the phone in her office on the sixth floor of the McLean, Virginia, headquarters of the CIA, then looked up and across her desk to Matthew Hanley. Usually the DDO had loosened his tie and removed his jacket by now; it was after five p.m., after all. But though he was neither a slave to protocol nor to fashion, at the moment he wore his best suit, his crispest white shirt, and a muted blue necktie secured under his collar in a full Windsor.

Brewer was subordinate to the DDO, but she was supremely sure of herself. The DDO, on the other hand, wore his conflicting thoughts on his face. "We said we'd pull Anthem if the Russians found her. She just called you and told you the Russians found her."

Brewer did not hesitate in her reply. "It's too early to pull her. When she called a half hour ago, I told her as much."

"I agree, unfortunately." Then Hanley asked, "Where the hell was Violator tonight? He was supposed to be watching Anthem's ass."

Brewer said, "He was off scene, tailing someone else. He doesn't know anything about what happened to Anthem."

Hanley said, "It was the right call, unfortunately, not telling Court about Anthem's encounter with the Russian tonight. How is Zoya now?"

Brewer nodded. "I told her we'd put Berlin station on her to watch her back. That settled her down a little."

Hanley sighed. "Yeah, well, we can't do that, can we?"

"Of course not. Berlin station would be uncovered via PowerSlave, and that would compromise Anthem. Plus, we do not want to get into a war with Russian intelligence, even if this bunch after her are mafia hitters working in the interests of Moscow but not under their direct employ. This shooting tonight is going to make everything harder, I suppose, but it doesn't change our critical need for intel."

Hanley looked at his watch, then pulled himself up to his feet. "Well, I've got to get to the White House. I will be there the rest of the night." He paused. "Listen. I need everything I can get from both of the Poison Apple assets. By tomorrow morning I expect we are going to be dealing with a ticking clock."

"You still can't tell me what's about to happen tonight?"

He shook his head, then shrugged a little. "I can tell you that what we are about to do is as righteous as anything we've ever done, but it sure as hell is *not* about making this shitty world a safer place."

Hanley grabbed his briefcase and headed for the door.

When she was alone, Suzanne Brewer took a few calming breaths, and she thought about everything that was going on in Berlin. The Iranians were her enemy, of course, but as far as she was concerned, so were Anthem and Violator. Working with them in the Poison Apple program had unquestionably stunted her career, and she wanted nothing more in this world than to be away from Matt Hanley, away from Zoya Zakharova and

Zack Hightower, and far, far away from Court Gentry. It was the only way forward for her, but for now, she knew she had to be the good soldier and do her job.

Court lay on the sofa in Dr. Azra Kaya's small but comfortable flat, with an IV stuck in his left arm and a bag of antibiotics and saline hanging from a floor lamp next to him, dripping slowly but steadily through the line and into his bloodstream. He wore an ice pack on his forehead, and his pistol was hidden from the civilian in the small of his back under him.

The infusion of antibiotics did nothing to make Court feel better; that would happen only after weeks of regular doses. But the other things she had given him—anti-inflammatories, narcotic painkillers, B vitamins, and bottled water with electrolytes for hydration—were taking the edge off his aches, pains, and general malaise.

Azra Kaya had taken it upon herself to feed the injured operator, as well. While the IV emptied slowly into his arm, Azra made a simple dinner of pork cutlet and mashed potatoes with sauerkraut, and Court wolfed down his portion while she sat nearby at the table and ate.

He washed down a swallow of food with fortified water, but before taking his next bite, he said, "Something bad happened tonight, not far from here. It will be on the news. I want you to know, I had absolutely nothing to do with it." He motioned to his forehead. "This is not from that."

In truth, he *had* had something to do with the killing of the BfV man tonight. He hadn't shot the man he had been pitted against, but the man killed might have had a partner there to back him up if Court hadn't taken the other man's attention.

He didn't know, but he also didn't feel terrific about knocking the shit out of a German intelligence officer who had just been doing his job.

"What happened?" Kaya asked.

"A man was killed. A German government employee."

She put her fork down and turned to him. "If you didn't have anything to do with it, then why are you telling me?"

Court swigged more water, then shrugged. "I don't really have an answer. I guess I want you to know I'm not the kind of person who would do that."

But was he? he questioned.

Azra said, "My oath is to treat my patients to the best of my ability. I am doing that with you. I don't know who you are, or what you have or have not done. I can't even let myself care."

Court sensed that she *did* care. But he said, "Okay, that's fair. But I'm here for good, not bad."

The doctor stood up from her empty plate, lifted the frosty bag off Court's forehead, and looked at the bruise there. He could see his reflection in a mirror behind the sofa. Though the ice was doing its job keeping the swelling to a minimum, it was still purple and slightly raised.

Dr. Kaya said, "I get the strong impression that someone didn't feel the same way."

Court smiled. "Clearly he did not." He looked up at her. "I don't get it."

She replaced the ice. "Get what?"

"Why do you do this? Why do you let fucked-up strangers in your house like this? I realize you are getting paid, but you don't seem the type."

"You don't seem fucked up."

"Oh, I guarantee you, I am."

She smiled at this, thought over his question for a moment. Finally she said, "Three years ago, when I was new at the hospital, a fourth-year med student and an old family friend, also a doctor from Turkey, took me aside and asked if I wanted some help paying off my school loan, to earn some extra money. He was retiring and moving back to Ankara. He introduced me to a Frenchman who said he would pay me a small retainer every month to be ready at any moment to treat patients outside the hospital system.

"I was scared, at first. But I needed the money, and I worried about what care these people would receive if they could go to no doctor at all. Plus, it's not illegal to give medical care to a criminal. So, I said yes.

"The Frenchman told me I might not hear from him for years, but just a month or so later, a call came late at night. A man was on his way to see me, and I needed to be prepared to treat a traumatic injury.

"I was off work that night and was afraid to try to sneak a wounded man into the hospital, but my apartment was quiet, and I could get whatever I needed from a minor care clinic nearby, where I worked on one of my rotations. So I sat here, and waited."

Court jumped in. "And I showed up."

She went back to her chair at the table and sat down. "I felt good about what I did because I could tell you were a nice man. That, and the money, ensured I would continue working for the Frenchman. It's been over three years now." Her face grew darker, and she let out a sad little sigh. "I've yet to meet another nice man doing this."

"I'm sorry."

Dr. Kaya shrugged. "I don't know who the people who are sent to me are, where they come from. What they have done. But there have been eight so far, all badly injured. One did not survive." She seemed pained by this. "I believe in the work. Everyone deserves a chance at life, and I can give them that chance. But the other men . . . have been more difficult." She looked up at him now. "Why were you different?" she asked.

He said, "That night. I'm used to stuff like that. But it was a tough time for you, I could see that. I felt bad." After a moment he added, "I was lonely. It's part of the job, but when you do meet someone outside of the work, it reminds you what normal people are like. You were normal."

"Are you still lonely?"

Court hesitated. "Sometimes." Then he added, "But that's not why I'm here."

She laughed nervously as she stood from her table again. "Yes, of course it's not." She came over and checked the IV bag.

The pain meds were kicking in, and he was fed and comfortable. He felt reenergized. He still needed sleep, or at least he needed the Adderall she'd given him to keep going, but he wouldn't take the pills yet, and he wouldn't sleep until he got back to his little flat in Spandau.

More than anything, though, he wanted to talk to Zoya. He knew what Hanley and Brewer thought of the matter. That it would be too dangerous for him to make direct contact with her. But he told himself there had to be a way, because Zoya was in too much danger now to keep going forward under cover.

German intelligence officers were definitely following her, and he thought it likely Russian assassins would soon arrive to kill her. And he had been compromised to some sort of paramilitary unit that was trying to kill him.

He needed to speak to Zoya, to convince her to get out of town before it was too late.

Dr. Kaya stepped back over and gently pulled the IV out of his arm, bringing him back to the moment.

He climbed to his feet and immediately realized he'd recovered a lot of his strength in the past hour. "I really appreciate it."

"You might feel a little euphoric, revitalized. But remember, you need to take it easy."

"Nobody sends me anywhere for easy." He pulled a wad of euros from his pocket. "Here's five thousand. Is that enough?"

She took the money. "That's plenty. For the week, two if you are around. Reach out whenever you need me."

She reached down and picked up a paper bag from the table. "Everything you need is in here. Use the Adderall sparingly. Twenty milligrams maximum at any one time, no more than twice a day. Remember, it's to keep you awake and alert, it's not to turn you into Superman."

"You got it."

He left Dr. Kaya's building just after midnight, climbed into a taxi nearby, and headed back to Spandau. He would walk the street for a while and then return to his spartan little flat. He had work to do still, and then he'd get a couple hours' sleep. Tomorrow, he told himself, he would execute his quickly forming plan to make contact with Zoya.

FORTY-ONE

General Vahid Rajavi looked at his diamond-encrusted gold watch by pulling back the sleeve of his white shirt, then he sat up straighter in the cabin chair of the Airbus A320 and smoothed out the wrinkles in his suit coat.

As the commander of the Islamic Revolutionary Guard Corps' Quds Force, he never wore military dress when he was outside official functions in Tehran. He instead preferred to blend in, at least as well as any man with eleven bodyguards can blend in anywhere.

He was the military intelligence chief of the Islamic Republic of Iran; the threats against him were manifest, so he and his team took every precaution possible.

The plane touched down at Baghdad International Airport at three fifteen a.m.; Rajavi was greeted by a Shia representative of the Iraqi government, and then they all piled into seven vehicles and left the tarmac in single file.

A minute later they were through the first gates and on Airport Street, an access road that would take them off BIAP property to the east on their way to the city. There was little conversation; it had not been a long or arduous flight, but the Iranians who climbed off the Airbus had a full day of clandestine meetings ahead of them, and while Rajavi was anxious to get started with them, his protectors were anxious to get him back onto the plane and back into Iranian airspace.

They rolled along in near silence. Next to them a Silk Way Airlines Antonov An-24 cargo plane landed on the runway, then slowed, turned onto a taxiway, and headed towards the terminal.

General Rajavi redirected his attention forward out the windshield as they drove to the airport exit.

The five men in the Quds Force commander's vehicle just looked out at the road ahead of them through their headlights, each with different thoughts, all kept to themselves, and then, one instant later, they simply ceased to exist on this earth.

As far as the commander of Quds Force and the rest of his entourage were concerned, when the missiles hit, there was no sound, and there was no light.

The noise and the light came after, but Rajavi and his entourage missed it all. The impact of the four Hellfire missiles, fired simultaneously from a pair of U.S. Air Force Reaper drones flying forty-two miles from Baghdad and thirty-five thousand feet above the desert, sent a shock wave across the airport and lit a row of glowing pillars of fire.

While the scattered remains of the victims lay motionless along the road and in the brown grass alongside it, fires burned all around, and wreckage blazed and smoked.

It would take little time for locals to confirm the death of General Vahid Rajavi. His distinctive watch was attached to a severed left arm found sixty-four meters away from his burning SUV, and a charred and still body missing the same appendage sat motionless in the center of the fire.

Matthew Hanley had been in the White House Situation Room with the president of the United States and other national security staff as they watched the feed in real time, but it wasn't until two hours later that official word came in. Hanley woke to the ringing secure telephone next to his bed as a summer storm whipped the air outside. "Yeah?" he said, battling with the hoarseness of sleep.

"Deputy Director. It's done."

"Confirmed KIA?"

"Confirmed."

"Collateral?"

"Eighteen dead, including bodyguards and an emissary from the Iraqi government. Someone from their diplomatic corps, as well."

Hanley nodded into the phone, then said, "To hell with them."

"I'd say that's a safe bet, Deputy Director."

Hanley hung up, then listened to the rain, the wind, and the rumbling thunder as the storm passed over D.C. He wasn't going to grieve for the fucking general of Quds. The man had the blood of hundreds of Americans on his hands, and that of thousands, tens of thousands, of other men, women, and children. Nor did he grieve for those close enough to Rajavi's inner sanctum of evil to be driving along in a convoy in Iraq, on a mission to sow only more discord.

But he was worried, because he knew this meant a response would be coming at a time and place of Iran's choosing, and he did not feel like his agency was adequately prepared to deal with it.

FORTY-TWO

The news from Baghdad filled Sultan al-Habsi with beaming pride. As he sat at a desk in the residential quarters at the UAE embassy on Hiroshima-strasse in the center of Berlin, his thoughts were on his plans—those already realized, and those still to come.

He considered calling his father right now but he decided to let the old man sleep a couple more hours. He would be told by his aides at the hospital upon wakening, and he would know for certain that his son had prognosticated this just days earlier.

Sultan, even as operational director of the Signals Intelligence Agency, had made tonight happen; he had personally orchestrated the killing of the man responsible for the deaths of both of his brothers.

His plan had involved using the Americans as proxies. He had no way to kill the most well-protected Iranian himself. His own intelligence outfit was struggling in Yemen; they were hardly capable of finding, fixing, and finishing a target as elusive as the commander of Quds Force in Iran.

But Sultan did have a weapon at his disposal. He was a key and respected informant for American intelligence; they relied on him for his knowledge of the region and its actors, and he could begin tailoring his intelligence product in a way that would, over time, place a large red X on the head of General Rajavi.

And this is exactly what he did.

It took five months, but a Quds Force operative in Baghdad spoke a cryptic code over his phone, a code the SIA had deciphered. The man told a compatriot in Tehran that everything was ready for "the visit," and then it was simply a matter of tracking the aircraft Rajavi always used to make his international flights on the night mentioned in the code.

Killing Rajavi had always been a possibility for the Americans, but in the past they had been leery of fomenting Shia anger to new heights. But when the Europeans relaxed sanctions, the Iranians killed American soldiers in Syria, and there seemed to be no way to stem the tide of a new Iranian ascendancy. The Americans, after listening to the good counsel of al-Habsi, the CIA's number one ally in the Middle East, decided a blow needed to be struck at the heart of Iranian military intelligence leadership.

And this they did.

It was all going to plan for Sultan, except for the American, Gentry, who had somehow appeared in Venezuela, and then again today here in Berlin. Al-Habsi had no idea what his knowledge was about all this, nor what his relationship was *to* all this.

Hades had lost another member of his team today attempting to take the former paramilitary operations officer down, and this noise and attention on the periphery of al-Habsi's operation was now a clear and present danger to the entire scheme.

Al-Habsi had PowerSlave operating, searching for the American, and he hoped like hell he could both (a) get another hit on the man's whereabouts, and (b) get Hades and his remaining operators there in time to eliminate him.

Otherwise, there was no telling how much trouble the Gray Man might cause.

He successfully pushed this one wrinkle out of his mind, and he thought about his ultimate objective.

He wanted war between the great superpower of America and the evil Shia regime in Iran.

And this would happen only after the next stage of his plan was initiated.

Al-Habsi felt betrayed by the Americans and the Europeans. The Americans talked a good game, diplomatically they pressured Iran to some degree, and they spent a lot of money spying on Iran's nuclear program, but getting the president to green-light this necessary targeted assassination had been like pulling teeth, and he knew Washington had no plans to escalate pressure on the Shias.

And the Europeans made no pretense but that they were all but allied with Iran.

Sultan al-Habsi realized that America and Europe were not his allies. They were, instead, impediments to his goal.

So he felt no qualms about them suffering collateral damage.

He was pleased his father had lived to see Rajavi's death, and he prayed the old man would stay around for the finale of the show.

Court slept on a pile of towels and clothing arrayed on the bathroom floor of his Spandau apartment, aided by the pain medication taking the brunt of the sting out of his shoulder and the spot above his right eyebrow that he had used to break the nose of a German intel officer.

He woke to the clock radio on the floor just outside his bathroom turning on. It was six a.m., which meant he'd slept almost four hours, and he felt . . . not good, but not too bad.

There was a bustle outside as people headed out on the street. Then he heard footsteps on the stairs right outside his thin walls.

He slid his hand up to his Glock pistol lying on the cheap vinyl floor next to his head and wrapped his fingers around the grip.

But the footsteps continued on past his floor.

The radio was turned to Deutsche Welle, a news station, and a breaking story began a few seconds later. It was in German, but Court picked up the majority of the correspondent's words.

General Vahid Rajavi, the Quds Force chief shithead, had been killed in a missile strike in Iraq. The German media speculated that the attack was carried out by either America or Israel, but as Court sat up, rubbed his eyes, and then massaged his shoulder distal of where he'd been stabbed, he had no doubt what had happened.

Matt Hanley had warned that something big was about to go down, something that would not necessarily make the world a safer place.

America had blown the Iranian general straight to hell, Court had no doubt.

Rajavi was a prick, this Court knew without question, so it was debatable as to whether this would have a net positive effect on planet Earth. It all depended on what Iran and its proxies did in retaliation.

There was speculation about this on the German news, as well. Protests were a given, violence was expected, and some sort of military response from Iran was all but assumed.

The second story was less surprising to Court, though it would be a shock to most anyone else in Berlin. A German government intelligence official had been murdered in the center of the city the evening before, the victim of a gunshot wound.

There was little information about the victim, and no description of the killer was given. He wondered if that would change, and he wondered if someone fitting his description might eventually be implicated.

Court pulled himself to his feet with the help of the sink next to him. He caught a glimpse of his face in the mirror; the bruise above his eye was just a faint dull gray, and he credited Dr. Kaya's care for that.

He'd thought through his next course of action while lying on the bathroom floor the evening before. He knew he was supposed to begin his hunt for Annika Dittenhofer; that was what Brewer and Hanley wanted out of him, but he'd come here to help Zoya. If Brewer was telling the truth, then Zoya would be holed up in her hotel suite all day.

A suite made safe enough with cameras and security, but a suite Court had no doubt at all he could get into.

He fished twenty milligrams of Adderall out of a bottle and popped it into his mouth along with an antibiotic and several anti-inflammatories. He'd stay off the narcotics throughout the day, despite the pain, because he needed to be extra sharp for what was about to come.

After a shower, he shaved off his beard for the first time in months, then took a razor to his head, buzzing the whole thing. He wasn't bald, his dark hair remained, but he looked completely different now.

If he'd been picked up on cameras around the Adlon the night before, he wouldn't be recognized there today.

Unless PowerSlave got him, he told himself with no small amount of concern.

He left the apartment at seven a.m., a man reborn via certain artificial enhancements, but a man reborn nonetheless.

Zoya Zakharova had slept on a row of bed pillows she'd lined up in the large walk-in closet in her large two-room suite. She woke at seven a.m., then reached up and fingered the small SIG Sauer P365 pistol she kept inches from her face.

All the thoughts from last night came back to her in a flood. The walk through the memorial garden, the confrontation with Sorokina, the gunshot and the shattering glass.

It was more than a minute before she started thinking again about the operation Hanley had sent her to Europe to undertake, and she wondered if she would ever get the intel on Shrike Group the Agency needed, especially now that she'd been so utterly compromised by the Russians.

Who had exposed her? She'd lain in her faux bed in the closet for over an hour before sleep last night trying to answer this very question. It *had* to have been Ennis, or this Miriam character, real name Dittenhofer, although she'd never met the woman. She didn't think it would have been Moises or Yanis, but she couldn't rule them out, either.

She checked her phone and found that a text had come in over the night from Suzanne Brewer. It was a link to a news article on UPI.

Iranian general killed in drone strike.

Zoya assumed this had happened in Yemen, but she clicked on the story. In seconds she saw why Brewer had sent her the piece.

Shit. So the U.S. fragged the commander of Quds Force. When Zoya spoke with Brewer last night, just after her encounter with Inna Sorokina, Brewer had promised her that Berlin station would put men on her, at a safe distance, to keep any Russian hit team at bay. It hadn't really calmed the Russian woman to learn this; she expected that Maksim Akulov and his team would run robust countersurveillance of their own operation and adapt accordingly. But even last night, Zoya had known her work was important.

Someone was killing enemies of Quds Force in Berlin, and now she'd learned that this had been going on directly in advance of an American assassination of the Quds Force commander.

This was no coincidence.

She sat up slowly, the stress firing burning acid throughout her stomach.

She told herself she was safe for now, at least in the hotel, and that exercise would help her calm down. She climbed out of the closet and headed to the bathroom, with plans to go downstairs to the gym.

At the far end of the hallway, inside suite 401, there was a flurry of activity. Semyon Pervak stood shirtless in the bathroom, using his big, brawny arms to hold the much smaller and utterly naked Maksim Akulov under an icy shower to revive him from the lingering effects of the night before. In the suite, Inna Sorokina and Anya Bolichova had dressed and armed themselves, and they had packed all their luggage save for what they needed for the assassination, placing all the Gucci bags by the door.

They then returned to the three laptop workstations on the kitchen table to monitor the various camera feeds split onto two of the computers as well as the real-time room service log on another.

Zoya had slept in her closet; this, both women assumed, was due to Inna's encounter with her the night before causing her enough terror to upset her normal routine. They'd only sat down and confirmed through the room service screen that Zakharova had yet to order her daily breakfast when they saw their target's closet door open on the bedroom camera. Zakharova stepped into the bathroom near the door, then exited it a few minutes later.

Her two watchers fully expected her to go to the room phone to place her breakfast order, but instead she got dressed in black tracksuit bottoms and a sweatshirt that read *Universität Heidelberg*.

Bolichova said, "She's adopting some kind of college student disguise, maybe?"

Inna did not reply, she only watched the feed.

Both Russian women next saw their target slip a holstered pistol into a backpack, along with a one-piece swimsuit, a room key, and a few other items.

Then she headed for the living room of the suite.

Both Inna and Anya rose to their feet; Bolichova ran to the door's peephole to look out and Sorokina hurried back through the bedroom, into the bathroom, where she encountered a very naked but surprisingly sober-acting Maksim. Semyon was no longer holding him; the assassin stood on his own two feet next to the shower, his impossibly lean and sinewy body covered with both scars and tattoos.

He raised an eyebrow at his intelligence officer, Pervak tossed him a towel, and Maksim nonchalantly secured it around his waist while she talked.

"Zakharova is in the hall. She's leaving."

"What's she wearing?"

"Looks like workout gear. Swimsuit in her bag."

"Then she's going to the gym." Maksim said it with confidence, then reached for his pack of cigarettes on the sink.

"Hurry up," Sorokina demanded, then looked at Pervak. "Put your shirt on. We can do this right now."

She rushed back through the bedroom and into the living room, then leaned over the other woman on the team, who was again seated at the computers watching the screen.

Bolichova said, "She got off on the second floor. Looks like she's heading to the spa."

"What would it take to shut off all cameras to the spa?"

"A press of a few buttons, but I don't advise it."

"Why not?"

"You'd also want to control the cameras for Maksim's movement into the location. Doing the job here on the fourth floor would be a lot easier. I've prerecorded the empty hall to play back during the hit. Hotel security won't see a thing. If you want Maksim to go down to the second floor, kill her in the health club, and then get out of the building, I'll have to bring the entire system down. Easy to do, but hard to fool anyone as to what is happening. Police will be here in minutes, and it definitely won't seem like natural causes when they find that the hotel cameras have been tampered with."

Maksim had followed Inna out of the bedroom, still wearing only the towel. "We go with the original plan. She'll be hungry after her workout, and she'll order food and coffee when she gets back to her room."

Inna looked again at Anya. "What about making entry on her room now? Lie in wait for her. I can open the lock."

"No," Pervak said. "This scenario benefits us. We use the time we have now while she's in the gym to get all the luggage out of the building except for two laptops and our weapons. When she comes back, we go in."

Inna turned to Maksim. "When she calls for breakfast, they'll tell her twenty minutes, but you go in fifteen. We cut the cameras seconds before we open this door, and you take the cart. This needs to look like suicide. The best way to ensure that is to overpower her at gunpoint, put her in the tub, then slit her wrists. When she bleeds out, you leave, then put the Do Not Disturb sign on her door. No one from the hotel will enter all day." She smiled. "We'll be in Moscow by then."

"What about the real room service?" Semyon asked.

Anya Bolichova answered this. "Just like D.C. I'll call and cancel it before it comes up. Spoof the phone in Zakharova's suite so they think it's her."

This made sense to everyone, Inna included. She turned to Maksim. "Put your room service attendant's uniform on, and be ready."

He saluted the woman sarcastically, then turned on his heel, leaving a cloud of cigarette smoke behind in the room as he left.

Zoya opted for a swim in the large indoor pool. She put her backpack in a locker, leaving the door open while she put on the one-piece suit she'd bought upon arrival here at the Adlon once she saw the great pool. She pulled her little SIG Sauer from the pack and slid it up through a leg hole in her suit, eventually pushing it up around her midsection. She wouldn't be able to draw it especially quickly, but, she reasoned, if she met any threats while she was in the pool, having a gun on her, though inconvenient to access, would be better than the alternative.

But she didn't really think it likely that she was in great danger now. Zoya knew a thing or two about Russian government-ordered extrajudicial killings, and all she knew on the subject told her there was no way Maksim Akulov would come into the center of a five-star hotel, full of cameras, for such a brazen hit.

No, if the Russians got her, she decided it would be by them running her down with an SUV as she stepped off a streetcar.

Still, the pistol gave her the peace of mind she needed to dive into the pool.

She swam laps, executed racing turns at each end, measured her breathing, felt the endorphins pumping into her brain.

Exercise always helped her relax, but this morning it was difficult to think of anything more than the fact that the fabled Maksim Akulov, an insane hit man of incredible skill, was here targeting her.

And the only reason he would know to come here, to be able to find her, was that her masters at Shrike Group had somehow slipped Moscow the intel. Wittingly or unwittingly, she had no idea, but for a woman who trusted no one, her mistrust had now reached a crescendo.

She swam faster and faster, anxious to get her workout in and return to her room.

Her plan to obtain intel for the CIA was thin today, this she knew, because her focus was fixed firmly on her other plan, her plan to dodge Russian assassins.

FORTY-THREE

Quds Force sleeper operative Haz Mirza climbed out of the Westphalweg U-Bahn station in Berlin's southern Mariendorf neighborhood, looked up at a low gray sky, and wondered how soon he would die.

It was only eight a.m., but Mirza had been up since five, when he'd received an encrypted text from a cousin in Tehran, telling him to check the news. *Any* news.

The twenty-four-year-old opened Twitter, and the first tweet he saw described the death of General Rajavi, no doubt at the hands of the Americans and the Jews. There were photos from the scene, and it was brutal. One close-in shot of the debris showed a severed arm at the end of which a graying hand wore Rajavi's distinctive watch.

Haz was an angry young man already; this, he knew instantly, would send him over the edge.

And over the edge was exactly where he'd wanted to go for some time.

As a sixteen-year-old boy he'd been trained by the Iranian military; he'd shown special aptitude and unique intelligence, so he left the infantry and moved into special operations. He fought in Yemen and Syria and Libya as a Quds Force paramilitary fighter.

Mirza had been recalled to Tehran three years earlier, shortly after his twenty-first birthday, and ordered to study German. Day and night, month after month. In addition to his studies, he also met with higher-level Quds operatives, and they taught him tradecraft, more advanced weapons, and technology.

When he was twenty-two, he was no longer a zealous war fighter. He was a highly trained operative. Yet he remained as fervent as ever. When he was deemed ready by his masters, he was secreted into Europe, given the papers he needed to find residence and work, and told to recruit a cell.

And then, this done, he was told to wait.

Mirza had been proud to serve on the vanguard of Iranian interests as a spy, but he became disillusioned with the work when there was no work to do. He got a job driving a truck, the men he recruited mostly worked in the trucking industry, and they all lived very normal, if very boring, lives here in Berlin.

Mirza wanted to serve, he wanted to martyr himself, and he wanted a mission so the men he led would not grow lazy and weak and become non-believers, like regular Germans.

In the last few months, Mirza himself began to question his own resolve. He felt himself softening by the day.

But no longer. First thing this morning, after the shock left him, he felt as if he'd been pumped full of a powerful drug.

He would seek his jihad now, there was no doubt about it. He'd drawn up plans years ago, before Germany and much of the rest of the EU relaxed their sanctions on Iran, and he merely had to receive his orders from Tehran. He and his men would no longer be told to remain in place, to abide by all local laws, and to wait for the day when they would be activated.

No, today he would be activated, he had no doubt. He just needed the call.

One of his plans was an attack against American interests here in the city. As he was certain America was the culprit in the death of the general, he expected this plan to be the one his orders centered on.

Yes, Germany and the rest of the EU had relaxed their sanctions, but Mirza didn't care about sanctions; he didn't care about politics; he didn't care about anything other than doing his job. And his job was that of an agent provocateur.

The West would call him a terrorist, but he knew that though his martyrdom would result in the death and destruction of many Americans here in Germany, he could never in a million years cause the terror that his people had undergone at the hands of the United States and its proxy dogs.

Today, though his brain raced, his mission was simple, because this was what he had trained for. He would reconnect with his team, make sure they were instilled with the fervency needed to act at a moment's notice. He would do this physically, as he almost always did, in order to avoid phones or e-mails, which could often be traced. He would reach out to each man at his home, or his place of work, or his place of worship, and remind him of his duties, tell him that the time for complacency and safety had passed, and that the reason they'd all been chosen and trained would, at long last, soon be realized.

After this, Haz and a couple of the others would jump into a car, then journey to his weapons cache outside of town, where they would load several duffel bags of equipment into their vehicle and return to the capital.

Haz Mirza was certain that, at long last, real action was imminent.

And he'd be ready.

Shortly before eight a.m., a man in a dark gray sport coat over a collared and starched dress shirt climbed out of a taxi in front of the Hotel Adlon Kempinski, pulled his sunglasses off, and waited for the driver to pull his roll-aboard out of the trunk. He paid the man, slipped his wallet back into his linen slacks, and wheeled his bag under the long red awning and into the lobby. He found the front desk and was beckoned forward by the polite staff member.

He provided a Canadian passport under the name Darrin Patch and made small talk in English with the desk clerk, mentioning he'd just climbed off a flight from Budapest and was happy he'd been able to book an early arrival time at the hotel. He was also hoping to get a room on the fourth floor, he said, because his wife would be joining him later in the day, and they'd stayed in room 407 for a few nights on their honeymoon years earlier.

With a proud smile the clerk confirmed to Mr. Patch that suite 407 was available and ready.

A minute later the man stepped into an elevator crowded with a family of six, all of whom were coming back up from breakfast. The father pressed the button for the fourth floor, and then asked the lone man which floor he was staying on.

"I'm on four, too. Thanks," he said, then looked around at the children.

The kids' ages ranged from four to twelve, and the man in the sport coat looked straight ahead while the parents began a conversation about visiting a museum later in the day.

The elevator stopped on the fourth floor, everyone stepped out and turned to the right, and the man with the rolling luggage followed behind the family towards the end of the hall.

Inside suite 401, Anya Bolichova spun around to Inna and Maksim, who were both watching local news, following the story of a murder the evening before at the edge of the Tiergarten. While they did this, Semyon was putting luggage in their car in the underground garage two blocks away.

Anya said, "The family in 403 is back, but there's another guy with them."

Inna rushed over and watched the man on camera. "He's not with them. He's got his own key card in his hand."

The family entered the door just to the left of Zakharova's suite at the end of the hall, and the man held the card over the lock of the door directly to the right of her suite, and then he disappeared inside.

"Did you get an image of his face?"

"Not much of one. He looks like he's just a guest."

Inna kept her eyes on the screen. "Look him up. Suite 407. What's his name? When did he book?" Inna turned to Maksim, who wasn't paying attention to the new arrival at all. She said, "Make sure you use the full suppressor, not the short version. The family in 403 is back from breakfast, and there is a new man in 407."

Akulov looked up from the couch. "You are telling me how to prepare my gun, Inna?"

Bolichova tapped keys on one of the laptops. After a moment she saw the booking. "He made the reservation online at one forty-five a.m. Darrin Patch, from Windsor, Ontario, Canada." The image on the screen from the passport scanned by the hotel showed a man in his late thirties or early forties with short hair, a beard, and glasses. He looked to all of them like some sort of plain businessman.

"Check open source," Inna commanded, and Bolichova searched for the man's LinkedIn listing. She found it, and saw that he was a food and beverage consultant. He had an Instagram page, as well, with lots of pictures of restaurants, food, and spirits. Interspersed were just a few pictures of himself with a family, and a few more that showed images of camping and fishing.

Bolichova said, "Either he's legit, or his cover is very well backstopped."

Inna thought it over a moment. "Okay. We can't discount him as a threat, even though it looks like he checks out. Semyon will go right behind Maksim, run rear security just inside the doorway to the suite. Anya and I will watch the cameras for any movement at all in the hall."

She looked to Maksim, expecting some pushback, but instead he just nodded his assent and headed back into the bedroom.

Zoya returned to her suite at eight twenty, energized from her swim and her workout in the health club. Before she even showered she placed an order with room service for enough food and coffee for herself, Moises, and Yanis: a cheese omelet for her, and two baskets of croissants, jelly, and butter for the men. She added a large flask of both orange and apple juice and a full pot of coffee.

At eight thirty-five a.m. she stepped into the shower, taking her SIG pistol with her and placing it on the soap ledge.

Even when she *didn't* know, without question, that hit men had tracked her down, she still kept a firearm in or near her shower when she bathed. She'd been trained to never be caught without a weapon, and though that concept was an ideal and not totally realistic, she did everything she could to be certain she kept a firearm or two within reach.

The new guest in room 407 sat on the edge of the bed, his eyes fixed on the wall in front of him, his mind on what lay beyond it.

He could hear the shower running, and he could picture Zoya Zakharova. The image simultaneously filled him with love, lust, and terror.

There were powerful emotions running through Court Gentry's mind, but for now he didn't act; he only sat there and took long, slow breaths. There was also medication running through him that made him more alert, more focused, and gave him energy, and for this he was thankful right now.

He'd used a CIA-backstopped passport to reserve the room, but he found this to be an acceptable risk. He knew the Agency could easily monitor guests here at the hotel; sitting right next to the U.S. embassy, it would be the height of malfeasance not to, but the legend wasn't tied to Court personally, since Hanley had it made for someone else and then gave it to Court.

The face on the passport looked something like Court, but the passport photo showed a bearded man, while Court was now clean-shaven. But it was not actually Court's photo, nor were the images on social media of Court, either.

He had decided, without doubt, to make contact with Zoya the evening before while he was at Dr. Kaya's getting treatment. He couldn't trust Brewer to run Zoya safely, and he couldn't trust Brewer or Hanley to tell him about the danger she might be in. The moment he worked out that this operation was more important to Hanley than Zoya's life, he told himself that it was up to him to be certain both goals were accomplished. And then, when he found out that the men from Venezuela had somehow tracked him here, he thought his proximity to Zoya might only put her in further danger.

He wanted to get her out of here. After that, he would stay and do whatever Hanley wanted of him.

He also knew he needed to make contact with her today without anyone from Shrike Group, anyone from Russia, anyone from the CIA, or anyone from German intelligence realizing he was doing so. Knocking on her door was out. He had to assume that someone would be monitoring the hallway cameras for visitors.

This left the window. Climbing along the outside of the building might have been the surest way to avoid surveillance, but it was certainly not the safest. He'd have to shimmy out his window, move laterally along a narrow ledge, and then somehow make entry to her suite. She didn't have a balcony, per se, but in her living room, just like in Court's room, she had large floor-to-ceiling double windows that opened inward like doors, with a metal railing in front of them. He decided this would be the easiest place to enter, although it was also much farther away than the first access point he'd come to on the ledge, which, according to his research on the layout of the suite, would be the bedroom window.

Court knew Zoya's senses would be on full alert, which didn't really scare him once she knew he was the one in her hotel room, but he did worry about that moment when he passed in front of her window. Someone trained, someone who was already anticipating an assassination attempt, who saw a figure outside, might well shoot him off the ledge right through the glass.

There were other drawbacks to Court's plan, as well, the main one being that he would have to execute this move on the fourth floor, which, in typical European fashion, meant it was five stories above the street. He would be in full view of anyone looking up from Unter den Linden, so he knew he'd have to be quick to avoid unwanted attention, and lucky to not catch any wandering eyes.

Still, scooting over to the next suite's window beat standing under the hallway cameras when he already knew German intelligence was surveilling her.

He listened to the running shower through the wall and drummed his fingers on the bed. Brewer had said Zoya told her that her colleagues were to arrive at ten a.m., and it wasn't even nine. He had time to get her out of here; he just needed to act.

Soon enough he climbed off the bed, threw his luggage on a table, and unzipped his roll-aboard. Seconds later he was changing out of his businessman clothes as he prepared to get down to his real business.

FORTY-FOUR

Bolichova hung up her call and turned to Sorokina, who sipped from a teacup while standing at the kitchen island. Anya said, "Suite 405's room service is canceled."

On cue, Maksim Akulov stepped out of the bedroom. He looked neat and healthy in his crisp white room service attendant's uniform, his hair was slicked back with gel, and he had a confident, determined smile on his face.

He was fine now, because the excitement filled his bloodstream like a drug. It wasn't the high he used to get from such endeavors—one needed more and more of a drug to have the same effects—but this was his best day, his best moment, in over six weeks.

The Russian carried three knives, a weighted throwing blade under his server's coat on his left hip, a second throwing knife just behind it at the eight o'clock position, and another hooked blade, stowed centerline behind his belt buckle. It was his intention to use this weapon to slit Zakharova's wrists after he got her into the bathtub.

In Maksim's hand he held an unholstered CZ subcompact pistol, with an Anschutz suppressor screwed onto the barrel. The Anschutz had a unique design that made it look like a long, fat drill bit. Concealing the weapon on his person would have been difficult, especially to an eye as trained as Zakharova's, so he slipped it under the linen draping the room service cart and adjusted the fabric to where the weapon did not reveal itself. Still, it would be easily accessible to him, and he'd have it out and in his target's face as soon as she opened the door. The target had the training, as well as the heads-up from Inna the night before with the offer to surrender, to know that an assassination attempt would be coming, so she'd likely be armed herself. But despite Inna's pleas for Maksim to respect Sirena's abilities, he had no doubt in his mind that he could get his weapon trained on her long before she could get hers trained on him.

The Russians were banking on her assuming they wouldn't dare make the attempt here in the hotel, since this wasn't typical GRU or SVR assassination technique for work in a European capital.

But it had worked in D.C., and Maksim felt comfortable it would work here.

Semyon also had a CZ pistol, and it was suppressed, as well, but he clicked it into an open shoulder holster, with the silencer pointing straight down, and then he put on his jacket, hiding the weapon.

For the first time in days, Maksim was back in charge. *"Dvah minut."* *Two minutes.* He walked over to the mini bar, unscrewed a single airplane bottle of Jack Daniel's, and downed it in one gulp.

He winked at Inna now. "Only one, dear. Keeps me steady."

Inna turned away, back to the monitor and the view through the two cameras in the hall.

Maksim rolled the cart up next to the closed door, scooted past it, and looked through the peephole. It was full of breakfast foods: an omelet, a ham-and-cheese croissant, coffee and orange juice, all resting on plates under domed stainless-steel plate carriers. Anya had purchased the food downstairs in the restaurant an hour earlier in anticipation of this morning's operation, basing the order on foods their target had ordered on previous mornings over the past two weeks.

Maksim and Semyon would have to remove all the food and the cart, along with the cameras, after the hit so as not to arouse the suspicions of the police or hotel staff, but bringing actual food would help them get through the door if a suspicious Zakharova ordered them to remove the plate covers while checking them out through the peephole.

Semyon stepped up close behind Maksim at the door now, ready to rush down to the opposite end of the hallway once his leader had made entry on Zakharova's suite.

Inna called to the bigger, older Russian male. "Don't forget Darrin Patch in 407. I don't like the coincidence of a fighting-aged male appearing in the room next to hers right before we launch."

Semyon did not acknowledge the intel officer; he just put his hand on Maksim's shoulder, gave the smaller man a squeeze, and counted down the time in his head.

Inna put her hand on Anya's shoulder, as well, and she looked at the CCTV feed piped in from the hallway. After a moment, she said, "Replace the real-time hallway broadcast with the prerecorded loop."

"Ponial." Got it. Anya tapped some keys, and Inna saw a quick glitch in the hallway cameras before they once again displayed a long, narrow, dim, and empty space.

"It's done," Anya said.

Maksim opened the door and began to pull the cart into the hallway, but he stopped abruptly.

Fifteen meters ahead of him the elevator chimed, and then he heard the doors opening. Quickly he stepped back inside the suite, shut the door, and looked out through the peephole.

Anya called out what she saw on her monitor. She said, "One man off the car, he's turned right, heading to the far end of the hall."

Inna asked, "Can you see his face?"

"Yeah, one second." She turned and looked at Sorokina. "It's Ric Ennis."

"Shit." Inna looked to Maksim. "Zakharova has company. We need to abort."

Maksim did not reply to this; he only continued watching through the peephole as the man walked away from him, nearing the door on the opposite end of the hall.

"We need to abort, Maksim," Inna said again.

Zoya had stepped out of the shower, wrapped her hair in a towel, and dried herself off with another. She entered the bedroom and chose a pair of black jeans, a white bra, and a white silk top from her closet. She began dressing at a leisurely pace, until she heard a knock at the door.

It could be room service, she knew, but Zoya wasn't taking any chances. She grabbed the SIG, still wet from its shower, and she pushed the weapon into her waistband at the small of her back as she walked through the living room to the door. She looked out through the peephole while securing a few buttons on her shirt, tucking the rest in front to clasp it shut, and then she stood upright, a look of surprise on her face.

It was Ennis.

Der'mo.

After checking the peephole again to be certain he was alone, she opened the door. Her gun was still on her, and her right hand hovered back near it; Ennis wasn't a Russian hitter, but she assumed he was the one who gave her up to Moscow.

Ennis moved in quickly with an intense stare at her but no words.

"You didn't tell me you were coming," she said.

"Yeah?" The man was agitated, this was clear. "Yeah? Well, you didn't tell me about last night, did you?"

"Last night? You mean about the Russian assassins who gave me one opportunity to go back with them to Moscow so I could be executed by firing squad? Who did you tell about me, Ennis?"

He cocked his head in surprise. "The *Russians*? They're here? They know?"

Zoya nodded. "Don't play stupid. *That's* what happened last night." She cocked her head, relaxed her grip on the weapon behind her. "What were *you* talking about?"

"Miriam called me a half hour ago. Her contacts told her that BfV was following both of us after dinner. You didn't go up to your room like you told me, you went for a walk. An intelligence officer following you was murdered. An officer following me was attacked and injured." He added, "You and I are both burned. Miriam wants us to get out of town."

There was nothing in the world Zoya would like more than to skip town now, but she knew she had to do her best to remain on her mission.

She needed to be here, in the middle of Shrike's intelligence operation against Iranian actors in Berlin, to find out what the hell was going on.

Ennis said, "We'll go together. Safety in numbers. Pack quickly, we can be on a train in a half hour."

Der'mo, she said to herself again. Her entire operation was falling apart around her.

FORTY-FIVE

In suite 401, Anya kept her eyes on the hidden cameras in Zakharova's suite down the hall. "It looks like they're fighting. Arguing about something."

Inna posited the reasons for the fight. "Ennis found out about the guy Semyon killed. He wants to know why she was running an SDR last night. She's angry because we are here, and she blames Ennis." Then she looked back to Maksim and said a third time, "Abort. We stand down till he leaves."

But Maksim shook his head. "*Nyet*. We're going."

Inna couldn't believe what she was hearing. "What's wrong with you? You know our orders; it's supposed to look like a—"

"A suicide? *Da*, it is." He spun to the other three dramatically, a flourish of his hand like an actor on a stage. "A sad, sad course of events. Two work colleagues are meeting for an early morning of intimacy, a clandestine affair no one in their office can know about. An argument breaks out between them. Infidelity, jealousy, a refusal to leave another and commit, whoever knows with these things? It gets heated. She pulls a gun on him, emotional; she doesn't mean it, but it makes her feel powerful to wave it around."

Anya and Semyon stared in rapt attention. Inna looked at him, as well, but she was clearly unconvinced.

"The gun goes off. Mr. Ennis is killed. Zakharova is stunned by what she's done, but ultimately resolute. The poor girl then turns the weapon on herself."

Inna Sorokina blinked in surprise now. "You are saying a murder/ suicide?"

Maksim nodded, a smile growing wider as he winked at Semyon, slapped him on the arm, and opened the door.

"That could work," Inna said, but she said it to Maksim Akulov's back, because he was already heading out the door with his cart full of food.

In suite 405, Ennis stood just inside the door and Zoya stood in the middle of the living room, her back to the open windows overlooking Unter den Linden. "I'm not leaving Berlin! I have a job to do for Shrike, and the killing of General Rajavi last night is only going to make Iranian operatives in the West more of a threat."

"We are blown! I'm blown by the Germans, at the very least. But you, you are compromised to Germany *and* Russia. There is no job here for you to come back to. You are a complete liability for Shrike Group. You're fired. I'm fired. We have got to get both our asses on the next train out of town."

She shook her head. "You go wherever you want. I'm not—"

"This is bigger than you know. This is more dangerous than you know."

"What are you talking about?"

Ennis seemed to weigh the option of saying more, before finally speaking. "The drone strike in Baghdad last night."

"What about it?"

"There is an assumption that the Iranians will retaliate. But what if I told you the Iranians are being set up?"

"What do you mean?"

"For the last six months, Shrike has been creating a trail between Iranian intel officers at their Berlin embassy, a trail that links them to Quds Force operatives in Europe. A link that doesn't exist."

"What?"

"Miriam was tasked with finding the Quds operatives, learning their patterns, putting them under surveillance. But I . . . my team, we were tasked with taking Miriam's intelligence and using it to plant physical evidence on the sleeper cell and on embassy intelligence staff here in the city. We created payment records, we've altered files in their systems. Our entire objective for the past six months has been to build linkage between the embassy and the sleepers. I thought we were just framing them to get Quds expelled and to get EU sanctions reinstated on Iran, but now I see the frame was so that the Iranian government would be tied to any attacks they carried out, even if the Iranian government didn't order the attacks."

Zoya nodded slowly. "Shrike Group, or its client, knew this was going to happen today."

He nodded. "Bingo. The cells we've uncovered across Europe are sleepers. They are connected to Quds Force, but they are more or less deniable. If the group here planted a bomb in the Reichstag, Iran could simply say the cell went rogue. Disavow them completely. But if Shrike was able to convince Germany that the cell was getting its marching orders, its money, its materiel, directly from the Iranian embassy . . . I mean . . . shit."

A knock at the door turned both their heads in that direction, just feet behind Ennis. Zoya kept her position, reached behind her back, and wrapped her hand around her pistol.

Ennis didn't even look through the peephole before swiveling back to Zoya, his face panic-stricken. "It's the BfV; I tried to run an SDR, but they might have picked me back up on the—"

Zoya said, "I ordered room service for me and the boys, but check it first."

Ennis looked out the peephole and blew out a relieved sigh. "Thank God."

By now Zoya had drawn her pistol; she held it behind her back, and she was heading for the door herself to check. She was halfway across the living room when Ennis reached for the latch.

"Wait, let me see," she said, but Ennis ignored her and opened the door.

Maksim shoved the door in with a shoulder, knocking Ennis all the way to the floor as he did so. The assassin brought the suppressed pistol up to his eyes, aiming it straight at Zoya Zakharova. The attractive Russian woman had raised her own weapon simultaneously, and she now pointed it at Akulov.

Neither fired.

Maksim had an easy kill shot lined up on his target, but he knew she would likely pull her trigger in reflex if he hit her. It was a standoff, muted somewhat by the fact Maksim was considering shooting anyway, so eager was he to die.

But he didn't press the trigger. This wouldn't be the clean kill his nation needed.

The American man stood back up, positioned himself within arm's reach of the Russian assassin's pistol, but Maksim wasn't worried about this. He was ready to move to the left towards the kitchen if the man made any muscle movement in his direction.

"What the fuck is going on?" Ennis said, his voice tinged with fear.

Maksim said nothing; he only held his weapon on his intended target, then took two steps back and shifted from a two-handed grip to a one-handed grip on his CZ. With his left hand he reached back behind him and unlatched the door. Semyon burst into the room, his own weapon's silencer scanning the scene before locking onto Ennis. He held his weapon steady as he pulled the room service cart inside to get it out of the hall, rolling it into the center of the living room next to the sofa and feet in front of Zakharova. Then he went back and shut and chained the door with one hand while his still-steady weapon was centered between Ennis's wide eyes.

Pervak looked at Zoya, then shifted his aim quickly to her.

Maksim smiled; he spoke calmly and confidently. "Are you going to shoot us *both* before we turn your pretty face into something ugly for the coroner to look at?"

Zoya lowered her pistol, then tossed it on the floor of the living room, next to the cart. She raised her hands.

"Very good." Maksim spoke two words in Russian now. *"Pristreli yego."*

Zoya understood, which meant she knew what was coming next. *"Nyet!"*

Semyon Pervak followed his leader's orders to "shoot him," shifting aim again, then firing once into Ric Ennis's right temple from less than two meters' distance. Ennis's head snapped to the side, blood sprayed the wallpaper behind him, and the man's dead body crumpled straight back over the sofa and down to the floor.

The bullet made a loud enough *thump* coming out of the pistol, but Maksim doubted, even in the next suite over, anyone would be able to identify the sound as having come from a firearm.

Still, he spoke into the earpiece, calling his team watching the cameras from the monitors back in 401. "Status?"

Inna replied. "The hallway is clear. Doors to 403 and 407 remain closed."

"Ponial." Understood. He turned his attention back to the woman.

"Now, Sirena. Let's deal with you."

Zoya looked down at Ric Ennis's body, then back up to the brain matter streaming slowly down the wall. Finally she turned her attention again to the assassin in the room service attendant's uniform. She forced her voice to remain calm as she spoke. In Russian she said, "You're . . . Maksim."

"Da," he replied. "And you're the traitor."

"Tell yourself that if it helps you sleep."

"Nothing helps me sleep, beautiful. Turn around," he ordered.

Zoya's back was to the open floor-to-ceiling window, and a concave metal railing a meter and a half in height just outside gave it the feel of a tiny balcony.

She did not turn around and face it, however.

She said, "You have a small pistol with a large silencer. You would have shot me between the eyes as soon as you came through the door if your rules of engagement allowed this. You have to make this look like I killed myself, don't you?"

"Clever girl."

"And how will you explain the extra body?" She motioned to Ennis, lying in a heap to Maksim's right.

Maksim said, "I don't have to. That's the very awkward job of the surviving relatives of both yourself and Mr. Ennis. Honestly, I don't envy them."

Zoya took a slow breath, then lifted her chin. "You'll need my help to make it look right." She stared down the pistol. "Good luck with that."

She was one hundred percent faking her self-assurance; she was terrified, and saw few, if any, options. But she needed to stall until she could find some sort of an opening, and while she and Maksim were talking, he wasn't in the process of murdering her, so she wanted to keep this dialogue going until an opportunity presented itself.

A moment later, however, it seemed the stalling would be coming to an end.

Maksim spoke to his colleague standing closer to the kitchen. "I have a new idea. Toss her out the window."

"Der'mo," she said.

FORTY-SIX

Court Gentry placed one booted foot directly in front of the other, then shuffled another step. It was slow going, but finally he made it past the windowsill outside Zoya's bedroom and back onto the narrow ledge. The larger living room windows were another twelve feet ahead, and moving at the pace he'd been going since leaving his own window, he figured he'd be exposed up here on the fifth floor for another thirty seconds.

He couldn't tell the status of the living room windows yet, since they opened inward and his face was pressed up against the warm stonework of the building's facade.

The amphetamines in his bloodstream managed to spike his adrenaline even more than a narrow walk on a sixty-foot-high ledge would have done on its own, and the feeling of helplessness up here shot pangs of anxiety through his mind.

He pressed his face tighter against the wall, scraping his cheek, and he told himself, not for the first time, that he should have become an accountant.

And then he took another shuffle-step closer to the window.

Semyon Pervak holstered his weapon under his arm, covered it with his jacket, and then moved forward, closing on the target. He was careful not to cross in front of Maksim's pistol; he knew Zakharova would dive for the handgun she'd dropped on the floor if she saw even a moment's chance, so the big Russian knew better than to give her any opportunity whatsoever. He stepped around the food cart, approaching her from her left side, and he spun her around roughly, twisting her right arm behind her back.

She fought back, and it took all his strength to overpower her.

"She's a strong one," he said to Akulov.

"If you're not stronger, I'll throw *you* out the window," came the reply.

Semyon Pervak began pushing Zakharova from behind, towards the opening five stories above the street.

"*Nyet!*" she screamed. She started to scream again, but the big man's hand slammed hard over her mouth and face, bloodying her nose in the process while he all but gagged her. This done, he used his other hand to shove her forward.

The Russian woman fought him hard for each step, but slowly she lost ground, her bare feet scooting across the oriental rug, then across the wooden flooring, as she was forced closer and closer to the window.

Behind her she heard Maksim Akulov speak, his voice still calm and comfortable. "Here's how it will be written, if you care. You couldn't make yourself put a gun in your mouth after you killed your lover, so you opted for a short flight instead."

Zoya was shoved all the way out, her thighs pressed hard against the railing. She clenched the steel bar tight with her free hand, screamed through the powerful hand covering her mouth, then tried desperately to shake her head free.

In doing this she turned to the left, then spun her head harder to the right.

There, less than ten feet away from her, a man stood on the narrow ledge in a black T-shirt and jeans.

She blinked.

It was Court; his eyes were wide in shock at what he was witnessing before him. His body was pressed tight to the wall, there were no handholds on the smooth facade, and she saw his bare face and short hair dripping with sweat. She tried to scream again but the hand had grabbed her face tightly once more, and then she was shoved again and again as the man holding her from behind, just out of Court's view, tried to send her down to her death. But with her body pressed against the iron railing and her hand clenching it as hard as she could, she knew her assailant would have to release the grip on her mouth and use both hands to shove her over.

This was the chance she needed, if she could hold her ground long enough for it to happen.

Semyon Pervak removed his hand from the surprisingly strong young woman's mouth to give a big two-handed push against her upper back, but she surprised him as he did this, ducking down and spinning away to her left, missing much of the blow, and then she darted a step back into the room. Pervak retained a grip on her left arm, ripped her silk shirt sleeve off, then tackled her onto the room service cart, sending food, drinks, silverware, plates, and plate covers in all directions as they fell over the top of it, onto the sofa, and then down to the floor, flipping the coffee table as they impacted with it.

They were three meters in front of Maksim, who was still positioned near the front door.

Zakharova kicked and threw punches, but Pervak weathered them all, used his weight to pin her amid the mess of the food and the dead body of the American man lying there next to them.

Inna came over Maksim's headset. "You're making noise!"

Maksim shouted to Sem. "Forget the window, we'll shoot her in the head." Then he stepped quickly over to the television, turned it on, and cranked it up to full volume.

The woman and Pervak continued fighting on the floor; her nosebleed smeared itself around the scene as she threw more knees and more elbows and more fists that did little other than glance off the big fifty-three-year-old. Maksim's strategic brain told him that once she was dead, he'd need to put some of that blood on Ennis's hands, to make it look like he attacked her before she shot him.

Despite the unexpected turn of events, Akulov had no concerns about his mission itself. Still, Inna was right. The noise coming from the room right now would make a covert exfiltration difficult, to say the least.

In his ear he heard Sorokina telling him to hurry. She was, no doubt, watching what she took to be a looming debacle on the hidden cameras, and he already dreaded hearing her harp on and on about how tough a target Zakharova had proved to be and about how Maksim had not listened to her.

Enough of this, he thought, and he moved forward, around the body and the coffee table, and began to kneel to help Semyon get the woman pinned down and a gun to her temple or under her chin to end this all.

His pistol with the suppressor was too large to holster, so he placed it on the floor behind him as he put his weight on her lower torso, giving Semyon some relief to concentrate on her upper body and arms. Semyon controlled her now with Maksim's help, his forearm smashing down on her mouth to keep her quiet and his right knee pinning her left arm. The big Russian used his left hand to move his pistol to the side of the muscular woman's head as she desperately tried to push it away with her one free hand.

Maksim snapped at his subordinate. "Do it already!"

He punched the woman hard in the thigh, the only part of her body he could easily reach.

He raised his fist for another blow, but before he sent it down again, his earpiece suddenly came alive with Inna Sorokina's frantic voice.

"Threat! Gun!"

This confused him. He could see Zakharova's hands, and she didn't have a gun. "Where?" he demanded.

"There's a man in the window!"

Maksim Akulov rose up on his knees. *"Shto?" What?*

Court kicked over the railing, drawing his pistol as he did so. He only had a fraction of a second to take in the entire scene; there was one man in front of him, and the sounds of a fight out of his view on the far end of the food cart on the other side of the sofa. He couldn't see Zoya, so he assumed she was in a fight for her life on the floor in the center of the living room.

He raised his weapon, acutely aware he was pointing his pistol in the direction of a thin wall with a family of six behind it, the one he'd encountered in the elevator. The one man he could see rising behind the sofa was wearing a room service attendant's coat. He had one hand inside it at his waistband; he seemed to be drawing a weapon.

Court sighted in on him quickly, but just as Court began to press the trigger on his VP9, the man spun away with extraordinary speed.

Court held fire and tried to track him with his sights. He didn't want to fire and miss. Even hitting the man dead center wouldn't ensure that his round would not overpenetrate and strike someone on the opposite side of the wall.

As the man came back around from his spin, Court saw an arm whipping in his direction. He sensed the man throwing something underhanded towards him, so he went from offense to defense, diving away quickly to his right. A black throwing knife churned the air as it whizzed by to his left, a foot from his face. The weapon embedded in the wall behind him, and Court tried to rush his weapon's sights back on his target while he dove through the air. He landed on the kitchen island, rolled once to his right, and came back up in a combat crouch by the sink, ready to finally dispatch this incredibly agile adversary by firing down on him from height and avoiding using the wall with the noncombatants behind it as a backstop.

But as soon as Court got his gun on his target, he saw something else in the air, already flying towards him, and before Court could shift into defense again, he felt a sharp sting on the outside of his right biceps. He dropped the pistol and it fell all the way down to the floor in the middle of the living room.

Court looked down and saw that a throwing knife had sliced him a few inches above the elbow. Blood ran freely down his arm onto the marble top. The blade hadn't embedded itself, he knew this much, although he had no idea where it had gone.

He looked up again and saw that the man who'd injured him had dropped back below the sofa, perhaps to go for another weapon. And to this man's right, an older, burlier man rose up from behind the cart, and this asshole already had a gun in his hand.

Zoya Zakharova finally saw an opportunity, and she knew the only reason she had been afforded this one slim chance was that Court had made it on the scene.

She was exhausted from the fight. She hadn't been able to match her opponent's strength or size; he'd had her on her back, and Maksim had been on her legs, but seconds earlier Maksim had stood up and begun spinning and whipping his body frantically. The man with a knee on her left arm and a gun almost to her head had sensed the movement, as well, and then he looked over the sofa. Instantly, he all but forgot about Zoya as he scrambled to get his gun aimed on a target.

Zoya used the opportunity to reach out on the floor around her, to find anything she could use to strike her enemy with before he could shoot the man risking his life to save hers.

Maksim Akulov ignored Inna in his earpiece when she told him Anya was on her way to provide support because Maksim was sure this fight was all but over. He had the man on the kitchen island dead to rights. He raised his pistol from the floor, planning on shooting this maniac dead, and then just shooting Zakharova, as well, who was on the floor to his right below Semyon.

There would be three bodies in the apartment after a very loud and nasty fight; he'd leave his gun in the new man's hand, and authorities would assume the man in the black T-shirt had been an assassin who ultimately killed the guest and her coworker.

Akulov sighted in on his target, but before the weapon snapped in his hand, the man on the island did a back roll with astonishing speed and crashed down into the kitchen out of view on the other side of the island.

Semyon did fire, however, though Akulov was certain he'd been too slow to hit the stranger.

Zoya hadn't been able to prevent the man above her from shooting at Court, but just as he got off a single shot, she scooted back a couple of feet and her fingertips wrapped around a stainless steel plate cover. She arced it through the air with all the force she could muster from the floor, and she struck the man in the arm holding his pistol. A second gunshot cracked, but it went wild.

She then flipped onto her stomach and began crawling away madly, knowing she had to keep throwing things at both men to distract them either until she could get to her weapon, lying somewhere on the floor on the other side of the sofa where she'd dropped it, or until Court could dispatch the two Russians himself.

Zoya scrambled almost into the corner, knocked over a floor lamp, then wrapped her left hand around a plate full of food that had skittered off the cart but was still covered in plastic wrap. She Frisbeed it back towards the two men in front of the sofa, the food spinning off the plate as it sailed.

She didn't wait to see if it connected, so eager was she to find more projectiles around her.

FORTY-SEVEN

Court saw Zoya; she was in the corner twenty feet across the living room, hefting a plate of food and slinging it at the larger of the two attackers, who now stood in the middle of the room. It wasn't much offense from Zoya, but he understood she was trying to distract the man while Court got his shit together, and he wanted to take advantage of it.

Maksim only had to step around the kitchen island to get the mystery man back in his sights, but after taking one step in that direction, a plate with food spinning off it whizzed right at his face. He knocked it away, then batted down a second projectile, this one a metal coffee urn Zakharova had flung his way.

He looked back and saw her there, over his right shoulder, but he kept his gun pointed towards the kitchen. This man had been so fast, Maksim knew shifting his fire to the unarmed Zakharova was too dangerous right now. He'd take a plate in the head, but first he was going to move around the right side of the island and pump a half-dozen rounds into Zakharova's would-be savior.

Akulov darted around the island and trained his gun on the space there, but his opponent was gone. A trail of blood led around the corner.

The wounded man was crawling back into the living room.

. . .

Semyon was in the process of shifting his aim back to their primary target, the filthy and bleeding woman on the floor. He'd almost lined up on her when she launched to her bare feet, dove onto the hardwood, and rolled forward. He fired high, and then she came up from her roll, standing well within striking distance. She threw an open palm into his jaw, knocking him back a half step, and then she grabbed hold of the hand holding on to the pistol.

She tried to flip the man over her hip and wrestle the weapon free, but only for an instant, because quickly he shoved her in the back of her head, sending her flying face-first down to the floor, almost all the way to the large open window. As she fell, however, she managed to strip the man's handgun, and it tumbled over the couch and clanged onto the floor by the food cart.

Court knelt at the end of the island, not far from the front door, but he knew he couldn't stay here. The man in the room service coat would be coming around through the kitchen to his left right now; Court needed to arm himself and get back in this fight before it was too late.

Ducking his head around the corner into the living room, he saw the attacker in the jacket drop his gun over the sofa while fighting with Zoya. It was fifteen feet from him, but he'd have to expose himself to both the larger and the smaller man in order to go for it.

And then he saw something else. Hidden under the edge of the food cart, a small black pistol lay on the floor.

He heard a Russian voice speaking English coming from the kitchen, steps from where he crouched.

"Poor valiant hero! When they find your body, you will be remembered as a cold-blooded murderer!"

At the same moment the big man saw Court, and Court saw him. The man reached to the small of his back, to pull either a gun or a knife.

Court knew he had to go for a weapon now, although he would be up against two armed killers in opposite directions. He saw little chance for success, but no chance at all without action.

Court threw his body forward and rolled towards the pistol, lying there by the island. His shoulder and his arm rioted in excruciating pain, even through the effects of adrenaline.

On his second roll he snatched up the CZ pistol, then rolled again, across eggs and toast and butter on the floor. He crashed into the food cart, causing it to lurch towards the window. As he raised his gun in the direction of the man at the sofa, who was now brandishing a small semiautomatic pistol, he kicked at the second pistol he'd seen lying there, sending it skidding across the floor to where Zoya had just risen into a seated position against the wall.

"Z!"

She spun to him, and he could see in her eyes that she understood.

Court stood and swung his pistol in a 180-degree arc as he pivoted away from the living room to aim at the target on the other side of the kitchen island.

He was giving his back to an armed man so that he could target another armed man, and he was putting all his trust in Zoya, betting his life that she would end the threat behind him while he dealt with the one in front of him.

Semyon Pervak had pulled his tiny SIG Sauer P238 up from the small of his back and lifted it towards the man three meters away on the opposite side of the sofa. He had two targets to choose from, but the decision was an easy one for his experienced tactical brain to make. He knew Zakharova was unarmed—she'd been flinging tableware and food around the room, after all—so he concentrated on the man who had just come out of a roll. He saw that the man was focused on Maksim, not him, so he lined up for an easy shot to the back of his head.

Fool, he thought.

Before Pervak could depress the trigger, however, he heard an impossibly loud unsuppressed gunshot. Simultaneously, he felt a blow to the side of his neck that dropped him to his knees.

Blood spurted obscenely from his throat just below the jawline, all over the sofa. He dropped his weapon to press against the wound. He tumbled down to his left, coming to rest over the body of the man he had himself killed moments earlier.

Zoya Zakharova had shot him, he understood this much. But as he died he realized he would never know where she'd found the gun.

Finally Court had his weapon up and aimed at a target. He'd managed to catch the man in the white server's coat as he swung his gun towards Zakharova, who he clearly knew now had a firearm. The man had his back to the wall in the kitchen, and the open window was a good six feet off to his left and ahead of him.

Court shouted at the top of his lungs, "Drop it, asshole!"

The would-be assassin's own weapon began to rise, but he seemed to realize he had no chance against two shooters.

He lowered his gun, and Court moved quickly between him and Zoya, who was now behind Court in the corner of the room. He was covering her with his body, and he was also preventing her from taking a clean shot.

He shouted to her, "Don't shoot! Don't shoot!"

"Why not?" Zoya asked breathlessly, the fight with the big older man having left her utterly wasted.

"Overpenetration." The room on the other side of the wall behind the man was where the family of six were staying. He said, "I'll fire if he poses a threat."

The surviving would-be assassin slicked back hair that had fallen in his face with his free hand. He dropped his gun to the ground, then looked up and smiled at the pair of armed opponents in front of him.

Zoya shouted, "Move! I'm shooting this bastard anyway!"

"No!" Court said. "We've got him. Where's he gonna go?" Court asked.

"Yes," the man said in panting English. "Where . . . can I . . . possibly . . . go?"

The only sound for a moment was the heavy breathing of the three people left alive, but quickly, with a continued smile towards both Court and Zoya, the man in the server's coat turned to the open window, and then he rushed forward.

He dove out, headfirst, over the railing, making not a sound as he did so. Zoya's fourth-floor suite was five stories above the street.

"What . . . the . . . fuck?" Zoya muttered.

Court dropped back on his butt on the floor in utter exhaustion, sitting down on the eggs and blood smeared all around. He lowered his pistol as he did so. "I didn't see *that* coming."

Zoya moved to him, but she kept her weapon trained on the door to the hallway. "There's at least one more of them out there, somewhere."

Court blew out an exasperated sigh and hefted his own weapon with his bloody right arm, and he fell down onto his left elbow; the rapid onset of the fatigue in his body made him worry he was about to faint. "Shit."

Inna Sorokina couldn't believe what she'd just seen on the monitor from her suite up the hall. Maksim had taken a nose dive out of the building. Quickly she shouted an order through her earpiece to Anya, who was moments away from entering the fray.

"Hold! Come back here."

"I'm at the door, I can—"

"Sem and Maksim are dead. Both hostiles have the door covered. Return."

And with that Inna pulled off her headset and quickly slammed the laptops shut, then shoved them in the two backpacks remaining in the room.

When Anya made it back up the hall, Inna met her at the door and handed her one of the packs. Anya slipped her Grach pistol into it, and the two women headed for the nearby stairwell. Along the way, Inna pulled the fire alarm, hoping the two of them could blend in with the crowd of evacuees and escape.

Zoya crawled over to Court and hugged him with the arm that wasn't holding the SIG pistol on the door. "What's wrong? Are you hurt?" she asked, clearly seeing his utter exhaustion.

"Not . . . not too bad . . . you?"

She looked down at herself. Her bloody nose had soiled her torn white blouse, she was covered in jelly that had broken from a jar, coffee and juice dripped off her, and bits of egg covered her arms. But she appeared to be otherwise fine. She said, "We have to get out of here, fast."

Court looked at the window the man had just flung himself out of, and he said, "Quickest way's not always the best way."

She helped him up to his feet, saw the blood running from his arm. "Tie that off. I'll fix it when we're clear."

It took less than a minute for Zoya to change into a black turtleneck and to throw her important belongings into a bag, while Court used the time to stagger into the bathroom and cinch a hand towel around his injury with the belt from Zoya's bathrobe. Soon the two of them moved carefully into the hallway. The space was already full of people, all of whom, they assumed, had heard the gunfire, but Court and Zoya were banking on the confusion buying them the time they needed to get out of the building.

Court ducked into his room for his backpack, and then they headed off with the crowd.

The stairwell was all the way down at the other end of the hallway, so they stepped into the elevator. They stood with several other people coming down from the fifth floor, and made stops along the way down, ending with a car full of guests obeying the fire alarm.

As they walked through the lobby, Court holding the towel with his left hand to help stanch the bleeding, Zoya saw the stairwell door open. Several guests came filing out, and then, right in the middle of the thick pack, Zoya saw Inna Sorokina and a younger woman. They both had empty hands, but they carried backpacks slung over their shoulders.

Inna and Zoya made eye contact across the crowd, both stopping and staring at each other.

Zoya took Court by the arm. "One o'clock. In the blue top."

Court followed her eyes. "Got her."

"She's one of them. The woman next to her. Looks like they're together."

Court said, "Nothing we can do about it."

Reluctantly, Zoya admitted to herself that Court was right. She wasn't going to get into a gunfight around one hundred people.

The two of them stepped out the western side doors of the Adlon, with Zoya looking back over her shoulder, all the way across the big lobby, where she caught a glimpse of Inna moving with the throngs out the east side, into the sunny morning.

FORTY-EIGHT

Court and Zoya made it to his Spandau safe house thirty minutes after leaving the Adlon. He parked his bike in a weed-strewn asphalt lot behind the building, the two of them climbed off, and he showed her the way upstairs.

He was winded on the climb. The fight had taken too much out of him, and even with the drugs in his system to keep him going, he felt utterly drained.

At the top of the stairs Zoya saw this. "What's wrong?"

Court wiped yet another heavy coat of sweat from his forehead; it replenished itself immediately, and he pulled out the key to his apartment. "We'll talk inside."

A moment later Zoya stood in the middle of the bare flat, and she looked around the drab space. "Living the good life, I see."

"I didn't get a fancy suite at the Kempinski."

"I hear one just became available." She stepped closer to Court, took him by the arm, and looked at the bloody hand towel tied there. "Although housekeeping might need a few minutes." She took off the towel and examined the wound. "Nice one. Do you have a blowout kit?"

"In the kitchen."

Together they stepped into the small kitchen, and here she opened a black bag full of trauma supplies that sat on the counter. While she did this, Court opened the refrigerator and took out two bottles of water.

While Zoya prepared the items she needed to dress Court's wound, she said, "Back in the suite. You wouldn't let me take the shot. Something about overpenetration?"

"I saw four kids go into the room on the far side of that wall, less than an hour earlier. Don't know if they were there still, but I didn't want to shoot one, and didn't think you did, either."

"Well, I guess it didn't matter, in the end. I'd heard Akulov was insane, but I didn't know he thought he could fly."

Court eyed her a moment while she began gauzing his biceps. "Akulov, as in, Maksim Akulov?"

She nodded. "That was him."

"No kidding?" Court said. "I've been hearing that name for years."

"Yeah, he was kind of Russia's . . . you."

"Well, I wasn't that impressed, to be honest."

"You didn't get him at his best."

"Suits me. I love assassins that suck."

She tied off the wrap, a little tighter than Court would have wanted, and then he went to the bathroom and grabbed a roll of toilet paper, then came back and wiped dried blood from her face that had dripped from her nose.

"Do you have any vodka?" she asked.

"I don't, no."

"Why not?"

"Because it's fucking ten a.m., Zoya."

She laughed at this, and he laughed, too, then said, "Hey, back there . . . did you throw a ham sandwich at one of those guys?"

"I threw whatever the hell I could get my hands on. I think there was a ham-and-cheese croissant. Which means, not only were they bad assassins, but they also got my breakfast order wrong."

"I think I saw an omelet in the air, too. Did Russia teach you that shit at spy school?"

She rolled her eyes. "I was throwing the plate, not the food *on* the plate."

"Whatever." He looked at her now. "It's good to see you."

They stepped back into the empty living room.

Zoya sat on the small wicker sofa. "You always turn up in the strangest places."

"Where I immediately bump into you."

"You didn't bump into anybody. You've been following me."

"You saw me?"

"No," Zoya admitted. "You're invisible when you want to be. But Brewer told you where I was, I assume."

"Yeah."

Court sat down next to her. Even with the sickness and the injuries that racked his body, he wanted to move closer, to press himself against her, to kiss her. But instead he kept a couple feet of distance, because he found her body language hard to read.

"How have you been?" he asked.

"Since you shot me, you mean?" Court had indeed shot Zoya in the hip months earlier in Scotland, the instant after Zoya shot Brewer because she thought Brewer was about to shoot Court.

With extreme understatement, he said, "Yeah . . . that was a mess."

He rubbed his forehead; perspiration dripped to the floor.

Zoya softened a little. "Something . . . something is not right with you. Are you sick?"

"Picked up a little infection. The fever comes and goes. I'll be fine in a couple of days."

She looked at him like she didn't believe him, then said, "You need to get to Templeton Three, in Maryland. They'll patch you up. Then Hanley will come yank you out of your hospital bed and throw you back out to the wolves."

Court sniffed out a tired little laugh. "That kinda sounds like something he might do." He added, "Hey, sorry about your friend."

"What friend?"

"Ennis."

She looked at him with confusion. "He wasn't a friend. He was my contact at Shrike."

"Okay," Court said, and Zoya cocked her head now.

"What?"

"I mean, last night, at dinner. It kind of looked like you guys were getting along."

Zoya pushed a long strand of dark hair back behind an ear. "I was working him."

"Okay."

"I *was*."

Court nodded now, took another gulp of water, and looked away.

When he did not speak, she said, "Ennis was my only route up the food chain at Shrike. He was also a gossipy fool, if you want my opinion."

Court said nothing.

Zoya cocked her head again, and a little smile grew. "You're . . . jealous?"

Now he turned away, but affected a laugh. "Yeah, that's it," he said, with poorly sold sarcasm.

"That's hilarious." She said this with a little smile, and then her smile went away.

It seemed every time Court encountered Zoya Zakharova, there was both affection and mistrust in the air. So far, on their previous meetings, he'd been able to eliminate the mistrust over time, but he worried this was getting harder and harder to do.

Shooting her hadn't helped, but that wasn't the only rift between them.

Zoya replied, "We *aren't* good, you and I."

"I know," he responded, though, in truth, her words saddened him.

"But," she added, "you saved my life back there. Not for the first time, either."

Court thought back to the mad battle in the hotel suite, running it quickly through his mind like an organized after-action report. "Well, you shot the big dude, and the little dude did a header out the window. I'm not sure I did anything more than create a diversion."

"Yeah. Well, you are my walking, talking flash bang grenade." She smiled at him again, squeezed his good arm. "It's good to see you, too."

Court's right arm hurt, his left shoulder burned, he was exhausted and feverish, but this small moment of human interaction made him the happiest he'd been in months.

Since the last time the two of them shared a tender moment.

He knew what this meant, of course. It meant he was in love with her, and he worried still that it would be his undoing.

He shook his head to clear these thoughts away, and she looked at him strangely, wondering what must have been going on in his mind. But before she could ask, he got back to business. "Anyway. You're out, now. This op is over."

"Oh . . . great. This is where you start telling me what to do, isn't it?"

"No, I just—"

She shook her head. "It's *not* over. Not even close."

"What do you mean? You're blown."

"I'm blown at Shrike, but I can't leave Berlin yet. Something is about to happen."

"Yeah, you're about to get shot by Russian assassins."

"Not with you watching my back."

Court shook his head. This was an insane argument. "I've got assholes running around Berlin trying to kill me, too, Zoya. Sticking around till one of us gets schwacked is the dumbest thing imaginable."

"So . . . you are leaving town?"

Court took a few slow breaths. "No. Hanley needs me to—"

"Right," she interrupted. "I can't handle it here. But you can."

Court didn't know what to say; he was trying to keep her safe, but she was taking it to mean he was trying to control her, to hold her to a different standard than he held himself to. He changed the subject. "What do you mean, something is about to happen?"

Zoya didn't want to change the subject; this was clear from the expression on her face, even to Court. But after a moment she said, "Ennis said the company's contract with their client will end. The Germans will be handed the intel they needed to put EU sanctions back on Iran."

To this Court shrugged. "Okay. Great. So, Shrike are the good guys. Why do we need to get in the middle of that?"

Zoya shook her head. "But that's not what this is all about. Shrike Group is running a scam. They're trying to set the Iranian embassy up to take the fall for some sort of future terror attack by Quds Force. Ennis told me this morning before he died."

Court nodded at this. "I have to talk to Hanley."

"No. *We* have to talk to Hanley. And then we have to find Haz Mirza, the Quds Force cell commander here in Berlin."

But Court wasn't having it. "The Russians know you're here, and if there aren't more than the two we killed already looking for you, and the two you saw in the lobby of the Adlon, you can bet there will be a shit-ton more in town by nightfall. You know I'm right. You aren't helping the Agency, you are jeopardizing this mission by staying here."

She put her head in her hands, and Court saw that she understood.

Court said, "I'll take over the op."

"Do you have any sort of a plan?" Zoya asked.

Court shrugged. "Not really. I guess I'll try to find this Mirza asshole."

"Ennis said Dittenhofer is the one surveilling the Mirza operation. Remotely. She's in one of his phones, she can hear his conversations."

Court nodded. Resolute now. "Then I have a plan. I'm going to find Annika Dittenhofer, shake her down for the intel that Hanley needs about Shrike, and get her to lead me to Mirza."

"And what are you going to do to Mirza?"

"I'm not going to throw a ham sandwich at him, I can promise you that."

Zoya rolled her eyes.

Court said, "I'm going to kill him, and then I'm getting the fuck out of here myself before the dickheads from yesterday track me down again."

She said, "That's a big operation for a sick man with a wounded right arm and a fucked-up left shoulder."

"I appreciate your confidence."

Zoya smiled a little now. "You'll need support in the field. If not me, you need to get Hanley to link you up with Berlin station."

Court looked at her like she was crazy. "Why would I do that? The station is burned to Shrike Group."

Zoya turned to face him. "What are you talking about?"

"PowerSlave."

It was quiet in the empty apartment for several seconds. "I'm supposed to know what that means?"

"Jesus." Court understood. "Brewer and Hanley didn't tell you because they didn't want you to know you were working without a net in Berlin." When she shrugged, he said, "PowerSlave is a tool stolen from NSA. A biometric database containing all American intelligence personnel, linked to a program that can identify them on camera feeds. Sort of a master key to expose spooks and operators in the field. It was created by an NSA official named Clark Drummond, who worked directly for Dittenhofer, and it's been up and running for most of a year for Shrike here in Berlin."

Zoya looked up to the ceiling. "I knew nothing about this. They told me I'd have support if Moscow found me. And when I told Brewer that Moscow found me, they told me to sit tight."

Court cocked his head. "You told Brewer that Moscow found you here? She didn't say anything to me about that."

Zoya put her head back against the wall and closed her eyes. "That's Brewer for you. You're right. Even without what happened today, I'm burned here as an asset to Shrike Group."

"You'd just make it more dangerous for me if you stayed, not less. The Russians aren't targeting me." He amended that. "Well, they aren't targeting me like they're targeting you."

Zoya didn't argue the point, but she did ask, "What about Hightower? Why isn't he here helping us?"

"Because he's in a jail cell in Caracas."

She was surprised by this. "What's he doing there?"

"Not a whole lot, would be my guess. SEBIN has him."

"At Helicoide prison?"

"How did you know?"

"I know a little about Venezuela. I did . . . a . . . thing there once." She shrugged. "Once or twice."

Court knew better than to ask. She wouldn't say, and he really didn't want to know.

She surprised him with her next comment. "If I could get him out, would he be able to help you?"

Court nodded. "Well, sure, I could use his support here, especially if anything kicks off with the Iranians, but I don't know how you are going to be able to—"

"I know some people." She smiled a little. "More importantly, some people know me. I'll call Matt and see if he'll approve it."

Court shook his head adamantly. "With Matt, often it's better to ask forgiveness than to ask permission."

The Russian brunette nodded thoughtfully. "That makes sense. I'll just disappear for a couple of days. I've got access to an Agency account in Cyprus. It's not a ton, but I could probably get the money I need to go down and get Hightower."

Court said, "And I have access to an Agency account in Antigua. I'll give you the account and routing numbers." He added, "But the most important thing is that you leave here now."

They exchanged contact information, and Court passed over his banking info. This wasn't a CIA account; in truth, it was his own personal money, but he'd amassed a small fortune there in his years as a freelance assassin, and he wanted Zoya to have all the resources she needed.

When this was done, both of them rose, each helping the other up. As they stood face-to-face, close for the first time, Zoya's expression turned even more serious.

"What is it?" Court asked, concerned.

Zoya didn't respond. Instead she grabbed him by the back of the neck and kissed him hard on the mouth. He kissed her back, and they lingered close for a long moment, wrapped in the silence of the morning.

Finally, she backed away a half step.

Court didn't know what to say. He felt that way a lot around Zoya.

She repeated herself from earlier. "We're not good, you and I."

Court nodded slowly, as if he understood. But he did not. Women bewildered him.

She said, "But . . . everything you do, Court, you do it with the best of intentions. You're not perfect. Sometimes, you're wrong. Sometimes, you're so *incredibly* wrong you fuck things up royally. But I've never met anyone in my life, other than my late brother, who is such a fundamentally good person."

Court didn't think he was all that great, but he appreciated her saying it. They embraced again; he was careful to keep his new injury out of her grasp as he did so.

Court shook away the soft stuff and got back to business yet again. "Get out of here. If you can get to Zack, send him this way. If you can't, then don't worry about it. I've made it this far on my own. Also, dump your phone. And remember about Hanley. You can trust him to do what's best for the USA, but you can't trust him to tell you the truth. About *anything*. He manipulates people like us into doing some crazy shit, and I think you need to try to get out of the crazy-shit business."

"Look who's talking," she said with a little laugh.

"Yeah," Court responded, and he motioned to his body with a wave of his hand. "Look who's talking." He was wounded and sick, and he looked like death warmed over.

"You make a good point," Zoya said, and she kissed him one more time, then headed for the door.

FORTY-NINE

Court dialed a number just minutes after Zoya left his little apartment. It was only five a.m. D.C. time, but he didn't care.

Hanley answered, and it was clear he was wide awake. "That you?"

Court said, "Violator. Iden Alpha, X-ray, Mike—"

"Skip it, it's you. I'm getting reports from the embassy about more gunplay nearby. What the hell happened?"

"The Russians made an attempt on Anthem. She's okay, but her contact at Shrike is dead, and she's been burned."

"Shit," Hanley said, and then he said it again with more conviction. "Shit!"

"Yeah."

"Where is Anthem now?"

"She's on a plane out of here. She didn't tell me where and I didn't ask. She dumped her phone so she can't be tracked." Court needed Zoya off Hanley's radar for a while, for her safety and also so she could retrieve Hightower and put him back into play.

He went on to tell the DDO about Zoya's thoughts that Shrike Group was creating false linkage between a Quds cell operative and the Iranian embassy.

Hanley sighed loudly. "What's our next play? Berlin station is burned by PowerSlave."

Court replied, "I'm going to go find Annika Dittenhofer, and I'm going to get her to lead me to Mirza."

"How are you going to get her to—"

"I'll give her five seconds to talk, and then I'll start breaking bones."

"Violator, you are not healthy enough to—"

"I'm fine. I've been getting a little treatment."

Hanley paused on hearing this, but not for long. "Approved. Whatever you have to do."

"Solid copy, boss. By the way, I guess congratulations are in order."

"For what?"

"General Rajavi. You put a warhead on his forehead this morning. Well done."

"Yeah, but this wasn't just a regular drone hit. We knew there would be implications. The president wanted the motherfucker dead, so I killed the motherfucker, but I knew we'd be paying for it for a long time."

"Was it the right call, then?" Court asked.

Hanley snapped back at him a little. "You'd have killed him, too, if you had him in your rifle sights."

"Yeah, I would have, but I'm not always smart."

"I hear you. Truth is, we might have just kicked the shit out of a bees' nest in our backyard. One full of bees that might have stung us once or twice each summer, pissing us off, but not really hurting us."

Court said, "Yeah, but in this case, you didn't destroy the hive, you just broke it open. Now we are standing here in the backyard asking ourselves if the bees are gonna be mad."

"Fuck yeah, they're gonna be mad," Hanley replied. "And that's why your work is crucial. With Zoya out of it, Shrike is a loose cannon."

Court hesitated, then said, "There is something you aren't telling me about all this, isn't there, Matt?"

There was a short pause. "Isn't there always?"

"Jesus, you don't even try to sugarcoat it anymore, do you?"

"You are too smart for that. I'm giving you everything you need to know to do your job. Find Dittenhofer."

Court hung up with Hanley, slipped his phone into his pocket, and winced with the movement. His right biceps stung like hell when he used it, and he'd had no concept of how often he used it until it got slashed open this morning.

He had Annika's home address in Kreuzberg, but he doubted she would be there, especially after the death of Ennis this morning, along with the death of the German intelligence agent following Zoya the previous evening.

He also doubted Dittenhofer would be at the Shrike Group office. He'd driven by the Potsdam building and found it all but boarded up. He saw no vehicles in the parking lot and no lights on in the windows.

No, he realized he needed to approach finding her from another angle.

Clark Drummond had told Court that he always met Miriam at the same Tunisian coffee shop, Ben Rahim, near Alexanderplatz. It was common for intelligence officers to meet an agent in the same place. Court had no illusions that she met others there, however, and since Drummond had also described the woman as a very skilled intelligence operative, he figured she was too smart to conduct clandestine meetings in a place she frequented on her personal time. And even if she had frequented Ben Rahim, now that the man she'd met there had been exposed to compromise, he doubted she'd go back.

But Drummond's small shred of intel did give him an idea. From a search of the Internet the evening before he'd located four other highly rated Mediterranean coffee shops, all within a couple miles of Ben Rahim.

His thinking was that the highly specific coffee served at Ben Rahim insinuated that Miriam liked Mediterranean or Middle Eastern coffees, and while she might steer clear of one establishment because of the Drummond compromise, she might not feel the need to go cold turkey on her beverage of choice for the sake of operational security.

This was thin, he knew, but he was playing a hunch, and that was all he had to go on. He popped an Adderall and a pair of hydrocodone, slung his backpack over his shoulder, and headed downstairs to his bike.

Between four and five p.m., Court entered all four establishments he'd pegged as being similar enough to the Tunisian café where Drummond always met with Miriam, and in each location he'd ordered a drink, sat at a table near a plant or a corner or some knickknack on the wall, and then, careful to remain clandestine, he placed a tiny wireless camera that had been given to him by Berlin station. Once each one was set, he looked at an app on his phone and judged the video coverage displayed, then moved the camera via swipes on his screen, either left, right, up, or down.

The last location he cammed up was Café Latrio, a Mediterranean coffee shop and deli only a few minutes away from Ben Rahim. He planted his device high on a small decorative bookshelf while feigning a search for something to read. He then sat back down, finished his Turkish coffee, and headed back to his safe house.

At six p.m. a woman using the passport of American Virginia resident Stephanie Arthur boarded an Iberia Airline flight at Schönefeld Airport, beginning thirteen hours of travel to South America.

Zoya had a lot to do between now and then, but she knew Court needed the support that she couldn't give him.

She owed him that much. In truth, she realized that despite the lingering bad blood between the two of them, she owed him everything.

Keith Hulett, call sign Hades, followed his target through Berlin's Gesundbrunnen station, following along through the flux of workers heading home during rush hour.

The man he was after today was well into his forties; he wore a black turtleneck and carried a leather folio over a shoulder, and his wire-rimmed glasses made him look, to Hulett, like some sort of Middle Eastern college professor.

All he knew about the man was what he looked like and what streetcar he would disembark from in front of the station on his way to his train to his home in Neuenhagen.

And he knew it was his team's job to kill him.

The target stepped onto the train. Apollo, Mars, and Thor were already on board, and Hades climbed in last.

The plan had been to tail the man back to his house and do him there, or on the street close to his home.

But the plan changed when their target stood from his seat and headed out to the bathroom between two train cars.

Mars came over Hades's earpiece. "Looks like an opportunity."

"Roger that," Hulett replied. "Who is closest?"

"You and Thor."

"Okay, when he gets out of the head, we knock him out. We break his neck and roll him out of the train onto the tracks. It'll look like he fell or jumped and got run over."

The two Americans positioned themselves outside the bathroom, reached inside their coats, and each pulled a set of brass knuckles they'd made out of bicycle chains. They put the weapons on their hands and then, when the door opened, both men dove on the man in the wire-rimmed glasses, bashing him in the side of the head over and over.

In the end, they didn't have to break his neck. He was dead in less than ten seconds from massive blunt-force trauma.

They hefted him up, opened the door to the train, and rolled him out, down a shallow, rock-strewn ravine.

Their mission accomplished, both men started back for their seats, but Thor took Hades by the arm. "Shit, boss," he said, nodding towards the open bathroom. "Blood."

Hades spent the next ten minutes in the locked toilet, wiping blood with every piece of toilet paper he could find, splashing water around the enclosed space, even taking his sport coat off and ripping out the inner liner, giving him more fabric with which to clean.

When the train hit its next stop, Hades left the bathroom and was first out the door and down to the platform. A light rain had begun to fall, but he and the rest of his team walked through it in the crowd, the men behind Hades watching to make certain no one was following their leader.

By the time they climbed into a taxi for the drive back to the safe house, they told themselves they were in the clear, and they'd eliminated another terrorist.

Yesterday they had both killed a man and lost a man. Today, in contrast, was a win, though Keith Hulett knew he wouldn't be satisfied until he found Court Gentry in his gunsights again.

Next time, he vowed to himself, he would take the fucking shot.

FIFTY

Inna Sorokina's phone rang while she sat in the passenger seat of the Russian hit squad's rented Mercedes coupe. She looked down at the number and saw it was Maksim's burner.

Again.

It was almost ten p.m. now; they'd spent the entire day sitting in the car in an underground garage a couple of blocks from the Kempinski, worried about vehicle checks on the road in the wake of the chaos in the hotel at Pariser Platz. Now they were tired and stressed and they hadn't been able to get a signal on their sat phone to send in a distress call to Moscow.

Inna knew she had to make that call, but she told herself she first needed to remain vigilant while Anya drove, to make certain they hadn't been tailed.

The call could wait. Maksim and Sem weren't going to get any more dead in the interim.

A steady rain fell, and as they headed south out of the city, the sky grew darker and darker.

A minute later the phone rang again.

Anya said, "Why don't you just answer it?"

Sorokina turned it off now. "Someone found it with his body and has been calling the last number dialed, probably the only number dialed, trying to find a relative or a friend of the idiot who put on a room service uniform, murdered one or two foreigners in a hotel suite, depending on whether they think Semyon was a victim and not an aggressor, and then died trying to escape out the window."

"If that's what the authorities think, does that mean we're in the clear?"

Inna shook her head. "Not at all. They will work out quickly that the man dead on Unter den Linden had confederates, and they'll be hunting for them. Pulling the fire alarm bought us some time; they'll have a lot of people to look over on the camera footage, but you can bet we're burned."

Anya turned right off Potsdamer Strasse and up the little driveway of a lake house on lake Templiner, south of the city of Potsdam. It was a wooded area with more houses dotting the shore, not as remote as Sorokina would have liked, but, she had to admit, Anya had found a safe house with a good balance between accessibility to central Berlin and an out-of-the-way location with multiple avenues of escape, if necessary.

They entered the four-bedroom home at ten thirty and immediately set up their computers.

Anya said, "You *have* to call this in."

Inna nodded and sniffed. "What do I tell them?"

"What happened, I guess."

"Right." Inna pocketed her phone, then stepped over to the little bar by the glass windows to the back deck with the view of the lake. "I'll send a distress call to Moscow. But first we can have a drink in honor of Maksim. The fool got himself killed, he got Sem killed, and he failed to eliminate his target, but at least he didn't get us killed." Anya gave a stressed laugh, then went over and drank a shot of tepid vodka with her team's intelligence officer.

"That man today," Anya said. "Whoever he was, he was extraordinary. Maksim in his glory days wouldn't have had a problem with him, but Maksim's glory days are long past."

"All his days are past," Inna said solemnly, then poured herself another drink.

Just as she brought the little shot glass back to her mouth, she and Bolichova simultaneously heard a noise near the front door. They produced their pistols in an instant and trained them towards the sound just as the door opened.

Both women had their fingers on their triggers, and when a figure stepped into the room, out of the darkness and the rain, both women let out a gasp.

Inna blinked hard, as if the image in her eyes would just reset, turn into something else, something that made sense.

But when she opened them back up, the image remained.

Maksim Akulov stood before them in a black raincoat, dark slacks, and soaking-wet dress shoes. He stepped into the room, under his own power, and in his left hand he held a bottle of cheap bourbon.

It was clear from the bottle and from the man holding it that a few shots had been downed already.

The two women just stared uncomprehendingly, until both slowly lowered their weapons. They looked at each other, as if to say, *Are you seeing what I'm seeing?*

Akulov stepped into the house fully, shutting and locking the door behind him.

And then he said, "I bet you two are just full of questions."

Neither woman spoke, so Maksim asked Bolichova a question of his own. "Who was he?"

She was still in shock, but she said, "We . . . can only . . . assume he was the guest in the next suite." She looked at her screen. "Darrin Patch, from Canada. I'm sure it's a pseudonym, despite his backstopped legend."

"He just appeared in the room. How did he get into her suite without you seeing it on the hotel camera?"

Inna said, "There's only one explanation. He went out his window, climbed over to hers."

Anya was still incredulous about this. "That's . . . a long way down."

"Tell me about it," Maksim said.

"No, Maksim," Inna said. "You tell *me* about it. How are you alive?"

Maksim moved slowly to a chair near the laptops. Anya pulled it out for him and helped him sit down.

Finally, he said, "It all went to shit. The woman was a fighter, just as you said, but we had her. It was going to be messier than I wanted, but with Ennis there, I wasn't worried about all the evidence of a fight.

"Then he appeared. Out of fucking nowhere. We fought a moment, I injured him, but he was slippery. He . . . that man . . . he was . . . he was like nothing I've come up against. Economy of movement, unreal speed, an efficiency in his decision making." He looked at the women. "He dove away from one of my knives, thrown from only five or six meters' distance. He almost avoided the second one completely, too. I've never seen anything like that in my life."

Both Anya and Inna were impatient, but it was Inna who said, "Tell us how you survived the fall."

"I dove out the window. I didn't mind dying, I just refused to die at the hands of another. I remember flying through the air, the falling, the wind rushing past my ears. I thought I would be at peace, but I felt no peace, because I didn't understand who this man was and how he made me fail my final mission. I finally felt it."

"Felt what?"

"The will to live. If only to kill Zoya Zakharova."

He paused again. Inna was about to walk over and slap him across the face, just as she'd done late the previous night, so he could snap out of his inebriation long enough to tell them what the fuck was going on.

But before she could, he shrugged. "And then I hit it."

"Hit . . . *what*?" Anya asked.

"I hit a flagpole. Don't know how far down it was, but it hurt. It snapped under my weight, but I got hold of the flag, and it tore immediately. Then I was falling again. Spinning." He looked off into the distance; he was reliving a recent memory through the haze of drink.

"I crashed into the canopy in front of the main entrance. A big, red, soft fabric, which tore in two, of course, with the force of my weight and my fall."

Anya cocked her head. "You crashed through the awning and hit . . . *what*?"

"A bellman was pushing a luggage cart into the hotel. I landed on it. The flagpole and the flag slowed me, the canopy absorbed much of my momentum, and a stack of Louis Vuittons took care of the rest."

Inna remained utterly incredulous. "That must have been eighteen, maybe twenty meters."

Maksim replied, "I'm no expert, but it felt like twenty-five."

"You weren't hurt?"

He rolled his eyes. "Of course I was hurt." He took off his wet raincoat with difficulty, opened his shirt, and took it off in front of the two women. Though he was covered in body art, when he lifted his right arm to them, it was easy to see it was horribly scraped and bruised. Vicious red and purple splotches covered the right side of his rib cage, as well. "But nothing broken, I don't think. If I sober up I might find out differently. I was helped up, someone ran to get me a doctor, but I just staggered off. Bought this coat, went to a bar, fell asleep in a park, went to a liquor store, came here." He sighed. "What a day."

He unscrewed the top of the bottle of bourbon, started to bring it to his lips, then looked at Inna. "With your permission."

She sniffed and looked away. "Doesn't matter now, does it?" She was still fixated on his story. "You are the luckiest maniac to ever live."

"Me? Lucky?" He snorted out a little laugh and took a long pull from the bottle.

"I'll get you some ice," Anya said, and she headed to the kitchen.

"Just a couple of cubes. I don't want to water it down."

Inna snapped at him. "She's talking about for your injuries, not for your Jack Daniel's!"

Maksim didn't acknowledge her, he just looked out the window towards the lake. "It's a shame about Semyon, but Zakharova would have shot me, instead, if he hadn't been there to take her attention while I fought the other guy. Poor Sem saved my life."

What a wasted pursuit that was, Inna thought but did not say.

Maksim drank while the two women tried to wrap their heads around the fact that their leader sat here before them, alive.

Inna shook the insanity of it all away, then pulled out her phone to call in to Moscow. Before she dialed, Maksim spoke, though it seemed as if he were talking to himself.

"The stranger. Whoever he was, he had one flaw, though. One easily exploitable weakness."

"Which was?" Sorokina asked.

"Virtue." He lit a cigarette from a pack he took out of his raincoat. "He went through all that to save Zakharova. And then, when he had me in his sights, he put himself between her and me." He took a puff and blew out smoke. "I don't know where he came from, I don't know who he is, but I am certain that he cares for her more than he does for his own life."

"You can identify love from actions in a gunfight?" Anya asked as she handed him a plastic bag of ice. He placed it between his ribs and his right arm, and used the arm to press it against his torso.

Maksim winced with the cold as he thought about the question posed to him. "*Da*, I suppose I can. He loves her. That's it. I felt it."

Inna had heard enough. "I'm calling Moscow so we can be exfiltrated."

Maksim took another drink from the bottle. "*Nyet*, I'll do it."

"Are you sure—"

"I'll do it!" He stood, turned, and pointed at Bolichova. "You got images of the man when he was in the suite, correct?"

"Yes. They automatically saved on my laptop."

"Send the images to Moscow; they can run them against the SVR, FSB, and GRU databases. Do everything you can to identify him."

"Yes, sir," she said, as she spun to her computer.

But Inna said, "Why? Sem is dead. We failed. All we need to worry about is getting out of here before we are captured or killed."

Maksim headed for the back deck, limping slightly as he walked. He pulled out his phone at the back door, then turned to the two women. "Indulge me. Put a name to that face. Put a biography to that name." He left through the door.

Anya Bolichova was already working on it. Inna just sat down on the sofa, still dumbstruck that Akulov had somehow survived.

Haz Mirza had spent the day as angry and as resolute as he had ever been in his life, but now, seconds after ending the call on his burner phone, he was even angrier.

Stand down.

That had been the message from his superiors. Yes, they were as angry as Mirza, they swore unto Allah, but there could be no violent retaliation, whatsoever, in Europe. Not now. The relaxation of sanctions was, Mirza had been told, simply too important to give up.

The twenty-four-year-old Iranian seethed. He wanted to act. He *needed* to act. The entirety of his time here in Germany, the entirety of his time fighting for the Shia realm in Yemen and Libya and Syria, it would all be just a big joke, a waste of life, if the West could simply be allowed to decapitate Iranian military intelligence without Haz Mirza doing anything more than going to his job at the trucking company like it was just another regular day.

He'd spoken to all nine of his men around the city today, before the stand-down order had been relayed. To a man they'd been furious at America because of the murder of General Rajavi, and they all agreed they would do whatever it was that Tehran wanted. But Mirza could tell that for some of them, their hearts weren't in it. Two of the group mentioned the easing of sanctions themselves, saying if this cell had had Allah's fortune to be stationed in D.C., and not Berlin, then they would have certainly acted in the first few hours to deliver Iran's crippling counterstrike.

"But Berlin, brother," one said, and the second echoed his sentiment. "This is not where the fight will be. Let's keep our heads down, wait for our chance to serve our nation."

Mirza had wanted to pull his Beretta pistol on the men who talked like this. Weak lambs.

He went to bed at one in the morning, but he couldn't sleep. His body communicated his need to him as strongly as his heart did. His hands were balled into fists, his jaw clenched, his blood pumping madly through him.

The thought of defying his masters came to him, and he discounted it the first time. The second time, he did the same. But the third time, he allowed his brain to linger a moment at the possibility. He had drawn up a plan himself for a brazen attack on the U.S. embassy. He had light weapons, he had nine mujahedin to fight with, though some of them were probably better truck loaders and forklift drivers than they were combatants.

If he went forward despite his orders to stand down, he and his men would be sentenced to death by Tehran for their actions, but Haz Mirza did not find this to be any great deterrent. He was no fool. He knew that ten men couldn't take over the U.S. embassy, not for any real length of time. No, they would all die in the lobby in a hail of gunfire.

But not before they had struck a blow against America, a blow that would send it reeling.

A blow that, in Mirza's racing brain, would lead to other Shiites around the world taking up arms in retribution for the death of General Vahid Rajavi.

He made no decision that night, but only by telling himself that his jihad was coming, one way or another, did he allow himself to finally close his eyes, to fall asleep, and to dream of glory.

FIFTY-ONE

Court woke before dawn, then changed the dressing on his arm, which he found to be a shame because Dr. Kaya had done an amazing job on it late the night before. Still, a little blood wept through the bandage, and he knew he'd have to clean it a couple of times a day, like it or not.

He didn't want *another* infection.

He'd visited the young doctor's flat just after ten p.m., where he received his transfusion, and she treated his fresh wound with no small amount of frustration that Court was still out there getting himself injured.

When she'd first seen the bandaging, she'd said, "I can tell this was wrapped by a man."

"Why do you say that?"

"It's done professionally, but roughly. You need a more feminine touch."

Zoya had been the one who dressed his wound. He smiled to himself.

Dr. Kaya didn't mention one thing about all the news. Court was certain there had been wall-to-wall coverage of all the killings in the center of the city, and she would know, without question, that the rough man who visited her at night to be treated for injuries would be involved in them, but she didn't say a word.

He felt bad for Azra, but he left her apartment feeling good, then went back to his safe house and crashed for a few hours.

Now, before dawn, Court sat on the floor of his third-floor flat on Bismarckstrasse in Spandau, a laptop open in front of him and the recorded camera feeds of four coffee shops playing out on a split screen. They'd been recording twelve hours already; the battery charges were good for twenty-four, and then he'd have to go switch them out.

Each time a female who looked anything like Dittenhofer entered a café, he tapped a key, bringing all four simultaneous recordings to a stop. And then, invariably, he'd determine that the woman was not the woman in the picture on the floor next to him, and then he would continue his scan.

It was tedious work, but it required constant focus nonetheless.

And then, shortly after eight a.m., he saw a woman fitting Annika Dittenhofer's general profile enter Café Latrio. He didn't have a good image of the coffee shop customer until she sat at a table and opened her own laptop. Then, using a function on the app to zoom in on and then sharpen the face, he checked her out more closely.

He recognized her both from the photo Drummond had printed for him and from older photos Brewer had sent along.

She reminded him a little of Zoya; they were the same age, and they both had a combination of soft feminine facial features and focused, intelligent eyes, although Dittenhofer's hair was somewhat longer and much, much curlier, and her eyes were aquamarine, whereas Zoya's were brown.

Court shook his head to clear it. Upon further inspection, she looked little like Zoya.

The woman before him had a look about her that said *all business, all the time*; she typed on her laptop, her ceramic coffee cup next to her, her oversized shoulder bag on the chair at the table.

Getting caught in the open by going to a café similar to the one she regularly met a compromised colleague at was not good tradecraft on her part, to say the least, which meant one of two things to Court. Either Drummond had misjudged this woman's abilities, or else this woman wasn't experiencing much or any counterintel threats in her work.

But Drummond had been NSA and CIA; he knew quality when he saw it, so Court assumed Miriam was simply confident Drummond had not compromised her before he died, and she clearly wasn't feeling any threats from any of her intelligence targets here in Berlin.

Court raced out of his apartment and down the stairs to his motorcycle, hoping he could make it to Café Latrio before she left her seat.

Since the moment Ric Ennis's body had been discovered in a hotel suite registered to Stephanie Arthur the day before, Annika Dittenhofer and Rudy Spangler had spoken to each other over a dozen times. Annika was desperate to get more information from the police, and Rudy was in full crisis mode himself.

Both of them suspected from the outset that a Russian hit team had come for Zakharova, and Ennis had just suffered the misfortune of being in the wrong place at the wrong time.

But this theory had one flaw. It didn't account for Zakharova's whereabouts now. Spangler speculated that the former SVR operative had been rendered back to Russia alive, and the operation was a kidnapping and not an assassination plot at all.

There was some evidence in favor of this. The entire camera network at the hotel had been brought down as the operation took place. It seemed like this was a step the Russians would only have taken if they were not going to be able to exfiltrate in a clandestine fashion.

Annika wasn't sure. She still felt Zakharova could have actually been the one who killed Ennis, although she couldn't figure out why.

Each time Spangler and Dittenhofer spoke, the owner of Shrike International Group urged his subordinate to stay focused on the company's mission. Spangler passed down a new targeting list to Dittenhofer, and when she called him this morning, his first question was about her progress.

"The names I gave you. VAJA men. Where are you on—"

"Rudy?"

"What is it?" he asked, his voice nervous.

"I have good news, for once. Haz Mirza received a hard stand-down order from military intelligence in Iran. They disavowed any actions he might take, and they threatened to send men to kill him themselves if he even contemplated doing anything to upset the Europeans."

"You picked up communications from Tehran?"

"We did. Mirza wasn't happy about it, but Tehran was very clear in their wording. No attacks are to take place in Europe."

Spangler said, "That is, indeed, excellent news. I told you, Annika, that something good was going to come of this."

Annika was dubious. She let out a little laugh. "So far, nothing has come out of our work, other than the fact that we know Iran isn't going to retaliate."

"My client is taking our information and processing it, and I expect all the Quds operatives to be arrested in short order."

"Okay, well, I'm not rolling up my operation. Moises, Yanis, and I are going to stay on Mirza today. Track his movements. We picked up chatter that yesterday he dropped in on a couple of the cell members; they were complaining to one another that he was wild with fury, insisting they would get a green light for one of their operations. This was before he was given the stand-down order, but he sounds like a loose cannon. I'm going to keep tracking."

Spangler said, "Don't compromise yourself. After what happened to Ennis and Zakharova yesterday, we need to be careful."

"You, too, Rudy."

Annika Dittenhofer hung up the phone, took her empty coffee mug to the counter, then left Café Latrio, anxious to meet up with Moises and Yanis in their surveillance vehicle to see if Haz Mirza was going to meet with any of his people today.

But first, she told herself she should run a short SDR. Normally she didn't bother; the Iranians were unaware of Shrike and its operation against them, but with the killing of Ennis the day before and the disappearance of Zakharova, she knew she had to up her personal security. Twenty or thirty minutes of random movements would alert her to anyone on her tail, she decided, so she got to it immediately.

Court Gentry watched her leave the café, and he fell in behind her, remaining careful not to underestimate her skill based solely on the fact that she'd fucked up on choosing a coffee shop.

And he was glad for this. He began to notice her taking stock of her surroundings as she moved, checking behind her a couple of times. It looked to be more of an automatic function ingrained in her, and less of a specific worry, but Court knew he could get caught just the same if he wasn't careful.

But Court was the Gray Man; he walked along unnoticed, stayed behind small clusters of pedestrians, moved diagonally to remain behind a bus stop advertisement when she reached a corner, always keeping something between himself and his target except for brief moments of time. He even crossed the street and moved one block laterally to her to avoid a choke point he'd seen ahead.

After a five-minute stroll she climbed aboard a streetcar and Court hopped on behind her, losing sight of her in the process, but checking at subsequent stops to see if she got off.

She made it three stops, switched trains, and started back in the opposite direction.

She ran an SDR for thirty minutes or so; it was competent, demonstrating to Court that she had, in fact, been trained, though she seemed to be a little overconfident in her abilities, or at least in the paucity of threats to her operation.

When she stepped off the streetcar on Fritz-Reuter-Allee in the gritty Neukölln neighborhood, she glanced behind her briefly, checking to see if anyone of interest got off to trail her. Court waited for her to do this, to satisfy herself she was in the clear, and then he jumped out of the last car just as the doors shut. Dittenhofer was a good seventy yards away by now, but he kept his stroll casual and his head moving, left and right, making sure he had both her in sight and himself in her blind spot in case she turned around.

It took another ten minutes, but the German woman finally arrived at her destination. She climbed into the back of a small moving truck on Gielower Strasse. Long rows of identical three-story apartment buildings were arrayed out in all directions on the block. Court presumed she was here, perhaps with technical staff, surveilling someone in one of the apartments.

He reached into his backpack, pulled out a device, and turned it on. While he did this he walked along the sidewalk, closer and closer to the moving truck.

His face displayed the countenance of a man lost in deep thought; he just strolled by like he passed this way every day at this time, and he showed no interest in anything or anyone around him.

Court had become an expert on planting bugs or tracking devices in plain view. He stepped off the sidewalk behind the moving truck and then, shortly before he came around the side where he could be picked up in the rearview mirror, he bent over without breaking stride and affixed the magnetic GPS tracker just under and inside the rear bumper.

Court continued on into and across the little street, then headed down a pedestrian walkway between two rows of apartment buildings.

He was clear in seconds, and minutes later he sat in a nearby café and ordered a coffee.

He didn't have a line of sight on his target, but he had positioned himself between her physical location and the closest streetcar stop and the closest U-Bahn station. With the tracker on her vehicle, he had her covered regardless of whether she left via the truck or on public transportation.

He'd like to have an eye on her right now, but in truth, he wasn't interested in monitoring her surveillance. No, he wanted to take her, to interrogate her. He considered just busting into the van, holding a gun on any cohorts she had there, and pulling her away, but realistically he knew he wouldn't make it far. He didn't have a vehicle with him at the moment. His best option, he decided, was to wait for her to leave, alone. He'd look for an opportunity to snatch her, and then he would take her to a dark and quiet place.

He caught himself wishing Zack were here. There was no one on earth better at interrogating intelligence away from a wily prisoner.

FIFTY-TWO

El Helicoide prison in central Caracas had originally been designed as a shopping mall, in a time when the Venezuelan government felt shopping malls were more important than prisons. That time had long passed, so the massive three-sided, pyramid-shaped structure had been converted into a detention and interrogation facility, some one hundred thousand square meters in size.

Venezuela had a lot of political prisoners, after all, and the numbers were growing all the time.

On a sweltering-hot morning a car pulled up to the entrance on Nueva Granada, and an attractive blonde with a large Coach purse climbed out. She headed for the outer-perimeter fence on foot and spoke poor Spanish to the guard, but he found it good enough for him to confirm that her name, or at least her alias, was on the day's visitors list.

He had her step through an X-ray scanner while her purse was placed on a conveyor belt so they could get their own scan.

On the other side of the gate, more guards took her purse over to a table, and the woman strolled over after a quick pat-down.

The contents of the purse were checked carefully, a phone was taken and placed in a small locker, and the woman's passport and visa were looked over for a moment. A large manila folder was pulled from the purse; it was stuffed full of something, so the guard unfastened and opened it.

He found stacks of twenty-euro notes, wrapped in bundles of one hundred notes each.

The man glanced up at the woman, but almost immediately a guard refastened the folder and placed it back in the purse.

Bribes passed through this security checkpoint all day long.

Zoya Zakharova was welcome here at Helicoide under the alias Tatiana Pankova. She'd been here a few times over the years while working with SVR, and there were still some people in the intelligence circles who owed her favors.

Or at least she thought they did.

She'd find out soon enough if her clout remained, even after her work with Russia's foreign intelligence service had ended. She was betting that her alias had not been burned in the few months she'd been out.

She wasn't trying to pass herself off as a current SVR employee—she wouldn't have been able to pull that off—but rather as a former SVR employee, here to collect on a favor.

And it certainly didn't hurt that she'd brought a manila envelope full of cash.

Zoya was escorted into the building proper; she walked through the halls to a staircase, since the elevator bank had an Out of Order sign on it, and with her minders she made it up to an office on the fourth floor.

The common areas of the entire building had a shopping mall feel to them, but the anteroom she entered gave off a typical developing-world government-installation vibe. Everything was metal and pressboard, file cabinets looked like they'd last been dusted in the 1980s, and other than a pair of large, cheaply framed photos of Venezuela's president and some general Zoya didn't recognize, the paneled walls were unadorned.

Her minders opened a door to a similarly shoddy office, and she went inside. They shut the door behind her, and she stood alone for a moment before she heard the flush of a toilet and then, thankfully, a sink running. Soon a middle-aged man with a big gut entered the room from a small side door. He wore the uniform of the Fuerzas Terrestres, the Venezuelan army, and carried the rank of colonel.

In English he said, "Colonel Hector Salerno, at your service." The two shook hands, but Zoya felt no warmth from the man.

"Tatiana." She didn't bother with a last name, because this man would know it wasn't real.

"Tatiana," he repeated. And then, in an almost bored and disinterested voice, he said, "I was told to extend you every courtesy."

Zoya only nodded curtly. *Let's get on with it,* she thought. This man clearly didn't like that he'd been told to do this woman's bidding, and for her part, this woman did not give a shit.

Salerno said, "I was also told you wanted us to release one of our prisoners into your custody." He stepped over to his desk and made a show of looking through some papers. She waited patiently while he pretended to read the name for the first time. "Zachary Hightower. The American."

Zoya imagined Salerno had thought of nothing else other than Zack Hightower since the day before, when her contact reached out to Salerno with the bribe offer.

Just as nonchalantly, he asked, "What is your interest in the prisoner?"

"I have no interest in him. I've been sent on an errand. Doing my job. As are you, Colonel Salerno."

The older man regarded the comment, seemed to think it over, as if there were a chance he wouldn't hand over the man. In truth, she knew full well that he was just beginning the process of jockeying for more money.

Zoya had been down this road a time or two.

She said, "The prisoner. How is he?"

"You have concerns about his health?"

"Only in that I would like him to be able to walk under his own power, and talk when necessary."

The colonel smiled. "It's not a health spa I'm running."

Zoya said nothing.

"I am told he is fine. He's only been here a number of days. Give him a month, maybe, and he'll be . . . different." The man smiled.

Zoya opened her purse and put the thick folder on the metal desk. "I'll take him as is. Now, as far as a holding and handling fee for Mr. Hightower, I am certain you will be pleased with this generous offer."

Salerno did not touch it at first. Instead he winked at her. "I don't accept rubles."

"Then it's good I brought euros. Fifty thousand."

He made a face as if he had been insulted by her offer. "One hundred," he countered.

Without hesitation, Zoya said, "Forty-five thousand."

"What?"

"Forty thousand. I'm on a mission for someone else, I don't care if you say yes or no."

"Wait. Wait! Okay! Make it fifty again, and I agree."

The woman shook her head. "Forty. I leave with him now and you get the money. I leave without him and you don't." The two of them stared at each other for a time, and then Salerno looked away, down at the folder, and he opened it.

Counting the money, he found exactly forty thousand euros. "How did you know—"

The woman interrupted. "I need to get him on a plane to Moscow by noon. May I have him delivered to exit processing? I can bring my car directly to the tunnel if you will ask your security officer to allow my entrance."

Salerno raised an eyebrow. "You know our system, and you know the layout of our facility. Interesting. Obviously, you've been here before."

"And I'll probably be here again, Colonel. Until that time, it's been a pleasure doing business with you."

She shook his hand; again there was no warmth, but Salerno was, at least, pleased with himself for scoring the big payday for some American, one whose own nation hadn't even asked about him.

Forty-five minutes later Zoya stood at the open back door of her Toyota Camry looking down a long, dark tunnel. A few guards stood around; Salerno hadn't left his office but he'd had one of his people bring her vehicle down from the parking garage while two more escorted her through the warren of hallways and staircases to make her way here.

She'd waited only a few minutes when she heard a heavy metal door clang, and then the rattling of chains, somewhere deep in the tunnel. Soon she saw Zack, shuffling along, with a pair of guards flanking him. He wore a light blue jumpsuit and his blond hair was disheveled but, Zoya noticed, he moved along at a strong pace.

As he got closer she noticed that his eyes were downcast, his face had no discernible expression, and, as near as she could tell, he hadn't even looked up to see her.

At the Toyota his shackles were removed, he was shoved closer to her, and still he stared down to the ground.

Zoya snapped her fingers in the man's face; he looked up at her and displayed no recognition.

"Hey!" she said. "Can you speak?"

After several seconds he said, "You won't get me to talk, either."

Only now did Zoya realize what was going on. She wore a blond wig, makeup that made her eyes look larger and her face appear older than it was.

He didn't recognize her.

She slapped him hard across the face, stunning him, and he didn't speak again.

One of the guards said something about the prisoner being "loco," and Zoya led him to the front passenger seat.

Minutes later the two of them were on the open road. They were clear of the prison gates, and yet the silence remained.

"You won't get me to talk," Hightower said again.

Zoya turned to him. In English, with no Russian accent now, she said, "That's the best news I've heard all day. Usually I can't get you to shut up."

Zack cocked his head, and his eyes cleared in an instant. "Anthem? I'll be damned."

"You're welcome."

"I didn't expect to see you here." She kept driving. "Why the slap back there? That shit hurt."

"Had to sell it, didn't I?"

After a long pause, Zack laughed. "Nah. You wanted to get a free lick in, didn't you?"

"You won't get *me* to talk, either."

They drove through the thick traffic. Zack squinted in the sunshine, the first he'd seen in days.

"How did you pull this off?"

"When I was with SVR I worked Caracas for a short time. Made contacts. One of those contacts is now in charge of SEBIN. I reached out to him; he was under the impression I was still affiliated with Russian black ops, contractually, anyway. Probably because I *told* him I was still affiliated with Russian black ops. I also gave him a bribe. My contact in SEBIN put the fear of the Lord into the warden, but I had to pay him just now, as well, to make sure it all went smoothly."

"Where'd you get all that money?"

She turned to Zack. "The money came from Hanley."

"Did you just get me in trouble?"

"I just got you *out* of trouble. Remember?"

"How much did Hanley have to pay?"

"One hundred thousand euros."

"That's it? Stingy bastard."

"Actually, Matt Hanley didn't offer a cent. I used his money without his knowledge."

"Figures. Well, I owe you." He reclined his seatback, closed his eyes. "Can't wait to be outta here. Gonna take a few days on my back porch with a beer in my hand and my feet up."

"No, you're not. You're going to Berlin. Now."

Zack raised his seat again slowly. "What the hell's in Berlin?"

"Court, and he's got his hands full."

"He's in the field? I thought he was out of commish."

"He should be. He's not."

Zack conveyed that he understood what she meant. "Fuckin' Hanley."

The Toyota rolled on to the airport in thick rush-hour traffic.

FIFTY-THREE

The three Russians in the safe house at the lake had been awake for hours, mostly drinking tea and perusing the news. Inna made breakfast for them all; it was something to keep her mind off the fact that Moscow hadn't contacted them again after Maksim's distress call the evening before.

Anya was on her laptop, waiting for a response to the query of the face she'd sent to Moscow over a dozen hours earlier.

Maksim, for his part, was in pain—his ribs and arm and hip throbbed. All his body parts functioned, some with more difficulty than others, so he still didn't think he'd broken any bones, but deep purple bruising covered a large portion of his torso and arms, and he didn't expect the pain to go away anytime soon.

Today Maksim seemed as sullen and moody as ever. He just sat on the back deck overlooking the water, smoked, and looked out over the lake. The bottle he'd walked in with the night before was on the kitchen counter, as yet untouched for the day, but Inna expected that to change soon.

At ten fifteen a.m., Inna opened the door to the deck. "Why haven't they responded?"

Maksim just shrugged.

"It's been ten . . . no, *twelve* hours. They should have at least communicated the exfiltration plan."

"Nobody has called. What do you want me to do about it?"

"Call them back, or I will."

The Russian man turned to his subordinate. "No, you won't."

"What are you waiting for?"

"It's fine. We're fine. We'll be okay."

"Tell Semyon that, Maksim."

The assassin glared at her, and he was about to respond when Anya Bolichova leapt up from the sofa in the living room and opened the back door. "Both of you! Get in here!"

The other two did, then looked to her in surprise. She was the quietest, meekest, of the team. She never spoke with such authority.

"What is it?" Inna said.

Anya stared at her screen. *"Der'mo!"* And then she spoke more softly. "I . . . I don't believe it."

"Well, we're here. Are you going to talk?" Maksim asked, crushing out his cigarette in an ashtray on the coffee table.

She looked away from them, outside the window of the lake house, then back down to her computer.

"I heard . . ." Her voice quivered a little. "I heard from headquarters. About the man in Sirena's hotel room. They got a hit on his face."

Sorokina instantly sat down. She knew from Bolichova's countenance that this was going to be important. Maksim, on the other hand, lifted his bottle with the arm that wasn't banged up, bit the lid off with his teeth, and spit it on the floor.

Before taking a drink he said, "Who was that bastard, then?"

"The same man was photographed two years ago. Near St. Petersburg. He was inside the home of Gregor Sidorenko."

"The mafioso?" Sorokina said. "Two years ago? Was this before or after Sidorenko's death?"

Bolichova hesitated again.

Maksim swigged the whiskey now; Inna couldn't tell for certain if he even cared, though he was the one who had demanded the unknown man be identified.

When Bolichova didn't respond to Inna's question, she posed it again. "Anya. Was the man photographed in the house before or after the assassination of Gregor Sidorenko?"

Anya's eyes flicked away from the screen and towards Sorokina. "It was . . . *during* the assassination."

Maksim's eyes narrowed now, and he slowly lowered the bottle in his hand. "Wasn't Sidorenko supposedly killed by . . ."

His voice trailed off.

Sorokina had all the gravity in her own voice now that Anya possessed. "*Da.* Anya is saying that the person who you fought against yesterday . . . was the Gray Man."

Maksim sat slowly on one of the sofas, brought the whiskey to his mouth just as slowly, and then took another single long gulp. When he lowered the bottle away, he looked down at it in his hand, then back to Sorokina. "He's not real. The Gray Man is just a fantasy."

"Is Semyon's death a fantasy? You said yourself you'd never seen anything like this man."

Bolichova sat back down at her laptop. "His name is Courtland Gentry. He is American. A private, freelance assassin."

Inna answered with one distracted word. "Kiev."

Anya said, "*Nyet.* Kiev was not the Gray Man. It was ten, twenty men. America's Delta Force, something like—"

Inna shook her head. "It was one man. It was the Gray Man. I didn't believe it then, but I believe it now."

It was quiet for a moment other than another gulp of bourbon that went down Akulov's gullet.

Inna turned to him. "Am I going to have to shoot that bottle out of your hand?"

He took it from his mouth. "I don't believe any of this."

She said, "Maksim. I told you Sirena would be working with someone else. I told you she was a formidable foe. I did not know how correct I was about both points."

Maksim said nothing, so Sorokina stood. "I'm calling headquarters back. They will send another team, or two teams, or five damn teams. They will take care of it. We are in no condition—"

Maksim Akulov flung the bottle hard across the room; it hit the stone fireplace and shattered into a thousand shards, and brown liquid shot in all directions three meters away.

"Nobody is calling anyone! We have this situation under control!"

Inna shut her eyes a moment. "In what way are we exerting control?"

"Anya," Maksim said. "Go take a walk."

Bolichova didn't have to be told twice. She slipped her pistol into her jeans and under her blouse, pulled her mobile off the table, and left the lake house, heading out towards the long driveway.

As soon as the door latched behind her, Inna said, "I am calling it in. I have to. At the very least, we need a replacement for Pervak. And sooner or later, Sem is going to be tied to the Bratvas, and the killings at the hotel and in the Tiergarten. They need to know what's coming their way."

"I will contact headquarters," Maksim said.

She cocked her head. "*Again*, you mean. You called them last night, right?"

He just shrugged and looked out the window.

"You didn't even call, did you?"

With a second shrug, he said, "I wanted positive ID on the man I faced before I decided if I was going to leave Berlin."

Inna closed her eyes. "The man who bested you yesterday. You want to stay here so that he kills you tomorrow. Is that it?"

"*Nyet*. I was given a mission, and that mission is the only thing that matters."

"Because that mission is what will lead you back to the Gray Man."

He moved closer to Inna. Leaned closer still, his breath hot and rank in her face. "I will call Moscow, right now. I'll say I want a stand-in for our dearly departed colleague, and I will say that we are on mission and fully capable."

"Why? Why does he matter? Why does she matter?"

"Inna, don't you see it?"

"See what?"

"This is the ending I've been dreaming of. I didn't care about killing some stupid SVR bitch who pissed off the wrong people at Yasenevo. Who fucking cares? But now? *Now* I have something to live for."

"Wow," Inna said. "Even when sober, you don't make any sense. This is something to live for, but it's the ending you wanted?"

"I will kill Sirena, and I will kill the world's most revered assassin, and I will go out on top."

Sorokina thought she understood. She said, "Go out?"

"I'll put a bullet in my brain, blast myself all over the bodies of my last, and greatest, victims."

She sighed. She wanted to tell him he needed a fast ride in the back of a van back to Mental Hospital Number 14. But she knew when to challenge him, and she knew when to back off. This was not a fight she would win. She could only do her best to steer her assassin back on track.

"Can you fight him? Like that?" She motioned to his shirtless body, covered in welts.

"I hurt him worse than he hurt me. Now that I know who he is, I will be ready to finish the job." He stood now, wincing with the motion. "When Anya gets back, she needs to work to get us a new fix on Zakharova. We find her, we find him, and I will defeat them both. In the meantime, I'll report in, and I'll start to heal from yesterday. I'll be ready."

He pulled out his phone. His decision had been made, and Inna would go along.

But she was more certain than ever that Maksim Akulov would end up getting her killed.

FIFTY-FOUR

Haz Mirza sat on his bed in his little flat at Gielower Strasse 41, doing his best to control his breath, to calm himself. Finally, he picked up a burner phone tucked in the sheets in front of him and tapped the icon to open Threema, the end-to-end-encryption private messaging app he used to communicate with the phones owned by members of his sleeper cell.

Mirza was using a solid approach to private communications, but he was unaware that Annika Dittenhofer had had him tailed months ago by a coordinated team of her denied assets. Through this she learned that he bought his burners at a small Chinese-run electronics shop in the eastern Winsviertel neighborhood, far from Mirza's apartment in Neukölln.

And then, after winning a fight with Rudy over the cost of the operation, Annika purchased one hundred of the phones, then had them specially altered. The new phones she repackaged in shrink wrap, so that they were indistinguishable from models for sale on shelves around the city.

She then had them slipped into DHL shipments heading to the electronics store. The Shrike-altered phones had an actual digital transmitter implanted in them, with a tracking device and audio pickups that allowed whomever was monitoring the line to hear both ends of a phone conversation. There was also a keystroke logger installed, and this gave her the ability to read the owner's outgoing text messages.

The operation had been a resounding success. Less than a month after the units were put in place, one of Mirza's men entered the store and bought eight of the burners.

Within two weeks, Haz Mirza himself began using one of the eight.

Now four of Mirza's nine subordinates carried Annika's phones, giving her incredible access to the cell. Sometimes Mirza placed his phone in a Faraday cage, a small box used to block electromagnetic fields, and when he did this, he went dark, but he had to take the phone out to use it, so she always picked him up when he made calls or texts.

A similar operation, inspired by Annika's work, was conducted by another Shrike intelligence officer, and this endeavor put phones in the hands of sleeper cells in three other European countries.

With these two initiatives, Shrike now had deeper knowledge of Quds sleepers in Europe than the Germans or the Americans by a wide margin.

Haz Mirza was unaware of all this, of course. He'd been here in Germany for over two years; if anything, as far as he was concerned, there was less heat on him now than when he arrived. Today he simply sat on his bed and smoked while he waited for the other end to answer the Threema call, with no concerns whatsoever that he was being listened in on.

And as soon as he placed a Threema call, Annika, Moises, and Yanis all sat up straighter in the moving truck three blocks away, and they scrambled to put on their headphones.

After several rings the call was answered. "Hello?"

"Babak?"

"Yes."

"Hello, brother," Mirza said. "It's me. We have a green light for today."

There was a long pause. "What? I thought we were to stand down."

"New orders."

A long pause. "What . . . what is the target?"

"The embassy. Pariser Platz. Five p.m. There is a change to the Marine guard force then, and it is also when many embassy staff are leaving work."

Mirza could only hear breathing over the phone for several seconds. Finally, the other man said, "We don't stand a chance, Haz."

"We will throw our bodies on the barbed wire so others can cross over us."

A pause, then, "What does that mean?"

"I am saying that we will die in our attack, for certain, brother. I will not lie. But we will, by our actions, cause an uprising in the West."

"I . . . I don't know."

Mirza stood from his bed, began pacing around his room. "What don't you know? You don't know if you will follow an order from Tehran? You don't know if you will follow an order from your leader? What don't you know?"

The phone clicked off. "Babak? Babak? Coward!" he muttered to himself before hanging up.

He dialed the next man.

As soon as Yanis relayed the conversation in full to Dittenhofer, she exited the van and stormed south on the gritty street, in the opposite direction of Mirza's flat and in the direction of the streetcar stop. She yanked out her own phone and initiated her own end-to-end-encryption app as she walked at a brisk, almost frantic pace.

She dialed Spangler, who was by now used to hearing from his star employee multiple times in an hour.

Dittenhofer spoke softly. "Haz Mirza has been told to stand down."

"You told me that."

"*Ja.* But he is going ahead anyway. He is planning an attack on the American embassy."

"When?"

"Five p.m. It seems he's having some problems getting his personnel together, as usual, but he's a zealot. He'll do it alone if he has to."

Spangler said, "I understand." He thought a moment.

"Say something! What is there to consider? We have to notify the Americans."

"No, we have to notify our client. He will take the necessary steps."

"We don't have time for that."

"Annika. Darling. Just trust me. Our client is here in Berlin. I will be speaking with him in moments."

Dittenhofer stopped walking, right in front of a Thai massage parlor and a low-end coffee shop. "Why is he here in Berlin?"

"For a meeting with me."

"Was the meeting planned before the Rajavi assassination?"

"Yes. He told me the day before yesterday."

She gasped. "Our client knew about the hit on Rajavi. Obviously."

"*Nein, Annika.* Our contract is drawing to a close; he wanted to come and wrap things up. That's all."

She continued like she didn't hear him. "But the client is Israeli, not American. Right?"

"We don't know that."

"Bullshit, Rudy. We now have actionable intelligence about an imminent terror attack hours from now, one that will be carried out by a cell we have under surveillance."

"And our client will stop that attack, I assure you. Now, I'm just getting to the meeting. I will call you after lunch." Spangler hung up, but not before Annika heard some background noise. It sounded like a car door shutting, and then she heard other street sounds in the background.

She hung up the phone, walked with it in her hand for a moment, then decided on a course of action.

Quickly she placed another call.

Court had been surprised to see Dittenhofer through the grimy café window, but he'd simply looked down at his coffee cup after doing so, counting off seconds in his head. When he reached ten, he stood, turned for the door, and exited fifty yards behind his target.

She'd made a relatively short stop at the surveillance vehicle, less than a half hour, but Court didn't know the significance of that, nor did he really care. He wanted a quiet place to snatch her off the street, but he didn't see an opportunity now, so he just followed.

The woman headed over to Fritz-Reuter-Allee, her phone to her ear, and Court assumed she was returning to the streetcar stop. But instead Court watched as she tried to flag down a taxi. It passed her by, but she immediately began looking for another.

Shit. Court turned away and began frantically searching for some means of transportation for himself.

...

Annika Dittenhofer held her phone to her ear, willing the other end to answer. She was reaching out to Spangler's driver, Wolfgang Wilke, whom she knew well enough to call, but perhaps not well enough to successfully socially engineer like her hasty plan called for.

He answered, as Germans do, with his surname. "Wilke."

"*Guten Morgen*, Herr Wilke, it's Miriam."

"*Hallo*, Miriam."

"Sorry to bother. I know you just dropped off Herr Spangler. I have something I need to bring to him, but forgot to mention it when we spoke. He must be heading into his meeting because he's not answering. If you tell me where you are, I can bring the package to you."

Wilke obviously had no suspicions at all about the request. "He's at Charlotte and Fritz in the Regent. I'm out front. He expects an hour or so for the lunch; will you make it by then?"

The Regent hotel was the same hotel she'd met Rudy at for breakfast just days earlier.

"I'll try. If not, I'll get it to him later."

On her third attempt, Annika Dittenhofer successfully flagged down a taxi and told the driver to take her to the Regent on Charlottenstrasse.

Today, she told herself, she would finally meet the client whose bidding she had been doing for the past two years.

Rudy wouldn't like it, this she knew, but right now, she didn't care.

FIFTY-FIVE

Sultan al-Habsi entered the Regent hotel at one p.m., in the center of a group of five bodyguards. The men wore suits just as nice as their boss's, however, so they didn't stand out as security. Still, they kept vigilant eyes moving all over the room as the entourage made its way to a nook in the rear with three large round tables.

Here Rudolf Spangler and his four security men stood. Rudy stepped around the table to shake the hand of the man he knew as Tarik.

"Welcome to Berlin, Tarik."

"Thank you, Rudy. Shall we sit and talk?"

The pair sat at the large table. Spangler said, "I just spoke with Miriam. Again. She is very concerned. She thinks Mirza is going forward with an attack. The U.S. embassy. Today. Five p.m."

"I won't allow that to happen."

"Then you will notify authorities here so they can stop Mirza? We would be happy to do this, if you prefer."

"No need. Remain vigilant. You will see."

"We *are* vigilant. More so, with the American attack in Baghdad yesterday. We have identified Quds operators. We have identified VAJA officers. This is actionable intelligence we can give to German intelligence forces, a way to deal a real blow to Iran."

"Not yet, Rudy. Something *will* happen, and then all will be illuminated."

The German leaned closer. "Did you have Kamran Iravani killed?"

"I don't know who that is."

"The student, the hacker, the anti-regime activist. The man you ordered us to follow. He was murdered two days ago."

Tarik shrugged. "Sounds like he lived a very dangerous life."

It was neither a confirmation nor a denial, but Spangler was no fool. He was certain his client had been killing people, using the intelligence Spangler provided. But he possessed plausible deniability, and he did *not* possess the psychological underpinnings to have any real empathy for those killed.

The Middle Eastern man held up a finger. "After the death of General Rajavi, it is only a matter of time before Iran will retaliate."

Spangler shook his head. "None of my operatives in Europe are hearing anything about Iranian-sanctioned retaliation."

Tarik said, "In days, we will have all the information we need to deal Iran a crippling blow. The Europeans will resume sanctions, the regime will be squeezed tighter than ever before, and all our hardships will prove to have been worthwhile."

Our hardships? Spangler thought. He doubted Tarik was facing much hardship himself. But he said, "This is all happening in Berlin?"

Tarik grinned now, the epitome of confidence on his face. "Be aware, my friend, that your firm in Berlin is not the only one working on this problem of protecting the world from Shia expansion. Your work is important, but you are a piece of the puzzle, and the puzzle is not laid out before you." He added, "It is, however, laid out before me, and I am telling you all Shrike Group's diligent work over the past two years will be put to good use."

Spangler took this all in. Despite what the Emirati was telling him, the German believed Berlin was most definitely the center of this entire thing, otherwise Tarik wouldn't be here now.

"You will see," Tarik said. "Our cause will finally be realized, my friend."

The German cocked his head. "*Our* cause? Tarik, I don't have a cause. This is your cause, and you are my client."

Tarik's confidence remained, but the brightness with which he'd been treating this entire conversation waned. "We are in this together. Until the end. You will endure great strain in the coming days. Much will be asked of you. Things will come to light that will scare you."

"*Scare* me?"

"You will want to distance yourself from that which must be done. It is only natural. But remember, Rudy. You have been destroyed, twice in your life. You were spent, thrown in the trash by your own people, and then I came along to pick up the pieces. Look where you are now." He pointed at the German. "You can stay there." But then he rethought his comment and pointed into the air. "No, you can go higher. Much higher. More of that respect you covet in the intelligence community. Worldwide acclaim. See yourself as a man reborn. Not just as a successful business owner, but as a spymaster. Who on earth would have believed you could be at the cusp of such greatness, after all you've been through?"

Rudolf Spangler wanted all of this. The entire second half of his life was based on a longing for what he'd lost in his early thirties.

But for the first time in his life, he found himself terrified of what he would have to do to achieve that which he coveted.

Court Gentry sat in the backseat of a 1998 lime-green Volkswagen Lupo, a two-door compact that smelled like someone lived in it.

He'd stopped a pair of young men as they were tossing their backpacks into the hatchback, and he offered them five hundred euros, cash, if they would take him somewhere.

They looked at the American like he was an idiot until he waved the cash, and then they looked around them, wondering what the trick was.

Only when Court stuffed the money in the front breast pocket of the driver, then asked him how good it felt there, receiving a smile from both men in return, was he invited to squeeze himself into the tiny bit of space in the rear of the Lupo.

Once in the car, the man behind the wheel said, "Okay. Where are you going? And don't say London."

The other laughed.

"Right in front of us is a taxi. I need you to follow it."

The passenger laughed as if this were all a joke, but the driver fired up the engine, and the lime-green piece of junk lurched out into the road.

"What is this?" the passenger asked after a few seconds of silence. "Are you some sort of a private investigator?"

"Exactly. Insurance fraud case back in the U.S. My partner has the car and I need to see if this lady is actually going to the hospital like she told us when she came to Germany for treatment."

Court was talking out of his ass, but he was good at it, and the boys asked no further questions.

They told him they were students at a nearby agriculture school, just leaving class on their way to lunch when he'd stopped them, and Court assured them that the woman wouldn't be leaving Berlin, so they'd still have time to make it back to class.

Twenty minutes later they pulled up behind the Regent Berlin, keeping far enough back until Dittenhofer left her cab at the restaurant entrance and entered. Court said *auf Wiedersehen* to his two new friends, who, he had no doubt, would be skipping class the rest of the day to blow their five hundred euros, and he climbed out, then walked straight through an employee access door of the hotel. Here he slipped behind a man mopping a kitchen, pulled a cook's coat out of a dirty clothes hamper as he passed, and stepped into a dry-goods storage area, where he quickly put it on.

He was betting that the hotel was large enough for there to be a multitude of cooks in multiple restaurants, and therefore no one would notice him as someone who didn't belong.

A minute later he marched quickly down a dark hallway in an employee-only area, and soon after this, he was in the kitchen of Charlotte & Fritz. It was roughly lunchtime, so he thought he'd check here first to see if Annika had come for a meeting.

. . .

Annika Dittenhofer walked through Charlotte & Fritz at one twenty p.m., heading purposefully for the corner table where she knew she'd find Rudolf Spangler.

And he had company.

Spangler's four Israeli security men sat at a large table near their boss, but Annika found several other burly forms in total between herself and her employer. The other men were Middle Eastern, and they sat nearby, staring at her as she approached. Only when she got as close as she could without resistance from the men did she notice that a middle-aged, Middle Eastern–looking man sat with Spangler.

Spangler's security didn't get up as the woman they knew as Miriam approached, but one of the other bodyguards stood and put a hand out to stop her.

She stopped and looked past him, towards where Spangler was seated, deep in conversation. It took several seconds for the German to look up from his tablemate, but when he did, Annika caught his eyes.

She could see the nervousness on his face, unsure if it had been there before she'd arrived or if, in fact, it was her arrival itself that was causing his distress.

He recovered well enough. Standing, he said, "Ah, what a surprise. Annika." He looked to the man seated with him, and said, "She works for me. May I introduce you?"

With a nod that showed just a slight hint of annoyance, Tarik ordered the guard to let her pass, while he, too, stood.

Annika had been raised in Israel, and she was certain this man was not Israeli. Nevertheless, in Hebrew she said, "It is a pleasure to finally meet you."

The man just shook her hand. In English he said, "You must be Miriam."

"And you must be our client."

The man smiled at her, but she felt nothing but coldness from his eyes.

"Rudolf has told me of your excellent work. As our business relationship draws to a close, I want to thank you for all of your efforts."

"I only hope our efforts are being put to good use."

The man nodded. "I hear a cell of Quds Force is preparing to act against our friends the Americans. I do understand your concerns with us playing this subtly, but I want to assure you I would never let an attack take place."

"Have you notified the Americans?"

"They will be ready."

She nodded, then glanced at Rudy, but he only looked back at her. She said, "We have Haz Mirza's physical location. Right now. There is no reason to wait for him to get to the embassy."

The unidentified man nodded at this. "Give me the location. I will pass it on to my American contacts."

Court Gentry grabbed a pitcher of orange juice in the kitchen of Charlotte & Fritz, and with it he walked out into the dining room, intending to take it to the bar. The waiters working the floor were all wearing black coats and ties; he was dressed as a line cook in a white coat, but he told himself he'd be able to sell his ruse long enough to scan the tables to search for Dittenhofer.

His tiny digital camera was already turned on and recording, even though right now it was still inside his right front pants pocket. He knew he didn't have much time, and he also knew he had to keep moving with purpose, otherwise he would not fit in here for long.

After dropping off the OJ on the other end of the bar from the slightly bemused but also very busy bartender, he turned and headed in a different direction through the restaurant. He saw Annika in a rear corner, as well as the two men standing at the table, but he did not move to them yet. Instead he simply stepped back into the kitchen, passed a pair of waiters, both of whom glanced his way as they rushed by with plates, and then he retrieved his camera, set to an eight-power optical zoom. A second pass through the restaurant would be risky but, he determined, worth it, because he knew he needed images of Dittenhofer's lunch companions.

He followed a third waiter back out into the dining room, grabbed a folded napkin and silverware from a plastic bin, and veered right towards the back corner. He held the camera pinched between his fingers, with only the lens exposed, as he added the place setting to an empty table thirty feet away from Dittenhofer. He didn't glance over to Dittenhofer and the others to his right, because he imagined that the two tables of security men had locked their eyes onto him. Instead he remained focused on his work, and when he stood back up from the table, he held his hand down by his side, the camera slowly panning back and forth behind him for a few seconds.

Less than fully confident he'd gotten good images, but certain he could not safely film any longer, he went back into the kitchen and pulled off his coat, then headed down the darkened hallway for the employee exit.

Annika gave the client the address of Mirza's flat on Gielower Strasse, and the client put it in the notes in his phone. This done, he turned to Spangler. "I better make some calls. Rudy, we will be in touch very soon."

They shook hands, and the man left without ever introducing himself to Annika.

When she and Rudy were alone, Dittenhofer said, "Your meeting is over? You just arrived twenty minutes ago."

"Clearly, he did not like the fact that you were here. And I don't, either. Sit down." They both did so. "You should have known better than to come unannounced."

Annika ignored the comment. "He's Saudi. Or he's Omani. Possibly Emirati. Qatari, even Kuwaiti, perhaps. But he's *not* Israeli, and you knew that all along."

Spangler shrugged. "Not all along. But I have known for some time. It doesn't matter. His mission is against Iran, and he pays very well for our assistance. When this is all over, when all of Germany learns what Shrike International has done to thwart an attack in the capital, you can be sure you will be proud of your efforts."

She just shook her head softly now, and her eyes adopted a distant gaze. "I no longer believe that you believe that. You know we are part of something very sinister. Very dangerous. But you think your reputation and your legacy are more important than human lives." She flexed the muscles in her neck as she said, "What have you become, Rudy?"

Spangler sighed. Sipped his orange juice. Annika had never seen him so angry, or so stressed. Finally he said, "Ennis's death. Gretchen's death. The others. It's been a very trying time for you. For anyone in your role. Our work with this client has come to an end. Take a vacation. Get out of town. Relax. One week, one month. However long you need. You've earned it."

Annika Dittenhofer stood. "What a wonderful idea," she said, and she turned and headed for the exit.

FIFTY-SIX

Court climbed off the U-Bahn at Spandau station, then walked back in the direction of his apartment, making a few movements around the neighborhood first to be certain he hadn't picked up a tail. He arrived back at his place just after two p.m. and immediately sat down on the floor by his laptop and attached his camera via a Lightning port.

Minutes later he realized he had captured reasonably good images of each of the men who met with Annika Dittenhofer. He took still images from the best parts of the video, then looked at both men carefully.

He didn't recognize either.

And this meant there was only one thing for him to do. He pulled out his phone and dialed his handler.

"Brewer."

"Violator. Alpha, Mike, Mike, two, eight, Lima."

"Go ahead."

"Sending you two images for analysis."

"Ready to receive."

Court waited several seconds, then heard, "I don't need to run the first one. That is Rudolf Spangler. CEO of Shrike International Group. Our intelligence from Berlin station indicates he no longer holds an active role in the day-to-day actions of the company."

"Dittenhofer hauled ass to him this afternoon for a meeting, all the way across central Berlin. My guess is it was work related."

"Anything's possible."

"What about the other dude?"

"I don't know. Stand by, I'll run it."

Court went to the kitchen and grabbed a bottle of water. While he waited for Brewer to return, he pulled pain pills from his backpack and took one, and then something extra for his fever, which seemed to be creeping back up.

He still was under some of the effects of the Adderall he'd taken in the morning, so he opted against another amphetamine.

He looked out his little window idly, then went back to the living room, where he sat on the bare wicker sofa, in the exact spot where Zoya had sat when she was here.

He closed his eyes and thought of her.

He told himself that someday the two of them would see each other in a place where nobody was killing anyone, and they weren't being chased or hunted.

And then he opened his eyes, looked around, and told himself the truth.

In truth, he doubted there would ever come a day when all this would end and they would live in peace. He'd die on the job, and she would, too, and that would be that.

Brewer's curt voice startled him. "Transferring you."

He tried to catch her. "Transferring me where?"

But she clicked off before responding. He took a sip of water, but this time he only had to wait a few seconds to be connected.

Matt Hanley's voice boomed over the phone; he sounded especially stressed. "Violator, that image. That is real time?"

"Negative. Forty-five minutes ago."

"Are they still in the same location?"

"Unknown. I didn't want to get made. I've got a tracker on Dittenhofer's surveillance victor so I can pick her back up when I need to."

Court could hear Hanley breathing into the phone.

Court said, "Standing by for orders, boss."

The DDO spoke in a low, grave voice now, almost threatening. "Listen very carefully. I give you a lot of latitude in a lot of ways, but I need you to do exactly what I tell you to do right now. No back talk, no lone singleton-with-a-conscience bullshit, no trying to outthink me on this one. Do what I fucking say. You got it?"

It was a weird ask of Hanley, Court thought, because Hanley knew Court was always going to do things his way. Still, he said, "Sure, Matt."

"I need you to break off coverage of Dittenhofer, of Spangler, and of anyone else with Shrike Group. No coverage of *anyone*. Just back . . . the fuck . . . away . . . from the op right now."

Whoa, Court thought. "Shit, boss. Who the hell *is* this guy?"

As surprised as Court already was, Hanley stunned him with his next comment. "I'm on the way as soon as I can get a Gulfstream tasked to me. Expect me there by dawn. You, in the meantime, cease all surveillance operations. Get back to your safe house, and sit there until we speak again."

Court was already sitting in his safe house, but now wasn't the time to quibble. "Yes, sir. Understood." Court was his own man, but there were notes of both terror and menace in the normally controlled voice of Matthew Hanley that he found unmistakable and deeply troubling.

He hung up the phone, wondering what the hell he was supposed to do now. Zoya was gone. His mission had been pulled right out from under him. Checking his watch, he saw that Dr. Kaya wouldn't be off work for another six hours, so there was no sense in going to her for his infusion now.

Court Gentry was a man wholly unaccustomed to free time.

He stood up from the sofa, deciding to walk down to the street to find some food and a beer.

One hour later Matt Hanley sat in the back of an armored Chevy Tahoe, one of three in a convoy that raced along the Potomac River, on its way east towards Reagan National Airport. The traffic was typically heavy for a morning drive in the D.C. area, but the big black vehicles had government plates, flashing lights on the grille, sirens, and drivers who'd driven much rougher roads than the George Washington Memorial Parkway, so the deputy director for operations knew he'd get to his aircraft in good time and in one piece.

While the motorcade raced down the shoulder at forty miles an hour, Hanley fielded calls, desperately trying to organize his workspace so that he could take an impromptu intercontinental trip. It was chaos, and in the twenty minutes they'd been on the road he'd spoken with the director of the Special Activities Center, the White House, his chief of staff twice, and Suzanne Brewer three times.

He'd just hung up with the Pentagon when his line beeped again. "Yeah?"

This time, it was his secretary. "Sir, I have a call for you. He didn't give a name, but it's a number from your approved list."

"Send it over, Estelle, and call the director. Tell him I should be back by Friday at the latest."

"Yes, sir."

The motorcade was waved through an open gate to the DCA tarmac, then headed at speed towards a white Gulfstream G400. Hanley looked out the window and saw two big Chevy Yukons parked closer to the aircraft, and a group of men pulling gear from the back.

Finally, the call came through, and Hanley heard a familiar voice, though he couldn't place it. "Matthew?"

"Speaking."

"Matthew. It is al-Habsi. I hope you are well, my friend."

It took a lot to excite Matt Hanley, but he felt his heart pound now, and a fresh anger welling within him. Affecting a calm countenance in his voice, he said, "Oh, hi, Sultan. How is your father?"

"He is hanging on, for now, my thanks to Allah."

"I wish him all the best. What can I do for you?"

"My friend, I have just uncovered something distressing. I had to inform you directly. Time is of the essence."

"By all means. What is it?"

"I just received a call from a trusted contact in Yemen with knowledge of an upcoming attack in Berlin. A sleeper cell of Quds Force operatives is about to strike the United States embassy there. We expect it to be an attack of very low sophistication, small arms only." He added, "I believe my sources to be excellent. I am sorry that I don't have more information for you, but I thought it best to notify you immediately."

Hanley steadied himself before speaking, fighting to keep his tone measured. "When will this attack take place?"

"I am also *very* sorry I didn't have more time to warn you."

"When?"

There was a slight pause, then the Emirati said, "Only twenty-five minutes from now. Five p.m. local time."

Hanley responded quickly. "Thank you for the information. Where are you now? Dubai?"

"No, I am in Abu Dhabi, but, as I said, the attack will take place in Berlin." When Hanley did not reply, he said, "I am having meetings at the palace today. The same place where you and I had dinner together last year."

Hanley's pause was short now. "I need to contact the Marine guard at the embassy."

"Good luck, my friend."

Hanley hung up, then placed yet another call, this time to his chief of staff. "Impending small-arms attack on U.S. embassy, Berlin. Time, twenty minutes."

"My God. I'm on it."

Hanley knew the Marines would be warned in Berlin, so he hung up and turned his attention back to his surroundings.

The motorcade pulled to a stop at the nose of the Gulfstream, and Hanley didn't wait for his security man to open his door. Instead he climbed out and marched over towards the group of men hauling gear out of the Yukons. When he was still twenty yards away, he shouted, "Travers, on me."

Chris Travers was the team leader of this eight-man cell of CIA Special Activities Center (Ground Branch) operators. Young for the job at thirty-five, he'd proven himself to Hanley numerous times. He raced over to the DDO now while the others moved to load the aircraft cargo hold with huge duffel bags and backpacks.

"Sir."

"You and your men will replace my security staff for a hop over to Berlin. I've got word of an impending attack in the next few minutes, but I'm speculating there's gonna be more trouble to come."

"Understood, sir," Travers said, and then he added, "I, I *can't* say I understand why the DDO is coming along for the ride, though."

"I've got a man to see over there."

"Is it the kind of thing where you might need *us* to see him, too?"

Hanley looked at the bearded operator. "It might be that kind of a thing, Chris. I'll let you know."

"Solid copy, sir." Travers helped his men with the last of the load while Hanley headed for the jet stairs.

FIFTY-SEVEN

Haz Mirza had spent an hour shaving his body earlier in the day, in keeping with his religious beliefs. He would die within hours, and he wanted his corpse purified in Muslim tradition. He was certain he'd be denied a proper burial by the men who would kill him this afternoon, so as a display of personal purity for his trip to heaven, he shaved and cleaned himself thoroughly.

When this was done he'd dressed himself in a crisp white shirt, light green denim pants, and his best pair of Adidas running shoes, then checked his equipment in his backpack. His folding-stock AK was loaded with thirty rounds, with a second thirty-round magazine taped to the one in the magazine well for a quicker reload.

There were more magazines of 7.62-by-39-millimeter ammunition, as well as a Beretta semiautomatic pistol, loaded with 9-millimeter hollow points.

The pack also contained two improvised explosive devices that were small enough to be hurled once the delay fuse was struck. He didn't know if he'd have enough time to set the fuses and to throw them, but he liked the idea of the potential damage the pipe bombs could add to the equation.

The rest of his team would be similarly armed, although two men also wore large, bulky suicide vests.

Of his nine men, he'd managed to cajole five into the operation. He was confident that four of that number would actually go through with it, but the questionable cell member, Mirza decided, would not dare threaten the operation by going to the *polizei*.

Today's objective was not to achieve a tactical victory; with five or six men and no support from Tehran, this would be impossible. His objective was, rather, to make a loud and violent political statement.

And he was confident he would achieve that mission today.

At four p.m. he climbed aboard his red Vespa Primavera scooter and headed towards the center of Berlin, and at four fifty he sat outside a café on Wilhelmstrasse, just around the corner and down the street from the rear of the U.S. embassy. His heavy backpack rested on the sidewalk between his feet, and an Americano coffee remained untouched on the table in front of him.

He'd placed his mobile on the table next to it, with his Threema messaging app open. A new message flashed on the screen, and he lifted up the device.

The text filled him with excitement, pride, and terror.

Ten minutes, brother. In position.

His second-in-command would lead the first wave, though in truth, it wasn't much of a wave with only four men. Still, Mirza's plan had been designed to create maximum chaos with minimum personnel. The four men would park their car on Unter den Linden next to Pariser Platz, as close to the embassy as possible. They would climb out as one, and then they would all four spray Kalashnikov rounds at the men and women in sight at the front gate, and then at the windows on the upper floors beyond that.

Mirza knew the upper floors contained the offices of the senior members of the embassy, including the ambassador, Ryan Sedgwick. Sedgwick was a close friend and political confidant of the president of the United States. And although he held out no hope his operation would kill the ambassador himself, by targeting the upper floors, he knew he increased the likelihood he would kill someone in a position of power and thereby cause real pain to America.

Mirza would be a part of the second wave, or perhaps he alone would serve as the second wave, depending on whether Faisal showed up here at the café in the next five minutes. Either way, Mirza would wait until five p.m. exactly, and then he would sling his backpack in front of his chest, climb onto his scooter, and make the two-minute drive to the rear of the embassy. By then the attack would have begun in the front. He planned to pull his rifle even before he stopped, leap off the bike as it was still moving up the street, and shoot the two or three guards who stood on the sidewalk there. Then, if he was still standing, he would rake the upper rear windows of the embassy and shoot any Americans he saw running out the rear of the building.

If Faisal came, then they would double the damage, but even if he didn't show, Mirza felt powerful, a warrior who could almost single-handedly bring the Great Satan to its knees today.

This was a martyrdom mission, for all of the men in the cell. Mirza held no illusions otherwise. But the twenty-four-year-old Iranian felt confident that his act of bravery would spur others on around the world.

Haz Mirza also knew that Tehran would vilify him, disavow him, discredit him. But he didn't care. His God was not the god of European sanctions relief; his God was Allah, the one true God, and he only lamented that his nation's leadership had replaced Allah, sacrificing Him on the altar of open trade.

He looked down at his phone and typed out a response.

I will see you in paradise, brother.

He took a deep breath in and exhaled slowly.

Mirza was in the middle of this calming technique as a man in a business suit appeared from behind him, stepped in front of him, and sat down at his little table. The Iranian was taken aback, but he tried to hide it. *What does this asshole want?*

"*Ja und?*" *Yeah?* Mirza said in German.

The man leaned closer and gave off an insincere smile. In Farsi he said, "Good afternoon, brother. My name is Tarik. I know you don't *think* you have time to talk to me right now, but I assure you, this is a conversation we need to have."

Mirza started to reach for his bag on the ground between his feet.

The man wagged a finger in the air in front of him. "There are two men with rifles pointed at your head. If you draw that Beretta pistol you keep in your messenger bag, they will have no choice but to kill you, and that would be a great shame."

Mirza swallowed hard, then did as he was told. Somehow, he and his men had been uncovered.

He had no idea who this stranger was. He wasn't German, and he wasn't American. He appeared to be an Arab, but he wasn't speaking Arabic. In fact, he spoke excellent Farsi.

"What do you want?" the Iranian asked, his hand still lingering next to his backpack under the table.

"What you and your brothers are about to do is admirable. I support it in theory, even though your own nation does not." He smiled. "I have personal experience with my nation's leadership not appreciating me and my talents, but I won't bore you with my story."

Mirza moved his hand closer to the bag again. His Beretta APX Centurion pistol was in an outside pocket, just out of reach. "I don't know what the fuck you are talking about."

Mirza's eyes narrowed. "Do not reach for that gun, brother."

"And if I do?"

"Do I really need to remind you of the men with rifles?"

"You are bluffing. There are no men."

The man calling himself Tarik smiled, and he raised his left hand. One second later Mirza squinted his eyes shut in pain as multiple lasers targeted them. When he turned away from the light, the lasers turned off as quickly as they'd come on.

"Satisfied?"

Mirza thought of going for the gun anyway, diving to the ground. Surely he could get a single shot off into the chest of the man sitting at the little table here before he was killed.

But he didn't move. "What is this about . . . *brother*?" Mirza asked, his voice dripping with sarcasm on the last word.

"Your nation has turned its back on you. It is weak, you said it yourself last night."

"You are listening to my—"

"We know *everything*. And we can help you. This act today that you have planned, you think it is a blow to the enemy's gut, but it is nothing. You and your men will all be killed before you make it to the gates. There will be no Shia retaliatory uprising. There will also be no glory in having your body ripped apart by lead in the open street, shot by eighteen-year-old American Marines on a rooftop."

Tarik continued. "But if you simply come with me now, then I will help you exact the retribution you seek from the Great Satan."

Mirza looked around. Rush-hour traffic clogged Wilhelmstrasse. He asked, "How will you do that?"

"You are strong-willed, well trained. Motivated. The rest of your team . . . lazy fools. I know you fought in Afghanistan, then led a platoon in Libya, a company in Yemen. You are a leader. You just need a different set of men under you."

"My men are brave lions."

Tarik sniffed out a little laugh, looked down at a Hublot watch on his wrist that Mirza imagined cost more than he'd make in five years driving tractor-trailers in Germany.

The Arab said, "Not for long, they're not."

"You will see," Mirza said, but he recognized that the fact that this man knew about the impending attack made it likely others would know, and the four men rushing the embassy in three minutes would be cut down as soon as they climbed out of their car.

Tarik said, "Let me tell you what we are going to do. You and I will get up together, and we will go somewhere to talk. Your men will act without you, and they will fail, but you will live on to fight another day."

"Why? Why are you doing this?"

"All will become apparent when I take you to see what I have prepared for you."

"You want to attack America, too?"

"Of course I do. More than you, perhaps, my young friend. But where you have all the heart in the world, I have the resources to put your talent to use."

Mirza was bewildered by all this, but he looked over his shoulder, in the direction of the embassy. "If you have the power to save me, why don't you save them?"

"Because I don't need them. I need *you*, a leader. And *you*, the leader, you need men. I have men for you. Good men. Trained men. Your men."

"*My* men?"

"Quds Force operatives. Strong. Brave. Committed. Forged by combat. Just like yourself."

"Where are these men?"

"Here, brother. We will go and meet them today. And tomorrow, tomorrow you will do that which your nation is too afraid to do. That which you could never do alone."

The two men stood slowly; Mirza could feel his legs shaking under him. It wasn't fear, not completely anyway; it was the sense that everything was now out of his hands.

Tarik said, "Leave your pack and your phone. One of my men will get them."

A black four-door BMW pulled to the curb, and an Arab man in a dark blue suit climbed out of the rear passenger side, stepped over to the table, and hefted the backpack without looking at the Iranian sitting there. He snatched the phone off the table, as well, and returned to the car.

Behind the BMW were three Mercedes SUVs, their windows blacked out. A rear door opened on the first SUV, and Tarik led Mirza towards it.

The young Iranian felt naked and alone as he walked, but he saw no other options.

And then, just as he lowered his head to fold himself into the vehicle, he heard the sound of gunfire over his left shoulder. It was blocks away. Still, it thumped loudly on the street.

Mirza could instantly identify the sound of one of the guns from his time in Afghanistan. It was an M249 Squad Automatic Weapon.

His men did not have this gun; it was an American gun.

Tarik stepped up behind him. "They are martyred to give you the opportunity to fulfill the mission that they themselves could not."

Mirza looked at the Arab, and then he climbed into the car, pounding gunfire still buffeting the street around him.

. . .

Hades and Thor both took their eyes out of their rifle scopes as soon as the SUV door shut and they lost sight of their target, then began breaking down their operation as they looked back over their shoulder towards the sound of gunfire.

Thor said, "Hope them Marines fuck up those terrorists."

"Sounds like they're doing just that."

"Get some!" Thor shouted now.

They headed back to their transport vehicle as Tarik, the man Mirza had been speaking with outside the café, and the rest of Tarik's men all rolled off to the south.

"What do you think all that was about?" Thor asked.

"Dunno," Hades answered, then added, "Don't care."

"I heard that. What's next?"

"Tarik said we go back to the safe house and prep ourselves for extract."

"We're going back to Dubai?"

"Eventually, yeah. We wait for Tarik to finish whatever the fuck he's doing here, and then we'll fly back on his jet."

"Shit, I was kind of liking it here."

"Same," said Hulett. "Still, we've wasted some terrorists, and we were even nice enough to leave a few for the Marines. I'd say we can be happy about what we've done."

"And we got paid," Thor added.

"Shit, yeah, we did," said Hades with a grin.

FIFTY-EIGHT

Sultan al-Habsi's four-car motorcade arrived in Pankow, just to the north of Berlin, under low gray skies and mist, and then the rain kicked off in earnest as the vehicles made their way onto quiet, two-lane Hauptstrasse. Three minutes later, when they turned off the street and onto a gravel driveway that ran between a pair of high brick walls, thunderclaps and lightning rattled the motorcade.

A large brick warehouse sat eighty meters back from the road, hidden by the wall and by a scattered row of spruce trees. The vehicles rolled into the open front door of the sturdy but old building, a former tank repair shop for the National People's Army, the military of the DDR.

When his SUV stopped, Haz Mirza stepped out, flanked on both sides by bodyguards who were, he had decided from their look and countenance, probably from one of the Gulf States. He'd determined the man calling himself Tarik to be from the same area, which made him an enemy, but the young Iranian couldn't fathom a reason why an enemy would go to the level of trouble Tarik had obviously gone through to bring him here.

The group of men all walked over the concrete floor to a doorway, and then up a set of metal stairs. They came to a door on the second level, and here Tarik stopped and addressed Mirza for the first time since leaving Berlin.

"I will open this door, and it might fill you with more questions than answers, but I assure you, all will soon be explained. I will give you ten minutes before continuing the tour."

With a flourish he slammed the latch down and pulled open the door.

There, in a large, well-lit room full of military-issue cots and plastic picnic tables surrounded by plastic chairs, Haz Mirza found fourteen men standing, ready to meet him.

Mirza looked the men over as the door was shut behind him. They were in their twenties and thirties; most had dark hair and some had beards, and they all appeared fit, well fed, and comfortable enough, but he didn't immediately recognize any of them, so he couldn't say if they were actually Quds.

Until a voice called from the center of the room. "Haz?"

He looked over the man who had spoken for several seconds. Finally, he said, "Ali?"

"It's me."

Mirza stepped forward with utter shock, then embraced his friend. When he stepped back from him he said, "I heard you died in Yemen."

The man said, "Yes, I think that I did, brother."

Others laughed a little. Mirza recognized a second man now; he was older, his face wrinkled through stress and hardship, but Mirza remembered him from Afghanistan. A third man he recognized as someone he served with in Libya years ago.

The men sat down at the cluster of tables, and Mirza did the same.

Mirza was going to ask what was going on, but then Ali asked him the exact same question.

Haz Mirza remained in a state of shock about all this. "I . . . I don't know. I have been in Berlin for two years. Commanding a sleeper cell. Tarik and the others, they kidnapped me at a café an hour and a half ago. Brothers, I was five minutes from attacking the U.S. embassy with members of my squad."

Ali leaned forward. "Why were you going to attack the embassy?"

Mirza was disappointed the question was even asked. "Obviously, since the death of General Rajavi, I knew we had to deal a quick blow to—"

A man stood from his table. "What are you saying? Rajavi is dead?"

Mirza looked around at his countrymen. "You didn't know?"

The shock, fury, and even sadness in their eyes told him they did not. He said, "I swear I know nothing more than what I have told you about what is happening here. Tarik said something about us attacking America. What can you all tell me?"

Ali and the others spoke of their release from the black site, their journey here, and that they had been waiting here for the last three days, informed only that they would soon meet their leader and receive their orders.

At this Mirza raised an eyebrow. "Orders? Tarik is giving the orders?"

Ali said, "Tarik has ten men here with guns. SIA security men. We talked about rushing them but . . ."

"But what?"

"But, brother, we want to see about this operation. What if Tarik does have a job for us that will deal a blow to America? Wouldn't we want to take part, especially now that we learn Vahid Rajavi is dead, killed by the Americans?"

Another man shouted, "If Allah wills it, we will fight."

A thunderclap outside echoed the verve Mirza saw in the unit before him, and in a way he never felt with his own cell of men, he was certain he now held something powerful in his hands.

A few minutes later he sat in a small warehouse-floor office, across a dusty desk from Tarik, who looked utterly out of place in his pinstriped suit.

Mirza knew now that the man who had snatched him off a Berlin street actually worked for the spy service of the United Arab Emirates.

And even though he couldn't help but hold out some hope that he and the men in the room upstairs would actually be given a real retaliatory mission against America, he was cynical and mistrusting enough to suspect Tarik of playing some sort of a game.

"The men. What do you think?" Tarik asked.

"They are in good spirits. They believe your story, or at least what you have hinted at to them."

"And they are wise to do so."

Mirza lifted his chin. "I was in the war in Yemen."

"I know this. My nation has a file on you."

Mirza took time to think about this, then said, "I fought in Aden, in Ataq, in Sana."

Tarik looked into Mirza's eyes, and he spoke slowly. "My brother fought in Ataq. He died there."

Mirza clearly did not care. "I had friends who died there." The two men stared at each other for a long moment before Mirza said, "We are enemies, you and I. Enemies make terrible friends. Dangerous friends."

To this Tarik nodded. "We are only dangerous to each other if we do not work together. But we are dangerous to our mutual adversary if we do. Are you ready to see the reason I brought you here?"

Mirza was confused. "I thought you brought me here to meet the men."

The Emirati shook his head. "The men are a crucial element in all this, but they aren't the main element. Neither are you, in fact."

"I don't understand."

"Let's go." The two men walked with Tarik's assistants and guards arrayed around them across the dank warehouse floor, towards a door at the far end. Their footsteps echoed in the empty space, even over the sound of rain pounding on the corrugated tin roof, two stories above them.

Tarik opened the door without fanfare and beckoned the twenty-four-year-old Iranian inside.

Mirza stepped into a darkened room; the sound of the rain on the roof indicated that this, too, was a massive space, but only when someone flipped on the overhead lighting did he see that it was identical to the first cavernous warehouse floor.

The difference, though, was immediately obvious. The floor here had been cleaned spotless, and on the floor in front of him were two diamond-shaped patterns of objects, each a meter in width, and a half meter in height.

Mirza was instantly familiar with the design. They were quadcopters, drones, and a quick count told him there were forty in all.

He stepped forward to the first device, knelt down, and then finally dropped all the way to the floor to look under it.

After a few seconds Mirza said, "Antipersonnel?"

Tarik smiled. "That one is armed with antipersonnel munitions, yes. Others are high explosive, a few are armor piercing."

"Size of the warheads?"

"Two point five kilograms for each drone. Hardly a nuclear device, but efficient."

Mirza rose back up to his knees and inspected the device more carefully. "These are Kargus. Turkish made, autonomous attack drones." Mirza stood back up. He ran his hand over the camera ball of one of the units. "These are much better than anything I've ever used in battle. Easier to operate, or so I've read." He fought a little smile, but the glint in the Emirati's eye showed Mirza that Tarik had picked up on his excitement anyway. Mirza added, "From what I've read, the Kargus can fly in a swarm. Up to fifteen units operating together."

Tarik shook his head. "Twenty. You have two full squadrons here."

Haz Mirza was like a kid in a candy store, and he could no longer even attempt to hide it. With his eyes wide, his pupils almost dilated with delight, he said, "With some training, I can pilot these."

Tarik replied. "I know you *can*, but *will* you?"

"I think now is a good time for you to tell me our target. The embassy?"

Tarik said, "The U.S. ambassador, Ryan Sedgwick, is the best friend of the president of the United States. He is also the chief symbol of America in Germany, and one of the most prominent members of the American government in all of Europe."

Mirza said, "I know this. Everyone knows this." He shrugged. "Still, even with the drones and the men, targeting one man deep in the massive U.S. embassy will be difficult, impossible perhaps."

Tarik put his hand on the man's shoulder. "That's why we are not going to the embassy. We are going to Finkenstrasse 23."

Mirza thought a moment, then sucked in a quick breath. "The American ambassador's residence? We are going to kill Sedgwick?"

Tarik surprised him by shaking his head. "Not *just* the ambassador. The day after tomorrow he will be hosting an art exhibition at his home. One hundred or so members of the American government and military. Another hundred prominent Western diplomats and bureaucrats. It will be a huge party. And we, as the Americans like to say . . . are going to crash it."

Mirza cocked his head. "How do you know about this party?"

Now Tarik smiled the widest grin Mirza had ever seen. "Because, brother, I was on the guest list." He shrugged. "I sent my regrets."

The two men were back in the warehouse office minutes later, and their discussion had turned into a philosophical one.

Mirza said, "I am a Shia who will kill Christians for a Sunni who wants to destroy Shias. It is a circle."

Tarik shook his head. "It is *not* a circle. Look who we are targeting. America. The regime that killed Vahid Rajavi like he was a stray dog in the street."

"But Iran is your enemy, too. Don't deny this."

"Not the Iranian people. The Iranian regime. The regime that controls the freedom-loving people of Iran with an iron fist. The regime whose actions have caused the entire world to impose crippling sanctions on your peaceful countrymen.

"You and I are not the same people, of course this is true. But you and I have common enemies, and I take you as a man smart enough to understand that our relationship is beneficial to us both. Beneficial to everyone you love in this world. Beneficial to Allah."

Mirza countered quickly. "The Emirates are not enemies of the West. In fact, you are a pawn of the West. You are a pawn of Israel."

"I am a pawn of no one, my young friend. The crown prince of the Emirates has sent me personally on this mission. Our relationships with other nations provide me with the best cover imaginable." Mirza said nothing, so Tarik leaned forward over the table.

Tarik said, "My brother. Are you willing to martyr yourself for your people?"

"One thousand times over."

"As am I. What more is there to know?"

"There *is* one thing more I need to know. Why do you need me and my men?"

"Obviously you and your men are the bravest fighters."

Mirza said, "That's not what's obvious to me. What *is* obvious is that you want me and my men to do this, because you want Iran to be implicated in this attack of yours."

Tarik sat back slowly. Mirza got the feeling he wasn't supposed to work this part out on his own. The Emirati said, "Does it bother you that you will receive credit for your sacrifice?"

"No, but I want to understand your motivations."

Tarik nodded; he was clearly impressed with Haz Mirza's intellect. "Yes, America will learn, as part of my plan, that you and your men are Quds Force operatives. It will heighten tensions between the two nations to a level never experienced.

"We will deal a crippling blow to them, a blow they will have no choice but to retaliate against. Your nation will fight them, they will be forced to do it, because America will attack them first."

Mirza said nothing.

"Listen to me, brother," Tarik said. "You hoped your death today would convince others to join you in battle. But there was never any chance of this. *Think*, man. You lying dead with your intestines on the street around you wasn't going to spur anyone on to do *anything*. But with *my* plan? With my plan there is a guarantee of follow-on attacks after you are martyred, because the act you are conducting will lead right back to Tehran, and America's president will demand retribution for Sedgwick and the others."

This was convincing to Mirza, but quickly he added, "How do you know America won't just fire nuclear missiles into my nation and kill every man, woman, and child, friend and foe alike?"

"The American president will take pains to show that his quarrel isn't with the people there. The fools in Washington learned in Afghanistan, in Iraq, and in other places that managing the victory is just as important as achieving the victory, if not more so. Trust me, there will be major conflict, all over the world, but the fighting won't be in Iran." He raised his hands as if in surrender, and he clarified. "Actually, if the wars of the past twenty years are a guide, then I imagine American special operations teams will come in small numbers, but the Iranian military is not the Taliban, not the fools in the ISIS caliphate, not even Saddam Hussein's bloated and overrated army. Your nation will fight them off.

"It will take years, perhaps, but the road ahead for Iran is going to be paved with victories."

Haz nodded. He was sold, and Tarik knew it. Then the younger man said, "There is a part in this process where you will feel the need to remind me that I must martyr myself. Show me some respect. Don't remind me. I know I cannot be taken alive, because if I were, it would be discovered I've been disavowed by Tehran. I am a rogue, working for an Emirati spy pretending to be a friend to his enemies.

"My force and I," Mirza said, "we will all die in battle against the Americans."

Al-Habsi beamed the smile of a proud father. "I knew the moment I met you that I had the right man for this important work."

Mirza stood. "I will join your mission, Tarik. As will my men. I would like to address them now."

Tarik stood himself. "I will take you back to them immediately."

FIFTY-NINE

Dr. Azra Kaya had Wednesday night off, so Court paid her a visit at nine p.m. He was in the middle of both his infusion and some Indian take-out food when his phone buzzed. He received a text on his Signal encrypted app, and when he read it, he smiled.

"Good news?" Kaya asked.

"Yeah. I'm going to see an old friend." He checked his watch. "Would it be okay if I came back in a couple of hours and finished the treatment?"

"Sure. You have another fifteen on this antibiotic, if you can stay. I'll switch the bag to the other antibiotic for when you come back."

"Good."

"You seem happy. Must be a good friend."

Court thought this over. "He's good to have around in certain situations."

"And I guess you can't tell me who it is?" Court just looked at her, and then she laughed a little. "Dumb question?"

"It's better if I keep my work out of your life."

She was genuinely amused. "Your work is very much in my life. The cut on your arm, the bruises on your face, the infection in your bone, the surgical wound that has reopened every day since you showed up in Berlin."

"Good point."

But she wasn't finished. "The drugs I give you to keep you moving, the constant news on TV about combat in the streets of Berlin. Face it, sir, you aren't exactly keeping me away from your work life."

"Yeah. I'm sorry. I owe you a lot."

"You would pay me back by getting a safer job. I worry about the day you don't come back to see me. Not because you are too healthy to need me, but because your health no longer matters."

Court thought about this. "Honestly, I'd rather bleed out in the street than on your sofa."

She looked at him with incomprehension. "You would rather die alone than with a friend by your side?"

She hadn't intended it, but her comment got to Court. He fully expected that was how he would go, surrounded by enemies, not friends. He tried to play it off with a joke.

"You have such a nice sofa, I'd just hate to ruin it."

She rolled her eyes. "It's a settee, and you aren't the first oddball who's bled on it."

"That's comforting."

"But . . ." she said, "you will be the last."

"What do you mean?"

She shook her head. "This was exciting at first. Now it is just stressful. Scary. Heartbreaking when I lose one of you or, in your case, when I see you go back out, day after day, for more abuse when you should be convalescing."

"I have to—"

"I know you *think* you have to. That there is no one else on earth who can do what you do. But your actions will lead to a lot of sadness for your friends and family when you die. Maybe you should think about them."

Court didn't know what to say. He wasn't around many people who gave a shit about him, and even those who did, like Zoya, lived lives similar enough to his that they understood why it was hard to walk away.

Azra said, "Yes, I lose patients in the hospital, but when I save them, they don't usually go back out and throw themselves to the wolves again the very next day. I will treat you as long as you need me, and then I will leave the network behind."

Court thought this to be an excellent idea. He needed people out here in the field ready to treat him covertly, when he needed them. But this young woman was too good for this type of work, and too pure for men of his ilk.

As soon as he left Dr. Kaya's flat, Court took a streetcar to Tegel Airport, and immediately conducted a thirty-minute SDR around the terminal. This done, he walked back outside into the rainy night and then into a parking garage. On the fourth level he stepped out of the stairwell and headed straight ahead. There, all the way at the end, was a black Audi A6 sedan. He opened the driver's door and sat down, checked the center console, and retrieved the key that had been left in the car for him.

He got out, popped the trunk, and looked in before sitting back down behind the wheel.

Court knew he was taking a chance using Berlin station again, but Hanley had given him a number to call if he needed supplies, and he was banking that neither Hanley nor Brewer had contacted them to tell them he was no longer sanctioned to operate in Berlin. He'd called the number, given his identity code, and referenced a number Hanley had given him that provided the authorization code Berlin station needed to authenticate him, and then he simply told them what he wanted and where he wanted it all delivered.

He started to check his watch, but then he saw a man approaching the Audi through the driver-side mirror.

Seconds later, the passenger door opened and the man climbed in.

"Dude, I'm starving! Been eating beans covered in shit for the last week. We've got to stop at KFC or something before we do anything else."

Court laughed despite himself. Zack Hightower was in his fifties, but he'd been like this for the ten or more years Court had known him.

Now Zack looked around the vehicle, seeming to notice it suddenly. "Pretty sweet. Agency ride?"

"It is. Got it just for you."

"It's a little European. I'm more a Silverado guy, myself."

The Audi was already moving for the exit. "A Chevy pickup would be a touch conspicuous around here." Court looked to his passenger. "Not that you aren't conspicuous enough on your own."

Zack shrugged.

"How was the clink?" Court asked.

With another shrug he said, "What do you think? Third-world prisons aren't nearly as much fun as everyone makes them out to be."

"That's too bad. I was planning on getting arrested in Quito next week."

But Zack had moved on. "So, Anthem says Hanley is out of the loop on me being over here."

"He is—for now, anyway. I know you pride yourself on being a good soldier. Is that going to be a problem for you?"

"Anthem also said Hanley left me out in the jungle to rot." He looked in the glove compartment, started feeling around, searching for something. "So . . . my loyalty is to you now, Six, as long as the op is legit."

When Hightower had been Court's team leader, his call sign was Sierra One, to the much more junior Court's Sierra Six. Zack still referred to Court as Six instead of his real name, or even his Agency code name.

Court said, "As soon as we have an op, I promise it will be one hundred percent legit." When Zack reached under his seat, still searching with his hand, Court said, "Center console."

Zack opened the console and retrieved a pistol in a holster. He drew the weapon and looked at it. "What is this bullshit?"

Court glanced towards Zack, then back to the exit ramp in front of him. "Looks like a Steyr. M9."

"I know it's an M9. Got eyeballs. Since when did the Agency start fielding these?"

Court shrugged. "Dunno. I've been out awhile. There's a pair of UMPs with all the fixings in the trunk."

Zack reholstered the weapon and slid it under his shirt in the appendix position. "Damn, it's good to see you, Six. You all healed up from that blade you caught in LA?"

To this Court replied, "Not really." He changed the subject. "What about Zoya?"

"What about her?"

"Did she tell you where she was heading next?"

"She didn't say, and I didn't ask. Just that she was burned here, and she was pretty damn concerned about you." Zack winked. "I told her I'd take care of you."

Court looked out at the night as they hit the highway, filling Zack in on the status of the operation as he drove. He told his former TL that Hanley himself was on his way here to Berlin, apparently because Court had ID'd some unknown subject for him earlier in the day.

Zack turned to face Court. "The big man coming out himself? That's weird."

"Tell me about it. Anyway, we're on stand-down till he gets here, but as soon as his plane touches down, I'm going to ask for approval to snatch this Dittenhofer woman. She's got answers about Haz Mirza."

"Mirza was the leader of the cell that attacked the embassy today?"

"Affirmative. Four terrorists dead, no other casualties. I don't think the Iranians got more than a couple shots off before the USMC splattered them across the square. But Mirza wasn't there. He's still on the loose."

"So . . ." Zack said, "you're basically saying this Mirza cat was the leader of a gang of dipshits. What are we getting all spun up for? He's all alone. Can't do too much without his men. Sooner or later, Hanley and his boys will roll him up."

Court shook his head. "No, we are missing something. Somebody went to a lot of trouble to tie Mirza with the Iranian embassy. I can't believe it was all to implicate members of his cell in today's shitty little attack. There's got to be something else coming. Something that involves Mirza, who has been disavowed by Tehran."

Zack shrugged. "Whatever, man. I just work here. What's the first thing on our agenda?"

"I have to go to an apartment on Tiergarten Strasse for about an hour. You can come with me and wait in the car, or I can drop you off on the way."

"Who's there?"

"A woman who has been helping me out."

Zack cocked his head. Soon he gave a knowing smile. "Listen, man, I think it's awesome how you discovered sex in your late thirties."

Court fought a laugh, because he knew it would just encourage his old team leader to continue with the razzing. He said, "She's a doctor. I've got an infection."

"I do believe it's called an erection, Six."

"Just stop. She's treating me."

"Treating you well, I hope," Zack said. Court couldn't tell if the man was kidding or if he really did think there was something else going on.

Court abruptly changed lanes, headed for the off-ramp. "I've made the decision for you. I'm dropping your ass off at the safe house."

SIXTY

Maksim Akulov hadn't touched a bottle all day, and though his body craved alcohol, his mind remained surprisingly clear.

He had an objective, a raison d'être, and this kept him going.

He'd spent the past day convalescing from his injuries sustained jumping out the high window of the hotel suite, not because he particularly minded the discomfort and lack of mobility but because he wanted himself in the best possible condition the next time he encountered the Gray Man.

And his two colleagues were working on arranging that meeting for him now. Anya had been going back and forth with SVR in Moscow, desperate to find any intelligence about Court Gentry. And Inna had stayed in contact with the team's handler in the Solntsevskaya Bratva, just waiting for word on where Zakharova would go next.

Maksim was sharpening a throwing knife on a whetting stone in the kitchen when Inna entered from the back door of the property. She called out to him from across the living room. "I just heard from St. Petersburg. They have no new information on Sirena's whereabouts. She dropped off the map after the gunfight at the Adlon, and no one has heard from her in days."

Anya was sitting at her laptop on the sofa. "Probably because Semyon killed the guy that was providing us the intel."

Inna thought this over. "Yes, that's possible that the informant was Ennis, but St. Petersburg won't give me that information. The other possibility is it was someone else, and Sirena is just smart enough to go to ground, not to trust anyone."

Maksim asked, "What do we know about the operation she was on?"

"Shrike International Group. She was working as a case officer. Her target, from what I've been told, had been an Iranian embassy staffer suspected of working for VAJA."

The Russian assassin said, "We can put surveillance on him."

"She's not tailing him anymore. She's disappeared. Remember? We have to entertain the likelihood she simply left town after the attempt was made on her. I know I would."

"Well, you don't have the Gray Man to protect you. She's still here." He said it confidently.

"Maksim, Moscow is sending another team after her. We've been ordered to stand down."

He stopped sharpening his knife and looked up at her. "What?"

"It's for the best."

"*Nyet*. It will take a new team at least a day to get on their mark here, especially with the added security around Berlin with the attack. That buys us time. I want twenty-four hours more. You give me that, and then I will go home. But I need both of you helping me."

He held up his throwing knife. "Get me in front of him, and I will do the rest."

Inna snapped back at this. "You mean *her*. Zakharova is the target, or have you forgotten?"

"They are both my targets. And I will see that they spend eternity together. You just have to find Sirena."

Inna relented reluctantly. "Twenty-four hours. And then we're on a train to Moscow."

"All I ask. *Spasibo*." *Thank you.*

Inna then said, "We are open to suggestions of how to find them."

"I hurt Gentry. I don't know how badly, but I saw the blood trail, so I know one of my knives cut him. We know he's not aligned with the CIA, and we know there is no way he would walk into a hospital, or any medical facility that was run aboveboard. So, ladies, the question is, if he were to go somewhere in the city for medical treatment, where would he go? Where is safe harbor for a man like him?"

Anya and Inna exchanged a look. Anya said, "I will make some calls."

"Excellent," Maksim said. "And I will continue to sharpen my blades."

Matthew Hanley and his team of Ground Branch paramilitary officers landed at Berlin's Schönefeld Airport shortly after six a.m., where they were met by Berlin station officers in a trio of silver nine-passenger Volkswagen vans. Once the team's bags were off the aircraft, Hanley, Travers, and the others climbed into the vans and they all rolled off towards the city.

Hanley had chosen to avoid going into the embassy for this trip. The DDO appearing at a station caused a lot of fanfare, and he needed to avoid that. And the DDO would have to call in on the ambassador, and that was something he desperately wanted to avoid having to do.

Ryan Sedgwick was an asshole in Hanley's eyes. A longtime Agency critic, he had the president's ear like no one else, and Hanley knew that Sedgwick asking a bunch of questions right now would involve Hanley telling a bunch of lies, and that would lead to trouble.

Hanley wasn't here for scrutiny, he wasn't here for meetings, and he wasn't here for glad-handing. His objective was open-ended, but his objective was concentrated on one issue.

On one man.

Other than a few of his close operational staff at Berlin station, no one else from the embassy would even know he was here.

The vans delivered the new arrivals to a CIA safe house in Lichtenrade, not far from the airport and a straight forty-minute shot north to the center of Berlin and the U.S. embassy. It was a five-bedroom home, fenced in, and it backed up to an open field of barley. Hanley eyed the safe house guards that the entourage passed on the way in, and was pleased to find the Berlin station security team inconspicuous in work overalls, with their submachine guns well hidden.

Hanley was more concerned with operational security than he was worried about threats to himself. He'd worked in Haiti, in Somalia, in Iraq and Afghanistan and Libya and a dozen other locales around the world.

Berlin was as safe a place as he knew. He needed this location to meet in a clandestine fashion with people in the city, and he couldn't very well have his arrival here at the quiet safe house broadcast with an overly robust security profile.

Once he and the others settled in, he received his first visitor. The senior operations officer who had been the lead at Berlin station in charge of looking into Shrike Group had been ordered to run a two-hour, early-morning SDR before arriving at Hanley's safe house, so by seven thirty a.m. the man had traversed some eighty miles of train tracks, city roads, and shoe leather.

He met with the deputy director in a room in the house that had been swept for electronic surveillance.

In the end, however, the meeting had not been nearly as fruitful as Hanley had hoped. Yes, Berlin station had been looking into Shrike for a few months now, but they still believed it to be an Israeli intelligence operation, something Hanley knew, without question now, was not the case.

The DDO recognized that his station knew very little about what was going on save for the fact that a senior employee of the company had been murdered two days earlier, shot in the temple in a hotel next door to the embassy. The officer offered, helpfully, that he had actually heard the gunshot himself, but this told Hanley the man had been sitting in his office in the embassy and had not been out in the field where he could be of any use.

Berlin station had been using cyber and signals intelligence intercepts to look into Shrike, the officer explained, for the very simple reason that every single time men and women were put in the field around Shrike's offices, police showed up within minutes to see what they were doing.

Hanley knew the rules about operating in Germany. Officially speaking, anyway, it was verboten, more so because the U.S. ambassador—to Hanley's way of thinking, anyway—was bending over backwards to placate the Reichstag, so he couldn't very well get too angry with his subordinate for adopting a policy of extreme caution.

Hanley had always placed a premium on human intelligence, so the theft of PowerSlave had effectively crippled his operation here in Germany.

The fact remained that Berlin station had been no help at all. No, Hanley realized as he watched the man leave that what he really needed was to talk to the one person in his influence who had the closest relationship with whatever the fuck was going on over here.

A call to Suzanne Brewer arranged the meeting, and at eight forty-five a.m. a motorcycle appeared at the front gate to the safe house. A man climbed off and was searched just inside the wall, then led not into the home itself but around to the back garden.

The man was directed to a picnic table, and he sat there alone for a few minutes, looking up at the clear morning sky. A guard brought him a paper cup of bad coffee, and he sipped it while he waited.

Matt Hanley appeared in the sliding glass door just a few minutes later, wearing casual clothes from REI. He had a coffee in his hand himself, and he sat down in front of the new arrival before speaking. Finally, he said, "Shit, Court, these transatlantic hops get tougher and tougher each time. I feel like I just fell down a flight of stairs."

Court Gentry had a few aches and pains to complain about himself, but he didn't bother. Hanley was management; he wasn't supposed to hurt like labor.

"Brewer said you caught another knife. You just trying to add to your collection?"

Court held up his bandaged biceps. "It's fine."

"And the shoulder? The infection?"

"I'm doing okay."

The older man laughed. "I told you last week that you had one week to get your ass back to the doctor." He shrugged. "Now I wouldn't let you go home if you wanted to."

"I don't need to go home. I need to know what's happening."

"Same."

"Why the hell did you race over here the moment you saw a picture of that man standing with Spangler and Dittenhofer?"

Hanley took a slow sip, then looked down at the cup like it was strychnine. He said, "I wasn't going to read you in on this, but it looks like I have no choice. Berlin station is compromised to Shrike, we all know that." He heaved in a massive sigh and let it out. "It appears that Shrike Group's client, the entity who is orchestrating this plot involving the Islamic Republic of Iran, is the SIA."

Court drew his head back in surprise. "Emirati intelligence? Not Israel?"

"Affirmative. The man you saw talking to Spangler helped put some of the pieces of the puzzle together for me. His name is Sultan al-Habsi, and he's SIA's deputy director of operations, but he secretly runs the whole thing. He was the source of the initial intel that led to the Vahid Rajavi drone kill. He has decent assets in Iraq, still, a lot better than ours these days. Anyway, we kept him in the loop as to our plans regarding the general."

Court was putting the puzzle pieces together himself. "So, you are saying he knew when the attack was going to happen?"

"Yeah."

Court then asked, "How is it that the deputy director is the guy at the helm?"

"Well," Hanley said, "his father is the crown prince."

Court closed his eyes now. "That figures."

"And that's not all. The old man's got one leg in the grave. Terminal stomach cancer. It's up to the crown prince to name a successor, and it's no secret that Sultan has been out of his father's favor for many years. But both his brothers were killed in Yemen, so he's the only heir to the palace. Our intelligence told us that one of his cousins would be appointed by old man al-Habsi before he died, but now we're not so sure."

"Why's that?"

"Iran is the crown prince's biggest enemy; they killed both his other sons, so now we have to ask the question—"

Court asked the question himself. "Is this entire operation a way for Sultan to earn back his father's trust and win the throne?"

"Bingo. Looks like he's currying favor with his dad, trying to deal some massive blow to Tehran before the old guy kicks the bucket."

"Unreal," Court said. "But what *is* the plan? Quds Force already attacked the embassy."

Hanley shook his head. "That was nothing. My guess is that was to clear the playing pieces off the chessboard, so al-Habsi could take control of the game."

"I don't get it."

"The Emirates are planning on some sort of major attack they can blame on Iran, and those guys were just truck drivers and freight loaders. They weren't soldiers who could get it done."

Court thought it over. "Well . . . the UAE are our allies. Can't you just tell them you know what Sultan is plotting?"

"No, I can't, as a matter of fact, and that's the problem."

"What do you mean?"

"We have a long-standing order at the Agency." He waved his hand. "Not just the CIA, all U.S. intelligence agencies. We do not collect intelligence on the UAE. We do not analyze intelligence collected on the UAE from our allies."

Court was surprised to learn this. "Shit, boss. We conduct ops against all our allies. Israel, the UK, even Canada. What makes the UAE so special?"

"A lot of things. This was the agreement we came to with them to ensure they would do our bidding in the war on terror. The president agreed to this, and the president is not going to appreciate learning we've gone behind his back here."

Court said, "Look, you're the DDO, I'm just a dumb trigger puller, but I don't get why you don't just go to the president, say you picked up some credible information from an outside source, something that fell into your lap." Hanley was already shaking his head, but Court kept going. "You can expose what the UAE's up to without having to reveal you picked up the intelligence from your own HUMINT operation."

"We can't implicate SIA in this at all, Court. That's the problem."

"Why the hell not?"

"Because we fucking *made* them!"

"Who did?"

"The Agency. We stood up Emirati Signals Intelligence fifteen years ago. We recruited Sultan al-Habsi, and hundreds like him in the UAE, brought them to the U.S. for training, taught them everything they know. We paid for everything, gave them everything, and we turned them into the group they are now. We are inextricably tied to them. If they go down, we go down with them."

"We created them, and then they fucked us over?"

Hanley waved a hand in the air. "Congratulations, trigger puller. You just managed to articulate the complete history of the CIA in one sentence. Look, the idea was that the UAE would be our proxies. They'd be our little brother in the middle of that shitstorm that is the Middle East. But then they got good. They grew and grew, and they started pushing back on us. They didn't give a damn about AQ, about ISIS, about the Sunni groups. No, they only cared about slowing Shia expansion. There was a lot of pressure from them for us to drive a hard line with Iran. We did it, at least as compared to the EU, and the UAE became our most trusted intelligence source on the mullahs, on Quds, on the proxy fighters in theater.

"It got to where we needed the UAE as much as they needed us. And that was about the time when al-Habsi started calling the shots. He knew we needed him, and he got his dad to demand from the president that we didn't spy on the UAE."

"So . . . it's a presidential order?"

"Damn right, it is. The USA does not run any intel collection on the UAE. Full stop. We can't touch them, and we sure as shit can't reveal that we used a black operator to spy on a nation we can't spy on in another nation where we aren't supposed to be spying."

Court said, "But, Matt. You can't just sit back and let us get drawn into a war because you are worried about the CIA being dragged through the coals!"

"I know that!" Hanley exclaimed. "That's why I'm here. I'm going to figure this shit out, and I'm going to stop the attack, and I'm going to keep the Agency's reputation, such as it is, intact."

Court didn't understand all the intrigue, but he did understand one thing. "If al-Habsi is the one orchestrating this plot, how about I just take him out? That would end it. Right?"

Hanley drummed his fingers on the side of his cup for a moment. "It might come down to that, but my concern is the die has been cast. We are looking at some sort of an attack, whether or not Sultan is around to take the fall for it."

"What do you mean?"

"I got a call while en route. BfV raided an apartment belonging to one of the Quds men killed in front of the embassy yesterday. They found some notes about a second attack on the embassy. It indicated that Mirza himself would lead this wave."

"With other personnel?"

"Affirmative."

"How many?"

"We are estimating a force of about twenty-five strong."

"That's a hell of a lot more than yesterday. Small arms, again?"

"And suicide vests."

Court thought about this. "AKs and S-vests sounds like something the Marines can handle."

Hanley responded, "But the embassy has to go into lockdown until it happens."

"If they go into lockdown, it won't happen."

"Which buys us time to find Haz Mirza. We are proceeding with the mind-set that the man might be working as a rogue agent for the SIA, and not for Quds Force. The entire Shrike operation was to eliminate German informants around Mirza, to find official cover operatives for Iran in the city, and to create fake linkage between them and Mirza."

He added, "Stopping al-Habsi won't prevent the attack, but stopping Mirza just might."

Court felt like he was back on firmer ground now. A riddle he could solve. "If I capture Annika Dittenhofer, take her to a cold cellar somewhere, I'll get you Haz Mirza."

Hanley nodded slowly at this, then said, "Approved. Travers and his boys are here, too. If you need them, they're yours."

"Good."

"Although," Hanley said, and his tone of voice turned suddenly accusatory. "From what I hear, you are already getting a little help." Court did not respond, so Hanley said, "Caracas station, what's left of it, found out Zack Hightower was released to a former member of Russia's foreign intelligence services. A female." After a pause he said, "I guess Anthem just happened to be in the neighborhood."

"Guess so."

"And how did she know Zack was in the care of our friends in Venezuela?"

Now Court came clean. "I told her about Zack. I also told her to get out of here. That's where she went, apparently."

Hanley said, "Court, you do good work, but you are more than a little . . ."

Court thought about what Dr. Kaya had said to him three nights earlier. "Relentless?"

Hanley shook his head. "I was going to say impulsive. But instead I'll say you are a loose cannon rolling around the deck of my battleship. You are a potent, vital tool, but first I have to get you tied back down and pointed in the right direction."

"I'll get you intel on Mirza, and Zack will help me. Then we get Chris and his boys from Ground Branch, and we go take Mirza and his crew out."

Hanley snickered. "You make this shit sound so easy."

Court shrugged. "The hard part will be al-Habsi. Be thinking about him, and what we do when Mirza is no longer the top item on our to-do list."

Hanley stood up from the table, letting Court know the meeting was over. "I will." He added, "Good luck. You don't need me to tell you, but remember . . . Hightower can run one hell of a tough interrogation."

"I was thinking the same thing."

"And also remember," Hanley cautioned, "Zack is a blunt instrument. You are a sharp instrument. Sometimes a hammer will work, sometimes a scalpel is called for."

"Got it."

The men shook hands. "Good luck, Violator. Let's get this done, and then let's go home. You look like shit."

"Yeah, well, I've been stabbed twice and I have a raging infection. What's your excuse, boss?"

SIXTY-ONE

Annika Dittenhofer pushed a hand out of the bedsheet and reached for the phone, both to answer the infernal ring and to see what the time was. In her line of work it was hardly out of the ordinary to get a late-night call, but since she'd told her technical team that she was taking a few days off, she really didn't expect them to bother her on the first evening of her hiatus.

She answered. "Dittenhofer."

"Miriam? Hi, it's Moises."

"What time is it?"

"It's almost eleven. Were you asleep?"

Annika sat up. "Yeah. What's going on?"

"I know you said you were taking leave, but I just wanted to ask your opinion."

"On what?"

"We broke off coverage of Mirza yesterday, like we'd been instructed, but about an hour ago his phone started pinging its location."

"The burner phone? The one he got rid of?"

"We only thought he got rid of it. It stopped pinging its location mid-afternoon yesterday. But it's back on. Yanis thinks Mirza might have put it in a Faraday cage before the operation at the American embassy, and only just took it back out."

"But he wasn't at the embassy."

"Operational security, I guess. Dunno."

"Where is it pinging now?"

"It's heading out of the city. In the direction of Fürstenberg."

"That's more than an hour and a half to the north. Right now? At eleven p.m.?"

"Yes. Yanis and I thought we'd take the van up there and have a look. Normally we'd get a physical surveillance request approved by the case officer assigned to us, but since you went on vacation, we're kind of on our own."

Miriam was already out of bed, racing to her closet for some dark clothing. "Approved. I will meet you there. Call me the second he stops."

Moises was pleased. "We were hoping you'd say that."

Court didn't wince as Dr. Azra Kaya pulled the needle out of his arm, though the sticks into the veins sure were adding up. She put a Band-Aid on the tiny wound; he thought it was funny that it was just a couple inches away from the large dressing around his biceps, but he appreciated her care nonetheless.

"There you are. You look like you're responding well to the treatment, but it's imperative you keep it up."

Court nodded, then stood slowly. Just then his phone buzzed in his pocket. It was the Signal app, he could tell by the pattern of the vibrations.

"Sorry. It's work."

Dr. Kaya nodded and led him to the door.

Court answered the call, realized it was Zack, and then rushed out into the hallway. "What's up?"

"Yo, Six, the tracker you put on the Shrike van is indicating movement. Heading due north, out of the city."

Court looked at his watch. "It's eleven p.m."

"No shit, it's eleven. Wrap it up with your girlfriend and let's go take a peek at what these shitheads are up to."

Court first saw this as potentially a perfect opportunity to snatch Dittenhofer, but soon he had another idea. He felt certain this must have something to do with Mirza, that perhaps she was following him, and he wondered if he and Zack could take the Iranian terrorist and his cell down tonight, and derail al-Habsi's entire plan.

For this he would need Chris Travers and his team, but Court wasn't ready to spin them up just yet. He wanted to make certain he had a target for them to hit.

He reached into his pocket and pulled out an Adderall, then said, "You load the Audi up with all the gear. I'll meet you at the safe house in thirty. Be downstairs and ready to go."

"Hell, yeah, brother."

One minute later Court climbed onto his motorcycle, fired up the engine, and took off in the direction of Spandau.

When the darkened street was quiet again, a woman stepped out of an alcove a block to the south and pulled out her phone. "Inna? I saw him. Yes, tell Maksim." Anya Bolichova added, "He's gone now, but I put a tracker on his motorcycle. I'll follow him at a safe distance, put trackers on any other vehicles he has, and report his location as soon as I know it."

Moises and Yanis parked the surveillance van in a campground in the forest meters away from Röblinsee, a small lake to the north of Berlin. They were just outside the town of Fürstenberg, in the Mecklenburg Lake District, and both the lake and the forest were shrouded in a thick, almost impenetrable mist at this time of night.

The men had tracked Haz Mirza's phone to an abandoned animal feed warehouse less than three hundred meters away, nestled between the Havel River, Röblinsee, and the train tracks. There it stopped moving, and it had remained stationary for the past forty minutes.

There was no light at all evident over the water from the warehouse itself, but the phone was definitely located there, so they determined they would park here to wait for Miriam, and to listen for any audio picked up by the phone.

In all their surveillance on the Quds men, they'd never been anywhere near here, and they didn't have a clue what could be going on across the water in an abandoned complex.

Annika Dittenhofer arrived in her car just fifteen minutes later and immediately asked for an update from her team.

Yanis joked, "You don't act like you're on vacation."

She smiled at this, then said, "Pay attention. What's going on inside?"

Moises replied, "The phone is in there. Hasn't moved."

"When did you get here?"

"About fifteen minutes ago. We aren't picking up any audio from it at all. If there is anyone in there, then they aren't talking, and they aren't moving around."

Annika thought it over for a moment. "This might be some sort of a staging area. He dropped his burner off with some other things and left." She looked out the smoked window here in the rear of the van. "There is nothing going on on this street. Let's give it another thirty minutes."

"Until what?" Moises asked.

"Until I go over there and take a peek."

Upon hearing this, Yanis looked out the front windshield. "It's black over there. Run-down. Abandoned."

Moises echoed this. "Scary."

Dittenhofer belted out a scoffing laugh. "If there is no noise and no movement, then that means there's no Quds Force. We will wait awhile to be sure, but I'm not afraid to walk over there." She waved at the audio gear in front of them. "Just pay attention to your headphones."

Court and Zack had turned the Audi's running lights off as soon as they got within a half mile of the now-stationary tracking device, and they rolled to a quiet stop in a small residential community just a couple blocks north of the lake. Parking in an elementary school parking lot, the two men were struck by the heavy mist hanging over the lot and the adjacent two-laned street.

They opened their car doors quietly; Zack had already disabled the interior light. They were stealthy here not because they were worried that Annika Dittenhofer or even Haz Mirza might hear or see them but rather because, even in the heavy mist, there were a lot of homes in sight, and they didn't want some busybody coming out and confronting them or, worse, calling the local police.

At the rear of the vehicle, Zack said, "Do we gear up?"

The two men had Heckler & Koch UMP submachine guns and extra magazines in the trunk, and chest rigs with body armor inserts, in addition to the pistols they wore on their bodies.

Court thought it over. They had a few blocks to walk still, and they would have to pass numerous homes between here and their objective. He didn't see any way they could kit up with big ceramic plates in their chest rigs, magazines strapped to their bodies, and subguns on their shoulders. Instead he said, "UMPs and extra mags in our backpacks. No armor. We're doing a recon. If we have something to hit, we'll call Travers."

Zack said, "Roger that," and both men got to work collapsing down the guns and loading the mags into the packs.

This done, they put in their earpieces and Court called Zack to open a phone line between them, and then they set out in the darkness towards their objective.

A half hour to the minute after Annika arrived, she pulled a flashlight out of a utility pack in the van and turned back to the two young men. "I'm going to take a look."

"You sure about that? This guy is Quds Force, or used to be, anyway."

Miriam said, "I'm not going to get too close. I'll put my earpiece in, and you guys can call me if you hear anything."

"Be careful," Yanis said, and then Annika climbed out of the van. Looking up the dimly lit street through the nighttime mist, she felt the scene to be like something out of a Cold War spy novel.

Soon she began walking slowly through the vapor.

SIXTY-TWO

When Court had checked the GPS while Zack drove, he'd noticed that the tracking device was parked next to a lake and near a very large structure. From the satellite imagery on Google, it seemed to be some sort of abandoned factory.

The two men followed the tracker on Court's phone up Kiefernweg to the lake, and then they turned left. Squinting into the thick fog, the men knew they were close. They separated, one on each side of the road, both ready to duck down in foliage for concealment if necessary.

When they were only forty yards from their target, Zack balled his fist and held it above his head, and Court stopped in his tracks.

"There it is," Zack said softly into his mic.

"I see it." The blue moving van was parked under trees, its nose pointing towards the black lake and its rear towards the street.

Both men moved into bushes on opposite sides of the road, and they maintained communication through their earpieces.

Zack said, "You want to just hit it? If our girl's got company, we can just gag 'em and zip 'em."

Court was still taking in the surroundings, making certain of his and Zack's immediate security. While doing this, he looked up the dark road, and he saw movement there.

"Hold," Court whispered, and Zack said nothing in return.

A few seconds later two forms took shape in front of Court on the road. "I got two pax moving in from the east, heading in the direction of the van. Backpacks, ball caps, hands empty."

"Roger that. I got them." Zack watched them for a moment. "They look a little squirrelly."

Court replied, "Amped up, yeah. I see it."

While both men watched, the men came flush with the van, then left the road, walking towards the back door of the vehicle.

Zack said, "Surveillance techs?"

Court didn't answer; he just watched while one of the men reached for the latch on the door, then looked back to his partner, who stood fifteen feet away on the road in the darkness.

Zack said it first. "Oh shit."

Then Court recognized what was about to happen, as well. "Son of a bitch."

The first man opened the door, and the second drew a pistol from his bag and opened fire. His weapon didn't even flash as he dumped round after round through the long suppressor and into the occupants of the van; the sound of several loud thumps echoed around the trees.

Court and Zack just watched helplessly from forty yards away.

There was a sharp tinkling of spent shell casings on the asphalt, and then it was quiet on the scene for a few seconds, until the body of a young man with dark hair tumbled out of the rear of the van. The body wore headphones, which were snapped back by their cord, and then hung there over the body by the rear bumper.

The two men shined flashlights inside the van for a moment, and then they began walking back up the street in the direction they came.

"What do you suppose that was all about?" Zack asked softly.

"I got here the same time you did."

To this Zack replied, "I sure as hell wish I knew who the good guys were."

"That's us. I don't know about anybody else." He thought a moment. "These guys might be the same jackwads I ran into in Caracas. And a few days ago, on the Ku'damm. They were no slouches. Do not engage till we get more information."

To this Zack whispered back, "Only way we're gonna get more information about those assholes is to see where those assholes went."

"Let's do it," Court said, and the two men moved out up the street, now one hundred yards behind the two killers.

"What about calling in Travers?" Zack asked.

"Negative," Court replied. "This is still recon. If a helo full of gun monkeys shows up, it's going to make a lot of noise; they might scare them away. Let's find an enemy and fix them to a location before calling in the shooters."

"Roger that. Hey, Six, you know what would be cool right now?"

"What's that?"

"A boat. We could come at them across the lake."

Court thought it over. "You want to steal a boat?"

"Yeah, like a speedboat, something with some power. But something quiet." Without waiting for Court's approval, he began walking towards the lakeshore, just a few dozen yards off his right.

Court followed along through the heavy mist, mumbling under his breath. "Fucking Navy guys."

Annika Dittenhofer arrived at the front gate of the massive animal feed factory, and even through the fog she could make out a dark array of broken-down buildings strewn with garbage and graffiti. She saw no lights or vehicles ahead, and she'd heard no warnings from Moises and Yanis, so she decided to keep going in search of Mirza's phone.

The tall chain-link gate was closed and locked with a rusty padlock, but part of the nearby fence had been pulled back, giving her enough room to slip through.

She was dressed head to toe in black and gray, so she felt stealthy enough, but for the first time in her career, she wished she carried a gun. There could be all types of ne'er-do-wells to deal with in here, but she felt an overwhelming need to press on.

A minute later Annika still hadn't heard from Moises or Yanis, and she took that to mean she was clear to move forward. The signal from Mirza's phone was being broadcast from the inside of the building closest to the water, so she walked quietly and carefully through the ruined streets around the fenced-off area towards the mouth of the Havel River.

She, of course, had taken into account the possibility that this was some sort of a trap, but she thought it much more likely the phone had been dumped here. She couldn't know for sure until she found it, but it was her hope to find a weapons cache, or some other intelligence that she could take to authorities so they could track down Haz Mirza and any surviving members of his cell.

She wasn't doing any of this tonight for Shrike International, nor was she doing this for Rudy Spangler. This was Annika going rogue, for the first time in her career, with the unwitting accomplices in the van on the lakeshore helping her find information that would lead to the capture of an on-the-loose terrorist before he could perpetrate another attack.

She'd devoted her adult life to intelligence work, and it would culminate, she hoped, in finally stopping the last remnants of the cell she had been keeping tabs on for over a year, now that their leader had proven a willingness to act.

Just outside the main building she pulled out her phone and dialed Moises. She was surprised when he did not immediately answer, and more surprised when the call went to his voice mail.

This wouldn't be the first time she'd had comms trouble in the field, however, so she pushed any worry she had to the back of her mind. Thinking it over carefully, she decided to press on ahead, knowing she could be only meters away from the phone and whatever else Mirza had left here in the abandoned factory complex.

She entered the main building finally. Her flashlight was off but held at the ready, both to help her avoid obstacles and to use as a blunt instrument if she encountered someone. There was a little light here and there when the moon shone through the clouds and the lake mist, and then through the massive shattered windows high on the concrete walls, enough for her to pick her way carefully around the trash and debris on the floor.

Still, her footfalls made noise, amplified by the cavernous hallways and other empty spaces around her. If there had been any hint whatsoever from the audio feed from the passive receivers in the phone, she wouldn't have dared go forward, but so far, anyway, Moises and Yanis hadn't called to report any issues.

Soon she found herself in the middle of a large, open room, a factory floor where the grain was milled and mixed and packaged. She could smell the river and knew it was just past the far wall, so she pressed on, but it was darker here; the moonlight came and went with the cloud cover through the windows high over the catwalks and just under the ceiling, some three stories above her.

There was a hole in the floor on the west side of the room, and she nearly fell into it. As she moved around it and continued forward, she recognized it as a staircase, perhaps down into a basement level, and she shuddered, hoping like hell she wouldn't have to go down there to find the phone.

She kept going, slow, careful steps in the low light, making her way to the middle of the large factory floor. But after a long period of heavy cloud cover, shrouding the scene in near total darkness, Annika saw no choice but to take a chance and turn on her flashlight for the first time.

She clicked the tail cap, and a white beam shot out across the dusty space.

And instantly she screamed out in surprise, her cry echoing all around.

Men stood on a metal catwalk twenty meters in front of her, one story off the factory floor. They all had rifles pointed at her, and when she dropped her flashlight to the floor, they turned on their weapon lights, blinding her with thousands of lumens.

"Don't move!" a man shouted in English, and she recognized an American accent.

She heard rushing footsteps behind her now, and soon a pair of armed men appeared on her shoulders and yanked her forward.

Yet another pair of men were there, on the ground level below the men on the catwalk. They wore rifles on their chests, and the bearded man on the left held a pistol in his right hand.

She was brought directly to the man on the right.

"Your name is Dittenhofer, and you and I need to have a little convo."

She had no idea what was going on. These weren't Mirza's people, no way. They were American, big and brawny; all the ones she'd seen had beards and hard faces. She wondered if they were CIA. Another possibility, she realized, was that these were the men who'd killed Drummond, and they worked for Shrike International's mysterious client.

But, if so, what did they want with her?

And then he told her what he wanted, but it did nothing to elucidate the situation.

"Where is Gentry?"

Annika cocked her head. "Who?"

The man slapped her across the face, knocking her to the floor.

SIXTY-THREE

Zack and Court did not find a boat with a motor as Zack had hoped, but they managed to steal a small rowboat from a dock on the way to the abandoned factory, and they used it now to approach the location from the south instead of the west, where they had seen the two men heading.

Rowing out into Röblinsee, shrouding themselves in the mist as they proceeded in an arc to stay hidden, took time, but they didn't like their chances of sneaking up on anyone in the ruins, so certain were they that the sound of their footfalls on the debris all around would carry across the empty buildings and alert anyone there to their presence.

After nearly ten minutes they brought the boat towards the shore, out of the mist, with Zack rowing and Court holding his weapon up with a left arm that tingled and a right arm with a deep slice in his biceps.

They came ashore inside the factory grounds, and both men crawled up a rocky bank and onto a parking lot full of cracked asphalt and growing vines and brush.

Zack whispered to Court. "Wish we had NODs."

Yeah, Court had to admit it, night observation devices would be handy as hell right now.

"And body armor. Good call on keepin' it low profile, Six. Any other bright ideas?"

"Just one. Thinking about taking your ass back to jail in Caracas."

Zack laughed softly, but his focus was on his gunsight and what lay beyond it.

Neither man activated the flashlight on his weapon, certain that using the darkness and the vapor to approach was preferable to a light show, but this was a large space, with a six-story main building on their left and a long two-story structure on their right. Unsure where to go, Court led the way to the main building, and Zack stacked up on his right shoulder.

The two men had done this countless times together; there was no discussion, they just went to work, moving as one, splitting up the sectors of fire automatically, dependent on where they stood in the stack. Court was responsible for six o'clock to midnight, 180 degrees of scanning as he moved, and Zack was responsible for twelve to six. This was so only because they knew they had their backs to the water, and there were no threats in the water, but once they entered the structures they would have to automatically change tactics. Court would take point, scan nine to three, and Zack would pull a moving rear security, covering three to nine.

They found a metal door into the building, and considered it. Alternatively there were open windows farther down the building, where the parking lot rose on a gentle hill.

Their third option for going internal on the structure was a pair of long-shattered low windows down at the asphalt, obviously leading to a basement or a crawl space below the building. It was covered by weeds and brambles, but Court and Zack both had fit themselves through tighter spots while on the job.

Court knew to defer to Zack on most things tactical. The former SEAL Team 6 member and longtime CIA paramilitary team leader knew more about these things than most anyone on earth.

Court took a knee, keeping his rifle up and sweeping the scene in front of him. "Three ways in. A, B, or C?"

Zack also took a knee next to him, his eyes straining open to take in as much light from the scene as possible. "I wanna say D, none of the above, but I guess we've come all this way so—"

A woman's scream and the shout of a man told them the building they'd been planning on entering was exactly where they needed to go.

Zack didn't hesitate. "Let's take the basement; we give up the high ground, but it will keep us covert until we're internal."

"Roger that," said Court, and he pushed through the brambles to the broken window flush with the pavement, and pulled his rifle sling off his neck so he could shimmy inside.

Zack covered for him until he disappeared in the darkness, then followed suit.

Annika Dittenhofer had no idea who these Americans were, nor did she know a thing about anyone named Gentry. She had climbed back to her feet; her hands were up in front of her face to shield her from both the blinding lights pointed at her and any more blows from the man in front of her on her right.

She asked with genuine confusion in her voice, "Are you with the American embassy?"

The man who'd slapped her was clearly the leader; he was the only one talking.

"We are asking the questions. Who knows you are here now?"

She said, "My teammates are in a van, two hundred meters away."

The American only said, "Not anymore, they're not."

She didn't know what this meant, but she was too afraid now to ask.

"Anyone else? Courtland Gentry. Where is he?"

She shook her head. "I don't know who that is. I am following a man named Mirza. An Iranian terrorist. He left his phone here and I thought—"

The man pulled a phone from a pouch on his load-bearing vest. "You mean this one?"

Annika looked at it for an instant, but then the American tossed the phone back over his shoulder; she heard it crash down the metal staircase into the basement.

"How did you get it?" she asked.

"We brought it here. Left it in a closet until you and the others showed up in the van. I'm told you were on leave from Shrike, so that makes me wonder why you are here right now. Makes me wonder if you are working with Gentry."

She was confused. "I . . . don't know Gentry. I work with no one except Rudy Spangler, and he knows what I am doing."

The bearded man on the leader's left holstered his pistol and stepped forward. He struck her across the face, knocking her to the dusty floor again.

Court and Zack moved slowly up the rickety metal stairs from the basement to the main floor. They had fixed at least two voices to a location on the ground floor, so they stepped as quietly as possible.

It was a difficult ascent; the staircase was steep and rusted, and the bolts groaned under the weight of two men, even two men moving at a glacial pace. Court didn't trust the integrity of the stairs, but when they heard the echoing voices coming from above, they decided to bank on the conversation masking some of their noise.

Court heard a German woman speaking English, and then he heard an American male speak. It sounded like a normal conversation at first, but when he heard the sound of a hand slapping a face, he knew it was a violent interrogation.

Was this Annika getting tuned up by a group of Americans? He couldn't surmise what the hell was happening, but he didn't want to witness another cold-blooded murder like he had with the two men in the van, so he rose slowly up the stairs, the holographic optic of his HK subgun to his eye.

The stairs did not lead to an enclosed stairwell; instead they led straight up to the open factory floor, terminating at a large opening near the center of the room. With only the top of his head exposed, Court took in the scene and, next to him, Zack did the same.

It wasn't hard to see where the action was coming from. Men on a catwalk twenty-five yards away from Court and Zack shined lights from their rifles down onto the factory floor, where a woman stood in front of two more men, their backs to the two new arrivals on the scene. These two were no more than ten yards away from the barrels of Court's and Zack's submachine guns.

All the men they saw appeared to be carrying AR pattern rifles, which indicated to Court they were likely American.

Zack whispered, "My count is six, all armed, plus the woman."

"Same," Court confirmed. And then, "We've never had much luck with odds, have we?"

"You kidding? This is a target-rich environment."

Court kept trying to decipher the scene unfolding in front of him, but he said, "General Custer said that once, I'll bet."

"Just once," Zack joked.

Just as Court refocused his attention on the woman, confirming this was, in fact, Dittenhofer, the man to the left in front of her reached out and slapped her hard across the face, dropping her to the ground.

Zack spoke softly to Court again; their shoulders were touching as they knelt on the unstable staircase. "Hold."

"Copy," came the reply. Court had already decided that if he and Zack were going to have to engage this much larger force of men, first they would need to take the last few steps up and out of the stairs so they could either find cover on the factory floor or go prone. There was a real chance of the staircase collapsing, especially if he and Zack started using it as a gun platform in a six-on-two firefight.

Zack was thinking the same thing. "We need to get off these stairs."

"Copy." But Court didn't rise up immediately. One of the rifle lights on the catwalk had shifted a little, and now he thought he might be visible to the men ahead facing this direction if he tried to move.

He could hear the voice of another man now. "Dunno, boss. I think she might be telling the truth."

The man standing over Annika on the left paused several seconds, then said, "Agreed. It was worth a try. I'd love one more shot at Gentry, but she ain't gonna be any help." He looked to the man on his left.

"Thor."

"Boss?"

"Kill her."

"Copy."

The man to the left raised his pistol without hesitation; the woman on the ground shielding her eyes from the flashlights lowered her hands a little and shouted, *"No!"*

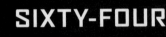

SIXTY-FOUR

Court fired once at the man with his pistol pointed at Dittenhofer's face, striking him squarely in the base of his skull. The operator dropped his weapon as he pitched forward, landing next to where Annika had crawled up to her knees.

Court had already shifted his aim to the leader of the team, but Annika was just beyond him so he didn't take the shot.

Hightower, on the other hand, opened up with fully automatic fire on the four men above on the catwalk, sending one of them tumbling backwards over the side.

The other men returned fire on the muzzle flashes in the dark, and dust and debris kicked up on the ground around the stairwell.

Court shifted fire to the catwalk, as well, but he only managed to squeeze off one ineffective round before his footing became unsteady. Bolts on Zack's side of the stairs broke apart under the combined forces of the weight of the men, their movement, and the vibrations of the gunfire, and the entire rusted iron structure dropped a foot down on the right-hand side. Court fell into Zack, and Zack slammed against the railing.

They didn't fall over and the stairs didn't give out completely, but if they wanted to continue to engage the men on the factory floor they'd have to climb out, exposing themselves.

Court said, "Going for the package!"

"Move!" Zack shouted, and Court pushed off his former team leader, climbed the last couple of steps up, flipped on his light, and sprayed automatic fire above Annika Dittenhofer's head towards movement along the wall where men had been retreating to cover. He raced forward, as low as he could, and by now Zack was out of the stairs and prone on the debris-strewn floor, sending enough rounds towards the men on the catwalk to hopefully keep them on the defensive and scattering to cover, as well.

Return gunfire had begun by the time Court got to Annika, who, to her credit, had already begun running over the rubble on the floor in his direction. He took her by the hand and pulled her back towards the stairwell as Zack's weapon ran empty, and they passed him on the floor right as he pulled his pistol and used it to keep up the suppressive fire.

Zack had long told Court that if you can't make hits, then you can at least make noise, and that appeared to be his philosophy as Court rushed past with the woman.

Annika stumbled right before Court made it to a low broken wall made out of cinder blocks not far from the stairwell out of the basement, and when he pulled her upright again he could feel her limping with each step on her right leg. He got her around the three-foot-high wall and pushed her down onto the rubble on the other side, and then he spun around and began dumping a magazine across the floor, giving Zack the opportunity to get off the ground and bound back to Court's position.

Zack ran towards his fellow Poison Apple asset's gunfire, which was safer than running towards enemy fire, but not by much. He leapt the cinder-block wall and then slipped on an old dust-covered tarp when he landed on the other side. He came crashing down in a heap next to the German woman just as Court expended the last of his mag.

Both Americans huddled low behind the wall as incoming fire sprayed in their direction.

Zack was closer to Annika than Court, but Court knew she had stumbled as they ran. "Check her for holes," he instructed, and Zack crawled to her, slicing his forearms on broken stone as he did so. With a flashlight in his mouth he felt all over her, then crawled back to Court.

"GSW, right calf. Not a big deal, we'll all have a lot more than that to worry about if these assholes regroup and come at us."

Court said, "I only saw one muzzle flash. Left wall. Our ten o'clock. Through a doorway."

"Affirm," said Zack. "I saw one go into that door, two more take the catwalk up to a door on the second floor, right side. Our eleven hundred high."

"That's three. Should be four."

Zack thought it over. "You popped one and I popped one. You're right."

"Where's the other fucker?"

"Probably flanking our asses."

"That's what I'd do."

Zack said, "Let's separate. I go right, head for that iron vertical beam, 'bout thirty feet away. I'll watch our six for flankers. You keep Eva Braun right here and stay low, but keep up the fire."

Court checked his load out. He had one more UMP magazine, and his HK pistol with two mags. Zack did the same, and found that he had half a mag in his subgun and one pistol mag left.

"Take my UMP," Court said, and he handed it to Zack, who in turn handed Court his last pistol mag.

Court looked at it. "Steyr? I'm carrying an HK."

"Strip it for rounds if you need to. You're the dumbass that wanted to hit this on the light side."

Zack climbed up to a crouch, fired a short burst over the wall, then took off to the right. Court held his VP9 over the wall and fired a half-dozen rounds.

He couldn't see if Zack made it; cloud cover had all but blacked out the light on the factory floor, so he called out to him.

"You good?"

"I'm here!" The men were speaking louder than necessary, a result of all the gunfire.

A voice shouted out from the darkened room off the factory floor some thirty yards away, surprising Court. "Hey! Hey! Are you motherfuckers American?"

Court did not respond, but after a few seconds Zack shouted back. "Who's asking?"

There was a long pause, and then the same voice said, "Who are you working for?"

Zack replied again. "America, dipshit. Who are *you* working for?"

"America, too."

Zack said, "Tell you what. You boys drop your weapons, thread your fingers behind your heads, and walk backwards towards us, one at a time. You do that, and we can all hang out and talk about apple pie and Ford trucks."

The voice from the other side said, "I'm a GM guy myself. And I'm on the job, otherwise we could party all night."

Court spoke for the first time. "Whatever job you're on, it's going to get you killed."

"There's five of us and two of you."

Court only knew of four. He looked over to Zack and could just barely make out his partner's silhouette, happy to see he was sweeping his rifle behind him, watching out for anyone flanking through the doors on the west side of the factory.

He said, "There used to be eight of you."

"Seven."

Court thought about what he'd seen of these men in action. He was playing a strong hunch when he said, "I bet that shithead I killed in Caracas would be pissed to know his TL had forgotten about him a week later."

Now there was a longer pause than before. "So . . . you're Gentry? The fucker from Caracas that killed Ronnie?"

"I didn't catch his name," Court replied.

The German woman remained huddled next to Court, pressed low below the cinder blocks, but she said, "Why are you making him angrier?"

Court whispered, "We can't attack them, there are too many. We can only defend. But we've got to get you out of here. I'm either going to scare him off or make him attack us."

"You want five men with guns attacking us?"

"No, I want to be home on the couch watching TV, but I'm working with the situation in front of me."

Court quickly fumbled in a pocket and retrieved his phone, then placed a call to Zack. They both had earpieces in, so he knew Zack would hear the call. The two men were only thirty feet apart, but Court wanted to communicate covertly.

Court came up to a low crouch. Still whispering, he said, "We've got to get her out of here. Any ideas?"

Zack didn't sound very confident. "You can go for the doorway behind you. Twenty meters of open ground. I'll cover you till I run dry, but I've got known threats on two compass points, one of which has the high ground, and I have two missing enemy."

The man who had been shouting out before now said, "Look. We've got CIA backing for what we're doing here."

Zack snapped back, "Yeah? I'm thinking you don't!"

Before the man could reply, Court shouted out now. "I know you're working for Emirati intelligence. Trust me, they do *not* have CIA backing for what's going on here right now."

"Dude, my work in Yemen was cleared by the Agency. You can't tell me it wasn't."

Zack shouted, "Look around, genius! Is this Yemen?"

Court spoke to Zack softly through his earpiece. "This guy is *not* going to listen to reason."

Zack said, "Shoot him a couple times in the cranial vault, I bet he'll come around."

The shouting from the dark continued. "We are a private military corporation working under contract for an entity that has CIA approval for its actions. That's all I need to know."

Zack came back over the earpiece. "Jesus, Six. This op has it all, doesn't it? Assassins, mercs, spooks, terrorists. Shit, I should have stayed in jail."

Court yelled back across the factory floor. "Listen very carefully to me, man. You are working for the SIA. The SIA is here in Berlin to set up an attack on—"

Gunfire from the far side of the floor interrupted Court's words and put an end to any possibility of negotiations. Stone chipped the cinder block in front of him, and he shoved the German woman down hard into the dust.

More rounds rained in from the second level now, and Court recognized this for what it was. This was assault by fire. He felt certain some of the men would be advancing right now, using the cover of their teammate's continuous gunfire.

Zack shouted over the phone. "Here they come! I'll suppress high ground!"

His UMP began barking, and Court knew his partner would be firing at the men in the room upstairs.

This left Court with the responsibility of covering the factory floor with his handgun. Not wanting to stick his head over the wall that was now being targeted with gunfire, he pulled his handheld flashlight and turned it on, then placed it on the three-foot-high wall, facing the open room. Then he rolled to his right, over garbage and decades of dust, and came out past the end of the low structure. He saw a muzzle flash in the same doorway as before, and then, in the flashlight's beam, he saw a man running forward, his weapon at his shoulder.

Court shot him in the legs, sending him tumbling into the debris on the floor, then shot him in the abdomen when he tried to get up.

He kept up the fire on the one doorway where he saw muzzle flashes, praying he had enough ammo to stay in the fight, that the men upstairs were being dealt with by Zack, and that the missing operator wasn't sneaking up behind him right now.

A round hit the flashlight, spinning it away across the room and then quickly extinguishing it.

The slide of Court's pistol locked open on an empty chamber. He dropped the magazine and slammed his last mag into position, then released the slide and fired a pair of rounds.

To Court's right a rifle with a weapon light glowing from under its barrel tumbled from the second-story landing and crashed onto the floor, and the light clicked off. Court took this to mean Zack was getting shit done in his sector of fire, too.

Zack called to Court now. "I dropped both targets upstairs that I know about."

"I got one down here. Another is still in the room at ten o'clock. But we're still missing one or two. How are you on ammo?"

"Winchester on the UMP." Zack was telling Court his submachine gun was empty. "Five in my Steyr."

Just then, the American mercenary's voice echoed across the factory. "You must be running out of ammo by now."

Court shouted back, "Not as fast as you're running out of dudes. You might want to do a quick head count."

There was no response to this. The massive room fell deathly quiet as, Court assumed, the man attempted to establish comms with members of his team.

The stillness continued for nearly a minute, with Court and Zack both spending the time scanning the darkness all around for threats. Finally, they heard an engine turn over and rev up outside the windows. Tires peeled out on rubble, and the engine faded away.

"Guess they weren't having fun," Zack said.

Court and Zack reconverged behind the wall. Court said, "We don't know if everybody hit the road or not. Keep your eyes open."

"Don't worry about me, I'm not reholstering this sidearm till I'm back in Virginia."

Court pulled Annika to her feet. "Can you walk?"

"I . . . I think so. Who are you?"

"Well, we're not about to shoot you in the head like those guys were, so I *guess* you could call us friends."

She was in a state of shock, but she managed to mutter, "Thank you."

Court moved her along towards the east side entrance of the factory floor, to a darkened doorway there. Zack hit it with his flashlight, but there was no movement, and they'd heard no noise, so they passed into a hallway.

As soon as they did so, all three of them stopped and Annika cried out in surprise.

A man sat on the hallway floor; an AR-15 rifle was slung around his neck, and his back was against the wall. Zack shined the light directly on him while Court trained his pistol, but it was soon obvious the man was dead. His throat had been slit, and his shirt and pants were covered in dark blood. He was a member of the mercenary team, that was clear, and it was also clear he'd flanked Court, Zack, and their prisoner, and had only to pass through the doorway to be in a position to kill them all from behind.

But what was not clear was what the hell happened to him.

A voice in the dark soon rectified this.

"Hey, boys."

Zack shot his light up the hall to his left while Court tracked the beam with his HK. There, Zoya Zakharova stood in jeans and a dark tunic, a pistol in one hand and a long knife in the other.

Before either man could speak, she said, "I don't want to tell you two studs how to do your jobs, but you might want to cover your ass next time. I'm not always gonna be there for you."

Court had lowered his pistol, and for a moment he just stood there in silence. Then he said, "What are you doing here?"

"I put a tracker in Yanis's laptop case two weeks ago. Got back in town this evening and checked it. Came here, hoping to find this one." She motioned to Annika. Then she looked at Court. "And where there's trouble, as usual, I run into you."

"Why are you back in Berlin?"

She shrugged at this. "Apparently to save your life."

"You're Zakharova," Dittenhofer said. "The Russian. You work for Americans?"

"Why not? You're German and you work for Middle Eastern terrorists."

"That is a lie!"

The sound of police sirens rolled in from over the lake.

Zack said, "Kraut po-po is en route. Think we can pick up this chat again back at the safe house?"

To Zoya, Court said, "Our wheels are a half mile away. Tell me you've got something closer."

"My car is next to the lake."

Court grabbed Dittenhofer by the arm, and all four of them headed for the exit.

They made it outside into a parking lot near the river, all three of the Poison Apple assets scanning the walls and windows and open ground for threats. Zoya had a four-door Fiat parked next to the low building in the deepest shadows, and they ran over to it.

They passed an alcove in front of the entrance of the low building, and Zack quickly flashed his light there.

Another of the mercenaries lay back against the door, a pair of bloody bullet holes in his forehead.

Zack turned to Zoya and looked at her pistol. "Anthem, did you take off your silencer?"

She stopped, turned to him, and flashed her own light into the alcove. "That wasn't me."

The three CIA agents looked at one another for a split second, and then they turned their backs to one another, with Annika in the middle. With their pistols sweeping all directions, they climbed into the Fiat.

Maksim Akulov slid into the backseat of the Toyota four-door driven by Anya Bolichova, slammed the door shut on the misty night, and sat quietly for an instant as the vehicle raced away. In front of him in the front passenger seat, Inna Sorokina turned his way. "What happened?"

He winced with pain as he touched his rib cage where he'd been hit after diving out of the hotel. "You have ears, don't you? There was a gunfight."

"Between who?"

Maksim shrugged. "I saw Zakharova right as I arrived at Gentry's location. I didn't see Gentry, so I decided to wait for them to come back to the car. And then . . . and then it went to hell."

"Who was shooting?"

"I have no idea. I heard eight, ten guns in the fight. I found cover behind her vehicle. A minute later a man appeared, I thought it was Gentry. Shot him twice, he went down. Then I saw it was someone else." Akulov slammed his fist into the seatback in front of him, jostling Sorokina with the act. "What the fuck is going on? You're the intelligence officer! You can't lead me into a ten-man gunfight! What's wrong with you?"

Inna seemed to have trouble controlling her anger, but finally, after spending several seconds in silence, she said, "We aren't getting intel from Moscow or from St. Petersburg. It's just us out here, fending for ourselves. You wanted Gentry, Anya tracked his Audi here from his apartment in Spandau. The only thing we knew about that factory was that Gentry was there. I told you that before you left the car."

Akulov slammed his head back against the headrest now, then touched his rib cage again, once more grimacing from the pain.

"Are you hurt?"

"I'm fine. Gentry's vehicle. Is it still stationary?"

"It is. With all the sirens, we have to assume that if he is still alive, then he has left the scene. Maybe he left with Zakharova in her vehicle."

The Russian assassin looked out the window as police cars raced by towards the lake behind him. Finally he just nodded to himself.

"We know where to find him."

"His apartment?" Inna asked.

"No. If Sem were here, I'd try it. But Gentry will have all sorts of defenses at his safe house. We need to surprise him at the other location. Let's just hope when he is there, he thinks to bring Zakharova with him."

The dark gray Toyota turned onto the highway to the south, heading in the direction of Berlin.

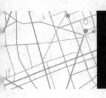

SIXTY-FIVE

Zack, Zoya, Court, and Annika made it back to the Spandau safe house at four thirty in the morning, exhausted still from the fight, the stress, and the late hour, with Court having the additional weight of his improving but continuing infection to deal with.

Court brewed a full pot of coffee as soon as they arrived, because he knew they had to get to work on Dittenhofer immediately and there would be no time for rest.

He had originally planned on a rough approach—or, more accurately, he had planned on turning her over to Hightower for him to work his magic on her psyche to get her to talk—but upon seeing that she was about to be murdered by the men working for the SIA at the abandoned factory, he determined there was a better way to get what he needed.

Zack treated Annika's superficial wound to her calf, and then Zoya helped her into the bathroom to clean up. When they came out, the German woman was teary eyed, drying her face with toilet paper. Zoya led her back into the barren living room and helped her down to the wicker sofa. She hadn't been tied or cuffed, but she'd seen what the three people in front of her were capable of, and it was obvious she wasn't going to pose any sort of a threat.

Annika now said, "You said back there that I work for terrorists. I have been doing exactly the *opposite*. Conducting surveillance on Iranian intelligence operatives and sleeper agents."

Court entered the room and passed mugs of coffee to Zoya and Annika. "I hope you guys like it black." Annika sipped it, then put it down on the floor in front of her.

Zoya began with the interrogation while Zack poured himself a cup in the kitchen. "Why were you at the abandoned factory tonight?"

She didn't speak at first. After a few seconds of silence, Zack Hightower entered. "Say the word, Six, and I'll go to work on her."

Court held his hand up to Zack, and Annika responded. "I will tell you what I know . . . but . . . I don't know who you are, so I don't know what you know."

"Just start talking. I'll tell you to skip ahead if I'm bored," Court replied.

"There is an Iranian named Haz Mirza who lives in Berlin. He is Quds—"

Zoya interrupted. "Skip ahead. We know about Mirza. We know you were tracking his phone."

Annika took a few breaths, then said, "Mirza's phone, we had it bugged and geotracked. It gave us the location of the factory."

Court asked, "Who knew that you had it geotracked?"

She thought about this, staring at a point on the wall as she did so. "Moises, Yanis . . . the two technicians you say were killed. Ric Ennis." She looked up at the trio standing in front of her. "And Rudolf Spangler. The owner of Shrike. That is all."

"So . . ." Court said, "you are saying that there is only one person on that list who is still alive."

The three stared down at her. She shook her head.

"*Nein. Nein,* you are wrong. Rudy is like a father to me."

Zack had been standing close to the balcony, keeping an eye on the dark street outside. But he turned around to face her now. "Yeah, then I'm just gonna say it. Your dad sucks."

She glared at him, but Court got the impression she was a very smart woman and was putting this all together about as fast as he and his mates were.

Still, she fought against her intellect. "I can't believe he would—"

Court interrupted. "Spangler gave those guys Mirza's phone, which means either he, or the guy actually calling the shots, has control of Mirza. Either way, your boss helped lead you there tonight so that those gun monkeys could kill you. You're smart enough to see that, aren't you?"

Dittenhofer looked at him, tears streaming freely down her face. After several seconds she nodded. "I don't understand why."

To this, Zoya said, "You know too much. The two technicians knew too much. You all had to be removed."

Dittenhofer sipped her coffee and stared at the floor. "I don't even know that much. They were asking about you," she said, with an accusatory finger pointed towards Court. "What do you have to do with any of this?"

Before Court could answer, Zack knelt in front of her. His voice dark and menacing, he said, "Tell you what, Fräulein. When you and two of your buddies snatch my friend at gunpoint, you get to ask him whatever you want. Until then, it's his turn."

She looked down to the floor. "Yes, I put surveillance on some Quds men, some VAJA men, even some MeK men. I recruited cyber assets into Shrike. But all I did was collect the intelligence product and pass it on to Rudy. I don't even know what Rudy was doing with the information."

"Do you know what Ric Ennis was doing?" Court asked.

She shook her head vehemently. "No. We were compartmentalized in our assignments. I have no idea what Ennis did, what the cyber team was doing."

Zoya said, "Ennis told me what he was doing."

And Court added, "Clark Drummond told me what he was doing."

"Why would they tell you that?"

Zoya answered. "Ennis knew a German intelligence officer had been killed while trailing our operation the other night. He was scared. The morning he died he came to my room, told me we had to run. I wouldn't listen so he told me what was really going on. He wanted me to know how incriminating this all was for Shrike. He said he'd spent months breaking into apartments of the Quds Force and VAJA men, planting evidence that would tie them together."

Annika bit her lip and sniffed hard, as if she could recoil the tears back into her eyes. "I knew it was something like that. Rudy would tell me to stop my coverage on Quds and the Iranian embassy spies, usually for just two or three hours at a time. I asked him about it but he said the client was directing us to do so and he did not know why." She looked to Zoya. "If Ennis was doing black-bag work, then that was Rudy giving him the instructions. Ennis didn't know the client any more than I did."

This was obvious to Court, but Annika clearly still had trouble wrapping her head around the fact that her surrogate father was as dirty as he clearly was.

Annika now asked, "But . . . what is the objective in all this?"

Court knelt right in front of the German woman now. "You said you were surveilling anti-regime operatives."

"*Ja*. Three of them. They were all killed this week."

"Why would someone kill them?"

"The only thing that makes any sense is that the client was trying to help Mirza and his cell." She sipped more coffee. "All three of the MeK men killed were informants for BfV. Kamran Iravani was himself bugging another one of Mirza's phones. If they hadn't been killed, then they would have been able to go to the German authorities and implicate Mirza and his men in an attack."

Court said, "Or . . ." He snapped his fingers. "If Mirza didn't attack, then they could go to the German authorities and tell them that, too."

Zack said, "What do you mean, if Mirza didn't attack? I thought he was a terrorist."

Annika understood what Court was getting at. "His handler in Tehran told him to stand down the day before yesterday. They said they would disavow any attack, and if he tried to defy them, they would kill him."

"But apparently he *did* defy them," Zoya said. "He assaulted the embassy."

Zack shook his head. "But Mirza wasn't there. It might have been his plan, but a trained combat veteran and a zealot like that would have been right in the middle of that mission if he could be. He's not a mastermind. He's a ground-level fighter. He'd be with his troops, unless someone or something prevented him from doing so."

Zoya said, "Do you think Tarik got to him?"

"Who is Tarik?" Annika asked.

Court answered this for her. "He's your puppet master. The one who has been giving orders to Shrike Group. Deputy director of Emirati intelligence."

She did not respond to this, so Court said, "You met him at the Regent along with Spangler yesterday."

Annika leaned her head back against the wall; it was obvious a sudden realization had occurred to her. "Of course. That's it. I told him myself exactly where Mirza was. Just a few hours before the attack."

Court put the puzzle together from this. "At which point Tarik sent his American mercenary force to go round up Mirza."

"But why?" Zoya asked. "And . . . if he wanted to save Mirza from the embassy attack, why did he let the attack go on without him? He could have stopped—"

Court had it, and Hanley had been the one to give it to him. "Because fucking Tarik, whose real name is Sultan al-Habsi, personally tipped off the CIA about the attack. He was further establishing his bona fides as a friend to America, while secretly he's been planning something else with the Iranian terrorist."

Zack just muttered, "What an asshole."

Annika now asked, "But, again, what is the plan? Mirza is only one man; most all the surviving members of his cell have been arrested." She repeated, "He's all alone."

Zack shook his head. "To hell, he is. He's got another force."

"How can you know that?" Court asked.

"He ran a cell. The cell got rolled up and shot up. But he's still a leader. Like I said, he's not a mastermind, but he's also not a lone wolf. He's not about to strap on an S-vest and climb aboard a city bus by himself. What he *is* about to do will take manpower, mark my words. Just because we haven't ID'd the rest of the dickheads doesn't mean there aren't any other dickheads out there."

Court looked to Zoya and Annika now. "Trust Zack on this. He knows dickheads."

"Card-carrying member," Zack confirmed.

Annika was left seated on the couch, her right leg bandaged and her mug of coffee in her hands, while the three Poison Apple assets stepped out on the balcony and closed the door to talk more freely.

"What do we do now?" Zoya asked.

"You stay here with Annika. Zack and I will go talk to Hanley."

Zoya was confused. "Hanley's here? In Berlin?"

"Yeah." He explained the relationship between the CIA and the UAE, about how Hanley came to town on the down low to try to rectify the situation, and didn't even want the U.S. ambassador to know he was here.

Zoya rolled her eyes. "So Hanley isn't supposed to be here. Zack isn't supposed to be here. You aren't really supposed to be here. I was the only one sent to Berlin in the first place, and yet still you want me to wait back in your apartment while the rest of you figure this out?" She shook her head. "I'm going to take Annika and try to find Spangler. You guys do whatever the hell you want."

Court said, "We'll come with you, then. We can fill Hanley in later."

She shook her head. "We will be fine. Stay here. Get your strength up. A storm is coming, and I won't be able to handle it without you."

Court nodded at this. He was utterly exhausted, the lowest he'd felt since he'd gotten sick. He said, "I'll stay here, update Brewer on what we have so far, and she can tell Hanley and Berlin station."

Zack turned to Zoya. "If you guys can grab Spangler, I will use my good looks and charm to get him to talk."

Zoya opened the glass door now to head back inside. "We don't have that much time. It would be faster to torture him."

"More humane, too," Court joked.

SIXTY-SIX

Keith Hulett, call sign Hades, had never demanded anything from his employer, but one hour earlier he had insisted on a face-to-face meeting with the man he knew as Tarik. It was hastily arranged for eight a.m. in the Volkspark Hasenheide, a small green space in Reuterkiez, near the American mercenary team's safe house.

He'd notified Tarik, via text, about the failure of his small force to kill Annika Dittenhofer, due to the arrival of Court Gentry and some other shooters. Tarik had not expressed condolences for the deaths of all Hades's men, nor had he given Hulett any further instructions; he just acknowledged the report, and agreed to the meet.

Tarik and his Emirati guards were already parked alongside a quiet park road when the man who called himself Hades arrived on foot, still wearing the filthy torn jeans he'd worn in the abandoned animal feed factory, and the same boots, though he'd changed out of his tunic into a green T-shirt, and he now wore a ball cap and carried a backpack over his shoulder.

Tarik sat in the back of a Mercedes S-Class, and two more E-Class Mercedes sedans were present, each with three security men standing outside them.

Hulett was frisked and disarmed of his SIG P226 pistol, his backpack was taken from him, and then he was ushered over to and inside the backseat next to Tarik.

As was his fashion, the Emirati intelligence chief didn't seem to care about Hulett's team. He opened with, "What about Annika Dittenhofer?"

"I already told you when I called. She got away. Gentry and some others, I don't know how many, took her."

Tarik showed nothing but displeasure. "Then why are you talking to me? What are you doing to find them?"

"What am I doing? Are you serious? My entire fucking team is off the table."

"What does that mean, 'off the table'?"

"Dead or unaccounted for, which, in this case, also means dead."

"I can get you more men, but it will take a couple of days. In the meantime, my people are chasing down leads. When we have a target, we will call you, and you will go."

Hulett just shook his head. "Fuck you. I'm done with this bullshit."

"That is unfortunate to hear."

Hulett looked at Tarik now, judging his next words carefully. "Gentry said you were planning something. That you didn't have a green light from the Agency to even be running an op here in Berlin. That you'd duped me and my team into this bullshit. That true?"

Tarik sighed deeply now. "I would have thought that, with everything you've seen, you would know enough to not ask uncomfortable questions at this difficult time."

"So that means yes."

"No, actually, it means good-bye. Your services are no longer required."

Tarik nodded towards the door to the Mercedes. Hulett fumed, then looked at the Emirati bodyguard in the front seat who was looking back at him. Then he looked at the driver in the rearview, and their eyes locked on each other.

Hulett recognized the stance these men had. Even though they were seated and no guns were visible, these two were ready to intervene if there were any threats to their protectee.

The American turned away and opened the car door, then climbed out slowly.

Outside the vehicle, with the door still open, he was handed his pack and his pistol back; the car door behind him was still open. He paused a moment, then spoke softly to himself. "Fuck it." And he spun back around, pulling his pistol out of its holster as he did so.

The bodyguards were prepared for an attack on their principal, but their reactions were slower than Hulett's action. One burly security man dove in front of the open car door, and another reached for the gun, but he wouldn't have made it in time.

In the end, however, it didn't matter.

A single gunshot cracked in the trees; Hulett spun towards the noise as his gun came up, but then he staggered back a step on the road.

A second gunshot sent him collapsing onto the little road.

Tarik's bodyguards swept their guns in all directions now.

Haz Mirza propped his AK-47 against a tree, then walked out of the woods with his hands raised. The bodyguards knew who he was, and they knew he'd been lying in wait to kill Hulett when they left the scene, so they didn't impede his advance.

Mirza stood over the body, examining him for a moment. He then turned his attention to Tarik inside the car.

"You shouldn't get Americans to do your fighting for you. They can't be trusted."

Tarik nodded slowly. "You are right, of course."

The young Iranian seemed emboldened at having killed. "You will see tonight what good fighters can do."

Now the Emirati intelligence chief smiled. "I just saw what a good fighter can do. I am certain you all will be victorious tonight, *inshallah*."

"*Inshallah*," Mirza repeated with his hand on his breast.

He shut the Emirati's door, then was directed to a nondescript Nissan two-door that was just now pulling up behind the three Mercedes vehicles. It would take him back to his safe house, where he would continue his lessons in operating the autonomous attack drones, then watch the loading of the devices into the truck before going through final instructions with his men.

Al-Habsi's three-Mercedes motorcade left the park quickly; there had been no one around during the shooting, but the sound of the 7.62-millimeter round being fired from a short-barreled AK would have been heard by hundreds.

Only when they were clear of the scene did the driver speak to his boss. "Sir? The airport?"

Al-Habsi nodded. This had been a terrible start to the morning of what he was certain would be the best day of his life. He had planned on being right here in Berlin when it all happened tonight, ready to run to the Americans with evidence that the attack had been orchestrated from the Iranian embassy in southwestern Berlin, but the fact that Annika Dittenhofer had somehow escaped with the Gray Man meant that, until Rudolf Spangler himself tracked her down and somehow killed her, al-Habsi was not safe here.

Still, there was some reason for optimism. Mirza had helped him kill the last of the American mercenary force. Dead men tell no tales, al-Habsi well knew.

Mirza and his force of prison inmates would all die eventually, as well, which was fine with Mirza and great with al-Habsi.

Sultan al-Habsi knew Spangler would not talk. The German was as corrupt as they came, and the instant he realized he had been an accessory to a savage terrorist attack that started a war, he wouldn't say a word. Still, al-Habsi would have him killed, sooner or later, just to prevent any chance of a deathbed confession from the self-aggrandizing old spymaster years down the road.

Annika Dittenhofer and Court Gentry were the last true dangers, so Sultan al-Habsi would go home to safety for now.

It was no matter. He could watch his triumph on television wherever he was, because the operation he'd conceived and overseen here in Berlin was about to be the only news story on Earth. And then, when it was all over, he could run breathlessly to Matthew Hanley with the proof that this had been no rogue attack but rather a carefully orchestrated official Iranian initiative.

Matt Hanley had just stepped out of the bathroom from his morning shower when he heard several car doors shutting in front of the rural home he was using as a safe house. He put his watch on, a Tag Heuer Monaco, and saw it was only seven a.m. He'd scheduled no meetings first thing today, and the guard force switched out at six a.m., so he had no idea who had just arrived.

He headed for the door as he buttoned the cuffs on his dress shirt, but had only made it halfway across the floor when he heard footsteps outside in the hallway.

As soon as the knock came he said, "Chris?"

Chris Travers opened the door. The Ground Branch team leader and the rest of his men were serving as Hanley's bodyguards as cover for their trip to Germany, so Hanley knew Travers would be the first to alert him if there was any trouble.

"Deputy Director. You have a visitor."

"An unannounced visitor? The hell I do. Tell them to make an appointment."

Instantly, Matt Hanley could see that Travers was uncomfortable, and that sent his stomach into a nose dive. "Who is it?"

"It's . . . it's Ambassador Sedgwick."

"Son of a bitch." Hanley had hoped to avoid the American ambassador to Germany learning that he was here in town.

"He's in the library. He seems . . . a little . . . annoyed, sir."

"A little?" Hanley asked dubiously.

"More than a little."

"Right. I'm on my way."

Two minutes later Hanley was still yanking on his gray flannel suit coat as the door to the library was opened for him.

Sedgwick and POTUS had been fellow Yalies, law partners, golfing buddies, even brothers-in-law for a time when POTUS's brother married Sedgwick's sister, and even the disintegration of the marriage didn't blunt the friendship between the two.

Hanley had it on good authority that Sedgwick had been given one of the most coveted ambassadorships in the world by his friend the president to bolster his international relations credentials because he was being groomed to be secretary of state when the current secretary retired at the end of the year.

Hanley walked into the room with a smile on his face, but he knew it wasn't going to improve the mood of the heavyset Kentuckian standing in front of the darkened fireplace.

"Mr. Ambassador. So nice of you to—"

"Don't start shit with me. That way, I won't have to tell you to cut the shit."

Hanley extended a hand for a shake, giving himself about a fifty percent chance of reciprocity from Ryan Sedgwick. The ambassador did take his hand unenthusiastically, but his eyes conveyed nothing but malevolence.

As did his mouth.

Sedgwick said, "I learn the deputy director for operations of the CI-fucking-A is holed up in an Agency safe house in my town. I know you guys don't play by any rules of courtesy, but I do *not* like surprises. In fact, I often find them suspicious."

"I am here personally chasing down some intelligence related to the attack the other day."

"Without your station notifying the ambassador of your visit?"

"Didn't want to trouble you. Due to some sensitive matters, I didn't even want to involve Berlin station more than I had to. Me calling in on the embassy would have been a distraction for everyone."

The two men sat down on comfortable sofas. Coffee was brought for them; Hanley hadn't had his first cup of the day so he drank greedily while Sedgwick just looked at him.

Finally the ambassador said, "Well . . . you're here. I know you're here, so your plan to keep this from me is out the window. Might as well tell me what you're doing."

"We are concerned there will be another attempt on the embassy."

"By who?"

"We believe it to be an Iranian Quds Force terrorist named Haz Mirza."

"The guy behind that pissant attack the day before yesterday?"

"Yes, sir."

Sedgwick laughed angrily. "It takes a transcontinental trip by the DDO to tell me something I can read on Twitter? Everybody knows the ring-leader of those Iranian terrorists is still on the loose. And everyone knows there was intel collected . . . by the *Germans*, I might add, indicating a follow-up attack on the embassy."

"That's correct. We do expect this next attempt to be much more ro-bust. Perhaps the first was simply a misdirection."

Sedgwick waved his hand in the air like he didn't believe, or didn't care. "Tell that to the terrorists our Marines killed. Four of Mirza's men are dead. Three more have been arrested. The intel I read is that Mirza only had nine to begin with. The other two degenerates are probably in a brothel in Hamburg trying to get off one last time before the federal *polizei* find them and throw them into prison."

"Our intelligence suggests—"

Sedgwick wasn't having any of it. "What intelligence? Intelligence that was so inconsequential that you came here without telling my office, with-out calling in on Berlin station? Come on, Hanley. I'm not an idiot. You don't want me to know what you are doing here because you know I will put a stop to it. Ever since your CIA was busted spying on Germany, in Germany, you've been told to watch yourselves. POTUS doesn't want to deal with another dustup like that.

"You know my relationship with POTUS; you know there is no one more closely tied to him in all of the government, so you sneak your ass over here so I don't know that you are running some sort of an operation in Berlin that—"

Sedgwick kept talking, but Hanley stopped listening. As he sat there, something suddenly occurred to him. The ambassador was right.

The single most important symbol of American power in Berlin, in Germany, hell, perhaps in all of Europe, was Ryan Sedgwick.

Hanley kept quiet, kept listening, kept nodding along to the man tell-ing him what a bunch of corrupt cowboys the CIA were, but he couldn't even hear the man, because inside his brain alarm bells clanged so loud he thought his temples might burst.

Matthew Hanley had found Haz Mirza's target. Sultan al-Habsi's target.

Hanley didn't know how, when, or where, but Mirza was coming after

Sedgwick. Al-Habsi would know that nothing on earth would draw the United States into war with Iran more assuredly than assassinating the president's friend and top political lieutenant.

Hanley finally interrupted; Sedgwick was saying something about the Agency's "runaway budget."

"Mr. Ambassador, we are working hard to assist the Germans with the Mirza investigation, but in the meantime, I think you should stay inside the embassy until this threat passes."

"You *just* said there was another attack planned on the embassy. You want me there when it happens, is that it? That's cute, Hanley. POTUS will love knowing you tried putting his former campaign chairman in the bull's-eye for the attack."

"I'd prefer you back in Washington, to be honest. But if you are going to stay in Germany, I think it would be best if you stayed in a place that was protected by a company of Marine guards, instead of home, or out to dinner, or driving from place to place."

Sedgwick waved that annoying hand in the air yet again, dismissing all Hanley had just said. "I can't stay at the embassy. I have things to do."

"May I ask what is more important than your safety?"

"Don't put words in my mouth. I will be safe wherever I go, especially now. My security has been doubled. Armored motorcades, the whole she-bang. These days I don't know if I'm driving the streets of Berlin or the streets of Mogadishu, since the CIA has done such a piss-poor job protecting American interests.

"And to answer your question about what is so important, I am hosting an art exhibit at the residence tonight. There will be dozens, hell, I don't know, hundreds of security there. It will be fine. I'm not worried about one idiot with a suicide vest; what I *am* worried about is the corruption of American diplomatic relations that I see when the deputy director of the CIA sneaks onto my turf to try to undermine—"

Yet again, Hanley tuned out and interrupted.

"This might be impudent of me to ask, Mr. Ambassador, but could I possibly attend your event tonight?"

Sedgwick had stopped talking, and now he looked at Hanley not like he was the devil incarnate but as if he were an idiot. He stood, shook his head in disbelief, and said, "Get out of my town. If you want to come back, notify my office. Don't skulk around like you are some old Cold War spy."

Ambassador Sedgwick left the library without another word. Hanley knew the courteous thing to do would be to escort the ambo to his motorcade outside, but he let him find his own way out. One call by Sedgwick to the president and Hanley would be a fifty-eight-year-old ex-spook looking for a new profession, and Hanley knew that call might well happen no matter what he did in the next day or two in Berlin. Still, he knew he had to ignore Sedgwick, stay here in Berlin, and then find, fix, and finish Haz Mirza.

Hanley had assets in place, he had lines into some intelligence about the plot and the players, and now, he felt reasonably sure, he had the time and location of the attack.

He knew what he needed to do. He needed to either keep Mirza away from Finkenstrasse tonight, or he needed Travers, Gentry, and Hightower to be there when it all went down.

He pulled out his phone and called Suzanne Brewer. He'd have her contact Romantic and get them here for a face-to-face chat. Hanley wished Anthem were in town still, too, but he understood her reasons for running.

SIXTY-SEVEN

Kevin McCormick sat in his office on the fifth floor of the U.S. embassy, with a view of the Brandenburg Gate out his window. As the local CIA chief of station, he had been working virtually nonstop since the Marines on the roof of this building successfully thwarted an attack two days earlier, and he expected his workload would not slack off at any time in the near future, all due to the killing of Iranian general Rajavi.

He knew that the intelligence for this week's attack had come in at the last second from the UAE, and he'd already sent his thanks to the local SIA office at the Emirati embassy on Hiroshimastrasse.

But still, the Quds Force cell leader was on the loose in the city, and all indicators were that he was not finished with his mayhem.

McCormick had other worries, too; office politics on a large scale. But he pushed these out of his mind and decided to call to his executive secretary to get his German counterpart at BfV on the line to see if there were any updates in the search for Haz Mirza.

But before he could do this, she leaned into his office. "Sir. DDO Hanley is on the line for you."

"Thanks, Brenda." McCormick sighed. Office politics. He'd been dreading this call. He'd found out earlier in the morning that the ambo was livid because he'd learned Hanley was in town, and Berlin station had been keeping this info quiet around the embassy.

The fact was, McCormick had no idea how Sedgwick found out about Hanley's trip to Berlin, but he knew this fact wouldn't get him off the hook with Hanley, and since he hadn't, in fact, notified Sedgwick of Hanley's visit, he'd be getting an earful from the ambo, too.

The call was put through, and the chief of Berlin station prepared for his first of two difficult conversations of the day.

"Good morning, Deputy Director."

Hanley wasn't one for chitchat in the best of times, this the CIA station chief already knew, but he was still unprepared for the berating to come. "Fuck, McCormick! You told the ambo I was here!"

McCormick said, "I absolutely did no such thing, sir. We've done everything in our power to keep this close to our vests."

"Oh, so it wasn't on purpose. It was a fuckup. Is that the defense you're going with?"

"I don't know how he found out. I called a meeting with senior staff an hour ago, and they assure me that—"

"Someone in your station either did it out of malice or out of incompetence. No other possibility exists."

"But—"

"Shut up, Kevin. Shut up and just listen."

McCormick had known Hanley for nearly two decades. He'd never heard him this angry, and he assumed it had more to do with the beating he'd taken from the president's top man in Europe than anything else.

Hanley was worried about losing his job, and right now, McCormick could relate. "Yes, sir," he said, sheepishly.

"Simple question, I want a yes or no answer. Would you like to have a career tomorrow morning?"

"Yes. Yes, I would. Very much so, in fact."

"Then I need you to do something for me, and I don't want any pushback."

McCormick had been handed a lifeline, and he lunged at it. "Anything you ask, sir."

"What I need is for you to get me an invitation to Sedgwick's party tonight."

"His party? I was unaware of—"

"Some art opening bullshit thing at the ambo's residence."

McCormick thought a moment. "That's right. I did hear something about that." Relief washed over him. "Shouldn't be any problem at all. I wasn't invited; I'm Berlin station, and Sedgwick hates us. But you're the DDO. I can reach out to one of the galleries providing the artwork and get you an invite."

"Good."

So happy he was to be let off the hook, McCormick said, "Is there anything else I can—"

"Yes, there is. I am going to send you two passports. I need identification made for these men. They are my personal security detail. I will be attending the event with them tonight."

"Certainly. With security badges they will be let in to any event at the ambo's residence as long as they're with you and you have an invitation." McCormick was even more ebullient now. "I'll run them down to personnel and get—"

"No."

"No?"

"They are not CIA personnel."

It was quiet a moment. "Your bodyguards aren't employed by us?"

"Long story. I need your art department to prepare these. And I need you to oversee it personally, and I need this to stay between you, me, and whoever in art that you trust." "The art department" was a nickname given to the forgers kept on staff at a station. Hanley was telling McCormick, without saying it outright, that the two people coming along with him to the ambassador's party would be using falsified CIA badges. And he was also telling Kevin McCormick that he would be complicit in this.

The chief of station's voice shifted from relief to torment. "Oh . . . Actually, I'm not sure that I can—"

"Two men who are Agency contract employees. They don't have security badges. I need them at the event, and they won't be allowed in unless they are on my detail. I need them on my detail."

McCormick sighed into the phone. "In good conscience, I don't believe I—"

"I don't give a rat's ass about your conscience! This needs to happen. If you don't do it for me, I'll call Benji Donovan at Prague station and have him courier them up to me this afternoon. But if I *do* have to call Prague, I'll have you made assistant to the deputy director of personnel in Port Moresby."

Hanley's voice lowered. "Tell me, Kev, have your past assignments taken you to Papua New Guinea, or will this be a first?"

There was a pause, but not for long.

McCormick asked, "Will these contractors be carrying weapons? There's a lot of documentation necessary for that, as you know, especially in Germany. Plus, I'd have to go through DSS and RSO." The Diplomatic Security Service was responsible for the ambassador, and the Regional Security Office assisted with local protectees. "I really do not think I can falsify that." He faked a little laugh. "I'd rather go to Port Moresby than prison, know what I mean?"

Hanley quipped, "So you *haven't* been to New Guinea, I see."

It was quiet another moment; Hanley pictured McCormick shitting his pants, and he enjoyed the image, so angry was he at the fact that someone at the man's station had outed the DDO to the ambassador.

But Hanley let him off the hook. "No weapons. The DSS and RSO will handle any tough stuff, I just need these men by my side."

Chief of Station McCormick relaxed, but only a little. "I'll take care of the badges, sir. Run down the images personally and stand there while one woman in art, who I trust implicitly, takes care of the entire job. No one else will know."

Matthew Hanley nodded to himself with the phone to his ear. He said, "Thank you, Kevin. Port Moresby's loss is Berlin's gain." He hung up the phone, and turned to Court and Zack, who had joined him in the library of the farmhouse.

"Violator, you and Romantic are good to go, but you'll have to go unarmed."

"That blows," Zack said.

"There will be seventy-five armed men and women at the event, I'm certain. I need your eyes, ears, and brains. I don't need two more trigger pullers tonight."

Gentry said, "I've heard that one before."

Hanley shrugged. "If the shit hits the fan, I'm sure you will have access to a battlefield pickup."

"That's your plan, sir?" Zack was incredulous.

"Mirza could be there as a waiter, as a member of another delegation, as a fucking artist there to talk up one of his paintings. I don't know. If he *is* there, and we have an opportunity, we can take him quickly and efficiently."

Court said, "What if Mirza comes with one hundred jocked-up Quds dudes wearing S-vests? You know he won't be there on his own. He has some sort of force multiplier up his sleeve."

"Berlin station has gone to red alert, and they know the party is a potential Mirza target. DSS knows it, too. The Germans are already on high alert knowing that he's loose in the city. Travers and his team will have a helo assigned to them, and they'll be fifteen minutes out. Even if Mirza does have some other men, even if he's got two dozen motherfuckers with him, they're *not* getting into that building."

"Unless they do," Zack said.

"Unless they do, at which point you'll have to stop him. You two, as well as myself, will be inside the residence. If an attack comes and all the armed men and women outside can't repel it, it will be down to us."

Court looked at Zack, hoping he wasn't about to say what he worried he would say.

And then Zack said it. "Sir, Anthem is here, as well. Do you want to roll her into this?"

Hanley cast a frustrated gaze at Court, who himself cast a frustrated gaze on Zack before saying, "I wasn't lying earlier, boss. She came back. Showed up when we were in the process of liberating Dittenhofer."

"Where is she now?"

"She is with the German woman now." He paused. "They're trying to track down Spangler."

"I will have Travers take you back to your place for a few hours, and they will collect Dittenhofer. She'll come here and I'll have Berlin station watch over her." He sighed. "And I'll call McCormick back and get Zoya a badge for tonight."

Court didn't say anything. He just looked at the floor.

"How copy, Violator?" Hanley asked.

Court shrugged. "Solid copy, boss."

Hanley looked at both men now with a finger in their faces. "Remember this. Failure is not an option."

Court sighed after hearing this cliché. "Failure is *always* an option, Matt. It's just not the desired option."

Zack said, "Six is not wrong about that. I've seen him fail."

Hanley let it go, and changed gears. "You still look like shit, Court. I'm going to need you to clean up before the party. It's an art show, can't have you walking around looking like you've got typhoid."

"Yeah, I'll get on that."

Court and Zack left Hanley in the library and headed outside, out on the driveway. Here they climbed into the back of a Suburban driven by one of Chris Travers's Ground Branch operators, with another in the front passenger seat, for the lift back to the Spandau safe house. Court was furious with Zack that he'd roped Zoya into this plan of Hanley's, but he retained the presence of mind to know that Zoya would have kicked his ass if he had kept her out of it.

Zack said, "We need suits and ties and shit for tonight, right?"

"Yep." Court said it distractedly, his mind somewhere else.

"Want to go shopping?"

"Not particularly. Last time I tried that, it didn't go so well." Court's focus was fully on Zoya now, on protecting her, and not on the mission at hand.

Zack nodded to himself, then smacked the driver's seat. "Teddy. How 'bout you and Greer drop me off at a mall somewhere? I'll get some duds for tonight for me and Six, then catch a cab back to Spandau."

Teddy looked in the rearview. "Roger that, gramps."

Zack smacked the back of the seat again, then turned to Court. "Dude, Mirza has got himself another crew of shitheads, and I agree they know something we don't about what's gonna go down, but if the shit hits the fan, we'll adapt and overcome." He added, "Anthem might end up being the help we need, just like last night in the factory."

Court nodded. Zack was right, but Court's affection for her still made him protective.

SIXTY-EIGHT

Court arrived at the safe house just after Zoya and Annika, who had been out unsuccessfully hunting for Spangler. The German former Stasi official wasn't returning Annika's texts or calls, his house was empty, and it looked to the women as if he'd left in a hurry.

Spangler, it was clear enough to all, had gotten the hell out of Berlin.

Annika Dittenhofer was shuffled limping into the Suburban with Teddy and Greer, and she immediately informed them she wanted them to take her to Chausseestrasse, the headquarters of German federal intelligence.

At this Teddy laughed a little, and Greer, who now sat in the back with Dittenhofer, politely but firmly explained that she had not, in fact, climbed into a taxi, and she'd be taken where she'd be taken, and neither of the men wanted to listen to any lip about it.

She puffed up her chest in a show of defiance, but a look from Teddy through the rearview at her convinced her to drop her protest.

The Americans had her now.

In the little flat on the third floor of the apartment building, Zoya checked Court's bandage on his arm and decided to re-dress it with clean wrapping. While she did this he told her about his conversation with Hanley.

He wrapped it up with, "So, he knows you are here, and he wants you to come tonight. Personally, I think—"

"Personally," she interjected, "I think it's the right idea."

"Right. Me, too, of course." Court wasn't going to argue with her. He knew where that would lead. Instead he looked at his watch. "It's almost two. Hanley wants us back at Tegel at seven."

She looked him over, touched her hand to his forehead, and asked him how he felt.

"I'm okay."

"You don't seem to have a fever, but your skin feels clammy. Your shoulder and arm have to be hurting from everything that happened at the factory last night."

"I'm on painkillers."

She nodded, then said, "Will you be on painkillers tonight?" There was no judgment in her voice.

"Of course not. I will keep them handy for whatever happens afterwards, though. Got a funny feeling I'll be needing them."

It was clear she didn't like the way he looked. "When was the last time you slept?" Zoya asked, and Court thought it over.

"Thirty hours, give or take."

"Come here," she said, and led him into the bathroom. Together they lay down on the bedding and clothing piled there. With barely enough room for both of them in the small space, they wrapped their arms around each other.

He moved to kiss her, and she kissed him back, but only for a moment.

"What's wrong?" he asked.

"Zack will be back soon. You need to rest."

He couldn't hide his disappointment.

"You're ill, you're wounded, you haven't slept in a day and a half, and you need opioids and speed in order to function. You sleep, I'll watch over you, and when Hightower gets here, I'll see that he doesn't disturb you."

Court didn't like this agenda. "I'm fine, Z."

"You are the opposite of fine. Hanley runs us all like rented mules, but you're the rented mule that goes off on his own and does other jobs." She sighed. "You're so . . ."

When she couldn't find the words, Court smiled. "Relentless?"

But Zoya shook her head. "I was going to say 'crazy.'"

"Right."

"Go to sleep."

She wrapped her arms around him tighter, and he fell asleep within minutes.

Court woke with his face planted in Zoya's thick hair. These were unfamiliar surroundings, to be sure, but it filled him with a sense of calm.

He realized with a sudden clarity that nothing on his body hurt.

All the pain, all the death, the danger, it had all been washed away, even if for just a few hours, and even if it wouldn't last long after waking.

He'd take it.

He'd spent countless nights in the past year thinking about Zoya, thinking about being with her, waking with his arms tight around her. It was happening, and he told himself everything else would have to wait.

He was going to enjoy this a minute.

He liked the feeling of her stirring in his embrace as she slowly woke, lifted her head, and looked around, almost childlike. He could tell she was in unfamiliar territory, as well. He was behind her, and soon she put her hands on his forearm over her body and squeezed it.

Her voice was raspy. "Hi."

"*Dobroye utro.*" *Good morning*, Court replied in Russian.

She checked her watch, then rested her head on his shoulder and giggled. "It's six fifteen p.m. I see sleep doesn't do anything to improve your Russian."

"And sleep doesn't do anything to curb your sarcasm."

They lay silently together a moment; Court tried to think of something to say, but Zoya spoke first.

"How are you feeling?"

"Never better."

She sniffed out a little laugh. "On a bathroom floor sleeping on your underwear. That doesn't say much for your life, does it?"

He laughed, too. "Right now, I've got no complaints."

The door to the bedroom opened with a squeak. Both Zoya and Court grabbed their pistols, but before they could peek through the bathroom door, they heard Zack's voice.

"Get your lazy asses up. An afternoon nap? What do you think this is? A Caribbean cruise?" When Court pushed open the door and squinted into the daylight, Zack looked at him and Zoya interlaced on the bathroom floor. "You two nutters are perfect for each other." He turned to leave the room. "On your feet. You need to be showered, dressed, and downstairs in thirty. Teddy will take us to Hanley, then we'll transfer vics and drive Hanley to the event ourselves."

His voice boomed, full of fake levity. "We're goin' to a party, y'all. Don't mind the fucking terrorists. Won't this be fun?"

SIXTY-NINE

Zack Hightower stopped the BMW 5 Series at the checkpoint on the corner of Clayallee and Finkenstrasse and rolled down his window. In the front passenger seat, Court Gentry pulled his credentials and passed them over, and a uniformed police officer looked at them, then scanned them with a cell phone.

A second officer, this one wearing a shotgun around his neck, stood by the front passenger window. Court made quick eye contact with the man, who only nodded back his way, then continued scanning the vehicle.

Zoya was in the backseat next to Hanley, and she passed her ID over to him, while he rolled down his window and proffered both their credos and his invitation.

While an officer checked Hanley's invitation and scanned the two IDs of the backseat passengers, Zack was instructed to pop the trunk and the hood. Men searched both for explosive devices, while yet another man used a mirror on a pole to look under the car.

The Germans did all this efficiently; there were a lot of diplomatic functions full of VIPs in Berlin, after all, so they had plenty of experience.

That was not to say this was a normal day for those charged with the security of the event. The American CIA had told the Germans they were worried about tonight at the ambassador's residence specifically, although the Agency people in the American embassy had admitted to their counterparts that they had been wholly unable to convince the ambassador to delay or cancel the event. Still, the normally robust security for a function like this had been doubled, and the police were on alert throughout the city.

When the BMW was waved on down Finkenstrasse to the next stop, the four people in the vehicle began talking about what they all saw.

"Eight city cops at the first stop," Zack said.

"That's my count," Zoya added.

Court was looking into the park on their right. "Looks like a half-dozen radio cars, two uniforms at each, parked on the southern side of the road. I see flashlights out in the trees, assume some foot patrols."

Hanley said, "Also assume checkpoints in the other direction, so double our counts for the total external ring security force."

Zack said, "Nursing home on the left."

Court quipped, "Matt, does Zack have time to run in and get a brochure?"

"Watch it," Hanley said. "I'm older than Romantic."

The man behind the wheel groaned. "I really hate that code name, sir."

Hanley didn't respond to this. Instead he leaned against the window and looked up into the dark sky. "I don't see any air. The Germans should have a helo or two up for this."

They stopped at a second checkpoint on the road right in front of the front gate, and here all four were asked to step out of the vehicle by an armed man in a black windbreaker. Once standing in the road, they were quickly wanded for weapons by Germans who looked like they might have been part of the Regional Security Office, local security officials who helped the embassy with such tasks.

A valet took the keys from Zack and drove the BMW to a parking lot in Finkenpark, while the four new guests walked to the guard shack next to the driveway, passing the open iron gate.

Court put his hand on the metal bars idly as he passed, and he judged them to be heavy-gauge iron and able to stop most any vehicle that might try to ram its way inside.

But only if the gate was closed.

The shack was manned by a half-dozen uniformed Diplomatic Security

Service personnel with MP5 submachine guns. Hanley and his small entourage waited in a short line behind other well-dressed guests, and finally their invitations and credentials were checked over a third time and they were welcomed to head up the driveway to the main house of the two-acre property.

The exquisitely manicured front garden had male and female security personnel standing around, all in suits and carrying subguns, shotguns, or pistols. Court could see their wired earpieces and the radios on their belts, and he was comfortable they would be in comms with the local police, the Regional Security Officers out front, and the personal protection detail of the ambassador inside.

On the roof of the old white mansion he could see movement, and he knew these would be DSS snipers, or perhaps U.S. Marines.

They walked as a unit. Zoya, Court, and Zack were supposed to be Matt's bodyguards, after all, so they were close enough together to speak without being heard.

Zoya said, "Easily seventy-five armed security personnel, when you include the *polizei*. Maybe one hundred."

"Yep," Hanley said. "But al-Habsi would know that already, and Mirza will be ready for it."

Zack said, "How the hell can Mirza get through this? I mean, unless he's already here."

Just then, a police helicopter flew overhead, and it shined a spotlight somewhere in the park across the street before flying off.

"Air. That's a positive development," Court said.

Zack threw some cold water on this, however. "Local police. They should have GSG9 in the sky and ready to hit." Grenzschutzgruppe Neun was Germany's elite special mission unit, some of the best paramilitaries on Earth.

They entered the front door of the massive, restored early-twentieth-century mansion at ten after nine, and they placed their covert earpieces in their ears, putting themselves in communication with one another, no matter where in the building they were.

Ingress complete, they began working on phase two of tonight's operation. They had to keep Hanley away from Ryan Sedgwick, or anyone who worked with Sedgwick who would recognize Hanley, and they had to do it while preparing for the potentiality of a terrorist attack.

Stage three was to eyeball every single person in the building and evaluate them as a threat.

And stage four was to stop a terror attack.

It was going to be a long night.

Zoya had been looking through the faces in the crowd in the living room, and she saw something that caused her to whisper into her mic. "I spy the Russian ambassador. He's here with a pair of security. They appear unarmed."

"Kind of like us," quipped Court.

Two unmarked and massive semi-tractor-trailers rolled north up Clayallee shortly after nine p.m., under heavy cloud cover that made the evening dusk near black. They passed the Museum of the Western Allies in Berlin and followed along with the speed of the light evening traffic, staying several lengths apart.

No one on the road paid any attention to the big trucks, not even when they slowed and made a left onto a two-lane, unlit wooded track. The vehicles rumbled at slow speed into the trees of Grunewald, the largest green area in the city of Berlin, leaving the lights of Clayallee and the mansions along the road behind, and continuing on through the trees for a hundred meters.

Both vehicles then slowed and pulled as far as they could to the right, onto the narrow shoulder, just steps from the parking lot of a Swiss restaurant. The pneumatic brakes on both vehicles hissed air as the trucks parked. Two men in the cab of the rear vehicle leapt out and ran to the back. The rear trailer's tail pointed away from the woods and back towards central Berlin, and when the men opened the heavy doors, they peered inside and saw nothing but darkness.

But only for a moment. Haz Mirza stepped out of the cab of the front truck, and he jogged back to the open doors of the second vehicle. He wore a small laptop computer on a sling so that it was propped against his chest; there was a tiny joystick attached to the USB port on the side, and once he had stopped jogging he focused his attention on the screen in front of him. He tapped some keys and soon dozens of little red lights began glowing inside the trailer.

The lights switched, one by one, from red to green.

Mirza looked back up the wooded road and towards Clayallee in the evening dim. There were a couple of cars heading this way, but nothing that looked threatening to him or his operation.

And if there *were* threats out here, Mirza knew the two men with him both carried short-barreled, folding-stock AKs under their light jackets.

He reached down to his keyboard, took a deep breath, and said *"Allahu akhbar"* while pressing a pair of command keys.

The high-pitched sound of one hundred sixty spinning motors echoed out of the large trailer, the buzzing so loud it was almost painful. He checked the road again and found the coast clear enough, so he tapped a few more keys.

At nine fifteen p.m., one at a time, weaponized quadcopters automatically disengaged from metal racks lining the side walls of the trailer and began flying slowly out the back of the truck.

The first meter-wide craft moved past Mirza and the two other men's heads at walking speed, and then it climbed just as slowly. There was a canopy of trees over the road, but the forest was well kept, and the limbs didn't cross the road until they were fifteen meters high.

The first drone stopped its climb at a height of just ten meters, and behind it, at a separation of twenty horizontal meters, the second drone flew out of the trailer.

Other than a small green light, visible only on one side of the quadcopter, the devices were all but invisible in the day's dying light, and they flew straight along the wooded road, passing over cars without anyone taking notice.

Mirza kept checking his computer, watching the camera view of the lead vehicle, which he called "the eye." This first drone would be Mirza's reconnaissance craft. Though all Kargu drones had cameras, this one unit would be kept above the flight, helping orient him as he organized the nonautomated portion of the attack to help him send each vehicle to exactly where it could do the most damage.

At this point Mirza was not piloting all the little aircraft himself; he was only commanding them to fly a prearranged pattern, with a series of execute commands. He could take over an individual quadcopter at any time and get it to do whatever he wanted it to do, but for now he was more a spectator to the programming Tarik's people had input.

Once out of the woods, the first drone made a left above Clayallee and shot almost straight up to 120 meters, then began moving horizontally at nearly fifty kilometers an hour.

Behind ship one, others came, each twenty horizontal meters apart, each churning the air with small plastic rotors.

With the sounds of traffic, even over this relatively quiet street, the quadcopters could not be heard at this altitude, and they were extremely hard to see under the clouds at this time of the evening.

It took over two minutes for all forty of the quadcopters—two squadrons of twenty—to leave their racks and fly off towards their destination, but the second they had done so, the rear trailer's doors were slammed shut. The two men who had come from the cab secured the latch, then headed back to the front of the rig, but not before Mirza embraced them both with a firm hug and a wide smile.

He said, "Paradise awaits," and the men responded in kind.

Then Haz Mirza ran up the street and climbed into the first vehicle, which, like the other, had been kept running. This vehicle had a sleeping berth, and Mirza crawled his way back to the small workstation he'd built there. Taking the laptop from around his neck, he put it on a table and plugged it back into the power and the three monitors secured to the wall in front of the bunk bed. Immediately he focused attention on the center screen to watch the eye drone's progress up Clayallee.

Both semis began rolling forward simultaneously, then pulled into the parking lot of the Swiss restaurant and turned around to follow after the two squadrons of attack drones.

Court wasn't here for the party—he wouldn't know a good party from a bad one—but he did have to admit to himself that everyone around him seemed to be having a good time.

The three Poison Apple contractors had done their best to stay near Hanley but not to loom too closely, while Hanley continued to do his best to avoid Ambassador Sedgwick as the Kentuckian walked through the large two-story residence shaking hands.

The home had been built in the 1920s for a wealthy German industrialist. It had been all but destroyed in the Second World War, but it was rebuilt as West German capitalism cleaned up everything to the west of the Brandenburg Gate. Composed of an entryway on the northern side leading to a long wide gallery going east and west, with the main living spaces of the home in the back, in the wings, and on the second floor, the home's wide and tall rooms were a perfect exhibition space for an art show, and Ambassador Sedgwick fancied himself an energetic supporter of the arts.

The home was nearly filled with artists, dignitaries from around the world who called Berlin home, and local elites, along with a security presence that did not go unnoticed by the gathering crowd. Court heard people commenting on all the armed guards, speculating it had something to do with the attack on the U.S. embassy earlier in the week, though no one seemed at all concerned about anything more than getting a good look at the art and snagging another flute of champagne off the next sterling silver tray that passed by.

Hanley walked through the long gallery, pretending to examine the artwork on the walls and on easels in the middle of the room, a collection of minimalist paintings by the late American artist Robert Ryman, while his three operatives scanned the crowd for threats.

In addition to the ambassador, there would be others here in the crowd who would recognize the deputy director for operations for the CIA, so Court half expected Hanley to get either pulled into a room by Sedgwick himself or asked to leave by one of Sedgwick's people, but so far the big DDO had managed to eat two plates of hors d'oeuvres while standing out in the evening air in the back garden.

The three Poison Apple operators weren't eating—it would have been off for bodyguards to snack while on the job—but while Hanley looked over the canvases, all some version of white with only faint shades of gray here and there, Zack, Zoya, and Court searched the crowd.

They were looking for Mirza, of course, but they were also looking for pre-attack indicators from others. The man passing the canapés, the woman walking by with the tray of champagne, the local security hired to stand near the pieces of art in the long living room or the main hall gallery.

Anyone could be involved in this.

Zack whispered into his mic for all three to hear. "Where's the art?"

Court felt the same as Zack. The paintings looked more like blank canvases that had collected dust to him, though he was no art critic.

Zoya was obviously annoyed with Zack, and she responded, "I think it's brilliant. Subtle, yet powerful."

"What do you think, Six?" Hightower asked.

Court cussed under his breath before responding, "I kinda like it." He didn't. But he didn't want Zoya to think he was a Neanderthal like Hightower just because he didn't see what the big deal was about a bunch of off-white squares.

Hanley had been listening silently to the discussion. He whispered but his voice was broadcast in their earpieces. "Stop looking at the damn art and start looking for our damn target."

"Sure thing, boss," Zack answered back.

Hanley's earpiece beeped, letting him know a call was coming through. He told the others to keep doing what they were doing and he tapped his finger to the little device. It was Brewer; she was filling him in on the German investigation.

She told him that a hard drive recovered from Mirza's little apartment revealed that notes the man made to himself on the day of the first attack seemed to suggest that the second wave would be at the embassy itself, and not here at the residence, some seven miles away.

Hanley reluctantly ordered Brewer to task Chris Travers and his team to the streets near the embassy. He thought the evidence found might have been a plant, but he did have to admit the security situation here at the residence seemed to be well in hand. Nothing short of a flight of attack helos could defeat one hundred security men, and he doubted Mirza had access to that.

He had warned the Germans, warned his CIA staff, warned the ambassador of a terror attack. He wasn't sure what else he could do.

He switched back to the previous channel on his earpiece and filled in the Poison Apple assets on his call, and to this Zack said, "All the evidence the Germans got from the sleeper cells points to another attack at the embassy. This might be a dry hole. Empty like these shitty paintings."

Hanley said, "We can only hope they hit the embassy. That place is on lockdown. Nobody for them to go up against but Marines in Pariser Platz, and I'd rather the jarheads dealt with Mirza now than a bunch of consular affairs folks a week from now."

"Roger that, boss," Zack said.

Zoya spoke with sarcasm. "So we pray for an attack on the embassy. That's the best-case scenario?"

"It is," Hanley confirmed.

"What is worst-case?"

"Stay tuned. We might all find out together."

No, they hadn't been able to locate Spangler, and no, Sultan al-Habsi had not been detained and interrogated, but Hanley didn't put much weight into either of these two losses. He felt strongly that Spangler had just been a local errand boy for al-Habsi's plan and wouldn't know details of any attack planned by Quds Force operatives in the city.

And Hanley also knew that he absolutely, positively, without question could not haul the deputy director of ops for the Signals Intelligence Agency of the United Arab Emirates, son of the ruler of Dubai and the crown prince of the nation, into a fucking black site and beat the intel out of him.

No, Hanley figured he was doing the right thing, in the right place, for right now. He was with his troops in the field, waiting for a potential enemy attack. He couldn't stop it, he couldn't do more to warn others, but he also would *not* run away from it.

He ordered his team to split up to cover more ground. Court and Zoya went back into the building, while Hanley and Hightower went down the stairs to the back garden and separated.

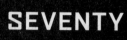

SEVENTY

The truck that had disgorged the Kargu drones headed north up Clayallee, just two hundred meters south of the turn onto residential Finkenstrasse. Already the two men in the cab could see the flashing lights of police cars blocking the road there in front of a large nursing home.

The men looked at each other, exchanged a nod, and began chanting prayers to themselves as the driver pushed down harder on the accelerator.

In the sleeping berth of the tractor-trailer one hundred meters behind the first truck, Haz Mirza looked at the screen on his left and used the touch-pad there to select ten targets. Three on the corner of Finkenstrasse and Clayallee, three more at the front guard shack of the ambassador's residence, and four more in the park on the south side of the street.

Quickly he swung his head to the right; sweat dripped from his face, a result of how amped up he was at this moment, and he looked at the screen on the wall there. He selected ten more targets, all for the second strike of the first squadron.

This done, he heard a shout over the radio in the cab of the truck in front of the one he was riding in. "Thirty seconds!" It was the driver of the first vehicle, a Quds Force operator from Qom who had once driven moving trucks for a living and whom Mirza had personally taught how to operate a big rig in the past twenty-four hours.

The driver of Mirza's own semi, seated next to the radio, shouted out, "Thirty seconds," as well, but he did it into a walkie-talkie for the twelve men in the back of the second trailer.

Mirza counted off seconds in his head, from thirty to twenty, and then he pressed a command button on his laptop. With his heart pounding and his breath short, he continued counting down towards zero.

One hundred twenty meters above Finkenstrasse, the first squadron of Kargu drones had been hovering twenty meters apart in a rectangular pattern. Upon receiving their terminal attack orders from the satellite uplink, ten of their number dipped and then dove in various directions.

The local police officers charged with the Clayallee checkpoint had just let a Range Rover carrying the ambassador to the Democratic Republic of Congo through, and the eight officers leaned back against their vehicles and resumed their conversation about an upcoming Hertha Berlin soccer match a couple of the men had tickets to.

But not for long. A few seconds after the Range Rover drove off, one of their number pointed south on Clayallee. *"Guck mal!"* Look!

A semi-tractor-trailer approached at high speed; the light traffic swerved out of the way as the truck's massive headlights bore down, blasting into rearview mirrors. One hundred meters behind it, an identical truck approached.

One of the cops reached for his radio while others hefted guns, but three seconds later all eyes turned away from the pair of big rigs and up instead into the dark sky. A whining sound came out of nowhere, grew and grew, and one man instinctively fired his Mossberg shotgun into the air at the origin of the sound.

The buckshot missed the streaking Kargu by several meters; then the device's warhead self-detonated when it was five meters above the collection of police cars and police officers, and it sent shrapnel straight down onto the group of men and women.

One hundred pellets roughly the size of buckshot tore into bodies, killing some outright, but then a second and then a third device followed the first one.

The second device was antipersonnel, just like the first, but the third was high explosive. It did not detonate in the air; instead it slammed into one of the police cars, igniting the gas tank and causing the vehicles so close together to erupt into fire.

"That's not good," Hightower said into his earpiece.

Everyone had heard something, even over the music from a string quartet and the conversation about the art throughout the house. To the trained ears of the Poison Apple unit, it sounded like a gunshot an instant before a series of three explosions in quick succession. Court started to run after Zoya, but he saw she had already approached the Russian ambassador's party and was moving them down a side hallway, presumably towards shelter.

Court himself began running through the living room towards the main gallery, but he only made it a couple of steps before more explosions, closer than the first ones, rocked the night.

The first tractor-trailer slowed on screeching tires before making the ninety-degree turn to the right. The neophyte driver bumped his left-side tires up onto the curb in front of the nursing home, and then he floored it, crashing straight into the burning wreckage of four patrol cars.

He barreled through, while outside he heard the impossible noise of seven more Kargus detonating up and down the street between his position and his target: the guard shack at the bottom of the driveway to the ambassador's residence.

Police officers all along the road were shredded with antipersonnel munitions, exploding at an altitude of five meters, giving the warheads a kill radius of twenty-five meters each. Along the park side of the road shrapnel ripped through police cars, through uniformed officers, through the leafy trees, all ahead of the tractor-trailer that now accelerated even faster, its grille aiming for the gate on the left side of the road forty meters ahead.

The guards at the guard shack who had not been killed by the munitions pushed the iron gate closed, desperate to keep the massive semi outside the property.

The first gunshot from the men and women on Finkenstrasse fired in the direction of the tractor-trailer came from a twenty-two-year-old female police officer who lay on the ground at the edge of the park with a mortal wound in her back from the ordnance exploding above. She drew her Glock 17 pistol with a shaky hand, pointed it at the front windscreen of the barreling truck, and fired a single shot.

She then dropped her weapon and passed out from blood loss, but her round penetrated the windscreen and grazed the driver in his right ear, causing him to jack the rig to the left. A sniper on the roof of the ambassador's residence fired an instant later, but had no way of anticipating the swerving truck, and it caused him to narrowly miss. Quickly he chambered another round, but by then the truck had disappeared behind trees between the front yard of the residence and Finkenstrasse.

The semi crashed into more police cars parked along a stone wall there, but despite the impact, the forward momentum of the massive beast drew it closer to the gate.

A dozen guns of varying type and caliber, wielded by the Americans of the Diplomatic Security Service and the Germans of the Regional Security Office, opened up on the cab of the vehicle, raking the occupants as the danger neared the ambassador's residence.

The truck itself finally came to a stop against the closed heavy iron driveway gate, with its load jackknifing behind it and sweeping a pair of running police officers away as if they were ants, just as the second tractor-trailer began to pass the burning wreckage of the cars back in front of the nursing home one hundred meters behind.

The Iranian in the passenger seat of the front rig had one job to do in the entire plan, and it was a job that he was told he could not possibly fail, because the mission's success rested on him. He'd been shot four times, his life's blood poured from his head, neck, and chest, but he kept his thumb pressed down on a kill switch he held in his right hand, praying that he could make it until the vehicle crashed into the gate.

He'd lost so much blood, and so much disorienting gunfire continued all around him, that he never knew that his truck had come to a stop within four meters of its target point. Instead he just sat there in a daze until he was shot again between the eyes, his brain ceased giving instructions to his body, and his thumb relaxed.

There had been a limited amount of room in the lead trailer for the explosives due to the tall metal magazine racks that housed the forty Kargu drones, but the fuel-oil-and-fertilizer bomb created by the SIA and delivered to Haz Mirza and his new cell of men at the warehouse was an efficient enough improvised weapon. Composed of three hundred kilograms of ammonium nitrate fertilizer, packed into three fifty-five-gallon drums and soaked with diesel fuel, and wired with blasting caps and fuses the Emiratis had purchased illegally in Albania, all it needed to initiate its detonation sequence was for the passenger in the cab of the tractor pulling the trailer to remove the pressure of his thumb on the dead man's switch.

And just as a dozen security men ran down the driveway, their weapons at their shoulders as they fired at the front windshield of the truck, the jackknifed trailer attached to it exploded with the force of 1,250 pounds of TNT.

The detonation killed every last man and woman within thirty meters, wounded most everyone who wasn't inside or in the backyard within fifty meters, and blasted the eardrums of everyone else on Finkenstrasse.

The iron gate disappeared; the guard shack and twenty meters of stone fence were destroyed; police cars flipped, exploded, and burned on the street; and entire trees in the park were ripped apart.

The upper-income residential neighborhood was now a brutal urban warscape.

Court Gentry had been in the foyer of the beautiful home, rushing along behind a cluster of armed security men, all ready to help thwart whatever attack was coming, but when the truck exploded, he was propelled straight backwards onto the marble floor and slid on his back ten feet before rolling to a stop in a heap by a staircase. More bodies fell next to him. He lay there, unmoving, as the sound of another massive truck approaching began rolling in from the west.

Mirza was still in the sleeping berth of the rear truck—now the only truck—and still designating targets by using the touch screen and the monitor from the eye drone, when he felt the hard pull to the right as his driver turned off Clayallee and onto Finkenstrasse. He knew he needed to activate the second wave, but he wanted to wait as long as possible to do so in order to catch as many security outside as possible responding to the explosion of the first truck.

He saw movement in the front yard of the ambassador's residence, a fifty-meter-square well-manicured hill with a driveway on the east side, and he deemed the movement to be uncoordinated security forces and civilians running away from the blast.

He turned his attention to the roof of the structure, and he hit the command button. Seconds later he could see the explosions as two of his drones' warheads detonated over the four snipers positioned there, putting an end to the danger they posed to his mission. He could feel the driver speeding up now, and he knew in seconds the man would slam down hard on the pneumatic brakes, so he reached out and grasped his little desk with all his might.

Court opened his eyes. His ears rang, he tasted blood on his lips but had no idea if it was his own, and he looked down at his dark gray suit and found it torn and splattered with blood. In front of him in the now-dark foyer, through the heavy smoke and dust, he saw motionless bodies, and he fought to retake control of his senses so he could move forward and get into the fight, although he had no idea what kind of fight he was in the middle of.

Crawling on his hands and knees, he made it to the first body on the floor, a man in a suit with an MP5 submachine gun around his neck. He didn't slow to check the man's vitals; instead he took the man's weapon, then reached into his jacket and pulled two more magazines from a mag carrier on his belt.

Two men passed him by at a run, both armed with M4 rifles, heading for the door and the carnage outside. Court struggled to pull himself to a standing position to follow them.

But his legs gave out halfway, and he began to fall back down.

Strong hands grabbed him under his shoulders before he could hit the marble, and he was yanked all the way back up to his feet.

Looking into the dust was hard, even to see the man holding him up, and he didn't recognize Hightower until the blond-haired man shouted at him. "I need your weapon!"

Zack had been in the rear garden when the first explosions kicked off, then in the living room when the truck exploded, and so he hadn't been knocked unconscious from the blast as Court had been. Court knew Zack was the better shooter right now, so he immediately passed the MP5 to Zack, who then ran for the front door, leaving Court behind to stagger around in his suit and tie, searching bodies in the smoke, desperate to clear his head, to find another gun, and to do something useful to thwart this attack.

SEVENTY-ONE

Zoya Zakharova had followed the Russian ambassador and his protective detail as they hunted for shelter, making their way towards the western wing of the old mansion. But once she saw that his men had the right idea about getting him to safety, she turned around and began running back towards the front of the home, hoping to link up with Court.

Then the truck exploded outside, and this knocked her off her feet, even though she was still a long way from the front of the house. When she climbed back up, she made her way through the dust billowing in from the outside, desperate to find some fresh air.

She found a shattered window and stuck her head out; she was facing east, towards the walls of the next mansion on the northern side of the road, but when she looked to her right she saw a little bit of Finkenstrasse down the hill through the trees. Just as she focused her attention on a police car speeding west towards the explosion, she saw something arc down from the sky at speed, then a bright light flashed above the patrol car, which immediately became engulfed in a ball of fire. The sound of a bomb's detonation followed. The car careened to the left, bumped up over the curb, and began rolling slowly through Finkenpark, its driver obviously dead.

Zoya turned back into the smoke and began running up the hallway.

She shouted into her earpiece for Court, but received no response.

Ditto for Zack. She was about to call for Hanley when the DDO came over the net.

"Anthem, what is your location?"

She answered at a sprint, fighting her way through well-dressed men and women desperately trying to push their way out into the back garden. "I'm heading for the front door. You need to be inside, not outside!"

"Why?" he asked.

"They're using armed drones!"

Hanley said, "Now we know what al-Habsi's force multiplier is. I'm going for the ambo, he'll be in a safe room upstairs in his office."

"Roger that. I'm heading out front to salvage a weapon. There will be a lot of dead security there."

Zack had run out into the front yard when, through the smoke and fire at the bottom of the hill, he could just make out another tractor-trailer skidding wildly to a stop in front of him, just behind the burning truck at the bottom of the driveway where the guard shack had been. The rear doors of the trailer burst open, and a flood of men, all dressed in black, leapt out.

The firelight glinted off the metal of their AK-47s, and though Zack didn't have a clue where Mirza had scored himself a platoon of armed terrorists, he didn't worry himself with this gap in his knowledge. Instead he dropped to a knee, brought the red dot optical of the MP5 up to his eye, and sighted in on the lead man, now picking his way through fiery wreckage heading towards the breach in the wall of the property.

But before he could squeeze off a round he heard a screaming noise above him. It passed over, heading west, and he tried to track it with his eyes. The fires from the burning vehicles ahead illuminated a meter-square quadcopter as it raced for a group of armed RSO men on the lawn, and then it exploded, its airburst sending shrapnel into all four men.

Another high-pitched shriek passed over Zack's head, then something detonated right at the front door to the mansion behind him as a group of men staggered outside with pistols and long guns.

Zack was alone on the driveway, and he figured this was the only thing that had saved him so far. He wasn't enough of a target compared to the groups of men the quadcopters went for.

As men in black breached the property wall just twenty-five meters away from him, spreading out in a not altogether coordinated fashion as they ran, he turned and sprinted back towards the house for cover.

Zack shot up the stairs, ten seconds after the drone peppered the men there with hot metal. The dead and dying covered the steps in front of the door. The Poison Apple asset leapt over a body at the threshold and entered the mansion to find a still slightly disoriented Court slinging an MP5 rifle around his neck and pulling a pair of extra magazines from the inside jacket pocket of a middle-aged security man who was quite clearly dead.

Zack shouted as he ran by Court, his voice broadcast on the communication network as well as across the room. "Dozen-plus armed pax coming up the lawn, wearing black! They've got drones with warheads, too. I'm heading for the roof to engage." He ran up the circular staircase, his rifle swinging in his right arm.

Court heard him through his ringing ears, but he still wasn't clear. *Drones? Did he say drones?* "You're going to engage the terrorists?"

"Negative! I'm engaging the fuckin' killer robots, Six! Those tangos are your problem!"

Court's MP5 was slick with the previous owner's blood, but he chambered a round and brought it to his shoulder as more explosions crashed outside the residence.

Haz Mirza's men had all left the trailer behind him; he could hear their outgoing gunfire just outside the cab, but he sat where he was, tapped a few more keys on his keyboard, and then closed his laptop and tossed it into a backpack staged there on the bed next to him. He'd just set the remaining UAVs, some twenty-five in all, to autonomous mode, meaning they would identify and attack targets on their own.

The UAE tech who had programmed the weapons had set their autonomous mode to launch strikes against any vehicles moving towards the ambassador's residence in a fifty-meter radius. Any force responding to Mirza's attack by vehicle would be identified by the squadron's computers, then destroyed.

This bought Mirza and his men the time they needed to focus on the ground battle.

Slipping the pack over his shoulder, Haz hefted his rifle, checked to make certain his chest rig holding his AK magazines was in place, then opened the little door to the cab.

Immediately he saw his driver slumped over in his seat. The man was alive, but barely, bubbles of blood popping from his lips. The man had done his job, and Mirza had no time for him now, because he had to go do *his* job. He climbed out of the sleeping berth, leapt down from the passenger door, and brought his AK to his shoulder. Scanning ahead through smoke and fire, he saw his men already running up the driveway, firing at any armed person they could find.

Mirza's radio was attached to the shoulder of his vest, and it crackled with traffic, but he couldn't hear over the noise as he ran forward, through the fire, trying to catch up with his advancing force.

His objective was the ambassador, and Mirza knew he didn't have to capture him in the opening assault, but he did have to have some access to the man so that he could communicate with him, so he pressed the talk button of his radio as he ran up the driveway. "Faster, brothers!"

The first men were at the entrance now, with others moving to both the east and west sides of the property to enter there.

Mirza himself broke left and began running through the yard behind a group of his men. Civilians ran from the home in all directions. As instructed, his men didn't waste time or bullets on anyone who clearly posed no threat, and the runners ran so frantically and haphazardly, they hardly looked like they'd be posing any defense.

He did see a man peer through a second-floor window with a pistol in his hand. Mirza raised his AK and fired, sending the man diving back inside, the glass shattering above him, and the curtains billowing in all directions from both the breeze and the gunfire.

But he did not stop. The ambassador was tonight's goal. Nothing else mattered.

And above him twenty-four Kargu drones remained, loitering at two hundred meters. Some were antipersonnel, some were high explosive, and a few were armor piercing. And they all scanned the ground below, looking for something to kill.

Court had wanted to get to the front door, or to one of the front windows, to engage the men Zack had warned were coming up the drive, but when another dive-bombing drone crashed through a front window and detonated its high-explosive warhead in the next room, he thought better of this plan. Instead he retreated north on the ground floor, through the long east–west gallery, and then up a little hallway that led to the expansive living room at the rear of the home. Here he took a knee, his MP5 to his eye.

This was as good a place as any to die, he told himself. He assumed the attackers would know they could flank the defenders by entering from the back or side of the house, or moving left and right from the front door along the gallery, out of Court's view. But he didn't know what else he could do other than defend this location until some coordination to the defense materialized.

The explosions outside seemed to stop, but there was still gunfire in the front. He'd heard no shooting from any other direction, but he expected that to change in seconds.

And it did. A volley of fully automatic AK fire came from his left, booming up a hall he'd seen Zoya run down a minute earlier when following the Russian ambassador.

In seconds a group of men in business suits and women in dresses ran out of the hallway into the large living room. Court shifted his weapon in their direction, but only for an instant, because he knew men could be coming up the hall in front of him. The group of civilians passed him by to run through the kitchen for the back door, but then someone knelt down next to him.

It was Zoya. She had a pistol in her hand, and she held it in the direction of the side hall. "Why aren't you responding on comms?"

Court looked at her. "What?"

She understood. He could barely hear. It would come back, but for now she had to shout into his face. "They breached a window on the east side."

Court nodded. He was hearing better, and the fog in his head was clearing. "That's what I'd do, too. Where did you get the pistol?"

"I pulled it out of the holster of a security man. He wasn't going to need it."

"Right."

"What's happening outside?"

"Zack said he saw a dozen pax. He says Mirza is using armed drones."

"Yeah," Zoya said. "They're going to take out any reinforcements."

Court just nodded. Anyone who responded to the scene would be in danger as long as there were still drones in the sky.

Zack climbed out of an attic window onto a flat roof and looked to the dark evening. A helicopter circled; he took it as a friendly but he had no way of knowing for sure unless and until it began shooting at him.

But he pushed that worry out of his mind in favor of a dozen more certain dangers, and he moved over to a pair of men lying motionless near the southern side of the roof. It was nearly pitch-black from the smoke from the burning truck blowing over the edge of the roofline, but Zack found what he was looking for.

A dead sniper lay halfway over his rifle, an M110 Semi-Automatic Sniper System. This SASS had a ten-round box magazine attached and, to Zack's great pleasure, a long-range thermal night vision sight, which would make target acquisition of a small machine in a dark sky easier than just looking through magnified glass. Zack dropped to one knee and then rolled the body off the weapon to heft it and move back near the attic window in case he needed some cover.

He paused an instant to regard the young man below him. Probably half Hightower's age, he was a DSS sharpshooter whose only mistake had been to be present at exactly the wrong place at exactly the wrong time. The man's spotter lay a few feet away; he groaned as if he were barely conscious, but Hightower knew he could either render aid or try to do something to blunt the attack from the air.

It was a call similar to those he'd often had to make as a Navy SEAL, as a CIA Special Activities Division team leader, and now as an off-book Poison Apple operative.

And though it was an ugly call to make, to Hightower, it wasn't a tough one. He opened the bolt far enough to make certain a round was chambered in the rifle, checked the safety to ensure the weapon was ready to fire, and then ran back to the window to the attic.

There had been no more explosions in the neighborhood, and already Zack could see police cars approaching up Clayallee in the distance. He wondered if the drone attack had been limited to the initial breach of the building, but he told himself to assume nothing and to scan the sky as best he could.

He hefted the weapon over his head and began looking at the black sky through the thermal sight on its lowest magnification.

And, to his surprise, it didn't take him long to find what he was looking for. A single quadcopter hovered over the park across the street, maybe one hundred yards higher than Zack's position.

The device was alone, which was good news, and it was low enough and perfectly still, which was even better news. This rifle had been sighted for another shooter, the dead kid on the roof thirty feet away, and Zack could only make assumptions about how it would shoot. But he'd snagged his share of battlefield pickups in his day, so he knew he would make the weapon work well enough for his needs.

He wrapped the sling hard around his forearm to steady the gun, and then he drew in a breath. He blew it out halfway, then held it. His finger pressed the trigger slowly, and soon a round pounded its way out of the gun.

At first he didn't know if he'd hit the device or not, but a quick flash of movement over the park caught in the firelight from the burning vehicles out front showed him something dropping from the sky. It slammed into the grass and broke apart.

"Too fuckin' easy," he muttered to himself, then continued his scan.

He soon realized tiny pinpricks of white in the thermal were not stars above; there was too much cloud cover tonight for that. He zoomed in the full five-power magnification available to the thermal setting on the scope, and by holding the weapon almost perfectly still, he could count over a dozen, perhaps two dozen, additional quadcopters. They were much higher in the sky; he estimated from their size at this magnification that they had to be three hundred meters above him, and they hovered in a large grid pattern.

Three hundred yards nearly straight up was an all but impossible shot, and one no sniper even trains for.

His hearing had come back to him, more or less, so he took the opportunity to call the others on the commo link. He heard plenty of gunfire below him, still, and he didn't know if Matt, Zoya, or Court was still alive. "One for Six. Six, you reading me?"

To Zack's relief, Court came over his earpiece. "I got you. What's the situation on the roof?"

"To be honest, dude, the fun factor is dropping and suck factor is rising. It's just like any other day with you. I took down a sentry quadcopter, but I am seeing another fifteen to twenty-five loitering in the sky above."

"Oh, fuck," Court muttered. "A drone swarm."

"Ain't that a bitch?"

"How long can they hover before they lose power?"

"The hell you asking me for? I just shoot the fuckers. That'll make them lose power."

"Get off the roof before you get spotted."

"I've got some cover in the attic window. I gotta stay up here to try to thin this flock before the cops arrive en masse. What's your status?"

"Anthem and I are down here, shooting at fuckers, too."

"Roger that."

Zoya had fired half a magazine at threats on the east side, wounding a man and keeping him pinned down behind a heavy oaken chest in the hallway there. She'd heard the majority of Zack's transmission through her earpiece, and she leaned back to Court.

"If they have that many drones, then we're on our own in here."

"Yeah. Travers needs to stay the hell away. He's got a helo, but there's no reason those UAVs couldn't target air-to-air threats." Court added, "This is what they call, at the CIA, a lack of imagination on our part."

"Matt's listening in," she warned him.

"It's not just Matt. It's me, too. I saw Mirza hitting us hard, but I didn't see him dropping bombs on us. Should have been ready for *that* curve ball." Court added, "I've got it covered here. Why don't you drop back and link up with Hanley."

She didn't move; this he could see in his peripheral vision.

"No?" he asked after a moment.

"No," Zoya said. It was clear to Court she wouldn't be following any orders of his that she took as him trying to keep her out of danger.

Fresh gunfire erupted in the gallery in front of him; Court saw flashes of light but no targets as of yet, and he held his position and his focus. He recognized that there were a lot of good guys with guns here in the building, as well as the bad, and he knew he'd have to identify friend from foe from noncombatant in the blink of an eye if he was going to get out of this.

Hanley's voice came over the net finally. "The ambo is secure in his citadel. Second story, top of the west wing staircase. I'm outside in the office with two armed DSS guards. There are a dozen other dips and vips in here with us, but only the two guns."

"How far out is Travers?" Zoya asked.

"Ten minutes."

"Matt," Court said, "they've got weaponized drones."

"Yeah, I heard. Can Zack really shoot them down?"

Court thought it over. "Doubtful, boss."

Apparently Zack had been listening in to the transmissions from up in the attic. His low voice grumbled over the net. "Ye of little faith."

Zoya interrupted. "I'll contact Brewer and tell her to hold Travers back until the threat from the air is neutralized." She began doing this, keeping her gun steady on the hallway while she dialed the number.

Zack said, "See, Six? Anthem has faith."

Court and Zoya made eye contact, and she just shook her head.

Just then, two men in black swung into the hallway from opposite sides, twenty feet from Court, eliminating any chance Zoya had to communicate with Brewer. Court opened fire from his kneeling position, struck one man high on his chest, and sent him falling to the hardwood flooring. The second man disappeared back around his side, chased to cover by 9-millimeter rounds from Court's MP5.

"One down, God knows how many to go."

Zoya still held her weapon on the east hallway. She said, "I need a bigger gun."

But before Court could respond, they both heard gunfire on the west side. Hanley's voice came back over the net. "Enemy in the west wing. Say again, zips in the wire."

"Roger that," replied Zoya. "East wing, as well."

"Watch out for flanking maneuvers."

"No shit," Court mumbled.

SEVENTY-TWO

Haz Mirza entered the building on the western side, through the kitchen, following behind three of his men. He'd seen a fourth Quds operative, a man in his thirties named Jamshidi, catch a shotgun blast to the stomach, and he now lay dying in some manicured bushes near the wall of the mansion. He had heard a report over the radio that another of his cell had been killed in the entry hall while entering the main gallery where the art was on display, and a third had been wounded trying to go around the back to make certain the ambassador didn't try to flee in this direction. This man was still in the fight, but immobile with a gunshot wound to his leg.

There was a lot of gunfire coming from the house now, but Mirza pushed forward behind his men. Tarik had told him the ambassador would be put in a locked room off his office, and this was up the stairs on this side of the home. He'd also given him a lot of detail about the safe room and the camera system attached to it.

Mirza and the trio with him were tasked with bypassing as much fighting on the ground level as they could so that they could quickly pin the ambassador.

They reached the stairs, allowing several civilians to pass after shining their weapon lights on them to be certain they were neither armed nor the one man they had come to find. But upon taking the staircase up, they found themselves under fire from the mezzanine. One of Mirza's men went down, shot in the back by a man with a pistol, but the other two Quds gunmen eviscerated the American security man and sent him tumbling over the railing, down to the ground floor.

More unarmed civilians appeared at the top of the stairs, and they were cut down by Mirza himself and another Quds man before they realized they were unarmed. When they stopped moving, the Iranians still on their feet reloaded their magazines, while the wounded man covered the ground floor.

At the top of the stairs Mirza and the others encountered a pair of men leaning out of a room with rifles to their shoulders. The Americans fired high and Mirza and his teammate raked the doorway, hitting one man in the knee and the other in the stomach and pelvis.

Both men dropped down, still alive but heavily wounded, trying desperately to keep their guns up and get them back on target.

Mirza continued firing, dumping a magazine into one of the men before he finally stilled.

Court listened to all the shooting near Hanley in the west wing. "Matt? You okay?"

There was no reply.

"Matt? How copy me?"

Still nothing.

He turned to Zoya. "We have to advance into the gallery, take it to the west wing, and go up the stairs there. You good?"

She dropped the mag in her pistol, looked at it, and snapped it back into the grip. "For four rounds I'm good, then I guess I'll just admire the artwork."

"We'll find you a weapon," he said, and then, "On me."

She put a hand on his right shoulder. Together they rose and began moving slowly up the dim and smoky hallway, their bodies close together.

Matt Hanley stood in silence, his hands raised alongside another seven men and women in cocktail attire. The two security men who had been in the room had both been killed at the doorway to the well-appointed office, but so far no one else had been harmed.

Hanley knew Sedgwick was behind the steel door inside the closet on his right, and he had two security men in there, as well. The ambo was safe, for now, but Hanley couldn't say the same for himself and those with him.

Hanley was unarmed, and he wished he had his trusty old Colt 1911 with him right now.

But he did have one thing. He had communication with the three Poison Apple assets who were somewhere else in the building.

Gunfire continued downstairs, and in different parts of the second floor, as well. This remained a fluid scene, but the four terrorists who made it into the ambassador's home office now had the door shut and blocked with a small but heavy wooden bookshelf, and they'd effectively cut off the ambassador from any hope of rescue.

At first two terrorists had entered the office; one he recognized as Mirza himself, and with him was an older man in black who appeared uninjured. Moments later, however, a man with an AK crawled into the room, a trail of blood behind him, and he rolled onto his side and pointed his gun back out onto the mezzanine he'd just left.

The ambulatory Iranian knelt down and patted the man on the shoulder to check on him, while Mirza held his gun on the group gathered here.

Within moments a fourth and then a fifth terrorist entered; it seemed clear to Hanley they'd all been ordered to come to this location, which meant Mirza had known the ambo would flee here to his panic room.

Hanley and all the others were searched for weapons and phones. No one had a gun, but all the phones were tossed into the corner. Still, Hanley's tiny, skin-tone earpiece was in place in his left ear, so even though his phone was not on his person, he could hear the Poison Apple team as they moved around on the roof and downstairs, and he could communicate with them if he had to, simply by speaking.

Haz Mirza immediately stepped over to Ryan Sedgwick's walnut desk and sat down behind it, and then he surprised Hanley by taking off his backpack and pulling out a laptop computer, as if he were at Starbucks doing his schoolwork, save for the polymer-and-metal Kalashnikov hanging on his chest.

He opened his computer and began typing, but soon he shouted in annoyance in Farsi to his men. Clearly he saw something on his laptop he didn't like.

Quickly the DDO realized what had the terrorist so worked up. Hightower had shot down his reconnaissance drone, which had been giving Mirza the clearest picture of the situation outside.

The Iranian went to work on his laptop, no doubt tasking another craft of the swarm to be his main visual reference point.

On the roof Hightower had taken a grand total of one shot at a one-yard-square target in the dark hundreds of yards above his head, and he'd missed. He had no way to determine if his shot was high or low, left or right, and he recognized the folly of this task. He figured he shouldn't do any more wild-ass-guess shooting up here unless he had to, because two dozen police cars were in view, approaching up Clayallee, and he didn't want to get sprayed with lead by Berlin's finest.

He did continue to scan the sky, and while doing this he saw one of the quadcopters leave its formation and descend straight down. It stopped over the park, roughly in the same spot as the drone he'd shot down, and now he realized he did have a chance to take down a second of what appeared to be about twenty of the unmanned aerial vehicles.

He lined up his shot as he'd done before, well aware that even though he was firing up, his round would still go somewhere if he missed, and he might end up shooting some poor hapless civilian in southern Berlin out on a Friday night.

But he put it out of his mind—Zack was a master at compartmentalizing his emotions—and he fired.

A second drone dropped to the ground in the park; this time its warhead detonated on impact.

He looked back up into the sky with his thermal optic. This wasn't a sustainable fight, Zack knew this. Soon, whoever was controlling the swarm would grow annoyed at the dickhead sniper on the roof shooting down his craft, and he would rain high explosives on Zack's position.

He had seen that the wounded spotter on the roof had been carrying a shotgun, and this gave Zack an idea. The weapon would be loaded with buckshot, and it would fire in an ever-widening pattern. If Zack had the shotgun handy, he might be able to take out more of the swarm if they came down within range.

He'd likely die in the process; he couldn't get them all before they got him, but he told himself fighting off a robot attack would be one badass way to go.

He ran across the roof now, his body low. On the ground in the front lawn of the property he heard someone yell at him in German, but he ignored it, just as he ignored the smattering of gunfire that continued below his feet in the building. He snatched up the shotgun, saw that there were extra shells in a carrier on the wounded man's chest, and ripped off the Velcro carrier and ran back to his attic sniper's hide.

He'd just made it back to the window when the screaming of four tiny propellers grew in his ears, and he dove headfirst inside as a massive explosion peppered the flat roof right behind him with shrapnel.

Zack rolled into a ball for a moment, his ears ringing again, then pushed himself up to his knees and racked a shell into the shotgun's breech.

"Fuck you!" he shouted, his eyes wild. Hightower was in a one-man battle to the death with the robots now, and it was as if he had lived his entire life for this moment.

SEVENTY-THREE

Court and Zoya passed several dead security officers before Zoya found a weapon that was both operable and powerful enough for her. She slid the sling of a Colt M4 with simple iron sights off the neck of a motionless Regional Security Office man lying facedown, then felt in his jacket for another magazine. This she stuck in her waistband next to her pistol, and she checked the rifle to make sure it was loaded and the safety was off.

They'd moved halfway through the long gallery; only emergency lighting high on the walls was still operational, so they cast long, incriminating shadows as they walked.

A group of people came out an open door on their right. Court trained his MP5 submachine gun on them but saw that they were State Department personnel. He motioned them forward, and they reluctantly moved out past the threshold.

Zoya whispered to them, "There are armed drones outside. You do *not* want to go out there and make yourself a target. Find a position and fortify it."

The little group moved past the two operators, back up the hall, and Zoya had no idea if they would listen to her or not.

She and Court moved on towards the west wing, past paintings and bodies, past discarded food trays and champagne bottles, past an American flag that had fallen on its side. A dead woman, a security officer from DSS, lay on her back, her eyes open and vacant.

They made it nearly to the end of the gallery when another door opened, and they saw a pair of men in black reach out with their AKs. Both Court and Zoya dropped flat behind an antique chest of drawers along the wall, then popped back up together, aimed their weapons across the marble top, and opened fire.

The pair of Quds Force men had separated at the doorway; one went left and the other right, and Court shot the one on the left through the mouth with a 9-millimeter round that exited the back of his head. Blood splattered a large, nearly blank canvas on the wall behind him, and the man went down.

Zoya fired a pair of three-round bursts at her target, killing the man on the right, then dropped to one knee and spun around, checking her six.

Court kept his weapon trained on the doorway in front of them, but when no one else came out, he and Zoya began moving forward again.

Before they entered the door, they each went to a fallen Iranian and relieved him of his Kalashnikov. The AK was much more powerful than Court's current weapon, so he slung his MP5 and fielded the dead terrorist's rifle, and he drew another magazine from the man's chest rig. Zoya put her M4 on her back and chose the other dead terrorist's short-barreled automatic rifle as her primary weapon.

She was Russian, after all, and had infinitely more experience with Mikhail Kalashnikov's AK platform than she did with Eugene Stoner's American-made AR platform.

She then looked up at the blood-splattered painting over the dead man's crumpled body.

Zoya whispered, "And, just like that, it's a Jackson Pollock exhibit."

Court had no idea what she was talking about, but he didn't ask. They moved through the doorway, weapons high, heading for the western staircase.

Mirza had spent the past minute on his computer, and he seemed frustrated by what was going on there. Hanley had heard another booming gunshot above him, and shortly after that he'd heard a loud explosion. He wondered if that meant Romantic had dropped another drone and, perhaps, Mirza had sent a drone after Zack.

Romantic wasn't transmitting at the moment, but Hanley knew he probably had a lot to deal with at present.

While the man at the desk kept his focus on his computer, one of the other Quds men pushed past Hanley and opened the closet door, his weapon in front of him. He found a steel door inside, and the latch was locked. They'd already searched the bathroom, as well.

After another explosion on the roof, Mirza shouted loudly, pumping his fists in the air. Hanley hadn't heard Hightower transmit over the commo net in over a minute, and he wondered if that meant Mirza had killed him with a drone.

Outside the sound of sirens grew and grew, but the DDO knew, as long as Mirza had a UAV swarm to call on, no one was going to make it inside this property.

It was down to whatever assets were already in the building, Hanley told himself, and then he reminded himself that he was an asset, too.

Zack tasted blood in his mouth, felt it running down his ringing right ear, and he looked down at his arm. A roofing nail had cut him from the wrist to the elbow and he bled all over his torn white dress shirt.

He pushed the wood and the roofing shingles off him and sat up slowly, rubbing his eyes.

Whoever was commanding the drones had just slammed his position with what seemed to have been some sort of a shaped charge that penetrated the attic, ripping a baseball-sized hole in the roof before detonating inside. Zack had moved to the opposite end of the room, anticipating a strike after his last quadcopter shootdown, but even though he was twenty yards from where the warhead detonated, he was amazed he'd not been even more badly injured in the blast.

Even so, he doubted he could survive another hit like that.

As soon as enough of the smoke cleared for him to see, he rubbed more debris from his eyes, ignored his bloody arm, then went back to his sniper rifle near the window and removed the thermal scope from the rail at the top. This he quickly mounted to the Remington 870 shotgun he'd taken from the dead spotter. It wouldn't be perfectly sighted, but at least he could see the quadcopters in the sky and fire at them if they came within range.

There was nothing sure about a shotgun, however. Nine .33 caliber pellets of steel would fly from it and spread apart, and he couldn't put any one projectile on a spot like he could with a sniper rifle.

Still, the spray pattern would increase his chances for hits, especially if the weapons he was targeting were moving.

He shouldered the shotgun, peered through the sight, and pointed the weapon out over the park, hoping to spy another recon drone. Zack didn't know a ton about unmanned vehicles, but he did know they would all have cameras, so the operator could, if he wanted, just fly one of the ships down from where they hovered at three hundred meters or so and slam it right onto Zack's position. Clearly Mirza or one of his people had just tried that twice, and the only reason they hadn't tried it a third time—they still had fifteen or more drones in the sky—was that they probably thought Zack had been killed with the last warhead.

Zack had a slight advantage due to this, but he knew it wouldn't last. As soon as he started knocking the little machines from the sky again, the operator on the other end of this fight would know where to send his explosives.

An SUV displaying the decal of the Berlin *polizei* raced with its lights out over the grassy park. Zack saw another just behind it, and he worried they would be too good a target for the UAVs to pass up.

He brought the thermal to his eye, scanned back and forth, and then he saw it. A pinprick of light—the reflection of the still-burning truck fire on Finkenstrasse against the ball-shaped camera on the bottom of a quadcopter. It was racing down, at speed, like a falling star. One hundred fifty meters away from his position, Zack knew he had less than a half second to stop it before it impacted with one of the vehicles.

He fired, pumped the shotgun to chamber another shell, and fired again.

The quadcopter detonated fifty feet over the SUVs, sending fire and debris down on them, but not destroying them or killing the occupants. They rolled closer to the ambassador's residence.

"It's on now, motherfucker!" Zack shouted, and he scanned the sky again.

Soon he saw another device lowering, as if homing in on a target. It wasn't moving as fast, and Zack didn't take the time to see what it was aiming to destroy, but at a range of eighty yards he fired three more shells, and this airship, too, detonated harmlessly in the sky.

Zack knew he had to move, so he jumped to his feet, ran across the attic to the other side again, and dove into the corner.

He'd shot down four drones, and his enemy had expended three more trying to kill him. He couldn't play this game all night but, he told himself, he wanted to take out at least one more quadcopter before yet another was spent taking him out.

Matt Hanley knew how to read people, and it was clear to him that Haz Mirza was out of his mind with both stress and fury at the moment. It was Hightower, Hanley knew; he was still up on the roof somewhere, blasting hovering machines out of the sky.

Mirza looked up from his computer for the first time in minutes, then stood and stepped away from it, walking over to his cohorts. There were four other men dressed in black and carrying Kalashnikovs now, and the injured man who had crawled in earlier lay still in the middle of the room. Hanley was pretty sure the man had bled out from his wounds, and his teammates obviously were, too, because they had disarmed him and left him there unattended.

Mirza spoke with his men for a moment more, then made a call on his radio that received no response.

Hanley put it together. These five shitheads were all that was left of the group, and as long as Mirza was not at his computer, the drones would leave Zack alone. Even if they were autonomous, they would be programmed to attack concentrations of individuals or moving vehicles; they wouldn't be set to detonate over a single man.

The leader of the Berlin cell turned away from his men, then headed towards the group of men and women standing against the wall near the closed closet door behind which the panic room was hidden.

His English was fair. "Ambassador Sedgwick is in his secure room, right there in the closet. He is a coward. While he watches you in safety, he leaves you to your fates."

Mirza turned around dramatically and pointed his weapon high in the corner of the home office. Hanley couldn't see a camera there, but the young Iranian seemed sure that there was one. He addressed a spot on the wall. "Mr. Ambassador, if you do not come out of that room, I will kill every last hostage."

Matt Hanley knew he had to buy time. He stepped forward, and an AK barrel was jammed into his chest by one of the Quds fighters. Undeterred, he said, "Please, listen to me. I can help you."

"How?" Mirza asked. He wasn't even looking his way; instead he was checking his laptop.

"I am more valuable than the ambassador. Take me with you. I am all you need to achieve your objectives tonight."

Mirza looked at the big American in the dark gray suit, then looked at his men and laughed, more relaxed than when he was focused on his drones. "You think you know my objectives?"

"I do."

"And how is this so?"

Hanley answered flatly, "Because I am the deputy director for operations for the Central Intelligence Agency."

Mirza's eyes widened in astonishment, and the other hostages let out a collective gasp.

"Liar," Mirza said.

"It's really not something I'd make up at a time like this."

The Iranian commander spoke to one of his men in Farsi. The man took out a phone and began typing in it.

It took Hanley a second to realize it, but soon he put together that the terrorists were Googling him.

Jesus Christ, he thought.

Mirza looked over the other Iranian's shoulder, then at the big man standing against the wall in front of the group. "What is your name?"

"Matt Hanley."

The cell leader cocked his head. "Matt? It is like Matthew?"

"That's right. Matthew Patrick Hanley."

The man holding the phone used a finger to scroll on his screen, and then Mirza looked up at the American. "That is the name. But there is no picture of you."

Hanley sniffed. "It's the CIA, kid. We don't do a lot of photo shoots."

"How do I know you are not lying?"

Hanley said, "Take me someplace private to talk, and I'll tell you everything I know about you, Mirza."

The Iranian sniffed. "You know my name. So does every television station in the world. Proves nothing."

"Yeah, but not every TV station knows the identity of the real mastermind of what is happening tonight."

Mirza's eyes narrowed in both confusion and anger, but Hanley said, "I'm the one guy here who knows that you, Haz . . . you are just the fucking errand boy."

Now the Iranian lunged towards Hanley and smashed the buttstock of his rifle into the man's ribs. Then, when the American was doubled over in pain, Mirza grabbed him by the collar and pulled him into the bathroom, shouting to his men in Farsi. While three of the four guarded the closed and barricaded doors, the other kept his weapon trained on the other hostages.

Hanley saw nothing else before Haz Mirza closed the door, then turned around, keeping the AK low in front of him, his finger hovering over the trigger. He faced Hanley. "You are not leaving here with your life."

"Neither are you, sport. But, in your case, I guess death in battle is more of a feature than a glitch, isn't that right?"

SEVENTY-FOUR

Court and Zoya stood at the bottom of the stairs, their weapons pointed up at the mezzanine. While they did this, Zoya finally had a chance to place a call to Langley.

"Brewer."

"It's Anthem."

"Iden check?"

"Screw that, Suzanne. Listen to me. Call Travers, tell him to spread his men out and approach on foot. If they aren't in a cluster together, there is less chance the drones will attack them. Romantic is keeping the drones too high to pick out individual targets."

"Got it."

Zoya continued, "The ground floor seems to be clear of hostiles. The DDO and the ambo are in the office upstairs. The DDO is a hostage. Romantic is on the roof; Violator and I will secure the office from the outside. We can hit it if we have to, but we are assuming a barricade situation. We need Travers to blow the door to get in there if it all goes to shit."

She hung up the phone, then looked to Court. "They could start shooting hostages at any moment."

Movement out of the kitchen surprised them, and they spun around with their eyes glued to their weapons' sights. Three figures, two men and a woman, appeared in the dim light. They all carried weapons but were wearing business attire.

"Hold fire," Zoya said. "Friendlies."

The three came closer, then lowered their weapons. They were all carrying Remington shotguns.

"Who are you guys?" the woman asked in American English.

"We're with the DDO of CIA. He's in the office with the ambo and a dozen others. Unknown number of hostiles."

The woman cocked her head, but a tall man in his thirties spoke next. "The DDO is *here*?"

"You guys are DSS?" Court asked.

"That's right."

"Yeah. Hanley is here. We're his security." Just then, several shotgun blasts boomed on the roof. Court pointed up with his AK. "He's with us, too."

"Shit," the other man said. "They are using some kind of UAVs to keep the cops back."

Court looked to Zoya. "Whatever Mirza is doing, he doesn't need a lot of time for it. This was a one-way trip, all the way."

Zoya said, "We've got to get inside."

The woman said, "We can help."

Another boom of the shotgun on the roof, and then another loud explosion up there, as if a drone had hit the building.

"Romantic. How copy?" Zack asked, but there was no response.

Mirza looked at the American CIA man with utter contempt. "What do you want to tell me about my mission, Mr. Hanley?"

Hanley said, "I want to tell you that you are being played."

"Being played? Playing a game?"

"No. You are being used. Your men are being used. Your country is being used."

Mirza laughed a little.

Hanley continued. "How do you think it was that your master told you exactly where to come in this house to find the ambassador? Where the safe room was, where the cameras are? Because he's been here. He's an American ally." Hanley laughed derisively. "Hell, the man running you now was *trained* by the CIA."

The Iranian shrugged. "That does not surprise me. But our objectives are the same. I do not care about anything more than this."

"That's just it. Your objectives are *not* the same. Do you even know the identity of Tarik?"

"Of course I do."

Hanley looked at him dubiously. "Sultan al-Habsi? The son of the crown prince of the UAE?"

It was clear to the American that the terrorist in front of him did *not* know this. Still, the young man played it cool. Said nothing.

Hanley added, "Al-Habsi wants Iran destroyed because he thinks it's the only way his father will make him the crown prince before he dies of cancer."

Mirza shook his head. "Always tricks with the CIA. Always tricks. Americans and Jews."

"Jews?" Hanley said, "Let's talk about the Jews. The UAE made peace with Israel. Do you know why?" He didn't wait for an answer. "Because the UAE was worried the West wasn't taking the threat posed by your people seriously enough. They wanted to partner up with the real anti-Iranians. With the UAE it's all about the danger your nation poses to moderate Sunni nations. Oil states, specifically. Your cause is not his cause, you just *think* it is. You want this act tonight to strengthen Iran against the West. The truth is, it will lead to Iran being wiped off the face of the Earth."

Hanley heard more shooting on the roof. Another explosion, louder, but farther away. This sounded to him like Hightower had tried to shoot down a drone but had been unsuccessful and it impacted with and detonated a police vehicle.

He continued telling Mirza what he knew. About Shrike Group, about al-Habsi giving the United States the intel it needed to kill the commander of Quds in Baghdad.

Mirza shook his head adamantly. "None of this matters. America won't invade Iran. They saw what happened in Iraq and Afghanistan."

Hanley laughed again. "And we saw what happened in Vietnam, and we still went into Iraq and Afghanistan, didn't we? You think we learn from our mistakes? No, sir. We make them over and over again, sure that the next time is going to be different." The big American shrugged. "And you know what? Maybe with Iran, we'll be right. We'll go in there and blow up enough shit to actually make a difference for once. Of course, you and I will be dead, so who gives a shit, but my bet is Shia expansion in the Middle East ends tonight. Just like your master envisioned."

"My only master is Allah."

"Bullshit! Sultan al-Habsi has his hand up your ass tonight, and he's playing you like a sock puppet."

Mirza was wild with rage; he took the butt of the short-barreled AK and bashed it into the fifty-eight-year-old's forehead, dropping him hard to his knees. More blows battered Hanley's head and back.

"Romantic? How copy?" Court asked over the net again.

A few seconds later he could hear Hightower coughing over his earpiece. Finally the man on the roof said, "I'm too old for this shit. I heard you guys. You want to try to hit the ambo's office?"

"Can you help?" Court asked.

"Talk me to the location; I'll come from the roof. Go through a window. All I have is a shotty with two shells remaining; I'm not going to fire near friendlies, but I can make some mischief for you."

Court nodded at this. "We have three DSS agents here assisting. They can help us with the breach. Find a way to that window." He paused, then spoke to Hanley. "Matt, if you can hear this, we need you to find a way to communicate with us. What we need is some intel on the layout and disposition inside."

Hanley had been pulled back into the office, thrown on the floor, and kicked a few more times by Mirza. As he lay in the fetal position, his suit coat up around his head, blood covered his face, matted his hair. He looked like he was completely passive, barely conscious. Apparently in shock, he began muttering softly to himself.

While he was doing this, Mirza looked into the camera broadcasting into the panic room. "We kill the deputy director of the CIA first!"

Hanley seemed like he was out of it, mumbling through bloody lips like a madman. He spoke too softly for anyone in the room to understand the words.

Mirza said, "Put him up against the wall and shoot him!"

Two men grabbed him and pulled him to his feet, as he kept babbling to himself.

Outside the office, however, his murmuring voice was coming through garbled, but intelligible enough.

"Five hostiles. Two right of door, three left of door. Hostages directly in front of door. Door lightly barricaded."

Zoya quickly conveyed all this to the DSS personnel. The DSS woman with the shotgun pointed her weapon against the lower hinge of the door, and the tall man in his thirties put his Remington against the upper hinge. The third man stacked up in front of Court and Zoya, with instructions to slam low against the door and clear the barricade with brute force while the DDO's people flooded the room.

Zack asked over the commo link, "Countdown from five?"

Court said, "From five. Five, four—"

In the office, a beaten Matt Hanley was propped up against the wall next to the window. Mirza stood in front of him, his rifle in hand. "So, Mr. Hanley. In the end, your bravery saved no one at all." Mirza smiled at this.

The big American pulled his shoulders back and stood erect. He smiled, as well. "It did have one effect, though."

Mirza cocked his head. "What is that?"

"It bought us some time."

Mirza raised his weapon to fire, and then the window shattered in front of him, just next to Hanley. Simultaneously, a pair of shotgun blasts blew the door off its hinges behind him, and then a man crashed into the room, pushing the bookcase out of the way with his momentum.

The five terrorists in the room spun towards the movement.

Zack Hightower crashed down onto the floor feetfirst, his suit coat off and his tie over his shoulder. Blood covered his right shirtsleeve. He had a rope in one hand and a Remington shotgun in the other, and he fired the big, powerful weapon one-handed, into the chest of a man near the door and hefting his weapon.

Another terrorist near the desk fired a round that missed Zack high, but Zoya moved into the room and went right, and she sent a burst of five 7.62 rounds into the man, splattering him against the wall.

Court dove over the falling bookshelf. In midair he fired at a man standing just outside the bathroom, killing him with a shot to the face.

Mirza opened fire at the doorway, hitting the DSS man who'd entered behind Zoya and spinning him onto his back, while the female DSS agent racked her shotgun and fired a blast at a Quds fighter near the bathroom.

Zack had chambered another shell; he pointed it at the last man standing across the room but found him too close to the cowering hostages to fire.

Court hit the ground hard after his dive over the bookshelf. Mirza had spun in his direction; he fired but missed just high.

Court returned Haz Mirza's fire, hitting him twice in the chest with his short-barreled AK. The terrorist sprayed his own Kalashnikov into the ceiling as he fell.

Zoya moved over to Mirza, who was lying on his back, facing up, blood pouring from his chest and back. She kicked his weapon away from him and held hers between the man's eyes.

Behind her, the female DSS agent shouted, "Clear!"

Hanley had been standing against the wall through it all. He now moved over to the dying Quds Force operative and knelt down. Through bloody lips, he said, "Too bad, Haz. We've known all along that you've been disavowed by Tehran. This will go down as a rogue band of crazies doing their own thing, and the world will forget about you in a couple of news cycles."

Mirza's eyes rolled up, his last breath came out through torn lungs, and he went still.

Hanley looked up at Zoya. "Think he caught that?"

She shrugged. "Who cares?"

. . .

Chris Travers and two of his men arrived moments after the raid. He looked disappointed that he'd missed the action. Zack said, "You know anything about drones, Travers? There are about a dozen of them hovering overhead."

Travers waved away any concern. "They will land when their batteries die. They won't detonate unless they have a target. I'll make a call, keep the authorities back. I'll recruit some civilians to help carry the wounded out up the street to ambulances."

Hanley looked to the panic room and saw that the door had not opened. He figured that Sedgwick would probably stay in there till morning, and Hanley was happy about this. The last thing he felt like doing right now was getting yelled at by the U.S. ambassador to Germany.

Hanley walked with Zack, Zoya, and Court downstairs and out into the garden. "'Thanks' doesn't quite cut it, but thanks."

Zoya started to treat the DDO's bloody face, but he waved her off.

Court said, "This is where you tell us to scram, isn't it?"

Zoya understood. "We have to be gone before people from the Agency arrive."

Hanley heaved his chest. "Zack's arm is pretty torn up. You guys have a way to treat that if I say you can't go to a local hospital?"

Court said, "I do. We'll take care of Zack."

"Good deal," Hanley said, then pointed to Court. "I want to meet with you in the morning. Airport. Eight a.m."

"Understood."

Hanley turned and went back into the ambassador's residence as Finkenstrasse filled with civilians carrying the wounded out of the ambassador's residence. Above them, attack drones hovered, still searching in vain for moving vehicles to target in a radius around the residence.

Court pulled off his rifle and threw it on the ground, then picked up a pistol lying next to the hand of a dead German RSO officer. It was a Glock 19, and he made sure it was loaded before sticking it in his pants. The other two dropped their rifles, but there were no other handguns around, so they remained unarmed.

Court said, "Let's get Zack patched up, and then we'll go back to the safe house. I need a beer."

"Same," said Zack while putting pressure on the deepest part of the cut on his forearm. They began moving together down the garden towards the broken stone wall and their car parked in a gravel lot a block away.

SEVENTY-FIVE

Dr. Azra Kaya had been listening to the news of the takeover of the U.S. ambassador's residence some ten kilometers from her apartment, and she'd had little doubt that the man she'd been treating was somehow involved. There had been wild stories of gunfights and terrorists for days across the city, right when the American had arrived, and though he'd confirmed nothing, he'd at least had the decency not to deny he was out there, involved in some sort of dangerous work.

She didn't think for one instant that he was a bad man. No, he was as good as they came, cut from a wholly different cloth than all the other men she'd treated in the last three years, and she only hoped he was okay.

She'd bought enough medical supplies to treat a small army, and though she hoped she wouldn't have to use them tonight, she knew it was best to be prepared for the worst.

She was making herself a cup of tea at eleven thirty p.m., weighing the chances that the American would come tonight, wondering if he could be even more injured, when her doorbell chimed. Someone had pushed the call button by her name on the ground floor, just like the American had done around this time of night all week. She was so relieved she didn't even go to the intercom box to check it. Instead, she launched to her feet, grabbed her keys, and headed for the staircase at a run.

Thirty seconds later she was at the ground floor, and she saw a figure in the darkness there. She turned the latch and opened the door.

Only then did she look at the man in front of her.

She deflated slowly, did not speak until she regained her composure, and then said, "I didn't get a text."

She remembered this patient. He'd been here over a year ago with a hand that looked like he'd broken it while punching someone in the un-yielding bones of the face.

He was an asshole, he was scary, and, she sensed, he was at least a little bit nuts.

And he was Russian.

"Good evening," the man said. "I'm sorry I did not notify your service I needed treatment."

She looked past the man, into the street, wondering if the American was coming or not. She deflated a little more, then said, "It's fine. Will you follow me?"

Even with a compression bandage on his arm, Zack Hightower continued to bleed over the car's interior. He wasn't in danger of dying from the blood loss, but it was making him a little dizzy and, to both Court's and Zoya's surprise, it made him quiet, rare for a man who never seemed to stop talking.

They pulled into the parking lot behind Dr. Kaya's flat and parked with the nose of the vehicle facing out. Zoya and Court helped Zack from the backseat, and they went around to the building's main entrance.

In the distance they could still hear sirens and swirling helicopters to the southwest as they arrived at the front door of the building. Court hadn't texted, so he pushed the call button next to the doctor's name, and he waited.

Zoya said, "You've been coming here every night?"

"Pretty much."

"And you know this woman, how?"

Court cocked his head. "I told you. She works for a service I used in the private sector."

Zoya was dubious, still. "And she . . . treated you?"

"She's a doctor. That's her thing." He pressed the call button again.

Court looked back to Zoya, who was holding Zack up by putting her head under his arm. "What?" he said, unsure why she was talking about this.

Zack Hightower broke his silence, and he spoke weakly. "Dude. She's jealous."

"No, I'm not." She said it defensively.

"A jealous Russkie is a dangerous thing," Zack said with a faint smile.

"I am just clarifying who this person is so that—"

The door clicked open remotely. Court found this odd; he'd learned to recognize and to trust patterns, and all the other nights since the first time he'd come to Dr. Kaya's flat, she'd come downstairs to let him in.

He opened the door, then paused.

Zoya said, "What is it?"

Court wasn't sure. He said, "You two stay here in the lobby. Lock yourselves in. I'll check it out upstairs and then come back down, help you get him in the elevator."

Zoya said, "He needs to be treated, now."

"Give me a minute. I'll be right back down."

Zoya put Zack down on the floor next to the elevator, and Court began climbing the stairs.

When he arrived at Dr. Kaya's flat, he was surprised to see that her door was cracked open. This he found odder still, so he drew his pistol and held it down by his side.

He knocked gently on the door, then moved away from it, back up the hall.

Dr. Kaya's voice cracked. "Come . . . Come in."

Something was wrong. Court raised the pistol now, lined up the front sight post between the rear sight posts, then slowly pushed the door open with his foot. Stepping into the kitchen of the flat, he did not see anyone in the living room, so still with his gun trained in front of him, he took a few steps forward and looked down the hallway to the bedroom.

There, down the hall and at the far end of the bedroom, all but shrouded in darkness, he saw a figure standing next to a nightstand by a bed. It was a female form, but quickly he recognized from the silhouette that there was a man behind her, holding a handgun to the side of her face, the barrel pressed against her jaw.

In this lighting, at this distance, Court did not have a clean shot at the man's head. Part of the man's body was exposed, but Court knew shooting the man would ensure that he would fire a round into his hostage at point-blank distance.

He heard crying and then the voice of Dr. Kaya. "I'm sorry," she said. "I'm so sorry."

He kept his weapon high. "You have nothing to apologize for." Then he looked at the gunman. "What's the plan, dude?"

The man holding Kaya spoke in a Russian accent. "I can tell you what the plan is *not*. I won't be jumping out of the window this time, I can promise you that."

Court's Glock lowered a few inches as he realized this was the man who'd taken a nose dive out a fourth-floor window at the Adlon four days earlier. With astonishment he said, "Maksim Akulov."

"You know me. I am flattered."

"How the *hell* are you alive?"

"I ask myself that a lot. I also ask myself a more important question. Why? *Why* am I alive? But I think I know the answer finally."

"Tell me," Court said.

"I am alive to kill the Gray Man."

"You know *me*, too," Court said. "And I couldn't possibly give a shit." After a second of silence he said, "Seriously. How are you alive?"

Maksim sniffed out a laugh. "Because I can fly, obviously."

Court turned his attention to the silhouette of the doctor, just in front of Akulov. "Azra. It's going to be all right. I won't let anything happen to you."

She sniffed and sobbed. "I believe you."

Zoya was downstairs, but neither she nor Zack was armed, and Zack was out of the fight due to his blood loss. Court didn't see a solution to the puzzle in front of him, other than hoping for a lucky shot if the man moved the pistol away from the Turkish doctor's face.

Akulov said, "Where is Zakharova?"

Court replied, "Brazil, last I heard."

"Liar. I have people down in the street. They confirmed that three of you, including Zakharova, entered the lobby five minutes ago. I will give you this girl, I will let her live, let her leave here right now. But only if you get Zakharova up here. Call her now."

Court said, "Fat chance, Maksim."

"Then I suppose the one noncombatant among us tonight dies. Isn't it always like that in our world, Gentry? We live to kill another day, and the innocents around us fall like lambs in the slaughter?"

Court's jaw flexed. "You better *pray* you can fly again, motherfucker, because I'm going to *throw* you out the window tonight."

Maksim laughed at this. "Pray? I don't believe in God."

Court just shrugged. "Doesn't matter, you won't be running into him where you're going."

The Russian laughed at this, as well. "Ah, yes. I understand. Perhaps it is the devil who will get me?"

"If I don't get you first."

"Take your best shot, Gentry."

Court did everything he could to calm his body, to remove any tension that could alter his shot, because he was pretty sure he'd have to take it soon. His eyes were slowly adapting to the low light, but still, Kaya and Akulov were so close together, and Akulov so well shielded by her, that he didn't like his chances.

But he faked utter self-assuredness in his voice. "I'll save my best shot for someone who warrants it. I can drop you anytime I want."

Court's pistol was in a two-handed grip, his arms fully extended, the sights of the weapon lined up in his eye, the barrel pointed at Maksim Akulov.

Court said, "You don't want to kill some random doctor. You want to kill me. Shoot her now and I drop you where you stand. And what will you have accomplished?"

"You are a long way away, Mr. Gentry. Don't try to scare me. We are both in the same line of work. I know it is impossible to shoot me in a way that would cease my motor functions instantly, which means if you shoot me now, then I shoot her. You know this. I know this. Let's treat one another with professional respect."

Court shrugged. "I barely know her."

It was quiet for several seconds. Finally, Maksim said, "Then why haven't you shot me already?"

This dude was smart, and he seemed to be pretty damn sure of the tactical situation before him. He was just missing Zoya, and as far as Court was concerned, that was a good thing. He answered, "I haven't shot yet because I don't want innocents to die if it can be avoided, and if you are any type of a man, you don't, either."

"A poor line of attack on your part, Mr. Cowboy. I have killed men, women, and children. Combatants and innocents alike. I question my actions, they haunt me, but that hasn't stopped me yet. I'll kill this bitch, and then I'll kill you."

Court slowly, reluctantly, lowered his weapon and stuck it in his jeans. "Okay. Let's do it your way. You have a shot at me now. Take the gun away from her head, point it over here, and let's end this whole thing right now."

Maksim did so. Azra cried out at this.

The Russian assassin smiled a wide, toothy grin now. The mathematical solution he'd been working through the last minute had seemed to partially solve itself.

"Now you are at gunpoint. Call Zakharova."

"It's *nyet* gonna happen, Maksim."

Suddenly, a voice called from the hallway, just next to the open kitchen door. It was Zoya. "Your equation is missing something, Maksim."

With new excitement in his voice, the Russian assassin said, "Yes, my beauty. I am missing you. You are the job I'm here for, not Gentry, or so our mutual friend Inna keeps telling me."

Court snapped at Zoya, "Go away. I've got this."

Zoya ignored him. "Maksim, listen to me. I can give you what you want."

"How will you do that?"

"If you let the doctor go, I will take her place. Don't you have a mission objective you care about? Or is this just about facing your most dangerous opponent? Are you a professional? Or are you just here because you are a fan of the Gray Man?"

Court couldn't believe what he was hearing. "Zoya. No. If you come in here, then he'll have both the targets he needs. Stay right where you are. *Please*."

Despite Court's pleas, however, Zoya stepped into the kitchen from the hallway, next to Court and in front of Akulov's sights. Her hands were over her head.

As soon as she entered the room Court redrew his handgun tucked in the front of his pants in a blur and got it back up on Akulov, although it was still a virtually impossible shot, with a very real chance of hitting Azra Kaya in the head.

Zoya said, "Here's what you have to do. Let her go, and take me hostage. You and Gray Man here can shoot it out with me in the middle. You have to admit your chance to achieve both your objectives today will improve."

Maksim nodded. "Come to me. I will let her go."

"You have a very narrow field of view from the back of that room and the hallway. If you fire at him, it gives me time to dive out of your line of sight. I am armed, and I will not disarm until I reach you. And if you fire at me as I approach, he will kill you."

"And piss on your body," Court said. He was furious at Zoya, directing it at Akulov.

Kaya sobbed audibly.

"Davay!" Come on! Maksim shouted.

"No, Zoya," Court said, but despite this, Zoya began walking forward. Court cussed, told her again to stop, but she kept going. She went down the hall, staying to the wall so that Court could keep Akulov in his sights. She made it into the dark bedroom, walked around the bed to the far corner, and only stopped when she was next to Akulov.

With incredible speed he pushed Azra away, took Zakharova by the neck, and shoved the gun to her temple. He frisked her body and realized she'd lied about having a weapon on her.

Court felt his hand trembling now. "Doctor. Come to me, please. It's okay." Dr. Kaya's curly hair was in her eyes, and tears streamed down her face, but she did as he instructed.

Dr. Kaya passed him by in the kitchen, then stepped out into the hallway, but Court could feel her presence still outside. "Azra. Get out of the building."

But she refused. Though she'd been crying, her voice sounded strong now. "I am staying. When you shoot him, you will need my medical expertise."

Court steadied his aim, took a couple of breaths to calm himself. In a voice laced with more bravado than he actually felt, he said, "When I shoot him, all I'm gonna need is your mop."

Maksim smiled. "You are fast, I've seen you in action. But you aren't so fast that I won't be able to fulfill both of my objectives tonight."

Zoya began crying now, the vision of vulnerability.

Maksim pulled her back to the far wall next to the window; she screamed with the movement, the pistol jabbed hard into her temple now.

Court said, "Zoya, we're going to figure this out and—"

She interrupted. "Court. I'm sorry. I have one final request."

"Of course. Anything." Court felt the quiver in his hands again; it came both from his supercharged emotions and from the fact that his arms were getting tired from holding the man at gunpoint for so long, especially after everything else Court had been through.

Zoya sobbed a moment, but then she lifted her head and faced him. Court could see that she'd shifted her head a little to the right, pressing it hard against the barrel of Akulov's handgun.

Her sobs disappeared, her voice strong now. "Just do me one favor."

"Anything," he repeated.

"Don't get it in my hair."

She waited a beat, long enough for Maksim to glance at her in confusion and, as he did this, he realized what was happening.

"No promises," Court said from across the room and, at the same time, Zoya dropped her head down in a blindingly fast motion, pushing against Maksim's arm around her. She exposed a portion of the Russian assassin's face in the process.

Maksim held her tight, however, and he recovered from the surprise of her action, and put his pistol back against her temple.

And then a single gunshot cracked in the night. Azra Kaya screamed in the hallway.

The bullet left Court's Glock and burned the air on its way across the kitchen and the living room, down the hall, and into the bedroom, where it struck Akulov's left eyeball. It tore apart flesh as it penetrated the eye, passed through the bone of the orbital socket and into the brain, where it passed through the Russian's medulla oblongata.

All motor functions in the assassin's body ceased in one tenth of one second, and he fell straight down, his pistol clanking on the floor. Unfired.

Zoya stood there. Court lowered his gun and raced to her, and they embraced in the dark.

Dr. Kaya entered the room a moment later, rushed over to her med kit in her bathroom, then ran back into her bedroom to check Akulov.

Court said, "Forget him. My buddy downstairs is hurt pretty bad. Please go help him. We will be down right behind you, and we'll all leave together."

"I am leaving?"

"Best thing for you right now. Police will be here in minutes."

She grabbed her kit again and started towards the door, but she turned around and looked at Zoya. "You risked your life for me. Why would you do that?"

"Because I trust this guy. We work well together. I knew we could end the threat and leave you out of this."

The doctor looked down at the body again, then turned and ran for the stairs.

Court said, "Maksim told me he had associates downstairs."

Zoya went to the window of the flat and opened it through the curtains, hiding her body from the street. "Help me lift his body."

"What are you doing?"

"I'm proving to Maksim's people that he can't, in fact, fly. Inna and the support staff will run when they know their trigger man is dead."

Together Court and Zoya rolled Akulov out the window, and he fell four floors before impacting with a loud thud against the sidewalk.

Across the street, a black four-door fired up, turned its lights on, and sped off.

Zoya said, *"Das vadanya, Inna."*

Court and Zoya kissed for a long moment, and then he said, "Should we go help with Zack and get the fuck out of here?"

Zoya shrugged. "I kind of like him docile." Then she smiled. "But we should probably go."

SEVENTY-SIX

Court stood on the tarmac at Tegel Airport at eight a.m. in a light rain shower, outside a beautiful Gulfstream jet that he was very confident he would not be boarding. Zoya was in the car in the lot; Hanley hadn't asked her to come to this meeting, and both she and Court took that to mean he would be getting a new assignment today.

She figured she'd get hers soon enough.

Hanley's two Yukons arrived. He climbed out of the rear vehicle and was surrounded by Chris Travers and his team. They walked forward, and the Ground Branch team began loading bags into the cargo hold while Matt met Court at the foot of the jet stairs.

The DDO asked, "How's Zack?"

"He'll be okay. We got him treated, then on a train to Dresden. He's in a hotel; I have a friend looking after him, she's a doctor. She's in the next room, which is a lot better than staying in her apartment in Berlin, where I blew the back of a guy's head off next to her bed."

"Makes sense."

Court said, "How bad is the fallout going to be from what happened here?"

"You mean, in addition to the forty-seven dead last night?"

"Yeah."

"The director wants me in his office the instant I land, so . . . it's not looking too good."

"Sorry, boss."

"Had to happen. Fucking al-Habsi."

"How long had he been planning this?"

Hanley shook his head. "We don't know it all, but here's what we figure. Originally, the plan had been to use Shrike Group to obtain intelligence on Iran's activities throughout the EU, for the purposes of discrediting them. They wanted to keep the sanctions strong. When Europe relaxed the sanctions, al-Habsi decided to hold the intelligence product Shrike had gleaned and to use it to move into a new phase of his operation.

"The plan was to tie Tehran to Mirza, and then to goad Mirza in a bold and brazen attack on the Reichstag. Tehran would take the fall, and Euro sanctions would be reinstated."

"But then Rajavi happened."

"That's right. When al-Habsi came across the intelligence that Rajavi would be traveling covertly to Iran, he told the Americans. This, as well as other intel he'd manufactured to make it look like Rajavi was planning an imminent strike against us, forced Washington's hand. We then killed the general, to al-Habsi's pleasure.

"But he knew this wouldn't start a war. Iran would never attack America with conventional troops. He decided to use his original plan, an attack by Mirza, to goad the U.S. into all but destroying the Shia nation. All he had to do was to change the target from the Reichstag to the U.S. embassy or some other symbol of America in Germany. If the attack was vicious enough, costly enough for America, and if Tehran was blamed for it, it would almost definitely lead to war."

Court said, "And the ambassador was chosen."

"One of POTUS's closest pals, a symbol of America, all that shit. Al-Habsi is damn good at what he does."

"I guess so. He got away."

Hanley shrugged. "Did he?"

Court cocked his head. "Did he *not*?"

Hanley looked off over the tarmac as an Egypt Air 727 landed. "I can't do anything about al-Habsi or the UAE. At no point can the CIA discredit the SIA publicly. It would come back on us, on the U.S., it would hurt intelligence efforts in the Middle East, it would damage a Gulf State economic ally, and it would get the White House so far up the CIA's ass for defying a presidential order that we'd probably be shuttered and mothballed. Sultan's got America, and the Agency, over a barrel, and he knows it."

Court sensed there was something Hanley wanted to say, and he correctly figured out what it was and said it himself. "But if a private contract killer were to take Sultan al-Habsi off the playing field, someone not associated with the Agency . . . then that would be beneficial to the U.S."

Hanley said, "Assassinating a world leader is a big deal, Violator."

Court nodded slowly. "He's not a world leader yet."

Hanley's eyes met Court's for the first time in the conversation. "I've been over to spend time with him in the UAE. Twice. He doesn't live in the palace. Not yet, anyway. His home is in Dubai, on Palm Island. Lots of windows."

"Windows?"

"Yeah. Looks out over the bay. The Palm Hotel is just across the water. Great hotel. Posh, but also quiet, and easily accessible."

Court was being given his operating instructions, and he was smart enough not to say anything about them directly. He did, however, speak in hypotheticals.

"I wonder how someone could get themselves into that hotel."

"UAE coastal patrol would look into the occupants of a boat if it sailed too close to the mansions or hotels on Palm Island."

Court nodded at this. "So if someone didn't really want to get checked by the UAE, they'd either have to hide out on the boat during inspection, or—"

"Or," Hanley said, "I guess they could probably go to Bahrain. Find a helo pilot. Someone who ferries people to and from cargo ships and oil rigs. For the right price, I bet that pilot could get someone onto the helipad of the Palm Hotel across from al-Habsi's place. Pretty sweet line of sight from that helipad."

Court nodded and started to make another purely hypothetical statement, but he shut up when he saw Hanley take a pen and a small notepad from the breast pocket of his coat. He looked up something on his mobile phone, and then he wrote down a note on the pad. He tore off the sheet, folded it in half, and then put the pen and notepad back in his coat.

"By the way," Hanley added as he did this. "You deserve a raise. A private shell company in Cyprus wired one million dollars into your Antigua account this morning. That money is there for anything you might . . . need."

Court nodded. Operational funds.

Hanley shook Court's hand. "All right, Violator, I have to go home and get my lashes from the director. Thanks for everything. Good to see you."

Hanley nodded, then dropped the paper on the tarmac as he turned around and headed up the jet stairs. Travers followed him up after shaking Court's hand, as well.

Court rolled his eyes a little, but then he knelt down and retrieved the little note. Opening it, he saw that it was a phone number with a 973 international country code.

Court thought a moment. Bahrain. An island neighbor of the UAE.

And then, under this, Hanley had scribbled one more line: *AW139.*

Court nodded. The AgustaWestland AW139 was a medium-sized helicopter.

Hanley had just given Court ingression instructions, and had just given him a green light to assassinate Sultan al-Habsi.

Or, Court told himself, it was more like a yellow light. The DDO had made it perfectly clear he did not want to be associated with whatever Court did, but that was standard operating procedure, and Court was well used to this.

He headed back to the car to tell Zoya he'd have to take a little trip.

SEVENTY-SEVEN

EIGHT DAYS LATER

Palm Jebel Ali is one of two man-made archipelagos in the shapes of palm trees in Dubai, United Arab Emirates. At the far tip of Frond J, a finger-shaped island that juts out to the north, a large mansion sits at the end of the street. It is gated and guarded at all times, but on this day there was even more of a security presence than before.

The homeowner was about to become the ruler of Dubai, after all, and until he moved into the palace, this home would be treated as such.

Sultan al-Habsi took the call about the death of his father at three p.m. this afternoon, some six hours earlier. He knew it had been a long time coming, but still, the Omani doctors had promised him they did everything in their power to keep him alive.

But Sultan was barely listening to this. Two days earlier, he'd met with his father in the hospital, and through sickening wheezes and long bouts of gasping for breath, al-Habsi the father told his son that, even though his mission in Germany had ended in failure, he would make him crown prince of Dubai upon his death.

But he would not become the ruler of the UAE. There were six royal families in the UAE, each one representing one of the Emirates, and, in a move that al-Habsi took as a brutal insult, his father had gone to the executive council of the nation and suggested that the ruler of Abu Dhabi take his place in overall charge of the Emirates.

And so it was decided.

Sultan al-Habsi would be the leader of his royal house, the leader of his emirate, but he would not be the leader of his nation.

He'd been thinking about this betrayal as he ate his dinner alone this evening, and not about his father's death earlier in the day.

He'd also been thinking about Berlin. The Germans had displayed proof that Mirza had been disavowed by Iran, and even though the bodies of the other terrorists revealed them to be former Quds fighters, the story being taken as fact was that they were all illegal immigrants in Germany, and there Mirza had recruited and brainwashed them, feigning to be a representative of Quds Force.

The drones from Turkey were shown to have been purchased and then reconfigured using money Mirza embezzled from the trucking firm where he worked, and al-Habsi knew without a doubt that this was disinformation by the Germans, because he himself had been the one who purchased the weapons and shipped them from Turkey.

The Germans were in full cover-up mode, this was clear, which told al-Habsi that either they or the Americans, or possibly even both nations, had discovered that the entire operation was orchestrated by outsiders, not Iran.

America couldn't touch him, so they were covering their own asses by covering his ass.

Still, Sultan wasn't taking unnecessary chances. The previous day Rudolf Spangler had been stabbed in the back in Athens as he walked from his taxi to his hotel. His wallet was stolen, and the SIA operative who stole it then tossed it into the Ilisos River.

Spangler probably would have held his tongue, but al-Habsi had determined it better to be safe than sorry.

Al-Habsi sipped his tea and looked out over the black water of the nighttime Persian Gulf a moment, and then one of his attendants entered the room. "Sir. Matthew Hanley from the CIA is on the line for you."

Hanley had al-Habsi's cell phone number; they'd worked together often enough over the years, but the call, for some reason, came in on the landline of the house.

Al-Habsi wondered if he was going to get some sort of a lecture, an admonishment about his actions, and he even wondered if Hanley was going to try to strong-arm him into a lopsided relationship, to blackmail the crown prince into providing more intelligence, to leverage what Hanley knew about Berlin into some capital.

But al-Habsi couldn't be sure if Matt Hanley knew anything at all about what had happened.

He threw his napkin on the table, walked over to his desk by the window, and picked up the phone. He stood behind the desk, facing the night, still looking out over the water at the lights of the Palm Hotel across the bay as the call was put through to this line.

A helicopter came in over the water from the north and landed expertly on the rooftop helipad of the hotel. The side door immediately opened, just visible to al-Habsi in the distance.

He spoke into the phone. "Matthew? How are you, my friend?"

"I am excellent. Never better, in fact."

The Emirati was surprised by the levity in the normally dour man's voice. He smiled. Either he'd been wrong and the Americans actually knew nothing about his involvement, or else Hanley was a good actor.

The new ruler of Dubai said, "Good. So sorry about all the troubles your nation had in Europe last week. I pray there will not be further attacks. How can I be of service this evening?"

As he said this he watched the helicopter. It wasn't shutting down; its rotor was still spinning as fast as when it landed.

There was a pause on the line, and Hanley did not respond.

"Matthew?"

Finally, Hanley spoke. "Ah, sorry. You asked how you could help me?"

"I did."

"You could help me . . . Sultan . . . by standing very still."

It was a million-to-one chance that al-Habsi had been looking at exactly the right place when the muzzle flash of a sniper rifle sparked in the darkened cabin of the helicopter three hundred meters distant, but he did see the flash of light. This, along with Hanley's strange request, would have led the newly minted ruler of Dubai to dive for cover if he'd had another moment to think about it.

But he did not. He said nothing, he did not move a muscle, he only stood there until the 6.5-millimeter Creedmoor round shattered the window in front of him, struck him just above his heart, and sent him tumbling back over the top of his desk, where he ended up in a heap on the floor.

He'd served as ruler of his emirate for a touch over six hours.

Three hundred meters away, the door to the helicopter closed, the aircraft climbed back into the sky, and then it dove for the deck and began heading north at top speed, low over the water.

Matt Hanley discarded the burner phone in a garbage can in the parking lot of the CIA headquarters in Langley, Virginia. The call had been untraceable, but Hanley knew he wouldn't need the phone anymore.

He was late to a meeting with the director, but he was glad he'd been able to fix al-Habsi to his desk by the big window for Violator to take the shot.

A pretty good day, so far, if he said so himself.

He'd met with the director upon his return to Langley, but he was confident he'd smoothed over the majority of the issues regarding Berlin. Interest had already seemed to move on, as the Germans were energized to prove that Iran wasn't, as a nation, responsible for the actions of Mirza and his men.

Today, Hanley expected, he'd be receiving a commendation for helping to protect the U.S. ambassador.

He was let into the director's office ten minutes later, and the heavyset man with a bad comb-over made clear immediately that this was *not*, in fact, about giving Hanley a fucking medal.

"Sit," he said. There was no handshake. Hanley did as instructed, and then the director sat in front of him.

"Tell me why you went to Europe."

"I . . . told you last week, and that was the truth. Is there a problem?"

"Tell me again."

"I wanted to follow up some leads on the Haz Mirza investigation after the attack. I thought my presence there, as quickly as possible and without worry about normal channels and such, would facilitate a quick under-standing of the event."

The director nodded. "Fascinating." Then he shook his head. "One hundred percent balderdash, but fascinating nonetheless."

"Sir?"

"I've had an in-house investigation done. The Gulfstream you flew to Germany was tasked to fly from DCA to Berlin over an hour *before* the attack on the embassy. The intelligence from the UAE came in eleven min-utes, thirty-four seconds before you took off. You were on your way to DCA, you were almost there to board a plane to Berlin, when Sultan al-Habsi tipped you off.

"You are going to look me in the face again and tell me you didn't know about the attack beforehand?"

Hanley deflated. "No, sir. I did not know about the first attack, specifi-cally. But I did know an attack was coming."

"One of your secret initiatives?"

Hanley went for a joke. A Hail Mary. "They wouldn't be secret initiatives if I told you about them, now would they?"

The Hail Mary was tipped out of bounds in the end zone. "The investi-gation also revealed that you have been conducting intelligence operations on the United Arab Emirates. Do I have that right?"

Hanley knew there was no answer that would save his career. If there had been, no matter how outrageous the lie, he would have told it with a poker face.

But instead, he told the truth. "I uncovered a plot by the SIA to goad the United States into war. It wasn't something I could sit on, despite cur-rent U.S. foreign policy with regard to the UAE."

"The SIA. The organization that gave us General Vahid Rajavi on a platter? The organization that warned us of the first Mirza cell attack on the embassy?"

"Yes, but they did this not to help us but to hurt us. The first act was to incite Iran. The second act was to establish their credibility before Haz Mirza's second attack, which was partially conceived and, I feel certain, fully funded by Sultan al-Habsi himself."

"The new ruler of Dubai? The man we trained from a college student into the deputy directorship of the intelligence shop of one of our closest allies? Do you have any fucking clue what you are saying?"

"Yes. I do. It's called 'the truth.'"

The director bit his lip. "And ye shall know the truth and the truth shall make you free."

The Bible verse John 8:32 was etched into the wall to the left of the main entrance at Langley, just inside the lobby and seven floors below where Hanley stood now. But Hanley didn't think the director was quoting scripture for benign reasons.

And he was right.

The director said, "I'm going to set you free, Matthew. You will be reassigned. Effective immediately. Obviously we will give you a few days to get your affairs in order here in Washington, but there is an urgent need of someone of your . . . caliber, at one of our foreign stations."

Fuck, thought Matt Hanley, but he didn't say this out loud. He did, however, ask the obvious question. "Where am I being sent, sir?"

The fat man sniffed, then looked around left and right, as if he were thinking this over. Hanley didn't buy it. Finally he said, "I'm wondering if, in all your travels that come with all your derring-do, you might have had occasion to visit the lovely city of Port Moresby. It's in Papua New Guinea. I confess I have not been there myself. To be honest, I had to look it up on a globe. Sort of the ass end of planet Earth. You should fit in quite well."

This was the exact threat Hanley had used on Berlin Chief of Station McCormick. Kevin had ratted on Hanley to the director, this much was obvious.

Hanley said, "Let me guess. I will be the assistant station director of logistics?"

The director made an astonished face, but only for an instant, because it was another put-on. "Oh, dear heavens, no. You will be the chief of station." The big man's face darkened. "The biggest fish in the smallest, dirtiest little backwater shit creek I could find for you."

Matt Hanley wanted to stand up and tell the director to shove the New Guinea assignment up his fat ass, but he didn't. He had hit speed bumps like this in his career. No, not like this, he had to admit. He'd never fallen nearly so far. But the U.S. intelligence community was a game you had to be in to play. He'd take the hit, and he'd take the shit.

"I will happily serve my country in whatever capacity you ask, Mr. Director."

"Good. Now, get out of my office. I have a meeting on the books now to speak with a woman about a promotion."

Hanley stepped out into the anteroom of the director's seventh-floor corner office. There, seated on a plush sofa with a tablet computer in her hand, was Suzanne Brewer. She seemed as surprised to see Hanley as he was to see her.

The administrative assistant took a call at her desk, and then she looked to Brewer. "The director will see you now, ma'am."

Brewer stood.

Hanley was gobsmacked. "*Et tu,* Brewer?"

Her eyes narrowed in confusion. "What's this all about, Matt?"

"It's very simple. I'm going down, and you're going up."

"I . . . I don't understand." He was somewhat heartened to see that she seemed to have no clue that any of this had been in the works.

He patted her on the shoulder, then leaned in as if he were giving her a hug. But when his mouth reached her ear, he whispered, "Congratulations. But just remember. Poison Apple hurts you just as much as it hurts me."

He was warning her to keep her mouth shut.

She nodded; she still appeared to be in a state of momentary shock, but then her head seemed to clear.

"I'm sorry, Matt. Is there anything I can do?"

This didn't sound sincere, but Hanley answered it anyway, forcing a little smile. "I guess maybe you could sign the order to upgrade the cafeteria at Port Moresby station."

He left Brewer with a confused look on her face, and he completely missed the knowing smile that she brandished as soon as he was out of sight.

Court Gentry reunited with Zoya Zakharova in Dresden, Germany, the day after the assassination in the UAE. Of course the murder of the brand-new ruler of Dubai was all over the news, all over the world. Many were suggesting there was infighting in the royal house of Dubai, but it was all speculation at this point.

He'd taken a room next to Zoya's, whose room was next to Dr. Kaya's, whose room was next to Zack Hightower's. The plan was for them all to stay here for a couple more days for Zack to get his strength back, and then the three Poison Apple agents would fly home on a commercial aircraft.

Dr. Kaya had been treating Court as well as Zack, and she pronounced his infection all but healed. She'd given him a few months of oral antibiotics, and told him he was far enough along in his treatment that he wouldn't need any more IVs.

Azra would soon go back to Berlin; she would tell officials there that the dead Russian outside her apartment had been a stranger who had followed her home from the hospital needing some sort of treatment, and another Russian had arrived moments later and killed him. She'd fled the city in fear, but had finally returned to the city she loved and the work she was born to do.

It was a story that was so much simpler than the reality that they all agreed the police would buy it.

Court was having fun. He didn't travel in packs as a rule, but he liked the company of all these people, Zoya most of all, and he found himself thinking about a future when there might be more of this, and less splattering of people's heads across artwork and rolling dead bodies out of windows to scare away Russian hit teams.

He enjoyed contemplating a more peaceful existence, even if it was just a dream.

The four of them had just eaten room service together in Zoya's room when the Signal app on Court's phone beeped. He answered it, heading back into his room to do so.

"Yeah?"

"Violator? It's Matt."

"Hey, boss. What's up?"

"Good work yesterday."

Court could discern a problem in the DDO's voice, so he answered with a questioning tone. "Thank you?"

There was an uncomfortable pause before he spoke again. "But . . . even though you did everything right, everything I asked, I do have to ask one more favor from you." He sighed. "It's a big one."

Court was about to get yet another mission. He was sad about the prospect of leaving the others and going off alone, but he hid it, not wanting Hanley to know that he was going soft. "Sure, boss. I'm good to go."

"That's just it. I need you to . . . I need you to go."

"What do you mean?"

"I need you to run."

"Run?"

"I'm sorry, son. The director uncovered bits of my operation into al-Habsi, he demoted me, and then al-Habsi was assassinated. The Gray Man is the only one who will be associated with that targeted killing, and since I'm the one who wanted him dead, that implicates me in your actions. You are a live grenade, Violator, and I can't get caught handling you."

"Because it would hurt your career?" Court said it with derision.

"My career is toast already. No, it would hurt the Agency if it came out I'd been running you. We've done so much good, throwing it away by having it revealed the DDO hired the assassin of the ruler of Dubai as a contract asset . . . Holy shit, Court. Do you know what that would do?"

Court lay back on his bed, stared at the ceiling. "So, you are saying that I'm an enemy of the state. Again."

"I will find some way to run interference for you here. But . . . yeah. The Agency will be back on you, hard, after the al-Habsi hit. Everybody will. Lay low. This is all going to be okay in time."

"How much time?"

"I won't lie to you."

"Why not? You do it every day."

Hanley sniffed. "I don't know, Violator. I've got my own problems around the office right now. I'll do what I can to fix this, but I'll need power to do so, and power is something I'm a little light on right now."

"Right."

"You do and do for your country, and your country always finds a way to shit on you."

Court's jaw muscles flexed. "Honestly, Matt, I'm used to it."

"Look, I've got to go. I have to pack my bags for New Guinea." He paused. "The fuck does one pack for New Guinea?"

Court answered distractedly. "It was hot as balls last time I was there. Pack shorts." Then he added, "And a gun. The streets can be iffy."

"Thanks, son. This isn't the end, Violator. I'll make my way back up, and I'll get you out of your purgatory."

"But in the meantime . . ."

Hanley said, "But in the meantime . . . run."

Court hung up the phone. Looked to the wall of Zoya's room. He heard laughter, and he sighed.

Inna Sorokina left the offices of Russia's Federal Security Service, the FSB, at one p.m., in possession, finally, of the one thing she had come home to Moscow to find. She walked through the rain in Lubyanka Square, hailed a taxi, and asked the driver to take her to her flat in Patriarch Ponds.

The driver asked for an address, and it took her a moment to remember it, so seldom was she home in Moscow.

As she rolled along she thought about the odyssey of the past few weeks. Not Berlin; she'd done her best to put Berlin out of her mind. But since Berlin she'd gone looking for answers. She'd been to the mafia, she'd been to the SVR, Russia's foreign intelligence service, and no one had been able to help her. But for the last three days she'd been here, at the Lubyanka, reaching out to domestic intelligence.

She'd worked her way up the operational chain, demanding answers about Berlin, going over the same ground, again and again, only to be told she needed to speak with someone else.

But finally, today, it happened. The deputy director of Directorate S, the "Illegals" department, agreed to give her a one-on-one meeting, and before she left his office, she had what she needed.

She was handed a small scrap of paper, upon which was written a number for a secure messaging app, through which Russian foreign intelligence received the intelligence about the whereabouts of Zoya Zakharova in Berlin.

Someone on the other end of the number in her hand, she knew, was close enough to Zakharova, connected to her in some way, to where they had set her up to be assassinated.

It was someone from Shrike Group, she was certain, and she could only pray that someone was still in a position to locate Zoya, and that they still had a desire to see her die.

Sorokina worked on the text in her flat while sheets of rain battered the window. Due to the end-to-end encryption she had no idea where it was going, or what time it was in the location where it would be received. She guessed Berlin—Berlin had been the center of it, after all—but she could not be sure.

She didn't know if she would get a response, but she decided she had to try. Someone had sent her and her team into a buzz saw by giving them Zakharova's location, and she knew she owed it to the others to at least attempt to find out who had done it.

It took her a while to compose her text, but when it was finished, she felt satisfied.

Tell me where she is. I can get her. I will assemble a new team, a better team.
Send me after her again. I know her, I know how she thinks. I will take charge.
All I need is a fix on her position.

She looked the message over many times, thought of adding more, but left it alone. She hit send, and Signal began its encryption process. A second later the message was confirmed sent.

Inna Sorokina put her phone down, rubbed her face in her hands, and then gave out a tired little sigh.

This wasn't over. She wanted Zakharova the way Maksim had wanted Gentry. The one difference being, Inna told herself, that she wasn't crazy and impulsive. No, Inna saw herself as slow, methodical, and clever.

If she received a response with any hint on where Zakharova had gone to ground, then she would hire a trigger man herself, and then she would go and find her.

There was nothing more she could do but wait on a reply, so she went to bed at noon, picking up a bottle of vodka from a table on her way there.

Washington, D.C., woke to a late-summer storm. The skies were deep gray, and the rain had fallen steadily since the first dusty light of dawn. A woman walked through Dupont Circle under her umbrella at a brisk pace, with a purse and a yoga mat slung on her back and a purposeful look on her face.

It was just past six a.m., and this, along with the rain, meant there weren't many people around yet today, but she followed a smattering of morning joggers and walkers on the sidewalk, stepped out over the gushing water in the gutter, and into the intersection of Massachusetts and Connecticut Avenues.

As she looked to make sure no traffic was coming, a phone chirped in her bag, barely audible under the rain on her umbrella.

She began crossing Connecticut as she reached in and pulled out her iPhone 12 with her free hand. But only when she looked at it did she realize the chirp had come from a different phone in her purse.

She slowed, stopped in the middle of the street. Only a honking car horn got her moving again.

The woman didn't pull out her other phone until she made it to the sidewalk. Here she stopped, rummaged through her bag with one hand while she held her umbrella with the other. She fished out the iPhone 10. Opening the secure text messaging app on it, the only app installed, she saw that she had received a single secure text.

She fought to control her nerves, and then she read it. She read it again. Read it a third time. The woman bit her lip and looked off into space a moment in the early morning.

Weighing her options.

Seconds later she began walking again.

Suzanne Brewer stepped to the edge of the sidewalk, knelt down next to a storm grate with ankle-deep water gushing in at speed, and tossed the cell phone into it. The device disappeared instantly and, with it, any evidence that Brewer had been the one to tip off the Russian government to Zakharova's activities in Germany.

Standing back up, Brewer began walking again at her regular pace, continuing towards the yoga studio in Georgetown.

Alone, through the storm.

ABOUT THE AUTHOR

Mark Greaney has a degree in international relations and political science. In his research for the Gray Man novels, including *Relentless*, *One Minute Out*, *Mission Critical*, *Agent in Place*, *Gunmetal Gray*, *Back Blast*, *Dead Eye*, *Ballistic*, *On Target*, and *The Gray Man*, he traveled to more than thirty-five countries and trained alongside military and law enforcement in the use of firearms, battlefield medicine, and close-range combative tactics. He is also the author of the *New York Times* bestsellers *Tom Clancy Support and Defend*, *Tom Clancy Full Force and Effect*, *Tom Clancy Commander in Chief*, and *Tom Clancy True Faith and Allegiance*. With Tom Clancy, he coauthored *Locked On*, *Threat Vector*, and *Command Authority*.

CONNECT ONLINE

MarkGreaneyBooks.com
f MarkGreaneyBooks
🐦 MarkGreaneyBook